not quite *perfect*

gretchen galway

NOT QUITE PERFECT

Eton Field, Publisher
www.gretchengalway.com

Cover Design: Gretchen Galway
Cover Graphics: Shutterstock

ISBN (Trade Paperback): 978-1-939872-10-4

Chapter 1

WITH CHILLY RAIN spattering her back, April stood on the front porch and stared at the old key in her hand, the same key she'd had since she turned eleven.

It was the right key. But it wasn't unlocking the door to her mother's house, the house she'd grown up in, the place she still considered home. *It's probably just the humidity*, she told herself, fighting down irrational panic.

At her feet, Stool—the three-legged dog she'd just adopted that morning after her boyfriend bailed on both of them—sniffed the welcome mat and wagged his tail, not a care in the world.

I used to be like that, April thought, shoving the key into the hole again.

Although the big house had a roof over the front porch, the wind was driving the rain at an angle, soaking her shoulders and backside. The dog, part Labrador retriever, seemed to enjoy the rain, and kept lifting his nose to the sky and lapping at raindrops.

The key still wouldn't turn.

Where else could she go? She glanced behind her to her car. Because the house was up in the cramped, winding Oakland hills overlooking the bay, the flat parking area was just a squat rectangle of concrete in front of the garage. Her old VW, filled with all of her boxes and bags, stared back at her with its cheerful round headlights and rounded grill as if asking, *So, what's the plan?*

The eternal question.

Feeling edgy—she'd already been evicted from one home that day, and it was barely lunchtime—she pressed the doorbell for the house she'd grown up in.

In an attempt to lighten the mood, she shouted, "I don't have any religious pamphlets, I swear!" A strand of her hair, curled into a tight ringlet in the humidity, stuck to her lips, and she brushed it away.

The door swung open to reveal a tall, muscular guy with blond hair and hard brown eyes: her oldest brother, Liam. The last person she wanted to see.

She bent over, grabbed Stool's collar, and dragged him into the house. "Hey," she said, kicking off her boots next to the hall closet and closing the front door behind her before her brother could see the contents of her car. She'd have to go back out to get her things—all of them—but he didn't need to see that. He wouldn't approve. Twenty-seven and moving back home with mom...

No, the perfect gold-medal-winning-fashion-CEO-mastermind and recent first-time-father, Liam Johnson, definitely would not approve.

"Where's Mom?" she asked, hoping he didn't notice the puddle she was leaving on the wood floor, or the river Stool was tracking in, because her big brother would have something else to add to the list of ways in which she didn't measure up, the list he kept in his head and added to daily. "And why'd she change the locks?"

"Lost her keys on a walk," Liam said. "What are you doing here? Whose dog is that?"

April strode over to a linen closet near the downstairs

bathroom and grabbed a towel to rub down Stool. "Mom?"

"She's next door," Liam said, at her heels. "Helping with the baby. Bev's walking the dogs, trying to get some air."

Liam and his new wife, Bev, had moved into the house next door a month before their first kid was born, after buying it from Bev's mother.

"If Mom's helping with the baby, then what are you doing over here?" She wiped Stool's paws. Putting her brother on the defensive was her only hope of getting him off her case. His first baby was just six weeks old, and he was probably determined to be a perfect father, since he'd been perfect at everything else so far. The weariness in his face, though, told her he was having trouble.

He loomed over her. "Don't worry about me. What are *you* doing here?"

Her soaked sweater and thin camisole clung to her back, cold and heavy. It was the first real storm of winter, and they needed the rain after months of drought, but she wished it could've waited one more day, when she didn't have to haul all of her measly possessions and a hungry dog across a San Francisco street into her double-parked economy car and then fight traffic across the Bay Bridge.

Her teeth began to chatter. Her dry clothes were in the car, and she couldn't get them without parading her homelessness past her domineering brother. He didn't mean to be a pain, but he was eight years older, their father had died years ago, and she was the youngest—and a girl—so he had stepped into the role.

"You look terrible," she said. His eyes were almost as red as the stained and wrinkled T-shirt he was wearing, and he hadn't shaved for a day or two. "Is the baby okay?"

His scowl faded. Rubbing his face with both hands, he sighed. "Merry's great."

"Still not sleeping?"

"Not that I've noticed. Bev says she sleeps while I'm out. Lots of newborns do it." He sank into a dining room chair and thunked his forehead on the table. "Maybe I should do the same. Catch some sleep where I can."

April, still shivering, went over and massaged his shoulders. He'd had an injury from years of competitive swimming, and she still remembered where the pressure points were for relieving the pain.

"Mm," he said, sinking lower. After ten seconds of massage, he said, "You can't move in. Mom's overwhelmed with the baby."

He didn't mean to be a tyrant. It came naturally. Their father had been the same but lacked Liam's nurturing, squishy center. Under there somewhere.

"I'll help," she said, digging a thumb beneath his shoulder blade.

He groaned in pleasure. "Mom's over there every morning as soon as she sees a light on—sometimes in the middle of the night. Changing diapers, rocking and walking, making meals, giving Bev breastfeeding advice—"

"Sounds like you'd want me to distract her. Isn't that driving you crazy? Mom used to get on your nerves."

He let out a ragged breath. "You'd think. But no. We're desperate. She's like an EMT. She should have a siren."

Voice trailing off, he sagged across the table. Eventually, she realized he'd fallen asleep. Stool had curled up on the floor beneath him with his chin over one of her brother's outdoorsy slippers. So forgiving, dogs. One man abandons him, and three hours later he's ready to pledge his loyalty to another one.

Not me. This time had been the last straw. She'd dated losers before, but this last one had been so low, he'd deserted a *dog.* A helpless, loving animal. Man's best friend. Sure, this one was missing a leg and liked to eat poop, but he still deserved love and respect.

And so do I.

She continued rubbing her brother's shoulders for another minute before jogging back to the front door, shoving her feet into her soggy boots, and bolting out to her car for her biggest duffel bag. The rain fell in uneven sheets, battered by gusts of wind, and she returned to the house as wet as if she'd fallen off the Berkeley Pier into the bay.

Liam stood in the doorway, arms folded across his chest, glaring at her through his heavy-lidded, bloodshot eyes. "Nice try," he growled.

Still holding the duffel over one shoulder—if she put it down, he might throw it out into the rain—she held up her shaking hands. "Look at me. I'm hypothermic. I need to change."

"You do need to change. I completely agree."

"I don't have anywhere else to go," she said.

"What happened to your apartment?"

"Lost the lease." She gritted her teeth together to control the chattering. Could she lose the lease if she'd never had one? Bob had seemed like a nice guy until he'd bailed in the middle of the night, leaving his dog, unpaid utilities, and an angry landlord who'd just discovered they had a dog in the place. Her creep radar had failed her on that one.

What radar? Time to admit she was flying blind when it came to judging men. It was past time she kept her feet on the ground.

"Stay with a friend," her loving brother said.

"Nobody can take me in with a dog," she said. "And if I don't take him in, who will? Look at him. He's an old mutt with three legs."

Her brother didn't budge.

"I'm going into shock, here." She held out her arms to show him the trembling had now spread above the elbows.

"Maybe you should've worn a jacket."

Her patience snapped. He wasn't her father, he wasn't her, he didn't know. "Get out of my way before I pass out." She pushed past him, using the bag as a soggy battering ram.

"Not moving in," he said in a low voice.

"It's not up to you, bro." That was bravado. He could stop her if he really wanted to, not by physical force, but guilt. If he really thought her presence would be bad for their mom, he'd convince April of it, too, and off she'd go.

"I'll make sure it's up to me," he said.

"If this is because I overstayed my welcome at your apartment that time—"

"Six months. If Bev hadn't moved in, you'd probably still be there."

"I couldn't afford my own place. So sue me."

"Get a job."

"I have—or had—a job. Lots of jobs." She'd been temping on and off now for over five years, a milestone that made her stomach hurt. Classmates of hers had founded tech companies and become oncologists. She made pretty spreadsheets. "You don't know what life is like for the little people, being a vice president your whole life."

"It was hardly my whole life. I worked my ass off to get there."

She pressed her lips together. Of course he had. Watching him work so hard for so many years, with so little happiness to show for it, she'd decided when she was very young to avoid his bad example. Was it her fault he got lucky at the last minute and found a woman who slowed him down and showed him joy?

In some ways, she understood his fears. He thought she was a parasite. A lazy leech who lived off her hard-working relatives. A hopeless slacker.

Compared to him, maybe she was. He didn't understand what it was like to be a normal person, a person who wasn't an Olympian or a self-made millionaire. The men in her family were driven and successful. She wasn't. She was just April. She'd made it through college but never made a splash. Her art, the one thing she was proud of, was good, but nobody had ever called her a genius. She wanted to find her footing, build a real career, but it was a lot harder than it looked.

She gestured to the kitchen. "Come on. I'll make us coffee." She'd planned on talking to him about her humble career, which was at the heart of his dissatisfaction with her, under better circumstances, but maybe his sleep-deprived stupor would be to her advantage.

"Only because I need the caffeine." He made a sudden move, taking the bag from her. "We'll leave this right here." He dumped it next to the door.

Well, at least it was inside. She strode into the kitchen, blessedly warmer than the foyer, found the beans and grinder, and got to work. April's teeth still chattered, but hot coffee would fix that.

Stool followed her into the kitchen and sprawled under the table, where he licked invisible crumbs off the tile. Her mother's three dogs, tiny little animals from a Chihuahua rescue, must not have left much behind, because he looked up at April sadly. She'd already fed him breakfast, but she found him a dog treat in the cupboard and dropped it between his paws. She still couldn't believe Bob had run off without him.

What did it say about her that she found that harder to

understand than leaving *her*?

"Hungry?" she asked.

"I don't know," Liam said. "I think I had dinner. Was that yesterday?"

She looked at the screen of the microwave. One o'clock. Could it have been only four hours ago since the landlord had knocked on the door with his ultimatum? Thank God most of her stuff was stored here at the house.

Opening the fridge, she found cheese and turkey, some spinach, pesto, and butter, and within a few minutes had two sandwiches cooking on the grill pan and fresh coffee in the pot.

When she presented the meal to him, the sandwich sliced and steaming with melted cheese oozing onto the plate, he inhaled deeply and said, "I didn't know you could cook."

"I've been learning," she said. She'd had to. Another strike against Bob: he'd been a worse cook than she was.

He made a face. "Hidden talents. What else can you do?"

She patted him on the back.

Frowning, he ate and said nothing. He'd given her an opening —why not strike now?

"Funny you should mention my talents," she began.

He grunted and kept eating.

"I have them, you know."

His left eyebrow arched. "Really?"

She felt her face warm. Being in her family was brutal on the ego. "Yes, and I've thought of something you can do to help me utilize them. For this career of mine you care so much about."

The other eyebrow went up. "Me?"

She gritted her teeth. "Maybe this isn't a good time."

He dabbed at his mouth with a napkin. "This is the only time you're going to get. Spit it out."

She'd expected him to be skeptical but not hostile. Fatherhood had made him grouchier than usual. She reached for her coffee, sucked down a mouthful, and sat down next to him with a big, forced, eager smile. "I want to work at Fite Fitness."

He stood up so fast, the chair tipped over. "No. I just got rid of Bev's sister. Months of pain and suffering—for everyone. No. I'm not going to do that to my company and everyone else ever again."

Shocked by the force of his reaction, she gaped up at him in dismay. "Please. Just—"

"No. No more relatives."

"I don't want to design clothes. I want to work in the art room. Doing graphics."

He was still frowning. "Art room?"

"Whatever you call it. Computer-aided graphics, sketching, surface design, whatever. I—"

"They have years of training, specialized training."

"You don't think I'm smart enough to—"

"Smart has nothing to do with it." He carried his plate to the sink and started washing it.

"Talent, then. When's the last time you saw my portfolio? I was an art major, you know, and I never stopped drawing. I go to an art studio every Wednesday night to share a live model, and I'd paint more if—"

"Commitment," he said, pointing at her. "It takes commitment."

She ran her fingers through her damp, curly hair, avoiding his gaze. "I can do commitment."

He snorted.

"I *can*."

"That department has trouble holding onto people. The last

thing I'd want to do to Rita, the manager, is dump another freelancer in her lap who's going to disappear a month later, after she's done all the work with the training. She's had that happen three times this year already."

"Maybe there's something wrong with her," April said.

"Who?"

"This Rita person. Maybe people can't stand to work for her."

He threw down the sponge and jabbed a finger at her. "You see? You're already blaming management."

She wished she hadn't said anything. "Sorry. I'm sure she's great. You wouldn't know this, but I get along great with my bosses, everywhere I've worked."

"Easy to do if you never stay in one place for more than a week."

"I'm a temp! It's not like I quit. That's how it's set up."

"You could take longer assignments," he said. "You must choose not to."

She forced herself to hold his gaze. "Only with temping. Spreadsheets are boring enough without having to do the same ones week after week. By moving between companies, I kept it interesting." That was a massive exaggeration. Interesting enough not to blow her brains out in the stock room from boredom during her thirty-minute unpaid lunch breaks. "That wouldn't be a problem at Fite, so I'd stay longer."

"Longer than a week? Wow."

Her plans were unraveling, and she hadn't even unloaded her car yet. "You're sleep deprived. Let's talk about this later."

He shook his head. "No, but I do have to get back." He looked around the kitchen, brow furrowing. "I came over here for something. What was it?"

"You can bring some lunch over for Bev and Mom."

"That wasn't it."

April had made a few extra sandwiches. Now she shoved them, in their ecologically responsible container, into Liam's hands. "They're probably as hungry as you were. Make sure they eat."

He took the container, still frowning. "It was something... something we wanted for the baby. But what would Mom have over here that would put Merry to sleep?"

"Music?" April asked, glad for a topic change. "I helped her copy all her CDs onto her phone. Bach could be soothing—"

"No, no. We've tried that. Oh, right. I remember now. A second rocking chair." He strode out of the kitchen, bumping into the doorframe on his way out and almost dropping the sandwiches. "I hate this. I keep forgetting things. I probably won't even remember seeing you here today. It's unbelievable. I'm losing my mind."

She followed him through the house and watched him put the sandwiches on the seat of the old-fashioned rocker in the living room, pick it all up, then maneuver the load through the front door, exclaiming as rain hit him in the face.

With her hand on the doorknob, she watched him hurry across the driveway to his house next door, grateful for his poor memory, and closed the door after him. He'd forgotten, or was too tired, to kick her out of the house. Her request to work had Fite had probably helped with that. She'd be grateful for small favors.

After rubbing some circulation into her cold arms, she lifted the duffel and hauled it upstairs to the bedroom she'd had as a kid, making a mental note to get a copy of the new house key. She put down a few pillows next to the bed for Stool, who liked his small comforts, and stroked his velvety black ears. "We'll be staying here for a while, doggo," she said, admiring the way he flopped onto his back, kicking his two front legs and the one in the back into the air, taking life as it came without complaining.

"Don't worry about *me* leaving you." April scratched his belly. "I don't get attached easily, but when I do, watch out."

Satisfied he wasn't going to panic at the sudden change in his dwelling, she went to the bathroom, still painted in 1980s aqua and purple, and turned on the shower. The damp had reached her bones in spite of the coffee. Existential angst was bad for a chill.

She stripped off her wet clothes and stepped under the scalding water. The joke about putting a bullet in her brain wasn't funny anymore. Temping was killing her, but what else could she do? Working at Fite was the only thing she could think of that was going to save her.

Liam assumed his declaration about her never working at Fite was final.

Luckily, she'd had years of practice doing the opposite of what he wanted her to do.

Chapter 2

Zack Fain, thirty-two-year-old widower, MBA, put his laptop bag on the battered oak desk Fite Fitness had given him and looked around the office.

He'd expected more glamour. Fite Fitness was an elite, trendy brand of athletic apparel. San Francisco was an expensive, world-class, fashionable city. Fite's headquarters, however, displayed the financial distress the company had been under for the past few years—one reason he'd been able to convince them to hire him as a consultant.

"Liam told me to tell you he'll be in around ten," the receptionist said. "I bet he was up all night with the baby. Bev had her baby a couple months ago. She's the owner, Beverly Lewis Johnson. She married Liam and now they just had their first baby. She is *so cute*. The baby, I mean, not that Bev isn't cute, because she is. Her name is Merry. Isn't that a great name for a person? She's like a hobbit. Did you see that movie? I liked the book better."

Trying not to smile during her speech, Zack gazed politely at her, making mental notes. Mid-twenties, olive skin, big brown eyes, and very, very geeky. Even without the hobbit comment. Her dark hair, far from the carefully styled locks he'd expect from a fashion industry receptionist, was pulled into a lopsided ponytail. Her lips were shiny with something sheer, but the rest of her face was bare. She wore a Minecraft T-shirt under a black cardigan, as if she'd known she was supposed to dress up for the office but didn't really know how.

He wondered who had hired her, and whether her unorthodox appearance meant she was related to somebody in management. Liam had warned him that the company had an unhealthy history of nepotism.

Related or not, she was a refreshing change from Manhattan. And change was what he craved. "Thanks. That will give me time to settle in."

"Don't let him scare you. Liam scares people sometimes. He has a way of looking at you that makes you feel like you're naked, though that could just be because I'm a girl." She smiled. "A woman, I mean. My name's Virginia. Anyway. Right. I'd better go." She tugged down her cardigan and turned to the door.

"Any chance you could give me a tour?" Zack didn't want to put her on the spot, but he also had no idea where anything was, even the bathroom. She'd walked him from the front door directly to this office ten feet off the lobby, and he knew there were several floors above them, all devoted to churning out yoga pants, running bras, moisture-wicking T-shirts, whatever else was hot that season.

"I'm sorry, but I have to stay at the desk," she said. "You'd better wait for Liam. He'll be in at ten. I told you that, right?"

He glanced as his watch. It was only 8:48 a.m. He'd have to wander around on his own. "You did. I understand. Thanks."

She shut the door behind her, and he waited a minute before walking over, opening it again, and wandering out into the hallway. Instead of taking the elevator in the lobby, he found the stairwell and climbed up to the second floor, thinking it might stress out Virginia if she saw him exploring on his own. He'd be sure to tell Liam, scary though he may be, that his receptionist had told him of his expected arrival time.

The lighting was much better on the second floor than the first. He squinted at the modern track lights, noting they were cutting-edge and energy-efficient. The flooring—blond laminate planks with faux distressed texture—was new, too.

He jotted these observations down in his palm-sized leather notebook.

Fite was coming out of a rough period. As a consumer who bought running shorts every year or two, he knew that Fite had gone downhill and was only now recovering. The founder had died and left it to his granddaughter, Bev—the one with the hobbit baby—and things were looking up.

That was the buzz, anyway. He wouldn't believe it without poking around for the next six months. He wasn't an accountant but an observer. He dug out problems in morale, organization, workflow, teamwork—and submitted a report when he was done. His quiet—and affordable, since he was a solo operation—work in the trenches was why people hired him. He'd told Liam and Bev Johnson that in his interview pitch, and refreshingly, they'd been receptive to criticism.

"One good marketing campaign isn't enough, I know that," Liam had said. "But we're doing other things."

"Morale is better, but we need to do more," Bev had added.

"I can make sure you're doing the right other things," Zack had told them. "Whatever they might be."

"I'm interested in doing more, but—look, we just had a baby. Six months from now might be a better time."

"Six months might be too late. Especially if you're distracted by your personal life," Zack had said.

Eventually convinced, they'd hired Zack, and here he was. Six months in San Francisco was just what he needed, and six months of him was just what Fite Fitness needed.

He was an expert on the effects of personal life on career. Since Meg's death, he'd had no personal life of his own, and his career had accelerated at twice the pace of another person's. Thirty-two and already telling businesspeople twice his age what to do.

The floor was quiet. Doors, most of them closed, broke up the walls on either side. He frowned. He needed an open-door policy when he was on site to get a feel for the place. Later, when he was gone, they could shut them again. He made another note in his book to remind Liam to send out an email. A second email, he hoped, since Zack already had asked him to do it once.

He wouldn't knock on doors just yet. Soon Liam would introduce him to the employees so they knew he had permission to nose around. He made another note to get a hard copy of the building floor plan. And a set of keys. The closed doors could be storage, for all he knew, or computer rooms.

One door at the end of the hallway was open, though, and he could see the edge of a cubicle wall inside. He glanced at his watch, saw he still had more than an hour to fill, and headed over to say hello, adjusting his new security badge so it was prominently displayed on the pocket of his suit jacket.

The first cubicle was empty, but the huge monitor and high-tech drawing pad in front of it told him this was some kind of computer design area. The cubicle across from it looked the same and was also empty.

It was 9:04 a.m., and lots of expensive equipment was going to waste.

He made another note.

Then he walked past the carpeted wall to the next cubicle and saw, finally, a living human being: a girl with curly brown hair, peering at a huge monitor.

He frowned. She looked really young, maybe nineteen. Although he liked to talk to everyone, he didn't do so until he'd introduced himself to the managers first, especially if the person was just an intern. In his experience, interns loved to gossip. Great for him, but it could get them into trouble.

"Oh! Hey," she cried, jumping away with a hand on her chest. "Is this your spot?" She wore a cropped denim jacket heavily adorned with colorful appliqués and jewelry. And cut-off red Bermuda shorts over knee-high combat boots.

Definitely an intern. "My spot?"

"Sorry. I was just curious." She moved to leave. "I should get back to work."

He didn't move out of her way. "This isn't your department?"

Her large gray eyes, heavily adorned with blue eyeliner, sharpened. "Not exactly. Who are you?"

"I'm a consultant."

"Ah, I should've guessed," she said.

"Oh?"

"The suit. None of the artists would wear suits," she said. "Were you looking for somebody? The folks in here don't usually come in until later."

"No, I was just taking a little unofficial tour. I just arrived." He wasn't sure why he was explaining himself. Time to kill, he supposed.

Her eyes danced. "I was kind of doing the same thing."

"Are you new?"

She gave him a mischievous grin. "I hope so." She leaned closer to him. "Don't tell anyone you saw me, okay? Please?"

"You're not supposed to be in here?"

"Are you going to tell on me?" she asked.

"I might." He had to bite back a smile. Something about her made him want to laugh.

Her grin widened. "But you might not?"

He sobered. *Get serious.* He couldn't treat this job as a paid vacation just because he was so grateful to get out of New York for a little while. If he was overwhelmed with amusement, it was only because he was talking to a teenage girl in combat boots who, for all he knew, had broken into the building. He should make a note about security.

"What's your name?" he asked.

"Like I'm going to tell you."

"Excuse me?"

"I think I'd better run, don't you?" As she asked this, she grabbed his shoulders, spun him sideways, and fled past him. She smelled like orange blossoms.

Caught by surprise, he grabbed the wall of the cubicle for balance. "Hey!"

"Enjoy the rest of your tour," she shouted from the hallway.

He blinked, not sure what had just happened. He picked up the landline on the desk, hit the reception button, and described the young woman roaming free on the second floor.

"Oh! You went upstairs?" Virginia asked.

"Yes. Do you know her?" How many teenage girls in combat boots could there be?

"Combat boots?" Virginia asked.

He pressed on. "Do you often have unauthorized visitors in the building?"

Silence.

"Virginia?"

"No," she said, her voice faint.

"Well, you do now," he said. "What's your procedure?"

"My procedure?"

"Not yours, the company's." He closed his eyes. This wasn't like him. He wasn't the police—he was a regular guy, the type of guy they could confess to, ask for help. To get that kind of rapport, he had to win them over slowly, not barge in with his notebooks blazing. "Never mind. Sorry to bother you."

She breathed out in relief. "Okay."

He hung up and let his gaze fall on the workstation. For a second, right before it disappeared under a screen saver of a cat flying past in a superhero suit, he glimpsed a window filled with multi-colored geometric shapes that formed the first three letters of the Fite logo.

He hit the mouse to bring the image back, but it required a password, and he was stuck watching the flying cat.

Either the curly haired intruder had been working on the design at the workstation, or somebody else had been here just before her. If he hung around, he might be able to ask who she was, why she was—

He rubbed his face. Later. Liam was due soon. This time he'd wait for him, and save his exploring for after a complete tour.

He exited the computer room, walked down the refurbished hallway, and returned to his office downstairs, unpleasantly distracted by the memory of shapely bare knees and combat boots.

He sat behind his new, empty desk, shaking his head.

Of all the times and places to discover his sex drive had returned. On the job with a teenager. Years of nothing—*nothing* —and now...

He didn't know if he should cry or thank God.

* * *

"Did you test the temperature?" April's mother, Trixie, pointed at the tiny bottle in her hand. They stood in the kitchen of Liam and Bev's house next door, listening to the rising volume of Merry's cries in the living room.

April laughed. "Listen to her. What a drama queen."

Her mom touched her arm. "Hold on, sweetie. We have to test it. It might be too hot. Dribble some of it on the inside of your wrist."

April's stomach tightened. She was an organic-hemp-wearing Northern California girl, but she'd rather not squirt her sister-in-law's breast milk onto her bare flesh. "Be my guest."

Her mother smiled. "You get used to it." She took the bottle, shook a few drops onto her own wrist, and handed it back.

The liquid inside the bottle was grayish white, not at all what color real milk should be. April had seen plenty of it before, but she never got used to it. "All right?"

"It's fine," her mother said.

"Thank God," April muttered, striding out to the living room, wielding the bottle at arm's length in front of her. Liam sat with Bev on the sofa. The baby, her face as red as a cherry lollipop under her jet-black hair, screamed in his arms. Liam had the expression of a man tied to the tracks in front of a speeding train.

"She sure can belt it out," April said. "Maybe she'll be an opera singer."

Liam snatched the bottle. "What took so long?" He aimed it at the little open oval of Merry's mouth.

Instead of sucking, she continued to howl. When Liam pushed the bottle deeper into her mouth, spiraling it between her lips, Bev reached over and pulled it out.

"She's too upset," Bev said, her voice rising. "Just wait a minute."

Liam reclaimed the bottle and looked down at his daughter. "Listen, sweetheart, I've got what you want right here."

April gestured at Bev's chest. "Maybe she wants it on tap."

Liam shot her a furious look. "Do you mind?"

"Just a suggestion," April said.

Tears trickled down Bev's cheeks. Bev had that combination of fair skin and smooth black hair that April had admired ever since she'd seen a print of the Mona Lisa as a kid. Bev was sweet, too, having taught preschool before inheriting Fite Fitness, and was possibly the nicest person April had ever met. Liam had totally lucked out, hooking up with someone like her.

Bev wasn't her usual happy self today, however. "The nurse said if she doesn't learn to like the bottle now, she might never learn," she snapped at Liam. "How can I go back to work if she never learns?"

"She's not even two months old yet," Liam said. "Are you saying we've already ruined her?"

April watched the two parents glaring at each other and thought they needed to learn how to chill. No wonder the baby was crying. "Can I have a turn?" she asked.

Liam aimed his furious gaze at her. Merry kicked her tiny legs.

"To give you a break," April continued, reaching out to rescue her niece from her brother. Poor thing. She knew what it felt like to have him on your case. "Go get a beer. Maybe a prescription sedative."

"You just want to show off," Liam said.

April smiled, flattered he'd noticed how she had a magic touch with the little squirt. "All right with you, Bev?"

When Bev bit her lip and nodded, April lifted Merry into the crook of her elbow. And then, plowing ahead with her theory that her niece was screaming because her dad was an uptight head case, she waved away the bottle and carried the baby out the front door. Stool, who'd come over with her from her mother's house with the Chihuahuas, followed her onto the landing. Ever since the morning she'd moved back home, he'd stuck to her like glue. Fear of abandonment could strike the hardiest of souls.

Perhaps it was the shock of cold wind blasting through the Golden Gate across the bay and into her little face, or perhaps it was the distance from her neurotic parents, but little Merry stopped crying.

"Oh," Meredith Bailey Johnson said. Actually, it was more like a gasp, but April decided it was her first word and smiled, rubbing the baby's soft, wet cheek against her own.

"Cold, isn't it?" April pivoted in her boots until they were aiming west. "The wind blows off the Pacific. That's San Francisco over there."

"Oh," Merry said again. "Oh, oh, oh."

April leaned back and looked into her face. "Are you cold?"

Merry gaped at her with her wide blue eyes as if she'd been drunk all night and just noticed she was in bed with somebody unfamiliar.

April totally knew *that* look.

"Wuh," Merry said. Her face was pimpled and splotchy.

"You don't look so good," April said. She flinched, realizing she'd insulted her only niece. "I'm so sorry, I shouldn't say shit like that."

The fight had drained out of Merry. She continued to gaze at April, but under flickering eyelids.

"I shouldn't swear, either," April whispered, glancing at the house. "Our little secret, okay?"

She had lots of those these days. Sneaking into Fite early every day was taking its toll on her cheerful disposition. She missed the sleep, hated lying to her mother about her fictional new obsession with sunrise jogging, and knew that any one of these days very soon, Liam was going to find out.

Silence. Merry was asleep.

"You seem smaller when you shut up." April kissed her on the forehead, right on the spots. "Good reason to keep making noise. Don't want people walking all over you."

Another gust of wind hit them, so April opened the door and stepped inside. Liam jumped up and strode over, reaching for the baby. He didn't say anything, but April could see his jaw clenching as he took Merry from her arms.

"She's asleep," April said.

"Probably went into shock," Liam said, tucking her under his unzipped sweatshirt against his chest. "It's November, not July. You've got to be careful with newborns."

Buried up to her chin under her dad's sweatshirt, Merry opened her eyes. Outraged by the relocation, she opened her mouth and sucked in a deep breath to resume howling.

"Oh, no," Liam muttered during the brief silence.

April grinned. "Thar she blows."

Merry's crying drowned out whatever Bev said as she came over and handed Liam the bottle. Poor Bev. She looked like she hadn't slept in a week, and crusty white streaks marked each of her shoulders.

April held out her arms. "Let me take her outside again. She likes it."

"Isn't it too cold?" Bev asked.

"I'll wander around inside, then," April said, clasping her finger's around Merry's little chest under Liam's sweatshirt.

"No—" he began, but Merry had stopped crying as soon as April touched her.

April lifted her all the way out, cradling her fuzzy head with one hand, and felt her own heart swell. Big blue eyes gazed into hers. She'd loved Merry before she was born, but the compliment her niece paid her by not crying whenever she held her was especially charming. What a fantastic kid. The best in the world.

"Let's bail this popsicle stand, kiddo," April whispered, walking away. Stool, as usual, padded at her side.

Liam stood and grabbed her arm. "Hold it. I think there might be something wrong." He leaned over and touched Merry's cheek. "She's all hot."

"She's been crying," April said. "And you had her in your sweatshirt."

"She needs to eat, that's all," Trixie said, shoving the bottle into Merry's newly closed mouth.

April pulled away from both of them. "Stop. She doesn't need anything. She's fine. Totally fine."

"She's right," Bev said. "Let April hold her. I just can't listen to her cry anymore."

"But we can't rely on her every time—" Liam began.

"I don't care about every time," Bev said. "This is right now. As in, right now I'm taking a shower. I've got dried spit-up in my hair." She got up, came over to kiss Merry on the forehead, and gave April a sad but grateful look before leaving the room.

April wandered around the house until Merry was deeply asleep. Then she tucked the limp little body into her car seat, set it next to the washing machine off the kitchen, and rejoined the others around the breakfast table. Bev, with damp hair and rosy cheeks, sat close to Liam. They held hands, looking happier than they had in months. Trixie was sipping her tea, smiling at them, then at April as she sat down.

"Mom was just telling us you used to babysit all the time

during high school," Liam said. "I didn't know."

"She was in very high demand," Trixie said. "With a wait-list and everything. I felt like her agent, fielding the parent phone calls that would come in."

April felt herself flush with pride. Back then, she'd loved being with babies. For a few years, she'd retreated from her own social life to babysit. Babies never asked stupid questions like *How's your mother doing?* (meaning: now that your father is dead); or *Are you as smart as your brother Mark?* (meaning: obviously not); or *Is Liam going to come home and show everyone his gold medal?* (meaning: I hope he'll have sex with me.)

"I made pretty good money," April said, taking the mug of herbal tea her mother poured for her. "Used to joke about becoming a nanny if art school didn't work out."

The table fell silent.

"Nanny?" Liam asked.

They were all staring at her.

The tea caught in April's mouth. "Joke. I was joking."

After a moment, Liam said, "So, you said you were sick of temping..."

Chapter 3

APRIL SHOOK HER head. "I'm happy to help out with Merry, no charge."

"Great," Liam said. "When can you start?"

"No, we couldn't," Bev said at the same time. "We'll find a nanny. Just because we haven't found one yet doesn't mean we won't."

"We need help *now*," Liam said. "You're trying to keep up with business at Fite and the baby and it's killing you. You can't do it all."

The new parents looked at each other. Then Bev turned to April. "We wouldn't take advantage. We'd pay you—"

"No. I don't want money to be with my own niece," April said. The warm glow of baby infatuation was still thick in her heart. She couldn't possibly turn that into a commercial transaction. "No," she repeated, pulling the mug up to her face.

"I'm sorry," Bev said. "Forgive me. I didn't mean to offend you."

"She's being irrational," Liam said. "April, look. You've got a skill. We require that skill. We'd be compensating you for being here with her instead of being at a paid job. Which, by the way, you don't have. It wouldn't be fair otherwise. Just because you're related—"

"I don't care about the money," April said, struggling to keep her voice down because of Merry in the other room. She went over to the sink and washed out her mug, even though she wasn't finished, just to have something to do with her hands.

"Fine," Liam said. "Do it for free, then."

"I will," April said. When she wasn't at Fite. Except he didn't know she was at Fite, because she was really just a loser who'd gone to high school with the receptionist.

"No." Bev stood up and walked over to look at the baby through the doorway. Her voice was soft but firm. "Even if it's okay with you, it wouldn't be okay with me. I can't go back to work feeling guilty about that, too."

Liam sighed. April felt flattered and disappointed at the same time. She wanted to be with Merry, but it was nice of Bev to try to protect her—even if, like Liam, Bev thought she knew better than April herself.

"There's a beautiful solution staring us in the face," Trixie said. She widened her smile when they all looked at her. "Surely you can see it, Liam. And you, Bev. You're such a genius about the people side of business."

Bev smiled but shook her head. "Help me out. I'm not running on all cylinders at the moment. I walked around with my breast hanging out all afternoon. Thank God nobody noticed."

"Oh, I noticed—" Liam began, his grin disappearing as Bev's open palm smacked him above the ear.

"It's a simple solution." Trixie stood up and carried the remaining mugs to the sink, humming under her breath. "Oh, April. We're going to have so much fun. Until you have your own baby, of course. Then it's not exactly fun, but I'll do my best to help you. And Bev, if she isn't busy with her second, if she has another"—she turned and gestured at Bev—"and I'm not pressuring you, because there's nothing worse than people bothering you about your reproductive choices, but if you *did* have another as the same time as April, and wouldn't that be wonderful—"

April grabbed her arm. "Whoh, Mom. Not pregnant. Not likely, either, because I'm not having sex again for a very long time, possibly ever."

Liam put his hands over his ears. "I don't want to know."

Her mother sighed. "And I do, but she won't tell me. Isn't that just the way the world works?" She squeezed April's shoulder. "Anyway, don't you think it's a great idea?"

"What? You haven't told us," April said.

"I'm sure Liam has put it all together, haven't you, honey?" Trixie asked. Their mother had an annoying habit of knowing everything and nothing at the same time. The problem was, you never knew which one it was.

"Mom," Liam replied, "when you act like this, I worry about what you're going to be like when you're old."

"And a backhanded compliment to boot!" Trixie patted her short hair. "Sixty is the new forty, you know."

Yawning loudly, Liam got to his feet and joined Bev in the doorway. April peeked between their bodies at the soft little pajama-clad feet sticking out from under the blanket in the car seat carrier.

Would it really be so bad? "I was planning on taking a break from temping anyway," April said quietly. What she meant was, she couldn't keep sneaking into Fite.

"Like I said, it's perfect," Trixie said. "You and Liam and Bev can take turns watching Merry and working at Fite, depending on what hours Liam can arrange for you, though of course he'll have to consult people."

"Mother," Liam said in a low voice. "Explain. Please. I'm too tired to translate right now."

"All that talent won't be going to waste anymore," Trixie said. "Artists aren't nearly as common as people think."

Bev's eyes widened. "Oh, I get it." She smiled at April. "That's a great idea!"

Trixie just smiled, eyes twinkling. "First Liam has to agree to the plan."

He groaned. "I don't even—"

"He agrees," Bev said, putting an arm around him and sinking against his side with a yawn. "Don't you, honey?"

"Ouch!" he cried. "Did you just pinch me?"

"Sorry. Your mom has a great idea," Bev said. "Say you agree."

"This is like a bad dream. Nothing makes any sense." He rubbed his face with his free hand. "If I say I agree, will you both leave so we can get some sleep?"

"Yes," Trixie said. "Fantastic. April, let's go. Tomorrow morning you can figure out the details—when you're here with the baby, when you're at Fite. And you get paid for both, because it's the only way that everyone will be happy."

"When who's at Fite?" Liam asked. Then scowled. "No. I can't have any more family on the books, I told you—"

"Nothing could be more perfect than having your talented, underemployed, hungry—as in eager, driven, capable—sister under the Fite umbrella," Trixie said. "Don't you think so, Bev? It is your company."

"What do *you* think?" Bev asked April. "We'd be taking advantage of you from both sides, work and home. Baby and business."

A theoretical day blossomed in April's imagination: half at home with Merry, half in San Francisco pursing a real art career.

"As owner," Bev continued, "I declare it a fantastic idea. And I'm sure Liam agrees with me."

"She'd be our nanny *and* work at Fite?" Liam asked.

"Yes," Bev said, kissing him on the cheek. "Maybe you'll finally get some sleep so you can follow a simple conversation again." She turned to April. "We'll have to get a permanent nanny when Merry's older, but we haven't found anyone we like enough yet. Will you help us in the meantime? Are you even interested?"

April sank into a chair. "Oh," she whispered, just like Merry had. "Oh, oh, oh."

* * *

"Incredible," Rita, the manager of Fite Fitness's graphics department, said. "You've done this before, right?"

April looked down at the printout of the variegated stripe design in black and neon-orange she held out. *Just last week, actually.* "I've had a little exposure here and there to software like this. But I have a lot to learn."

"That's all right. I don't know why Liam didn't ask you to work for us earlier. I've been complaining about the freelancers all year." Rita tucked a strand of blonde hair behind her ear, exposing large silver hoops and a tiny butterfly tattoo on her neck.

April smiled. "Baby on the brain."

Rita peered at the design. "Or he's just being an asshole again." Her gaze shot up to April, and her pale face lost what little color it had naturally. "Please forget I said that. I have a foul mouth. I love your brother."

"I love him, too," April said, "even though he is, quite often, a total flaming doofus."

Rita smiled and cringed at the same time. After an awkward pause, she took the printout and pointed at the stripe in the middle. "Can you vary the width on these a little bit? I can show you how if—"

"How much?" April asked.

"Well, I'm just guessing what the designer is going to say, but... maybe reduce to a half inch."

"No problem." April had been relieved her first project was just a stripe design for a T-shirt. Stripes were incredibly easy. She'd been trying to figure out how to do all-over designs the week before, until she'd realized the software for complex textile designs must be on a workstation she hadn't hacked into yet. The first one had been easy because some freelancer had left a sticky note with his name and password next to the phone. No such luck with the other computer.

The moral question of recruiting her other brother, Mark the computer genius, to help her hack into it had kept her up at night. When she'd decided he wouldn't do it anyway, she'd started using the Internet to research common office security gaps—common passwords, human habits (like writing down their secrets on yellow paper next to the keyboard), administrative overrides. Years of being an interloper at somebody else's desk through temping had taught her a lot of those tricks already. Many Monday mornings, she'd waited hours until somebody with time or a brain could help her log on to the company's network. Boredom, even when paid by the hour, got old pretty fast.

Today, however, she could sit down at her own desk—well, she wouldn't have to share it unless the workload got so busy they had to hire another freelancer—and type in her own name and password. No corporate crimes necessary.

Knowing it was terribly obvious, she'd chosen *Merryis#1* as her password. Smiling to herself, she typed it in, thinking she was probably the third person in the company to do so.

"Rita?"

April turned around to see a young woman with long brown hair in a tight black dress hurry past, waving a sheet of paper.

"Hi, Teegan," Rita said, rising to meet her.

"I'm really sorry, but Jennifer says this is totally, totally terrible," Teegan said.

April suppressed a retort. *Terrible? Like, dying from famine terrible?* She peeked over her shoulder. She knew that holding her temper with some of these melodramatic chicks was going to be a challenge.

"Something not working?" Rita asked.

Teegan waved the paper. "Look at the colors."

The words *FITE FITNESS* filled the page in a rainbow of color. "Yes?" Rita asked politely.

"It's a rainbow," Teegan said.

"The request sheet asked for multiple colors," Rita said.

"But not *those* colors."

"The request sheet didn't specify."

Teegan made a face. "Jennifer said she told you."

"What colors would you like?" Rita asked.

"The ones in the New York line. The palette is on the boards in the conference room."

"Which conference room?" Rita asked.

"The one off the lobby."

"When do you need it?"

"We needed it this morning." Teegan's voice tightened to a faint whine. "When can you do it?"

Rita gestured to April. "We'll do it right now. This is April, our new freelancer, she's just—"

"Great. I've got to run." Teegan hurried away, and the door knocked shut behind her.

"The assistants tend to be a little high-strung." Rita followed her, giving April an eye roll, and reopened the door. "We're supposed to leave all the doors open while the consultant is here."

April took a sudden interest in her monitor, hiding her face. She'd pumped Bev for information about the guy—his name (Zack Fain), how long he was staying (six months), if he was single (*I thought you were never having sex again, April.*)

"I wonder when he'll grace us with his presence," Rita continued. "I hear he's been shadowing Engineering all week."

April hadn't told Bev that Fite's new business consultant had watched her run out of the office like a looter stealing a high-end TV. She still didn't know what to say if she saw him. *Just kidding, I really do work here* was one possibility. *I bet you're a lot cuter out of that suit* was another. Not that she would say that. She wasn't going near a naked man until she had her life figured out.

"Will you go get the swatches for me?" Rita asked. "I'll have to rush to get everything done before my lunch date. "

"Date?"

"Don't look happy for me. It's just with my dentist."

"Sorry," April said.

"It's okay. He gives me nitrous oxide. Which is why I need to get everything done this morning. I love that stuff. Thank God you can't buy it at Costco. Did you hear what Teegan called the group? New York, first-floor conference—"

"On my way," April said, striding off.

She took the stairs down to the lobby and waved at Virginia behind the desk.

Virginia still hadn't forgiven her for almost getting her into trouble with the business consultant, convinced she'd almost lost her job.

She'd come around. In fact, she wouldn't have the job at all without April's help. When, months ago, Virginia had asked April to put a word in for her with Bev and Liam about a job, April had been skeptical—Virginia knew video games, not fashion—but she'd helped her out. In return, Virginia had smuggled her into the art room before hours without telling anyone.

"Morning, Virg," April said, patting the desk as she crossed the lobby to reach the conference room. "Plans for lunch?"

"I thought you were with the baby in the afternoons," Virginia said, not meeting her eyes.

"Not yet. I'm in training, learning the software for a few days. Later this week I'll cut back to half days."

"Actually, I brought something to eat," Virginia said. "I can't go out. I have to be at my desk. Eating what I brought."

The rejection stung, but April shook it off. After putting her friend in a bad position, she couldn't blame her for wanting a little space. "No problem," April said, smiling broadly to emphasize her good will, big heart, and general likability. "Some other time."

Then she hurried into the conference room, marched around the large oval table to the foam core boards hanging on the walls, and tripped over a man's feet.

"You again," he said.

Chapter 4

THE FIRST THING Zack noticed was that she'd upgraded the heavy boots to black high-top sneakers.

"Oh, damn! Sorry." She stumbled over him. "I didn't see you there."

He reached up to support her elbow, admitting to himself that the shoes were, in fact, the second thing he'd noticed. The first was her rear end encased in cobalt-blue skin-tight jeans—and about to fall into his lap.

His blood warmed. "I'll send up a flare next time," he said.

Her gaze met his, then flickered down to his hand on her arm. "Don't worry," she said. "I'm supposed to be here."

"Really." He amended his earlier guess about her age. She was at least twenty. Or maybe he was just trying to make himself feel better.

Her pretty—no, gorgeous—gray eyes narrowed like a cat's. "Really."

He released her arm. "I'm not." He mentally shook himself. Why had he said that? He'd been taking a break, that was all. He was allowed to take breaks. His productivity suffered without them.

She stepped back and looked him over. "I thought you were allowed to go wherever you wanted." A slow grin formed on her lips. She wore purplish lipstick, like a Hollywood vampire. "There's a rumor you've been in the women's restrooms."

He stood up and buttoned his jacket, unhappy about the gossip but not surprised. He'd been through it many times before, usually triggered on his first day because of the open door requirement. And yes, he did look into the bathrooms—how else would he know what an employer was really like? "Only once, and they were all unoccupied at the time."

She laughed. "I love it. You're turning over all the rocks."

Her insight surprised him. "Yeah. Something like that."

She had turned away from him and now was searching through the large presentation boards hung on the wall. "Have you seen New York?" she asked.

"Frequently," he said. He managed to say it without bitterness, but every day he woke up back home in California filled him with relief—then guilt. He knew intellectually he was allowed to be happy, but his conscience still didn't believe it. "Thinking of doing some travel?"

She smiled at him over her shoulder. "The name of the line or group or whatever is New York. There's a board here with some color swatches I need."

He rubbed his hand over his mouth, covering a grimace. *Have I seen New York? Oh, sure, lived there for several long, cold years, clinging to the fragments of a life I never really began—oh, you don't give a shit?*

"Got it!" She spun around with a board half as tall as she was in her hands. "Nice seeing you, Zack, but I've got to run." She lifted it over her head like a backwoods traveler hoisting a canoe and maneuvered around the other side of the table toward the door.

"Sorry, but I didn't catch your name." He walked parallel to her on the other side of the table. He made it to the door before she did, which was good, because he was pretty sure she was trying to escape again without telling him who she was. And he had a business reason for knowing. It wasn't just because the miracle of the week before seemed to be repeating itself.

It wasn't just the jeans. Thousands of bodies in tight jeans had paraded past him over the past few years, and not one of them had fired him up the way hers was.

She paused with the board on her head, looking as if she were tempted to bop him in the forehead with it to get out of the room. "Look, Rita Gronsky needs this right away."

"Rita Gronsky, manager of the graphics department?"

"No, Rita Gronsky, banjo-playing astronaut." She rolled her eyes. "Yes, in the graphics department. I'm April. I'm a freelancer here. If I don't get this to her in the next five seconds, I won't be."

He didn't move. "So, Rita Gronsky—manager, folk musician, and astronaut—would fire someone over a delay of five seconds?"

"Now it's more like five minutes. And she wouldn't, but the designers might get her into trouble, and I wouldn't want to be responsible for that." She went up on tiptoes, slicing the board over his head, and wiggled past him. Just as her body brushed his, she said, "Would you?"

A hot shiver ran down his spine, freezing him in place. In a daze, he watched her jog across the lobby and into the hallway toward his office and the stairwell. He'd noticed most of the young designers, patternmakers, interns, and freelancers skipped the elevators, preferring the speed of the stairs. Being the same way himself, he'd been bumping into them there all week.

He ran a hand down his chest, under his jacket, feeling the shocking return of life under his ribs.

Maybe he'd bump into *her* there. April. Still didn't know her last name. The memory of her body brushing his brought hot blood to his face.

He shook his head. What the hell was the matter with him? Since when was he the type of creep to fantasize about jumping the cute young thing in the stairwell?

He slammed his laptop shut and shoved it into his briefcase, trying to ignore the fantasy that hit him like a high-resolution video.

Since today, apparently.

* * *

At the end of the day, April logged out of her computer—she'd named it Jane and had attached a suction-cup bud vase to the monitor—and slung her backpack over her shoulder. It was heavy with software manuals and made her walk at an angle as she headed downstairs.

She'd mentioned her run-in with the consultant, Zack, in the conference room to Rita, who had freaked out and told her to give him as much time as he wanted the next time, rush color-matching project be damned.

"The designers are all bark and no bite," Rita had said. "This guy is all bite. Have you seen that notebook of his? Not a word, just scribble, scribble, scribble. You give him all the time he wants, and for God's sake, don't mention me next time. We'll make time for him, even if we're swamped."

"What are you so afraid of? He's just a guy in a suit. Besides, he can't be much older than I am. How powerful could he be?"

"He's an ax looking for a log, April. That's what these guys are. They look for people to get rid of. On his last day, he'll hand Liam and Bev a list. I don't want to be on that list. Got it?"

"You've got nothing to worry about. One reason Liam didn't want"—April had cut herself off here, realizing she shouldn't tell

Rita that Liam hadn't wanted his sister at Fite—"didn't want you unhappy was because you might quit. He's paranoid about you quitting."

Rita had waved that away. "Promise me you'll give Zack Fain whatever he wants."

"Sure," April had said.

She doesn't know what she's asking, April thought now as she stepped onto the first floor. She'd recognized that look of his. It wasn't the look of an ax—more like the look of a horny lumberjack who'd been in the woods too long.

Still, she hadn't treated him professionally, either, and it was time she did. So, assuming he was the type still to be at work at 4:55 p.m., she'd see him and clear the air. She smoothed her hair —hah, that was a delusion—with her palm before knocking on his door.

His *closed* door, the hypocrite.

Why had he been sitting in the conference room a few steps away, then, when he had a space of his own right here?

There was no response, so she knocked again. The door flew open while her arm was still raised, and she stood there in front of him, feeling like an idiot while he watched, scowling.

"Hey, there, big guy." She moved her hand to her forehead in a salute and snapped her heels together.

So much for the professional thing. She never had been very good with authority.

His eyebrows rose. He regarded her for a long moment before saying, "At ease."

Was he kidding? She glanced past him into his office. Harsh fluorescent ceiling lights flickered over dark-brown bookcases, stained carpeting, and a monster of an oak desk designed decades before personal computers.

"No wonder," she muttered, lowering her hand. She wouldn't want to hang out in there either.

"Excuse me?"

"Sorry. Nothing."

"What can I do for you?" he asked.

"I was going to ask you the same thing. I ran off earlier. Rita told me we're available at any time for you if you want anything."

"Tempting, coming from a musical performer."

Because he wasn't smiling, she said, "She doesn't really play the banjo."

"That's very disappointing." His dark blue eyes held her gaze. "And the career in space exploration?"

"Ended before it began."

His lips twitched. "I'll be sure to let either one of you know if I need anything, banjos and space excluded."

She still stood in the doorway. Her left arm had gone numb under the weight of her bag. "Great. Then we're good for right now?"

He looked away and took a deep breath. "What time is it?"

"Almost five."

"Five." He stared into space, rubbing his jaw. "Do most people usually go home at five?"

"I wouldn't know, I just—" *I just started today.* Except she couldn't say that, because he'd seen her last week. "I work part-time. Freelance. In the mornings, usually."

He took out a little notebook out of his pocket.

"Don't write that down," she blurted out.

His expression didn't change. "It's how I work. Nobody will see this but me." A tiny ballpoint pen appeared in his hand.

"That's b—" She bit her lip. Calling the business consultant a liar while he was taking notes was a bad idea. She shouldn't have gone out of her way to talk to this guy. She was only going to get herself and everyone else into trouble. "Beautiful. The pen. Can I see it?"

The eyebrows arched again. He studied the pen for a moment and then offered it to her.

It was a cheap travel-size ballpoint, red plastic with fake silver trim. She plucked it from his fingers and pretended to admire it. "Artists have an eye for good tools. This one has great, uh, proportions."

"I got it at the gas station near the airport."

She could tell by the tone in his voice that he knew she was full of shit. But he wasn't the only one who could keep a straight face. Without breaking a sweat, she offered it back to him as if it were made of platinum, studded with diamonds, and filled with ink derived from the tears of baby angels. Baby kitten angels. "Don't lose it," she said gravely.

"It's yours," he said, putting his hands—and the notebook—in his pocket. "I've got more of them."

"They sell cases of pens at the gas station?"

"I picked up several so I wouldn't run out." He leaned against the doorframe as if he were getting comfortable, as if their conversation were just getting started. "How long have you been a freelancer here?"

She'd been trying to decide how to deal with that question. Until recently, she'd never lied about anything—it was much more radical to tell the truth, and she always prided herself on being a rebel. "Honestly?" She leaned in, lowering her voice. "This is my first real... you know, *paid*... day here."

To her relief, he nodded in understanding. "Are there a lot of interns at Fite?"

She had no idea. She shrugged.

"Was it hard getting them to hire you?" he asked. The notebook was in his hand again.

"Don't blame them. Money's tight."

"Especially when you're just starting out, though, isn't it?" he asked.

"You mean me?"

He nodded.

This was more familiar ground. She knew she looked a lot younger than she was. "I'm twenty-seven. I started out a long time ago. Just not here."

The surprise on his face was the most emotion she'd seen him express yet. He ducked his head and twirled the pen—a different pen—in his fingers.

She pressed her lips together. Even if she dressed like her mother, people would still think she was sixteen. "Is there anything else you want to ask? I need to get home."

"Go ahead," he said, pushing away from the doorframe. "Thanks for coming by."

"No problem." She moved her backpack to the other shoulder and turned, grateful once again to flee his company.

"If I need anything else," he said to her back, "I'll ask you tomorrow. I'll be starting in your department first thing in the morning."

Chapter 5

TWENTY-SEVEN.

ZACK brushed his teeth, staring at himself in the mirror over the sink in his rental condo's bathroom. He spat and rinsed his mouth.

Only five years younger than he was.

He rubbed the deepening groove between his dark eyebrows, feeling ancient. His eyes looked like his dad's, blue but gloomy, hidden under heavy lids. His jaw was like his dad's, too, ready for a shave an hour after he'd used the razor. He loved his dad, but the old guy was pushing seventy. Should he look so much like him already?

Maybe his life after Meg's death had gone by in dog years. No. Too old. He'd be dead, too.

How could that combat-boot-wearing, energetic, rock star... *girl...* be his contemporary?

He had to admit that he was even more attracted to her now, knowing her age, than before. It hadn't been just the appeal of forbidden fruit, the hot young intern, an old man's fantasy. He simply liked her. If it weren't for his personal ethics about his work, he could ask her out. They might have sex.

He could have *sex*.

He splashed cold water on his face and rubbed it dry with the white cotton towel.

It had taken him three tries to get dressed that morning. He'd downgraded the slacks to dark jeans, switched them back to wool, then denim again. "It's not a date," he muttered, combing his fingers through his short hair.

Why had he said he'd be in her department today? The art room was a minor player in the company, only a footnote to the design and engineering teams, who themselves were secondary to sales and finance. He didn't need to be in the art room for any longer than the thirty minutes it would take to interview Rita, the manager.

He smiled. The banjo player. And astronaut.

There was a good reason for his joining their department today: he was sick of sitting in the basement, and his week interviewing everyone on the engineering floor had been tense. Adopting a low profile for a day or two, maybe longer, would help everyone relax.

He repeated that to himself during his twenty-minute walk from his rental condo across downtown San Francisco to the Fite building, but when he walked into the art room, with his laptop slung over his shoulder and a coffee in his hand, relaxed was the last thing he was feeling.

Rita hurried over to meet him at the door. "Oh, hello. Thanks for the email. Last night, I mean. Not that I wouldn't be here at eight, but—actually, you might as well know, I'm not usually here at eight. I have two kids, and Liam hired me under the conditions that I would work nine to five with a shorter lunch, if necessary, which it usually is, but the CDs don't usually drag themselves in until ten, even the ones without—"

"This is for you," he said, holding out the coffee. "I'm sorry for messing up your schedule. Tomorrow, please come in at your usual time."

Biting her lip, she took the cup from him. "I was blathering, wasn't I?"

"I have that effect on people. Comes with the job." He smiled and looked around. Where was April? He probably shouldn't ask. Even though most people seemed to find him completely opaque, he had to be careful. He shouldn't ask direct questions about April until her appeal had worn off—within the next day or two, he hoped, if he immersed himself in her department and the thrill of having functional hormones wore off.

"There's usually only one freelancer here at a time, so it was easy to find you space. I've cleared this desk for you," Rita said, ushering him to the cubicle across from April's. They'd be sitting back-to-back.

His heart began to pound. *Right now would be a good time to get a fucking grip.*

One or two days. That would do it.

Clenching his teeth, he set his laptop on the desk.

"Is it okay?" Rita asked. "I've got another spot over here, but it's cramped. Three monitors take up a lot of room."

"No, no, this is great." He met her gaze and smiled politely.

"Oh my God," a voice burst out from the other side of the cubicle wall. "I will never, ever, ever be a morning person, and if one of those early bird worm-loving freaks gets in my way, I'm not responsible for what happens."

Zack, a morning person, had sensed she had arrived even before she spoke—it wasn't just the fruity perfume she was wearing, but the squeak of heavy rubber soles in the hallway that gave her away.

"Good morning," he said. He could feel his smile brighten from polite to puppy-happy.

Be careful, you dork. He had a reputation for being about as flirtatious as a filing cabinet, with excellent results. He was young but serious and responsible. Sexual harassment was a claim he advised his clients to take seriously. He could hardly commit it himself, even accidentally.

He noticed her frown just as she tried to hide it by turning away to sit at her desk. "Morning," she said softly.

He untangled his laptop cord and plugged it in, adjusted his bag, phone, and laptop on the desk, and removed his full-sized notebook and one of his many pens from inside the bag. A glance at his phone told him it was 8:03 a.m., a typical start time for him. He let out the breath he'd been holding, telling himself it was funny, not terrifying, that he had a crush on a woman who wore a torn Beavis and Butthead T-shirt to the office.

The two women in the office with him didn't say a word for thirty minutes. He was lost in his own work, transcribing his notes from the day before, when Rita knocked on the hard edge of the cubicle to get his attention.

"Will you be needing me for anything? I have a meeting at nine, so if you wanted to talk to me, now would be a good time," she said.

He really did have to justify crashing into her office like he had. "I'd love a quick demo of the software you use. Not the off-the-shelf packages, but..." He trailed off. He wasn't convinced that all the specialized equipment Fite had was worth the fortune the company had poured into it. He knew how tempting shiny new software, computers, and toys could be—especially to fashion designers who made a living chasing trends and looking cool.

Rita's face tensed, as if she'd had to defend the expenses before. "I'll want to give you a proper demonstration." She looked at her watch. "Is ten fifteen all right? I just got called into a meeting. It's with the Men's team, and they're already upset with—well, they're always upset, honestly, but we have to get some revisions in the afternoon FedEx shipment to New York, and it really can't wait —"

Zack held up a reassuring hand. "You don't have to take time out of your day for me. I'll just watch"—he hesitated, as if not sure of her name—"April. While she's working. That way I'm not slowing anybody down."

Rita shook her head. "April hasn't learned FreePeat yet. That's the software you're talking about, I think, because it's so expensive." She ran nervous fingers through her fair hair. "Right?"

Zack glanced at April, who had her back to him. The monitor over her head was filled with black and pink stripes. "I think that was the name," he said. "That's not what she's using right now?"

"No, that's just Illustrator. For screen prints, we can use either." Rita looked at her watch again. "Look, maybe I can reschedule that meeting with the Men's team. They're probably just going to ask for a color change, and I can rush that over lunch—"

"Don't skip your lunch just for me," he said. "You already came in early. I'm really not here to cause trouble. I try to blend in. Impossible, I know, but don't change your schedule for me. I'll adapt. Is ten thirty a good time?"

"Yes, but are you sure?"

"Absolutely," he said.

Rita nodded, smiling tightly, and retrieved a tablet from her own cubicle before running for the door. "Be right back! April can show you what she's working on if you're interested."

When she was gone, April rotated halfway in her chair and met his gaze over her shoulder. A handful of her curly hair was swept up in a round ponytail at the back of her head that looked like a yarn pom-pom on a winter hat. Her gray eyes were rimmed with cobalt-blue eyeliner that was the same color as her skin-tight jeans. "Are you interested?"

His hands began to sweat. *Hell, yes, but why?*

He stood up and came over. "Do they usually hire freelancers who don't know how to use the software?"

She rotated away from him and grabbed the mouse. "I know how to use the software. See?"

"Not the specialized software, though. Is it that rare?"

"You'd have to ask Rita," she said. The window on her screen closed, opened, closed. Another graphic appeared, this one with the Fite logo in earth tones. It zoomed across the screen, F-I-T-E, and then disappeared. Her fingers tapped on the mouse.

She was nervous.

Why?

He'd allowed his resurrected sex drive to distract him from learning something important. Big mistake. In spite of the high flirt risk, he rolled his chair over from his side of the cubicle and sat down next to her. "So, April," he began. "What exactly were you doing in here the day we met?"

Her hands settled on the desk. After a second, she said, "Trying to learn the software so I could get a job in this department."

"Where were you working before?"

She didn't answer.

"April?"

"It's funny," she said. "I'm the one who screwed up, but if I tell you, other people will get in trouble."

He instinctively clicked his pen. "I'm not the police."

She rolled her eyes.

"I'm not," he repeated.

"Fine," she said. "Why are you here?"

"I was hired to find ways to establish the company's long-term financial health."

"In the art room?" she asked softly, raising one eyebrow.

His pulse accelerated. *She's on to you.*

No, she was just trying to scare him away. Donning his coldest, most filing-cabinet persona, he said, "Each license of that design software costs as much as the combined annual salary of two associate merchandising assistants," he said. "And yet you don't know how to use it."

"Big deal," she said with a shrug. "The combined annual salary of two associate merchandising assistants is about fifteen bucks."

"A little more than that."

"Not much more. Seriously." She snorted. "Why do you think I work in *here*?"

"That's what I'm wondering."

Her smile vanished. "I'm an artist. I have a degree. I'm good, ask Rita."

"Did you use to be a merchandising assistant?"

She ran her fingers through her hair, roughly releasing the fluffy ponytail. Brown curls floated around her face. Her eyes darted around the carpeted walls, settling nowhere. "I don't suppose if I tell you, you'll promise not to tell Liam? You can file it away in your notebook and move on to more important things?"

"I can't promise anything, I'm sorry."

"Then I won't tell you. I can't. Assume the worst if you have to, I'm not squealing."

He put the pen down, trying not to laugh. "This isn't the *The Godfather.*"

"You don't know my br—" She turned to the computer again and brought up the stripes. "Never mind. Do you want to see what I'm working on or not?"

"You do know I can find out all this in HR, right?"

"Go ahead."

He frowned at her, more confused than ever. Making a show of taking out his notebook, he asked, "What's your last name?"

"Shit."

"Unusual name."

"It's French," she said.

"April..."

"That's English, I think. Or Latin." She peered at the computer. "You could look it up."

He would. But in the meantime, he'd let her know what he suspected. "You know somebody who works at Fite. While you were visiting them—or more likely, that's why you were visiting— you poked your head in here to look around."

The corner of her mouth quirked up. "And then?"

"And then you got a freelance job. Either because of your recon mission or in spite of it."

"Will you tell anyone about your theories?"

"Why should I?" he asked.

"Isn't that your job?"

"No," he said. "In fact, it's not."

"What exactly is your job?"

He held out three fingers and ticked them off. "Process. Product. People."

She rolled her eyes. "Please."

Stifling a laugh, he said, "Seriously. It's in my brochure."

"Pencils," she said, holding up three of her own fingers. "Pillowcases. Penguins."

He held his straight face and pointed at the design on her computer. "Pants?"

With a grin, she turned to the screen and zoomed out.

"Pink!"

He waited a beat, then said, "Pretty."

She laughed. For a moment, his chest felt light—as if the anvil that had fallen off the cliff and crushed him into the dirt had been lifted. He didn't know his lungs could expand with so much air, that his ribcage was so flexible.

She sobered. "Seriously, I'd appreciate it if you didn't tell anyone you saw me in here that day. At least until I've been here a little longer." She held his gaze. "Please?"

Of course he couldn't promise. He didn't even know her last name.

"Okay," he said, feeling the pressure returning to his chest, the joints of his ribcage contracting. His filing cabinet unlocking. "As long as you show me those pretty pink pants."

Chapter 6

L ATE THAT T HURSDAY afternoon, April lay little Merry down into the bassinet attached to Bev's side of the bed. After spending her first three eight-hour days at Fite, she was happy to spend the afternoon with Merry. The workload had slowed, she could study the manuals at home, and Zack made her nervous.

Besides, the deal was she babysat in the afternoons anyway. It really didn't have anything to do with Zack. Or the way he watched her through his glasses with those curious navy-blue eyes and then flushed like he couldn't help himself.

You're thinking about him again, she berated herself, leaving Liam and Bev's bedroom to tell her mother she could stop playing the piano now.

Her mother had bought the piano for her first grandchild the day Liam and Bev told her they were moving into the house next door. Even before their furniture arrived, the piano store delivered a new baby grand, planting it right in the middle of the living room overlooking the Golden Gate. Her mother sat there now, playing Mozart softly in the upper register, little tinkling notes she insisted made Merry happy, brilliant, and sleepy. Proof of her skill at the piano, Stool curled on the floor near the pedals, finally letting April disappear into the other room without following her. The three Chihuahuas were curled up on the sofa. They had accepted Stool's existence as long as he kept his distance.

"She's out," April told her, patting her back. Her mother had broad shoulders, strong from gardening, dog care, piano, weight lifting (that had been the idea of Mark's fiancée, Rose), and mothering.

Trixie Johnson waved her arms a lot when she mothered.

Now she was resting her hands on the keys, gazing off into space. "What a magnificent child."

"Thanks," April said. "I learned everything I know from you."

She tilted her head back and beamed at her. "You're joking, but it's true. You're wonderful."

"Right back at you, lady."

"I haven't asked you about your work at Fite—"

"Which I appreciate," April said.

Her mother made a face. "But I've been very curious."

April sat on the bench next to her, bumping her hip against hers. "Yeah?"

"Mm-hm."

"You seem to know everything, even if nobody tells you anything," April said.

"I merely observe," her mother said. "Like Sherlock Holmes."

April smiled, imagining her tie-dye-wearing Berkeley mom in a plaid Victorian hat with earflaps. It was surprisingly easy to conjure the image. "You tell me, Holmes. How's it going for me at Fite?"

"You're doing very well with the artwork, of course..." her mother began.

April waited. "Yes?"

"But you're having social trouble of some kind." Trixie tapped her ribs with her elbow. "I'm good, aren't I?"

"That was an easy one," April said. "Interesting troubles are always social."

Her mother smiled. "I admit that."

"Seriously, though, I'm fine."

"What's his name?"

April groaned. "Why would you think there's a guy involved?" She shook her head. "Fite used to have one straight, single guy, and that was Liam. Now that he's married Bev, the company is all women, gay men, and married old-timers."

"Sure," Trixie said. "That makes sense. It's the fashion business."

"And I told you—I'm done with men for a long time. The binge is over. Cold turkey."

"Of course you are." Her mother began playing Bach's Minuet in G Major.

April listened for a minute. "I know what you're doing. Mark and Liam are hitched, so now you're going after me."

Frowning, Trixie stopped the minuet and struck a loud minor chord. "Mark isn't hitched *yet*. I don't know why people spend so long planning a wedding. It's been almost a year since they were engaged. It's not like it used to be—you can walk down to city hall and get married in a day or two, can't you? You don't even have to go to Nevada anymore—which, by the way, is right up the road. A few hours and it could be *settled*."

Mark and Rose had pushed their wedding to the following spring, after initially planning to get married the previous summer, around when Bev and Liam, with Merry on the way, had gotten married in a small family ceremony at the house. Mark said they didn't want to compete with Liam and Bev for any of the wedding glory, but April knew they'd seen how much work it was, not just for them but also for the guests who had to travel across the country, and they'd dragged their feet a little bit about their own big day.

"They wanted that particular winery for their wedding," April said.

"Why? Why does everyone make such a fuss about one little party? It's the marriage that's important. If people put half the time into planning that, nobody would ever get divorced."

"Never?" April asked.

Trixie played another gloomy chord. "Be quiet. What's his name? The man you aren't going to tell me about unless I make you."

"I don't know what you're talking about."

Another chord, louder than the others.

"Shh, you'll wake the baby," April said.

"Merry does whatever she wants to do with no input from any of us, just like you," Trixie said. Then she smiled. "It's wonderful. I'm so happy to see you two grow up together."

"Thanks. You just called me an infant. As if I don't get that enough from the general population."

Trixie laughed. "You're a late bloomer. Smart of you, given the two flashy acts you had to follow. I don't know how I could've handled having Liam or Mark as *my* brothers—winning gold medals, being in the news, making millions of dollars, and all so *young...*"

"Yeah, yeah, don't rub it in," April said.

"I'm just grateful you didn't move to Pennsylvania or Berlin."

"What's in Pennsylvania and Berlin?"

"Not you, thank goodness," her mother said. She resumed playing Bach in the high notes.

April listened for a full minute before saying, "There *is* a guy, but it's not what you think."

"Mm." Trixie kept playing.

"His name is Zack. He's a business consultant. He's at Fite for six months, is totally not my type, and is going to move back to New York, where he lives, as soon as he's done firing everyone at the company, which probably includes me."

"Zack," Trixie said. "Does he like dogs?"

"Sure, Mom. Rescued greyhounds are his favorite, but he'll tolerate a terrier mix if it's not much of a barker." April began playing harmony in the lowest register.

"Ask him to dinner," Trixie said. "I bet he hasn't had a good home-cooked meal in ages."

"We're not on those terms."

"For crying out loud." Her mother slapped her hands on the top of the piano. "Your father and I met, married, and had a baby within a year. He still died before you reached high school. How long do you think life is? It's short, April. Short. You have to seize it. You have to take it and grab it now. *Now*."

April stared at her. Her mother never talked like that. "Uh..."

"You know I'm right," Trixie said. "That's why you broke into Fite all those mornings without permission. Because you know you can't wait forever. Sometimes you can't wait for life to get out of your way. You have to barge right into it."

Goose bumps rose on April's arms. Not because Trixie knew about Fite, but because of the serious, urgent edge to her voice. "Is everything okay, Mom?" She lowered her voice to a whisper. "Are you okay?"

"If I told you I'd be dead next week, would you invite him to dinner?"

The goose bumps spread to the rest of her body. "Yes," April whispered.

Trixie sighed. "How about a knee injury?"

"You hurt your knee?"

"I could." She moved her hands from the keys to her thighs. "I'm not getting any younger."

"But you're not sick. Right?" April studied her mother, unhappy to notice she didn't look quite as baby faced and vibrant as the image April nurtured in her mind. Lines from unprotected sun exposure—which Trixie insisted was worth the vitamin D—creased her eyes, cheeks, mouth, and neck. Her hair had been white for a long time, but it looked a little dull and flat. "Right?"

"I'm not pooping as easily as I'd like," Trixie said. "And I almost wet myself laughing at a TV show last night. Does that ease your mind?"

"It depends," April said, swamped with relief. "So to speak. What was the show?"

Trixie laughed. "That's my girl. You're my lighthearted one, always were. Don't worry. I'm fine."

"Except for the peeing-in-your-pants thing."

"My grandbaby and I have so much in common," Trixie said, starting to play again. "Next Thursday is perfect. Do you know if Zack's a vegetarian?"

The craziness of the idea was so *her*. "Great idea, Mom," April said. "I'll invite the business consultant I barely know home to meet my mother—on *Thanksgiving*."

"Not just your mother," Trixie said. "Liam and Bev's mother, too. His clients. It's not such a strange request, see? You could pretend it's for business."

Luckily, Zack had told everyone he'd be gone the entire week for the holiday. He didn't specify where he was going, but she and Rita and Virginia had decided it was New York, his permanent base.

Gossiping about the dark-haired, serious young consultant had become a widespread hobby at Fite Fitness, and although

April tried to abstain, she found herself as curious and full of theories as everyone else.

"He's out of town until after Thanksgiving," she told her mother.

"Visiting family?"

"How would I know?" April turned the pages of the sheet music on the stand in front of them—beginner's music, for a child. Just in time for the two-month-old infant in the other room, who no doubt would be playing "Twinkle Twinkle Little Star" any day now.

"Didn't you ask?" Trixie swatted her hands away from the sheet music. "Never mind, you're right—a regular day will be more relaxing, less intimidating. You can invite him for a plate of my famous lasagna."

"Mom, seriously. I barely know him. And inviting him home to meet my mom—"

"Forget about me. I'll go out. There's a space movie I want to see. Those are always better in theaters, and I can avoid the crowds around the holiday weekend."

April looked at the couch next to the piano. It was the same one she'd slept on in Liam's condo in San Francisco during another one of her homeless periods. "How about you and I go to the movies together?" April asked. "Just you and me."

It had been ages since they did anything like that. April tried to remember the last time she'd been out with just her mom— away from the house, away from her brothers.

"You'd do that?" Trixie asked.

"Of course I'd do that. I want to do that."

"Just us?"

"Why are you so surprised?"

"I... I don't know. Movies are such a date thing with you.

Seems like a waste to go with your mom when you have boyfriends falling all over you."

That was her polite mother's way of saying she slept around. "They were all losers, that's why they kept falling."

"But this Zack guy sounds impressive—"

"Forget that guy. You and I will make a real date of it. We'll go to the salon beforehand. And dinner. Indian, and not just the lunch buffet. From the *menu*."

Interest glowed in her mother's eyes. "Do you think Liam and Bev could do without us that long?" She glanced over at the door to the bedroom. "We could try to bring Merry with us. We can practice using that baby carrier."

"No baby. Just us. We couldn't really do it right with her along."

"What about the dogs?"

"Stool has settled in," April said. "He gets along with the others pretty well." She glanced at the trio still snoozing in a puppy pile on the sofa.

"Wouldn't you rather do that with one of your girlfriends? You're surrounded by family day and night." Trixie glanced at April out of the corner of her eye. "I've heard some people don't like that."

"Let's do it. You and me," April said, thrilled finally to have diverted her from her fixation with Zack. "Saturday. I'll get us in at that salon on College."

Trixie beamed, touching her hair with the tips of her fingers. "I haven't had a proper cut in ages."

"Perfect. Me either."

"I'm so excited." Trixie laughed and stood up. "We'll both be gorgeous."

"Totally gorgeous."

Cupping April's cheek with her hand, her mother added, "And when Zack comes back and sees you, he'll know you're interested in dating."

* * *

The Monday after his long Thanksgiving holiday, Zack walked into the Fite building and felt the muscles between his shoulder blades loosen for the first time in eight days.

Why had he gone back? Meg's parents loved him—they often told him so—but at this point he'd spent more holidays with them than he ever had with his late wife. The painful absurdity of that weighed on him more every year.

I have to move on. He'd told them not to expect him at Christmas, which hadn't gone over well, especially with Meg's older sister, Sarah. Working in California for several more months was a good excuse, and he'd stuck to it—but what about next year?

He wished he'd never told them his own family didn't observe holidays—any holiday, even birthdays. As children, both of his parents had belonged to a church that didn't approve of holidays, and although they didn't belong to that particular sect anymore, the habits were there. Even before she died, Meg's parents saw it as their duty to make up for the first twenty years of his life. Just a couple of years earlier, they'd hired caterers and a band for his thirtieth birthday party.

Sometimes he felt like they loved him more than Meg ever had. It wasn't something he'd ever said out loud, to anyone, and he never would. It might sound like he blamed her, when all she'd done was hold on as tightly as she could, afraid of facing the darkness alone. If he'd been the one who'd found out he had cancer just as his first college loan payments were coming due, he might've felt his love for his girlfriend deepening, felt a need to hurry and do as much as he could as long as he could, right now, while he still could.

He didn't regret marrying her. He'd known he wanted to marry her on the fourth date. He'd proposed two months later.

But she'd said no. It was only when she'd gotten the diagnosis that she suddenly seemed eager to make it forever…

It's not only me who has to move on. But how can I do that to them? Take away another one of their children?

He greeted Virginia at the front desk as he strode past to his office. Just a quick stop to file a few things in the cabinet before returning to his cubicle in the art room next to April.

He would move out of the art room today. He'd decided that several times on the plane. Rita had shown him plenty, proving to him that the art room was more than pulling its weight, even with the expensive software and other equipment. They managed pretty well, actually, with less staff than they needed. Rita had told him about the freelancers she'd had to send home within the last year, assuring him that although April was new and untrained, she could draw and she showed up on time. None of the other freelancers had managed to reach that zenith of achievement.

The art room was empty when he walked in. Rita would come later, but he'd hoped to see April. Well, of course he'd hoped to see April.

It was good she wasn't there.

He looked at his watch. Why was she late? It was already 8:12 a.m. He'd noticed in the five days they worked together, she always walked into the office at 8:03 a.m., because of her train from Oakland, she'd said.

With an irritated sigh at himself, he sat down and opened his laptop to go through the morning email before he packed up his things. Nobody would be upstairs yet, anyway, and he'd want to tell Rita personally how much he'd appreciated her time and space.

"Welcome back," April said, walking past him to her desk.

His pulse kicked up. He sat up taller, sucking in his gut.

Oh, man. Still had a thing for her, it seemed. He'd thought it would've faded by now. Unable to resist, he turned to look at her. She wore all black, which was corporate enough, but the pants were tight and stretchy, like a yoga instructor's, and her shirt was sleeveless. Her hair seemed about four inches shorter, maybe more, yet somehow covered more of her face. It was as if the hair in the back had rotated to the front.

"Morning," he said. "Haircut?"

"I don't want to talk about it." Scowling, she plopped down in her chair and hit the power button on her computer. "I look like a stuffed animal."

He scanned the email in his inbox for a few seconds, deleting as many as possible and sorting the others into their action categories before asking, "Which one?"

"What?" She frowned at him from under her bangs. Her lipstick was red today, red and shiny, and it made her lips look full, ripe, and wet.

The room was too warm. California was too warm. He swallowed. "What kind of animal?"

"Hell if I know. Something too damn fluffy." She batted at the brown, bouncy curls on her head.

He wondered if they were as soft as they looked. Most women seemed to have straight hair these days. He couldn't remember the last time he'd seen a woman their age (he'd enthusiastically accepted they shared the same general one) with short, curly hair.

Realizing he'd been staring, he said, "You could wear a hat."

Her scowl deepened. "Thanks for the tip."

"Sorry," he said, turning back to his laptop. He wasn't trying to seduce her, but he could've managed something more tactful. The problem was, he was fighting the urge to say *I like it. It makes me want to touch you*, which would've been all wrong for several reasons. "Speaking of your hair, I'll be getting out of it today."

"Oh," she said. "You are?"

Did he imagine the disappointment in her voice? "I figured you'd be glad."

"Nope. It's been a great way for me as the new chick to make friends with people." She grinned. "They all want to know about you."

"Then why do they look so unhappy to see me?"

"They're afraid of losing their jobs," she said.

"Tell them I'm not a hatchet man. That's not what I do."

She studied him. "Honestly?"

"The last company I worked for didn't fire a single person after I made my recommendations."

"Yeah, but what were those *recommendations*?" She said it as if it were a disease.

He turned back to his laptop. "I didn't tell them to lay anyone off. Quite the opposite." Squinting at his screen, he dragged a few emails into his spam folder. "But, as it happens, they didn't agree with my assessment to cut the boss's salary and hire more entry-level admin."

With a laugh, she brushed the hair out of her eyes. "You said that?"

"The organization was as top-heavy as a three-scoop ice cream cone." He'd come up with that metaphor when he'd written the report. They seemed to have enjoyed it less than he had.

"You don't think that's good?"

"Why do you sound so surprised?" He rotated in his chair,

tugging both lapels of his jacket. "Is it my fancy suit?"

"Maybe."

"Two hundred bucks," he said. "Season clearance."

"That's still more than I spend on my outfits," she said.

"But I get to wear this almost every day," he said. "The average woman's wardrobe has very poor value if you factor in all the costs. I did a report—" He cut himself off. What was he doing? Bragging about how much he enjoyed writing financial reports? That one hadn't even been for school. He'd done it for *fun*. Instead of, as a normal guy might do, watching football or having sex with pretty girls.

Like her.

He cleared his throat. "Anyway..." His mind blanked. What had they been talking about? His suit. Ice cream. Women. "I should get back to work."

"By the way, which department will you be in this week?" she asked. "The assistant designers will ask me at lunch. If I keep feeding them secrets about you, maybe one of them will invite me to her birthday party."

The deadpan tone in her voice made him smile. "Do you *want* them to invite you?"

"I do love pony rides," she said with a wink. Then, flushing, she rotated away from him. "You're not the only one who should get back to work."

He stared for a moment at her back, encased in that black tank top. "I'll be in the Men's department this week," he said.

She nodded but didn't turn around. The software, which he'd learned was where they inputted their colors for the artwork they needed for different lines, appeared on her screen. "I haven't met the Men's designer yet," she said. "Darrin. I think I saw him last week at the coffee truck, though. He didn't look as scary as the stories about him."

"Scary?" he asked.

"Is that why you're doing his department while he's in New York?" she asked. "To avoid him?"

His stomach fell. "Darrin is in New York today?"

"All week."

He shifted gears. "Then I'll go to Women's. It's higher profile, and—"

"The Women's designers are in New York, too. That's why the vibe is so relaxed around here today."

"Right after Thanksgiving?"

"I know. I think they're just expensing their family vacations, but Jennifer and Darrin always get away with murder." She spun around and pointed at him. "Don't quote me on that. I'm new. They're wonderful. Creative geniuses. Quote me on *that*."

He pulled up his calendar on his phone, cursing himself for being so caught up in family—his dead wife's family—drama, he'd neglected some basic planning legwork. "When will they be back, do you know?"

"Next Monday."

"Damn it," he muttered.

"You could invade the trim office," she said. "Without zippers, there would be no Fite TrakrJak. That's the big silhouette this year, I found out. I'm working on the screen print for that sucker right now." She pointed at her screen. "Really going out on a limb, too. *Fite* in big letters. I'm a genius."

Me, too, he thought. *A goddamn genius*. "Guess I'll sit here another week, then." His voice was grim, but his body warmed at the thought.

<h1 style="text-align:center">Chapter 7</h1>

WHILE SHE WORKED on the third Fite logo color revision of her morning, April felt Zack sitting behind her at his desk, tapping away at his laptop.

She glanced over her shoulder. Was it possible the consultant had the hots for her? Or was she doing some terrible freelancer thing that was going to end up in his report? Something was going on inside that handsome head of his, she wasn't sure what.

She transformed the three-inch letter F on her screen to neon green. It would be easier to ignore the tempting idea of repressed sexuality coming at her across the beige commercial carpeting if her work were more interesting. Next week, Rita had promised, she'd start training her on FreePeat, the textile design software, but for now April was stuck with reworking block letters in solid colors.

Zack sneezed.

"Bless you," April said, making the T a lovely shade of blinding yellow.

He sneezed again. "Sorry," he said, sniffling.

She turned. "I hate flying. I always catch something."

"No," he said, looking up and meeting her gaze. "It's just allergies. This building's a little dusty."

Rita popped her head around the wall. "Oh, please tell them

that. Please? I've been begging to get an air filter in here." Rita's nerves around the consultant had calmed down as soon as he'd assured her, right before the holiday weekend, that the art department's accomplishments were impressive given its limited resources.

"To whom do you direct your begging?" he asked.

"Harry Charron," Rita said. "The facilities manager."

When Zack opened his small leather notebook in his palm and made a note, Rita flashed April a thumbs-up.

"Say, Zack," Rita said, smiling. "It's quiet around here today. What do you say we all go out to lunch together? Since you're done with us as targ—I mean, subjects—it might be nice for you to, you know, just relax."

"Lunch?" he asked. The look he gave April made her flush.

This was crazy. She was imagining things. He ran that probing look over everything, even the department water dispenser. "I'm sorry," April said, "but I have to get back to Oakland. I'm only here in the mornings this week."

"Oh, right. Sorry," Rita said. "I certainly wouldn't want to steal the bosses' babysitter."

After an awkward pause, Rita flinched and covered her mouth with her hand. Until now, they'd managed to avoid any references to April's family connection. Johnson was such a common name, and April so new, with a low profile, it hadn't come up.

"Babysitter?" Zack asked.

"I'm—shit," April explained.

Rita took an interest in the carpeting, as if searching for dust mites.

Well, it hadn't been Rita's idea to hire the owners' sister, and it was bound to come up sooner rather than later.

April put her hands on her hips, glad she'd worn Fite Fitness today, which should make her seem like a serious employee, a committed corporate worker bee, an ideal member of the team.

"I watch Merry in the afternoons," April told him. "Didn't I mention that earlier? That I'm only part-time?"

There. The truth, but kind of sneaky-like.

Zack frowned. "Merry?"

"Merry Johnson." Heart pounding, April sat in her chair and reached for her herbal tea. She didn't want him to know she was just a family hire. He wouldn't look at her the same way again.

Whatever way *that* was...

"My niece," she said finally. "You know, the baby?"

"Johnson," he said. His eyes widened as he figured it out. "You're Liam's sister."

She decided against faking too much innocence. He'd probably see right through it. "Yes," she said, and left it at that.

He leaned back in his chair and stared at the ceiling. April glanced at Rita, who mouthed *sorry*.

April waved it away with a smile and turned to her computer. It was for the best. Hopefully, knowing he was the client's sister, he might tone down the smoldering a little bit. If that's what he was doing. Tall and dark was hot, even in a suit.

Imagine what he'd look like in faded jeans and an old T-shirt. Or jeans and no T-shirt. Or no anything...

"That's why you were here when I met you. You're family," he said. "Why didn't you tell me? I thought you'd broken in."

"Sorry," April said, brushing aside the daydream. "You startled me."

"All this time I thought I was protecting—" He cut himself off, his gaze shifting to Rita. "I don't understand. Why the conspiracy?"

Rita, nervous again, twisted her fingers through her hair. "It was just a misunderstanding. I never meant to hide—"

"*I* did," April said. She should've told him on her first official day, when she tripped over him in the conference room. Now it had become a bigger deal than it needed to be. "Blame me. I don't tell anyone unless I have to. It's hard being in Wonderboy's shadow. I wanted to work here on my own terms."

"But everyone else must know," he said.

"Maybe, but I'm not the one to tell them," April said.

He put his hand over his notebook on the desk. "Wonderboy?"

"Gold medals, CEO, you know," April said. "I don't even know how to use FreePeat yet."

Rita dove in. "You will by Friday." She turned to Zack. "She's really good. Even if I got to hire her myself, I would."

"You didn't hire her yourself?" he asked.

April sighed. "Rita, didn't you have a meeting you had to go to?"

"As soon as Liam told me about her, I was glad," Rita continued.

"Which was how long before she showed up?" Zack asked, patting the notebook.

"Go ahead," April said. "Pick it up and write something down. You know you want to."

Ignoring her, he kept his gaze locked on Rita. "Has he ever done this before? Hired a relative without consulting management?"

"Please don't ask me," Rita said. "I don't want to cause any trouble. I really like working here."

"Except for the sneezing," April said.

"And forget I ever mentioned that about the air filter," Rita said. "I'm too sensitive. Just forget I ever said anything."

The notebook opened in his hands. "Do you feel that telling the truth about how often relatives are hired in this company could jeopardize your job?"

"Put that away," April said. "How can she answer that? You're trying to trap her."

"This wouldn't be the first complaint of nepotism around here," he said, scribbling with that little pen of his.

"That's unfair," April said. Her heart was pounding. Before Bev had inherited the company from her grandfather, Liam had been the only non-relative in a position of any power. Now he'd married the owner but did everything he could to keep family away from the company. "I made them hire me. If you want to blame anyone, blame me."

His pen hovered over the page. "Made who?"

She gritted her teeth. "You know."

"Liam and Bev?"

She nodded.

"How did you make them?"

"None of your business," April said.

Eyebrows arching, he continued writing. "They couldn't find anyone else to babysit their kid?"

Anger washed over her. Insults swirled over her tongue, but she bit them off. He was an officious dork—perfect. A few minutes ago, she'd been imagining him naked. Now she was having a fantasy about throwing him off the Bay Bridge covered in Shark Chow. Much better.

"Her name is Merry," April said tightly, "and it's my pleasure to spend as much time with her as I can. We don't all worship corporate America. Some of us want more balance in our lives."

"April," Rita whispered in alarm.

Zack put the notebook and pen in his pocket and regarded

April. "I'm sorry to upset you. I have to ask the hard questions. It comes with the job."

Not trusting herself to speak, April ground her teeth together.

"I unearth problems that a regular employee can't afford to unearth," he said. "When the dust settles, this will be a stronger company. And a better place to work."

"Easy for you to say. You won't know if it will be or not. You'll be long gone." April made a dismissive gesture with her hand and sat at her desk, spinning in her chair to give him her back. "We can't wait."

*   *   *

An hour later, when Zack finally got up and left his desk to bother some other innocent people, Rita tapped April on the shoulder.

"Coffee," she said. "Back alley. Now."

Assuming that Rita was worried about her job, April stood up and followed her down the stairs, past the offices, and through the storage area to the back door. She didn't regret a word she'd said to him. The coffee truck had been there long enough for the line to die down, and they got their own caffeine fix quickly. April tried to pay for Rita's, but she refused.

"Let's talk over here," Rita said, kicking aside a muddy paper cup in the gutter with her red-and-black ballet flat as she strode away. The shoes complemented the designer jeans and fitted red jacket she wore.

"You look nice today," April said, following her to a deserted, grubby stretch near an illegally parked sleek black BMW, probably belonging to one of the designers. "Job interview?"

Rita shot her a look over the rim of her coffee cup. "Watch it. I'm not happy right now."

"There's nothing for you to worry about. He's gunning for me, not you." April sniffed the dark, acrid liquid in her cup.

"I happen to like you."

"Not so much at the moment," April said.

"Why did you have to say that last thing about wanting him gone?"

"Because it's true." But April sighed. "I'm sorry. I hated the way he talked about Merry, like she wasn't worth any effort or sacrifice, like she was just a thing."

"Liam's not going to be happy. He's going to fire you, and then who's going to do those screen prints for Women's that are due tomorrow? I've got meetings all afternoon, and my daughter has a gymnastics show tonight I just can't miss—"

"I'll do the screen prints," April said. "Even if he fires me, which he won't. He'll just want more paperwork filed with HR to cover his ass. A copy of my diploma showing I actually have an art degree, color samples from my portfolio, notarized references. You'll see. If you think I'm doing a good job, Liam will find a way to keep me on that doesn't make him look like Mr. Roche, Bev's grandfather, the one who used to own this place. He let his daughter Ellen terrorize everyone. Including Liam."

Rita chewed her lips and fiddled with the rim of the cup. "You think?"

"As long as *you* want me here, he'll go along with it, even if some anal-retentive dude in a suit tells him it looks bad." In April's mind, Rita's opinion was the big thing to worry about. "*Do* you want me here?"

"Well, yes. The designers will dump a ton of work on us next week when they get back. Until I can find another freelancer or two with a little garment experience, you're all I've got."

"Then you've got me," April said, wishing Rita's endorsement had been a little more enthusiastic, a little less desperate, but she was willing to live with it.

She just needed more time to prove herself.

And she would.

* * *

Zack hadn't been this angry with himself since he'd forgotten to contribute to his retirement account before the tax-filing deadline. He tapped on Liam's door, which was nicely open, hoping the emotion pumping through him didn't show on his face.

Liam looked up from his computer with a scowl. His phone was ringing, but he made no move to answer it.

"Morning," Zack said, not intimidated. He was used to working with executives. "Got a few minutes?"

"Not exactly," Liam said. "More like two."

Zack looked at his watch. It was 11:36 a.m. April would be going home—to *Liam's* home, probably, to babysit—in twenty-four minutes. They should probably clear the air as soon as possible.

He walked across the office and stood in front of Liam's desk. "I'll be quick. I just discovered the woman I've been working with for over a week is your sister."

Liam's expression didn't change. "April."

"Yes," Zack said.

"Well?"

"Nobody told me."

"You didn't have anything bad to say about her last week," Liam said. "I read your email. You said Rita likes her."

"She seems to."

Liam stared at him across the desk. Unease flickered in his eyes. "Seems?"

"Rita would naturally feel pressured to like her, or say so, given the family relationship."

With a loud sigh, Liam buried his face in his hands. "Yeah," he said, his voice muffled. He looked up. "Do you think Rita's lying? My sister... well. She's... April."

Guilt made Zack pause. He didn't want to condemn anyone without a fair trial. "She seems to be doing her job. She's new, of course."

"And doesn't have enough experience." Liam stood up, glancing at his watch. "I can't resolve this right now. But if she's a problem, she's out of here. Tell people that. I'll tell Rita myself, but just so you know, too. I mean it."

"All right." Zack turned and walked to the doorway. His guilt snapped at him again. Had he really needed to talk to Liam about this now? In quite this way, as if it were urgent? He hadn't expected Liam to throw his sister under the bus so readily.

"Thanks for your time," Zack said.

Liam was right behind him with a tablet in one hand and large presentation board under the other arm. "Sorry I didn't tell you."

"Why didn't you?"

"It was a last-minute thing," Liam said. "But mostly, I wanted to know what you thought of her. Not knowing who she was."

"Any other family members here I should know about?"

"Not anymore, thank God." With a snort, Liam whacked him on the shoulder and strode off in the direction of the lobby.

Zack let out his breath.

Her brother.

That powerful, confident, mature leader of men—the client whose reputation would help him expand his business when he got back home to New York—was her *brother*.

She was totally, completely off limits.

Well, that was a relief. Now he could focus on his work, on what was important. He'd surely stop fantasizing about her now.

Chapter 8

No such luck.

The sheets twisted around his legs, damp and clinging. The tiny travel clock on the nightstand read 3:43 a.m.

The dreams about April had gone on and on and on, and he resented the moonlight that had ended them.

He kicked off the covers, squinting at the moon shining through the window like an angry face. In his drowsy delirium, the man in the moon looked like Liam Johnson.

What the hell did you just do to my sister? the brother-in-the-moon demanded.

She started it was Zack's lame reply. And she had. The dream version of April had licked, kissed, teased, and violated his body in every corner of the Fite building. He was just about to turn the tables and show her he wasn't the submissive type when the full moon woke him up.

He liked the condo he was renting, but the lack of window coverings was a problem. That moon would've woken him even if he hadn't been having futile sex dreams. He stumbled over to the window and frowned out at the night. Maybe the moon was so bright because it hung low over the San Francisco Bay, doubling its reflective power.

He'd get curtains tomorrow after work.

Work. The life he loved. Work, work, work.

He rested his cheek against the glass, watched it fog between him and the angry moon. In spite of himself, he smiled. His cheek pulled along the window.

"Damn," he whispered.

In his dream, she'd been just what he wanted, just what he needed. Sweet, enthusiastic, fun. That lithe body under his, above his, touching him, accepting him...

He closed his eyes.

Damn.

Twelve times over the past four years—well, two, since his friends had waited a couple of years after Meg's death to start interfering—he'd met and dated women who should've made him feel this way. Hell, he would've been happy with fifty percent of what he was feeling right now. Or ten. Two.

But for those smart, attractive, compatible, likable women: nothing. A glimmer of interest that lasted just long enough to get through the motions—he didn't like to think about how unpleasant that must've been for those poor women—and then the passion died, a weakly burning match in a gale of guilt and memories.

Of course Meg would want him to move on. He knew that. It was *him*, something about *him*. It was *his* fault.

Rather, it *had* been his fault. This was no flickering match he was holding—it was a flamethrower, and he couldn't find the power switch.

He got out of bed and staggered into an icy shower.

Four hours later, he sat at his borrowed desk next to April's, sipping his second coffee and rubbing his jaw. He'd forgotten to shave. Hours of nothing to do but wait for the dawn, and he'd managed to forget one of his basic morning tasks. At least he'd remembered to put on his glasses. Looking scruffy wouldn't stop him from working, but an inability to see would.

Scratching his nails along the stubble, he stared at the floppy white daisy attached to April's computer monitor, weighing his options.

Work was important to him and would always be important to him. Central to his life. The reason for being.

But...

Just at that moment he balanced on the precipice overlooking his life, April strode into the room with a red sequined tote bag slung over her shoulder.

"Morning, Mr. Fain," she said, saluting him. Her cloud of hair was pulled back under a thick silver band, her lips were painted a glossy fuchsia, and she wore a long, tight knit dress in the same shade of pink as her lips. His mouth went dry.

But this isn't the only job in the sea, he finished silently, rising to his feet. "Hi," he said, heart racing. "I was wondering if you'd have lunch with me today."

*   *   *

What did he just say?

April had never been a morning person, and last night she'd slept poorly. She hugged her tote bag to her side, suddenly wide awake.

"Excuse me?" Her voice came out more challenging than she'd intended, in part because she resented the way her heart skipped a beat at the sight of him. Was that unshaven jaw just for her? Because... damn. It worked.

"I owe you an apology," he said. "I know you don't have much time at lunch, so we could make it short—say, thirty minutes?"

"Uh..."

"My dime." He glanced down at the floor between them.

Suddenly self-conscious about the girly outfit she'd chosen that morning, April turned and put her bag on her desk, flicked on her computer, and tried to think of a diplomatic way to say no. She wasn't the most gorgeous babe on the planet, but she knew when a guy was imagining her naked. Even if he'd been a harmless barista at the coffee shop on the corner, she couldn't let herself involved. Not even for lunch.

But—damn, he looked good with a little shadow on that jaw. A little less corporate, a lot more corporeal.

She sat down and met his gaze. "I can't."

"Because of your other job?"

"Because I can't have lunch with you." She gave him a steady look that she hoped said *Or anything else, got it?*

He looked over the cubicle wall between them and Rita's empty desk, and then at the door, running his hand through his dark hair. "All right." He nodded and turned away. "Of course." The chair creaked as he sat down.

Within seconds, his laptop was open and he was typing something as if his request had meant nothing and her rejection even less.

Maybe it was her attraction she was feeling, not his. It had been an unusually long time since she'd gone to bed with anyone. Maybe she was hallucinating like a crazed traveler with an empty canteen in the Sahara.

She stifled a sigh. "What did you want to apologize about?"

His hands stilled over the keyboard for a moment. Then he hit a few keys and turned to her. "I spoke to your brother yesterday."

She couldn't resist. "Which one? I have two."

He raised an eyebrow.

"All right," she said. "I'll assume you meant Liam. And?"

"He's made it known he'll fire you the instant anyone complains about your work."

Her stomach flipped over. She stared at him for a second before turning away to mouth a string of foul curses under her breath.

The *instant* anyone complained? Anybody? Who could survive under that kind of edict in this place?

"I'm sorry," Zack said. He didn't look sorry, and his voice was emotionless.

She spun on him. "For what? Isn't that what you wanted?"

"Actually, no."

"Well, you got it," she said.

"I'll talk to him again and explain why letting you go probably isn't a good idea at this point."

"Probably." She grabbed a T-shirt hanging from an overhead cabinet and flung it on her desk. Hands shaking, she took out her ruler and slapped it over the shirt. The project request clipped to the hanger was to increase the gap between each stripe by fifty percent. She smoothed the slippery fabric flat with her palm and tried to line up the ruler precisely, because fifty percent of a pinstripe was hard to measure. It was probably in the computer from when it was originally designed, but she didn't have the first idea how to find it.

Because she was so new. And might never get a chance to be anything else. Her hands were trembling too much to hold the ruler steady.

"Can I get you a coffee?" His voice by her shoulder made her jump.

"Buy me whatever the hell you want, I'm not drinking it," she said.

He pulled up a chair and sat down, so close to her she could smell his shampoo. How could a little synthetic apple fragrance smell so good?

"I'll talk to him," he repeated. "You don't have to worry."

"I'm not worried. I'll just have to work twice as hard to prove myself." She flung the ruler aside. The stripe was microscopic. She'd have to find the original shirt design in the computer somehow. "Just please don't say anything else to him about me. You'll just make it worse."

"How could I make it worse?" he asked.

She looked at him out of the corner of her eye. *Because he'll think I used my womanly wiles on you.* During the months she'd lived in Liam's apartment, she'd brought a few too many guys home, and now he had the crazy idea she was some kind of femme fatale. "Just don't say anything else," she said. "Please."

"All right. Let me know if you change your mind."

"I won't. Now I have to get back to work, all right?"

With a nod, he stood up and rolled the chair back to his side of the cubicle. April began combing through the digital archives for the striped shirt on her desk, wondering if Liam had ever in his life, just once, felt stupid and useless. And if he had, why couldn't she have been there to see it and record it on video?

Half an hour later, Rita arrived, looking tired but beautiful in a Fite jacket over slim black Fite running pants—almost the identical outfit April had worn the day before. Somehow, on her, it was glamorous. Was it the hair? Her natural grace? April decided to ask her for fashion tips. Her own natural quirky style seemed to turn heads, but not in a good way.

"Morning," Rita mumbled as she strode past.

Zack rose to his feet and followed her into her cubicle. "I've already asked April, but she can't spare the time. Lunch today? On me."

Oh, sure. Now he was asking Rita to lunch.

April's stinging pride overrode her anxieties about designing stripes and looking good in running pants.

Chewing her bottom lip, April printed out the stripe on her screen. She was such an idiot. He'd obviously intended to ask Rita all along as well. It hadn't been a come-on.

"Thank you, that sounds nice," Rita said. "But you don't have to do that—"

"My pleasure. Twelve?"

"Twelve fifteen is better. I have an eleven o'clock meeting that will probably run over." Rita peered around the cubicle wall at April. "Are you sure you can't make it?"

April could see she wanted her there, and making Rita happy was her middle name. April Making Rita Happy Johnson. "You know, come to think of it, I bet my mom would love an hour with her grandbaby all to herself," April said.

Rita smiled. "Great. It's a date."

Zack returned to his desk and picked up his phone. "I'll meet you both in the lobby at twelve fifteen."

He left the office without another word.

"Thanks," Rita said, walking around the wall. "I'm not quite up for a solo flight today. Not after the shit hit the fan yesterday."

Me neither, April thought. "I'll call my mom. She won't mind." Far from it. Given Trixie's psychic powers, she'd probably guess she was having lunch with the mysterious Zack at work and would expect him to dinner any day now. For their engagement party.

"I, uh, heard from Liam last night," Rita said. "He called me at home."

April dragged the ruler between her fingers. "Zack told me what he said. You should know he probably means it. Liam. He never wanted me here to begin with."

Rita squatted down and looked her in the eye. "Don't take this wrong," she said in a low voice, "but this is one of those times your brother is being a complete asshole."

"He's trying to protect you and the company. I understand—"

"No, he's being an asshole," Rita said. "You're the only freelancer I've got right now. I'm not going to let some"—she lowered her voice even more—"some spoiled, shallow bitch get you banned just because you didn't color her stripes fast enough. I don't care what he says. I won't let him do it."

To her surprise, April felt her eyes get hot. Rita had kids, and as far as April could tell, no husband to help out. "Don't be stupid. You barely know me. Don't put your neck—"

"If I like working with you, I'm going to work with you. All right?"

"Why would you do that for me?" April knew her family would always be there for her, even if Fite didn't work out. Did Rita have that kind of safety net? "You shouldn't—"

"It's not about you." Nostrils flaring, Rita stood up. "It's about my authority here. I have to be able to choose my own people."

April didn't know what to say. She'd worked with a lot of people over the years, but none had fought for her in any way other than demanding another week or two of her services. "Thanks." Words caught in her throat. "I'll... get back to work then."

"Good." Rita tucked her hair behind her ear. "I've got sixteen more stripe layouts and a color-blocked jacket I need before ten."

* * *

Zack met them in the lobby at 12:14 p.m., almost inviting Virginia the receptionist along to make it very, very clear he wasn't singling out April for romance, conversation, or long, deep, hot kisses in the conference room—where he'd spent the rest of the morning thinking about doing just that.

With only thirty minutes available for their lunch, he took them to the popular gourmet sandwich place on the corner, waited in line for fifteen minutes until he could buy their sandwiches, which they ate in a crowded corner. They gave up on conversation within the first five minutes. It was noisy, their mouths were full, and they had nothing to say to each other, not really. He was just an outside consultant who made them uncomfortable.

And April was his client's little sister, who made him even more uncomfortable.

But he was getting a grip. She'd been horrified at the idea of him coming on to her, and that had been the slap in the face he'd needed. He ate his turkey and Havarti on one-inch-thick, fresh-baked whole-grain bread and kept his eyes on Rita as much as possible. Pretty woman, Rita. Blonde, fit, tall, composed—except when her job was at stake—but her good looks had no effect on the awakening monster that was Zack's libido.

He'd been ready to chuck his job here overboard for one date with the other one, though, the funny girl in a disco dress eating a chunk of avocado with her fingers. Her nails were painted black with white polka dots. Her bracelet was the kind a child would wear, pastel candy rings on a thin elastic band, and half were eaten.

What was it about her that drove him so crazy?

"These are good sandwiches," he said. "Thanks for telling me about the place."

"What?" Rita asked, hand to her ear. The line along the deli counter was snaking around them, forcing them to huddle together over the small table.

"Good sandwiches," he said, more loudly.

"Glad you like them," Rita shouted back.

April picked up another thick, green chunk of avocado and popped it into her mouth. Zack's food stuck in his throat, and he grabbed his bottle of iced tea to help him swallow.

Did she know how sexy she was? He glanced around. Did other men respond to her like this, or was it just him?

Men in suits, jeans, and uniforms crowded and talked around them, eyes on the menu on the back wall, on their buds and other women, apparently oblivious.

"I'm so sorry," Rita said, looking at her phone, "but I have to get back for a meeting. We were in line so long..."

He couldn't be alone with April. He pulled out his own phone. "Is it that late already?" He scowled in a show of alarm.

April shoved half a sandwich into her mouth and stood up. Around the mouthful of food, she said, "That's that. Shall we?"

Only ten minutes after they'd sat down, they maneuvered through the crush to the street, where he held out his hand to Rita.

"Thanks for putting up with me for a while. I'll be moving on this afternoon," he said, shaking her hand.

Her smile was genuine. "So soon?"

He understood the relief, but it did bother him a little how glad people usually were to see his back. "Yes." Next he held out his hand to April. "Good luck."

April pumped his hand with the relish of an elderly farmer milking his least favorite cow at dawn. "Because I'm going to need it?"

He shrugged. "I say that to everyone." Because Rita was already walking up the sidewalk toward Fite, he turned to join her, asking April over his shoulder, "Walking this way?"

But she waved and bolted across the street, her mesmerizing

figure in the bright pink dress disappearing behind a bus.

He'd be working in a distant corner building before she came back to work the next day. They might not see each other for weeks.

His foot caught the edge of the curb, and he stumbled.

Rita caught his elbow. "Careful."

Right, he thought. *Aren't I always?*

Chapter 9

THE SECOND SATURDAY in January, April watched her brother's fiancée twirl in front of the three-way dressing room mirror in a shimmering white dress.

Although she'd watched six of her friends get married over the past year and a half, and therefore thought she'd seen enough wedding gowns to satisfy her already meager liking of them for a lifetime, the getup that Rose was wearing made April gasp.

"Holy moly," she whispered. "You look like an angel."

Rose shook out her long blonde hair and adjusted the plunging neckline, revealing significant cleavage. She was big all over, but the chest—well. April had made a point of finding pride in her own natural B cup self, but Rose bursting out of that silk made April a little envious. No wonder Mark was in love with her. She was feeling kind of woozy herself.

Her brother, the lucky man, sat cross-legged on the floor holding a takeout coffee cup, looking like he'd been smacked in the head with a board.

April walked over and nudged him with her boot. "Say something. Doesn't she look incredible?"

He lowered his head and sipped his coffee.

April kicked him. "Hey, tell her she's beautiful."

Rose swished over, laughing. "He already did," she said,

tousling his floppy brown hair.

"I don't know why she puts up with you," April muttered in his ear. "Better learn some charm before she catches on and leaves you for a guy who knows how to talk."

Elbowing April away, Mark set down his coffee and got to his feet. Suddenly, like the alpha male at the climax of a romantic film, he took Rose in his arms and kissed her. April could almost hear the symphony.

After ten long seconds, he broke the kiss, and gazing into Rose's eyes, said softly, "Talking is overrated."

Rose's skin flamed hot pink against the white silk. "Oh, baby, let's get married yesterday."

"Okay," he said.

April put her hand over her heart and looked away, blinking hard.

Wow. She'd thought she was way too jaded to care about two people getting it on, but...

She hurried to the door, waving over her shoulder. "Three's a crowd, kids. I'll meet you out front in a few minutes, how's that?"

"I think we embarrassed her," she heard Rose say.

And then her brother's response: "Impossible."

He was right. She wasn't embarrassed. She didn't know what she was. Jealous? No, she was smiling. Happy?

No. She was crying. She paused and wiped her face before turning the corner.

Mark surprised her by joining her outside the dressing room. "It's never a good idea to start something you can't—hey, what's the matter?"

"I just needed a little air," April said.

The store was a small, cramped boutique in Oakland that specialized in plus-sized formal wear—proms and weddings, mostly. The only store clerk was busy helping another future bride and her seven best friends in the world pick out bridesmaid dresses. It looked like it was down to frothy pink or slinky black.

"I know how you feel," Mark said with a sigh. "She's something, isn't she?"

Rose had insisted on bringing Mark, not caring if he was surprised on their wedding day—they were inseparable. Rose's family was back East, and her best friend, Blair, had moved back there last summer with her fiancé, Bev's cousin. Aside from her future in-laws and coworkers, Rose was alone in California.

April couldn't imagine what that would be like. She still lived at home with her mother, for God's sake. She saw her brothers at least once a week, and embarrassing as it was, had to admit she'd miss them if she didn't.

Even Liam. Four weeks had gone by since he'd threatened to fire her if anyone complained about her. If anyone had, Rita had kept it to herself. April's devotion to Rita grew by the day.

"I hope she doesn't change her mind," Mark said, gazing toward the dressing room.

April snorted. Love sure could turn a smart guy stupid. "Of course she won't. I was just kidding."

"Every day she still wants me is a surprise," he said.

"You've got the self-esteem of a baked potato." April poked him in the shoulder. "Which is crazy, given your accomplishments."

"That has nothing to do with anything," he said.

"Please. You founded companies before you graduated from high school. You've got millions in the bank. Geeks around the world worship you like a god."

He flushed and looked away, shaking his head. "It doesn't matter, April. The only thing that matters is that I met Rose." He cleared his throat. "And that she's willing to have me."

April felt another wave of unidentified emotion wash over her. Tears pricked at her eyes. What was the matter with her? "You're a catch. Even if you weren't kind of good-looking, women would want you. You've done big things and still are true to yourself. You're not just some jerk taking advantage of people to get ahead, you're a real success."

He smiled down at her. "Gee, thanks, April." He put an awkward arm around her. "I think you're pretty great, too."

The unidentified emotion turned sour. She pulled away. "No, I'm the opposite of you. I've always had loads of self-esteem for absolutely no reason whatsoever."

He frowned, looking concerned.

She went on, as much to herself as to him. "I used to be able to comfort myself that you and Liam were accomplished but socially stunted. I, on the other hand, lived a life of emotional and spiritual meaning. I had friends, boyfriends, my art."

"I kind of thought the same thing."

She shook her head and looked at a yellow taffeta gown with a neckline so low the wearer would need a bikini wax.

She swallowed over her tight throat. It was their love that was making her cry. Liam had found the same elusive treasure with Bev.

Both Mark and Liam had been emotionally starved workaholics—yet they'd each gotten something she was no closer to having than when she was a rebellious, immature teenager.

It was her own fault. She'd done everything wrong. She'd hung out in bars, partied with friends, never committed to a career. She hadn't cared about winning gold medals or being admired or making millions—she'd just wanted to be happy.

But being a flaky chick without a job hadn't made her happy.

She needed a purpose in life. More hours with her paint and pastels, more hours with a computer stylus and tablet. If she developed herself as a person, maybe someday—and she could be ninety-seven, God knew she was a late bloomer—she would find a companion of some sort who could keep her company in her later years.

In the meantime, she was going to keep her head out of the clouds. Chasing worthless men was one reason she lived with her mother and couldn't afford high-end art supplies.

"I'm getting this one," Rose said, coming out in jeans and a sweater, holding the dress. "It shows a totally inappropriate amount of cleavage, but it makes me feel beautiful. And it's on sale."

"Don't worry about money," April said. "Tell her not to worry about money, Mark."

"Don't worry about money," he said, leaning over to kiss Rose. Now that his woman was back in sight, his conversation with April was forgotten.

"Honey, this is what 'on sale' looks like." Rose pulled out the tag and held it up to his face.

His eyes widened. "I sold my last car for less than that."

He'd sold it to April, who was grateful to have any car at all. "That's not saying much," April said.

The large group at the front of the store was migrating toward the back to get measured. "I'll wait for you two outside," April said, starting to walk away.

"Hold it," Mark said. "We were talking, weren't we?"

"Don't worry about it." April gave him a big hug, kissed Rose on the cheek, and left them to enjoy their bubble of happiness.

* * *

The following Thursday evening, April was wiping baby vomit off her fingers with an aloe-scented wipe when Liam stuck his head in through the bedroom doorway.

"Zack Fain will be here in ten minutes," he said. "Actually, next door. Mom's cooking lasagna."

April stared at him. He didn't *look* drunk. "Who?"

She hadn't talked to Zack since that quick lunch before Christmas. In fact, he'd been keeping such a low profile, she might've thought he'd left the company if Bev and Liam hadn't mentioned the reports he'd given them.

Ten minutes? She caught her breath.

As Liam's harried gaze moved to Merry, a smile broke out across his face. "Hello, sunshine." He strode over, unclasped the changing table belt, and lifted a naked, delighted Merry into his arms. Probably because of all the lessons April had given him about staying mellow, Merry didn't burst into tears, not even when he lifted her up and made a deafening raspberry on her baby potbelly.

Still finding it difficult to breathe properly, April plucked another wipe out of the box. It was amazing how much nastiness could come out of such a tiny, adorable creature. Although at four months, her niece wasn't so tiny anymore. She had Bev's dark hair but Liam's size, topping the growth charts at the pediatrician's office.

"That's my girl," Liam said, bouncing her in his arms. "What do you think, April? Wrestling? Basketball? Look at the muscles she's got. She's *cut*."

"Careful with the bouncing," she said, wondering if she'd heard wrong, if the vomit fumes had pickled her brains. "She was covered in spit-up a minute ago." She rubbed away the white muck that had gotten under her rings. She swallowed. "Did you say Zack Fain?"

His smile didn't fade, but he did move Merry away from his face. "Yeah. Should be here any minute." He gently bounced Merry up and down. "Did you have a big burp? What a special girl you are!"

"Very special. Check out the wall," April said. "Projectile. She let loose when I sat her up."

He made a face at the spatter spreading three feet. "She did that?"

"Gold medal spitter you got there," April said.

"Gold medal spitter," he repeated, laughing, nuzzling Merry to his chest for a moment before laying her down on the table. "Such a special girl."

April reached for a fresh diaper. She didn't appreciate how stimulated she got at the thought of seeing Zack again—and, bonus, he'd be out of his habitat, a suit released from captivity, like a tiger out of the zoo.

Please—a tiger? What was the matter with her? Not a sexy, dangerous predator. No way. More like... an owl. Or a ferret.

Still, she'd be happy to sit this one out. Creating her first pattern-matched sketches for impatient designers that morning had worn her out, and Merry had skipped both of her naps. She unfolded the diaper, lifted Merry's legs, and wiggled it under her little bottom. "I'll do this. You have to get ready for dinner."

He bent over and kissed Merry's forehead. "I'm fine. You might wear something a little less terrifying, though."

April started to defend her Buddha-in-a-bikini T-shirt before she realized what he was saying. "I'm not coming to your corporate dinner."

"Sorry, but you are. Rose and Mark will be there, and they don't even work at Fite. You do work at Fite, don't you?" He looked around the bedroom. "I put some clean baby onesie things in the dresser. Are any of them left?"

"Hold on, no. I can't go. I won't go."

"Mom already told him you'd be there," Liam said. "The whole family, she said. You know how she is. Somehow, she came by the office with Merry, met Zack in hallway, and one thing led to another."

"When? Merry's been with me all afternoon."

"Monday, I think. I only found out an hour ago when she called me to find out if Zack was a vegetarian."

"No," April said, "I can't go. It'll be too weird. You'll hate me for something or other—I'll say something, I'll do something—I can't handle the pressure."

"He's just a consultant, Ape. He works for Fite, not the other way around."

"You already told me to change my shirt," she said.

He rolled his eyes. "Fine. Wear whatever you want. Just help me find something for Merry, will you? Please? Bev seems to think I have no style, which is pretty hilarious considering I've been running that garment company of hers for a few years."

"I think we've got some baby yoga pants around here somewhere," April said, wondering why she was overcome with nerves. So a guy she met at work was coming to dinner, so what?

Her mind lingered over the memory of him sitting at the desk behind her, scribbling in his little notebook. She wondered if he'd bring it with him to dinner, take notes on the food, their conversation, the decor.

Liam was right. Why should she go out of her way to avoid him? She didn't care what he thought. Her name was April Keep Rita Happy Johnson, not April Impress Zack the Hot Anal Retentive Suit Happy Johnson.

Muttering the long name under her breath, she picked out

Merry's outfit—yoga pants and matching hoodie—and threw it on the changing table for Liam on her way out the door.

"See you over there," she said. "I've got to wash off the rest of this baby yuck before dinner."

And maybe find something else to wear.

Maybe.

* * *

Zack's finger hovered over the doorbell.

The whole family, Liam's mother had said. How had he been lassoed into that one? One minute he was congratulating her on becoming a grandmother, the next she was giving him directions to the house.

She looked like April. That might've been it. The shape of the face; the sharp, laughing eyes; the eccentric fashion sense. To visit Fite Fitness, Trixie Johnson had worn lime-green Crocs, bike shorts, and a floral sundress under a red-and-white ski jacket.

"I hate winter," Trixie had said. "I fight it with all I've got."

Then she'd smiled at him, broad and warm and fearless, and he'd seen April's face.

"When should I arrive?" he'd asked.

With a glance at his watch—waiting until the 6:29 p.m. turned into 6:30—he pressed the doorbell.

He heard little dogs barking, a long pause, and then he was standing directly in front of April in the open doorway.

He'd managed to avoid her for weeks. Now she was two feet away, unadorned with pink lipstick or silver headbands or tight, pink dresses. Tonight she was casual in a long-sleeved black T-shirt and faded jeans, no hint of the wild child he'd met at work.

The natural April was even more disarming than the decorated one.

"Hi," he said, holding up the bottle of wine he carried. "I

brought this."

She ushered him inside and closed the door. "I'm surprised you drink. Thanks."

His upbringing had created hundreds, if not thousands, of awkward encounters over the years. It bothered him to think those years still showed on the outside, after years of effort to blend in. "Why wouldn't I drink?" he asked, slipping out of his jacket.

"I don't know. I just got the impression you might not." She took his jacket and looked him over head-to-toe.

Her gaze felt like fingers. He froze, concentrating on keeping a blank face.

She looked away. "Come on, everyone's in the kitchen." She flung his jacket on a sofa and walked into the dining room.

He waited a second to calm his pulse. In spite of himself, he grinned. It felt good to be alive again, even if it hurt.

Even if she'd just looked at him as if he'd given her a quote on life insurance.

Liam, striding out of the kitchen, met him in the dining room. "Zack, thanks for coming." Liam, like Zack, wore a blue button-down shirt and khakis. Possibly the same brand.

No wonder April had looked at him like that. Zack looked just like her big brother.

As they shook hands, another tall guy and a large, stunning blonde woman came in the front door. Zack found himself staring at the woman—would his new found sex drive kick into gear with every female in this family?—but as beautiful as she was, in some clingy black dress that showed off her amazing chest, he knew the statuesque blonde wasn't the woman who'd be haunting his dreams tonight.

Liam herded them together. "Zack, this is my brother, Mark,

and his fiancée Rose. Guys, this is Zack Fain, the consultant we brought in at Fite."

They exchanged greetings. Knowing Mark Johnson's success at starting up tech companies, Zack shook his hand eagerly. He quickly pegged Mark as a geeky introvert, in high contrast to his ebullient fiancée, who smiled and made chitchat easily.

Zack, also uneasy in social settings, made as much cheerful small talk as he could, fighting his disappointment that April had disappeared somewhere.

"I can't believe Liam let Bev hire an outsider to poke around," Mark said. "He's never even given me a tour."

"Bev didn't 'let' me do anything," Liam said.

"Uh-oh, hear that, Rose?" Mark asked. "That's what happens when you get married. You don't get to do *anything*."

Rose kissed Mark's cheek. "You never want to do anything anyway. My big, handsome homebody."

Liam looked at Zack. "I agreed it was time to get a candid outside perspective. Zack made a convincing case."

Mark frowned. "Didn't Bev have to talk you into it, though? That's what I heard."

Rose elbowed him. "How about a drink, guys? I make a mean martini."

"Oh," Mark said. "I'm supposed to be sneaky about that stuff, aren't I? Sorry." He looked at the floor.

Zack smiled at Rose. "I'd love a martini." He'd planned on taking a cab to the BART station, where he could catch a train back to San Francisco. Where the hell was April?

No. He shouldn't be looking for the sexy little sister; he should be schmoozing with his clients. "Will Bev be able to join us tonight?" he asked.

"She's around here somewhere," Liam said. "My mother's up

to something. Whatever it is, I apologize."

April appeared in the doorway to the kitchen, sending Zack's body temperature up a few degrees. "Liam? Can I talk to you for a minute?" She glanced at Zack. "In here?"

Groaning, Liam nodded. "Excuse me," he said, joining April. They conferred with their heads together, too quietly to hear.

"Uh-oh," Mark said.

Rose hooked her arm in his. "Hush. Help me make the drinks."

Moving to a quiet corner, Zack clasped his hands behind his back and wondered how many minutes had passed since he'd walked through the front door. A 6:30 arrival, perhaps thirteen minutes of conversation accomplished so far, an estimated two hours seventeen minutes of faux camaraderie remaining.

April split away from Liam, who went into the kitchen, and she came over to Zack. He stared at her as she approached, told himself not to stare, stared anyway. Without the makeup and the crazy clothes, she was adorable. Well, she was adorable in the makeup and crazy clothes, too.

And he was just crazy.

"We're having a picnic," April said.

"Picnic?" Zack asked. January in California was still January. And it was dark.

"Don't worry. We'll be inside. We have a sun porch behind the kitchen. It's"—she twisted a curly strand of hair between her fingers—"it's usually where the dogs hang out, but tonight's something special."

"Okay," he said.

"Any back problems? We'll be sitting on the floor."

"I'm fine."

"Are you sure?" She gave him a hopeful look. "Even just a

twinge? Because if you did, then we'd get to sit on chairs." She caressed the sturdy-looking oak chair at the head of the dining table.

Sitting on the floor didn't sound so bad. It might be more casual than a formal setting. "Will there be a red-checkered tablecloth?" he asked.

"Damn," she said. "You saw it already?"

"No, just hoping."

She narrowed her eyes. "You got your wish. Red. Checkered. Tablecloth."

"What kind of dogs?"

"Do you like dogs?" she asked.

He nodded.

"Well, hopefully you'll like these anyway," she said. "Come on. The party's back here."

"Martini for you, April?" Rose called from the bar built into the wall.

"Nope, staying sober tonight," April said. "I'm no fool."

Not sure he wasn't one, Zack accepted his own drink and brought it immediately to his lips, unable to break his gaze away from April as she moved through the warm, cozy dining room to the well-lit kitchen beyond.

Chapter 10

SMILING HIS THANKS to Rose, he followed April into the kitchen as he took another sip, then another. He had only a second to take in the bright walls and savory smells of the Johnson family kitchen before April led him down a step into a walled-in porch overlooking the side yard and vast, twinkling night view of the San Francisco Bay.

At their feet, the checkered tablecloth was spread out on the floor and dotted with seven plates, bowls covered with cloths, a jug overflowing with silverware, and a half-dozen squat LED candles.

Trixie Johnson, her short white hair slightly mussed and standing up like she was '80s rock star, spun around with a bouquet of huge sunflowers in her hands. "Zack! I didn't realize you were here already." She handed April the flowers and reached out to him with both hands.

He wasn't sure if she wanted a hug or a shake. Feeling the buzz of the martini starting to hit him, he put his half-empty glass down on an end table, took both of her hands in his, and squeezed gently. "Thank you for inviting me. This looks fun."

"Fun!" She beamed. "It is, don't you think? I'm so glad you like it. My kids are pretending I'm crazy. I'm not. I'm a genius."

Her hands were soft but strong, holding him in place. He

looked past her friendly face to the distant skyline of San Francisco, the small rocky island of Alcatraz, the lights of the sprawling Bay Area freeways circling and crisscrossing the water. "Quite a view," he said.

Trixie gave his hands another squeeze. "It's so nice you could come. Where do you usually eat? I was worried about that."

"In dark alleys and parking lots, I'm sure," April said, thrusting the flowers back at her mother. "You know, scrounging in Dumpsters. Isn't that right, Zack?"

"Too close to the truth to be funny," he said.

Trixie nodded. "I thought so. I'll send you home with some freezer jelly. Do you have a kitchen where you're staying?"

"Sure. It's a condo. A regular home."

"Well," Trixie said. "Some homemade jelly will help."

He smiled at her. She reminded him of his own mom a little bit. A different kind of nonconventional from his mother's pious eccentricities, but it put him at ease. For no good reason, he found himself comparing her to Meg's mother, who'd always been as nice as anyone could be but had a stylish, wealthy demeanor both in her dress and her home that made him feel like he dragged mud over the floor whenever he moved. "What kind?"

"I only make strawberry," Trixie said. "Don't really see the point of other kinds, honestly."

His smile broadened. "My mom preserves strawberries every year. She always gets them from the same patch. Says they're the best."

Trixie looked delighted. "And where is she, then? Back in New York?"

"Oh, no. I grew up in Bakersfield. My folks are still there."

April made a surprised sound at his elbow. "You're from California?"

"Yup," he said.

"Huh," April said. "You seem so..."

He retrieved his martini and sucked down another mouthful. *Ridiculously sexy?* He looked at her. Without makeup, her face seemed vulnerable, sweet, inviting. Those big gray eyes...

He took another drink. "What?" he asked.

"Eastern," April said.

"Bakersfield is east of here. A little."

"Maybe it's because you've been living on the East Coast for so long," April said.

He tipped back his glass, discovered it was empty. "Maybe."

Trixie patted his arm. "You've run out. April, show him the bar, will you? I'm going to kick you two out of here while I get the lasagna plated up." She rotated him and pushed him toward the door. "The others are in the living room. Tell them it's time to dig in. No point standing around feeling uncomfortable beforehand."

"Nah," April said, walking up the stairs to the kitchen, "we'll save it for dinner."

"Give my little guys their dinner first, please," Trixie called after them. "They're in my bedroom."

"I better feed Stool again, too, before he eats something he shouldn't." April stopped and reached down to pick up a stainless steel bowl on the floor. "Stool is my dog. My mom has three Chihuahuas. Well, two are actually Chihuahuas. We don't know what Zeus is."

"A Greek god?" Zack asked.

"You wouldn't say that if you'd seen him. He's pretty ugly. In a good way." She held up the metal bowl and turned. "This will take me a minute. The bar is right over—"

"I remember," he said, and returned the way he'd come, through the warm kitchen to the dining room. Maybe another martini would be too much, at least the kind Rose made. In the neighboring room, he heard more voices, a baby, and a piano. He took his time pouring a glass of Pinot Gris, in no hurry to dive into another conversation just yet.

Trixie stuck her head into the room. "Could you help me set the table?" She laughed. "I mean, floor? It's hard for me to get up and down."

He went over, wine in hand, glad to be useful, and in ten minutes they'd carried in a hot ramekin bubbling with lasagna to each plate on the tablecloth, a large salad, a platter of steamed asparagus, a bowl of stuffed green olives, and a warm baby bottle filled with milk.

"Dinner!" Trixie yelled. Clapping her hands together, she sat cross-legged on the floor near the window, then said to Zack, "Sit here with me. I'll do all the talking."

The first to join them was Beverly Lewis Johnson, her baby daughter in her arms. He'd met Bev at Fite several times now, but hadn't realized he owed her his job. They were saying hello just as the others poured into the room, each with a drink in hand.

"Will the dogs be sitting at the dining room table while we're out here?" Mark asked, sitting with Rose near the door. "It's only fair."

"No, they're in my bedroom," Trixie said.

Liam brought in a baby carrier and propped it between him and Bev before sitting down. April was the last to come in, scanned the area, saw the only empty spot was next to Zack, and gave him a look that hit him like ten of Rose's killer martinis.

The other people faded to dust, the sound of cheerful small talk drifted miles away, the smell of garlic bread and bubbling tomato sauce evaporated. It was just April's gaze drilling into his as she moved closer, closer, until finally she sank down to her knees and was scant inches from him.

"Hi," she said.

He catalogued the now-predictable responses in his body. Accelerated heart rate. Cold palms. Parched mouth.

"Hi." He turned slightly away from her to drain his wine glass.

It was his own fault. For too long, he'd convinced himself he could live without sex and pleasure, and now he was experiencing a systemic breakdown.

Hoping his hand wasn't visibly shaking, he reached across the tablecloth for a large wooden bowl. "Salad?" he asked her.

"Get me the garlic bread first," she said. "Under the striped towel. If I don't get a piece now, Liam and Mark will eat it all first."

He found the basket and handed it to her as if he weren't fighting the urge to unravel a year's worth of plans.

No. He took on the job; he'd finish it. He couldn't get involved with anyone at Fite, especially not the client's sister. As soon as the six months were up, he'd pursue... a personal life. Not with April. He wasn't her type. He'd find somebody with whom he could have a normal, steady, quiet, mature relationship.

The Johnson family's conversation boiled around him, washing over him unheard. Vaguely he recognized talk about weddings. One soon, for Mark and Rose.

He glanced at April's profile. Her nose was slightly upturned. And her lips were full, talking and laughing and smiling, full of life.

She'd probably laugh at the idea of getting involved with a cold stick like him. Except... he didn't use to be cold. He'd been funny once. In fact, by the time he was nineteen, he could imitate two dozen of the most famous cartoon voices of all time—such an impressive feat that his college roommate made him perform for his parents.

He leaned toward April and asked, in his best Scooby Doo voice, "Pass the parmesan?"

She paused with a chunk of garlic bread sticking out of her mouth. "Wuh?"

He cleared his throat. Only a drunk guy would think the Scoob was irresistible. "Excuse me. Parmesan, please?" He pointed at the tiny grater and wedge of cheese on a board next to her.

She squinted at him for a full three seconds before handing it over.

The conversation about the wedding continued at the other end of the tablecloth.

"I'm kind of looking forward to it being over," Rose said. She sat curled up against Mark, her legs bent to one side.

"Over before it even began," Mark said with a sigh. "I knew it was too good to be true."

Rose laughed and sipped her wine. Her smiling gaze met Zack's across the tablecloth. "I'm a bridezilla, can you tell?"

"I doubt that," Zack said.

"I've already issued decrees about what color nail polish my honor attendants can wear," Rose said.

"You did not," April said.

"Other than you," Rose said. "I knew you'd rock it with the bridal style, Ape."

April tipped her glass at her. "Thanks. I hope black is okay."

"Nails or all over?" Bev asked, looking alarmed. "You don't want to look like the protest vote. The bitter, angry sister."

"I don't get it," April said. "The guys get to wear black. What's the difference?"

"You can wear black if you really want to," Rose said.

Liam lifted Merry onto his shoulder. "And then she can serve drinks to cut down on the catering costs."

"Costs, schmosts," Mark said, lifting his beer. "One server isn't gonna make a difference at this point, believe me. Not that it wasn't a good idea."

Zack glanced at April, alarmed to see the teasing was bothering her. Lips thinned, she stabbed her lasagna with her butter knife.

"Bridesmaid dresses are a very poor value," Zack said. "Making them black would do a lot to change that. Plus, you look good in black. I mean, everyone does, don't you think?"

April paused, knife in air. Zack realized he'd become the center of attention. He'd just told April she looked good in black. Very subtle. Maybe this would be a good time to lean over and stick his tongue in her ear, too. Pant a little.

He tried to drink from his empty glass.

Rose came to his rescue. "I agree. Black is the new black. If anyone, male or female, wants to wear black to our wedding, you have the bride's official permission."

Trixie tapped Zack's shoulder, a kind smile on her face. "More pinot?"

Nodding, he held out his glass. "Thanks."

"We hope you can come, of course," Trixie said as she poured.

He didn't know what she meant. Another picnic? "Excuse me?"

April's voice was ominous. "Mom..."

Oh, man. Did she mean the wedding? Mark and Rose hadn't heard her. He sipped his wine, pretending the same.

"You can be April's date," Trixie said. "She doesn't have one yet, do you, sweetie?"

Zack thought he heard the words *kill me now* come faintly from April's direction.

The picnic fell into another awkward lull. Then Rose said, "We'd love to have you just as you are, Zack. Right now our guest list is very heavy on my side—and very female. It would be great if you could come. No pressure, of course." She smiled. "And you can even wear black."

"Thank you, that's really, really generous of you," Zack said. "But I wouldn't want to mess up your guest list this late in the game. I know how tight the planning is. When we—"

Well, shit. He'd started to say, when he and Meg were planning their wedding, they'd had to call each invitee individually to find out whether they were coming, because the caterer was threatening to pad them five extra plates, which would've busted their already strained budget. And given Meg's cancer diagnosis, they didn't want to waste a dime...

"Thank you for inviting me," he said instead, holding up his glass in a toast. "To your wedding and to this great picnic."

"Fabulous," Trixie said. "I love it when everything works out."

"You're *coming*?" April asked.

"I'll get your address from Liam for the invitation, all right?" Rose asked. "So you know we're serious."

Perhaps, given April's obvious horror, he should've taken that moment to backtrack and give his regrets. They'd just met him and might wish later they hadn't been so hasty in inviting a stranger.

But Mark Johnson had founded tech companies, he was a wunderkind programmer that was famous in some circles, and he was a contact Zack had angled to make when he took the job with Fite. Being invited to his wedding was an incredible opportunity for Zack's business, one he couldn't possibly pass up.

And he looked good in black.

"I can't wait," Zack said, shooting April a smile.

* * *

April watched Zack in the kitchen after the meal, cursing the attractive shape of his back and shoulders as he dried dishes. Her brothers had set up a dishwashing chain after dinner, and Zack had somehow fit himself into the drying step of the process. Liam scraped, Mark washed, Zack dried. Zack Fain, the temporary, hired business consultant, fit into the Johnson kitchen as if he'd been there for years.

Mom had invited him to the wedding.

He'd said yes.

It was all very strange.

Something he'd said during dinner was bothering her, and she'd decided to ask him about it in private. Not here at the house where her psychic mother would pick up on it and interfere. Afterward, in her car, when she drove him to the BART station.

He'd kicked off his loafers. She wondered if he'd noticed that snazzy green-and-white striped sock of his had gotten wet in a puddle of dishwater, or if he was having too much fun laughing at Mark's story about founding a software company when he was a teenager and hiding his millions from them for years.

Ha-ha.

"Are you okay?" Bev asked quietly.

April shoved her hands into her pockets. "Fine." She felt Bev's gaze but didn't look at her.

"Thanks for cleaning up Merry's spit-up," Bev said. "Liam said it got all over the wall."

"It was impressive," April said. "If she'd been face-down, she would've blasted to the moon."

The humor in Bev's voice evaporated. "I wonder if I should take her to the doctor."

"No, I don't think it was bad or anything," April said. "I

looked it up online. Pretty common. She drank too much, too fast."

"You googled it?" Bev asked.

"Yeah. Turning on the image search was a mistake, though," April said. "It *was* pretty amazing. I was tempted to upload a picture myself."

They laughed. Zack turned at the sound, saw them, then looked at his watch. The water was off, the dishes were put away, he seemed ready to leave.

"Do you need a ride to BART?" April asked him. "I heard you were going to call a cab."

"Yeah, that would be great. Are you headed that way?"

April realized that he didn't know she lived at home. "I will be as soon as you get your shoes on," she said. "Let's hit the road, shall we?"

Trixie looked sad to see Zack go—but at least she didn't suggest he move into Liam's childhood bedroom, as she had with Bev years earlier—and the others seemed to like him, too, shaking his hand at the door and laughing like old friends.

Finally, Zack and April were in the car heading downhill through the narrow, wooded streets to the more urban, flatter neighborhoods below.

"I hope you realize you don't have to go to Rose and Mark's wedding," she said, braking as the car accelerated on the steep decline.

"Would you rather I didn't?"

"Why would I care?"

"I don't know," Zack said. "You brought it up."

She took a sharp turn too fast, making him grab the dash. "Sorry."

"I wouldn't mind if you slowed down a little," he said.

Because she did want to talk, she took her foot off the gas. They were still up in the hills, where the roads were narrow and winding, crowded with parked cars and driveways for the closely built homes.

"Thanks," he said, rubbing his temple. "I shouldn't have drunk so much. Your future sister-in-law makes a killer martini."

"And Mom's proud of her wine collection. She pushes it on everyone."

"Nobody pushed. I took it all willingly."

"Sounds kinky," she said. Then clenched her teeth. "Sorry. Forget I said that."

He chuckled softly. "Okay."

What was his deal? Why did she care? She was exhausted—she could be home in bed right now instead of hauling his khaki-clad ass across Oakland—but she was too curious.

She took a breath and dove in. "During dinner, after they asked you to come to the wedding, you said something that got me wondering."

He reached forward and adjusted the defroster knob. "Oh?"

"Have—have you been married before? The way you were talking, I got the impression that—"

"Yes," he said. "I was married before."

She felt guilty for prying, but also kind of proud of herself for getting it right. "I thought so. I'm sorry, I don't know why, but I've had that impression for the longest time. None of my friends have gotten divorced—yet, because there's one couple I know who never should've made the leap—"

"She died," Zack said. "Not divorce. Cancer."

Oh my God. After a pause to recover her voice, she said, "I'm so sorry. I am such an idiot." She stopped at the corner and looked at him. "Really, I'm so sorry."

Questions she wouldn't ask aloud ran through her mind: *How old was she? How could she die so young?* She'd lost her own father to cancer, but he'd been past middle age.

"It's okay." He was smiling a little, as if in apology.

"Was it—when did—" She shook her head. "Never mind. You don't have to talk about it."

"It was melanoma. Four years ago," he said. "It's all right. I wish I'd mentioned it earlier. I just didn't think of it. It was common knowledge back in New York. Even with my clients."

"How did they know?"

"Well... most of my work is word-of-mouth. After Meg died —her name was Meg—her father put the word out that I could use a hand getting my consulting business off the ground. So the work I had those first few years was pretty much his doing. He was a lawyer, knew a lot of people." Zack said. "So, you could say I got where I am today because of pity."

"Don't say that," she said. "They hired you because they thought you'd do a good job."

"How could they? I was way too young," he said. "I knew my father-in-law was behind it. But I made a name for myself eventually. For instance, Bev and Liam hired me without knowing my sob story—I sought them out personally when I saw the Annabelle Tucker publicity machine kick into gear. I'd had some garment experience in Manhattan, so..."

Annabelle Tucker was a teen pop star who recently had— thanks to Bev, her former teacher and babysitter—agreed to wear Fite clothes in prominent and evocative ways, resuscitating the brand and company in the process.

April reluctantly resumed driving. "I bet pity wasn't as much of a factor as you think. Maybe it got you the interview, but not the job."

"It's all right, I don't mind. It made them feel good. I was doing a public service."

"How old are you?" she asked.

"Thirty-two."

She bit back a sigh. Only five years older than she was, and he'd already been married, widowed, and founded a consulting business. "I just moved back home with my mother. After I drop you off at BART, I'm going right back to sleep in the same bed I had when I was twelve years old."

His teeth flashed. "Really?"

"You think that's funny?"

"I think it's cute." His smile vanished. "Sorry. That sounded patronizing."

It should have, but she felt something tingly and sweet. "I'm used to it. It's because I look twelve."

He cleared his throat. "Not twelve. Young, but definitely not twelve."

"How old?"

"I'm afraid to say. You seem unhappy already."

"Tell me. How old?"

He grinned again. "Nineteen."

"At least I can vote," she said.

His voice fell. "That's not all you can do."

Was he *flirting*? "Excuse me?"

"I'm a man. Your family got me drunk. This is what happens."

She zipped out into traffic. "Huh. Who knew?"

"When you're older, maybe you'll like it," he said. "Looking young."

They'd reached the busier, more urban part of North Oakland. She changed lanes to dodge a bus but had to brake for two women holding ice cream cones, who were crossing College

Avenue against the red. "I like it fine right now. I'm very positive about how I look. Very, very positive."

"That's good."

They drove in silence for a few minutes. "We're almost there," she said. "Is your place in San Francisco far from the station?"

"Just a block or two from the Embarcadero."

"I know that area well," she said. "Liam used to live near there."

"Exactly near there, in fact."

"Exactly?"

"Precisely. In every way."

"Hold on. You're renting Liam's condo?"

"It was his idea," he said. "They hadn't put it on the market yet."

Since she'd lived there herself for months, she suddenly had a vivid picture of Zack there in his suit, his khakis, his boxers, and then nothing at all.

When she had to stop at the intersection, she peeked at him and wondered how accurate her imagination was.

Mmm.

Damn that imagination. It was always getting her into trouble. "We'd better hurry," she said. "The last train isn't as late as it should be. You'd think they wanted us to drive everywhere."

He looked at his phone. "I should be fine. It's just up here, right?"

For a man who'd started a family and lost everything, he seemed so calm, capable, normal. She tried to imagine how Liam or Mark would behave if they lost Bev or Rose, and failed.

Humbled by her own small life, she pulled over in front of the florist's shop below the stairs up to the station. The cloudless night was cold, and she suppressed a shiver. "Here you are."

"I just realized," he said, turning to her. "If you live with your mother, you didn't have to go out. Why'd you offer me a ride?"

"Just being my usual selfish, obnoxious self," she said. "I wanted to pry into your personal life."

"Now you're the one who's being too hard on herself." The streetlights flickered across his face. His hair was mussed, his eyes slightly unfocused.

"And I felt like I should scare you away from coming to the family wedding," she said.

"Why?"

"To save you from my crazy family, I suppose."

"I like your family," he said. "A lot."

"Really?"

"Really," he said. His low voice seemed lower in the dark, small car.

Her heart started beating faster. She had to remind herself he was just being polite. "Well, that's nice of you." She shifted her gaze to a double-parked taxi across the street.

She waited for him to open the door, to say good night, to leave.

He didn't move. "I like you, too," he said.

The air squeezed out of her lungs. She opened her mouth to suck in a breath but made the mistake of turning toward him at the same time, which moved her face near his.

He had beautiful eyes, dark as a twilight sky. Knowing the shadow of melancholy came from a profound loss intrigued her, softened her toward him.

He wasn't like other guys she'd known. What would it be like...

His gaze flickered to her mouth. She could hear the raggedness of his breath as she drifted closer, drawn to the desire she read in his face.

He wasn't going to do anything. He wanted her, but he would need her to make the first move.

It was wrong. It wasn't part of her plan. It was a mistake.

Oh, hell. Since when had she been any good at following the rules?

She put her hand on his cheek and closed the gap between them.

Chapter 11

WHEN HE FELT her lips press against his, Zack suffered a moment of full-body paralysis. Arms to chest to toes, he turned to granite. Even his lips were numb, useless.

For a moment.

She'd kissed him. She was still kissing him. Her hand was warm and soft against his cheek, and she smelled like the spiced molasses cake they'd had for dessert.

His blood heated, shattering the icy prison that had captured him; he tilted his head to deepen the kiss and felt her fingernails dig into his jaw.

The evidence of her desire drove him to lick the seam of her lips and move his tongue between her teeth, where everything was as hot and wet as his favorite dreams about her.

A soft, high-pitched sigh escaped her throat. While his tongue slid against hers, he found her face with his hands and held her in place. He wasn't thinking about anything, he wanted her and he was having her. Her curls felt as springy as he'd imagined, her skin silkier, her kiss sweeter.

So many years he'd wanted to feel this way. Life rushed into him. His nerves shuddered with a sudden, electrifying current.

She moaned. Her hands moved over his body to his shoulders, down his chest, then up to the back of his neck, where she caressed him, opening her mouth wider for him, giving him everything.

She was more than a fantasy. He could hear and taste and feel her. She was real. How could he have lived so long without this? Instinctively he thrust his tongue deeper into her mouth, moving his hand over her chest to her stomach. He lifted her shirt and found her breast, then cupped it, rubbed his palm against the silky fabric of her bra until he felt her nipple harden.

A bus roared past them. Just past April's cheek, he glimpsed a trio of men walking past the car window with a pizza box and a case of beer.

What the hell was he doing?

He went still. Heart pounding in his ears, blood racing through his veins, his attention narrowed to the feel of her mouth under his lips and her breast under his right palm.

You can't do this.

The effort of not moving made him tremble.

What would be the harm? She was obviously interested, a consenting adult, the most attractive girl he'd met in a string of long, lonely years...

No. He'd just had dinner with her family. One brother was his current client, the other (if Zack behaved himself) a future one. Connections like Mark Johnson didn't come around often. He wanted to break into high tech. She was their baby sister. He saw how they looked at her, watched over her.

And he was feeling her up in the goddamn front seat of a late-model economy car on a busy street.

Exhaling loudly, he yanked her shirt down and pulled away. The space between them grew wider, colder. "I can't believe I did that. I'm so sorry."

She stared, touching her mouth.

"I shouldn't have drunk so much. I hope you understand—it's not you, it's—I never get involved with anyone at work. Never. I just—I'm sorry." He leaned back in his seat. He could still hear his heart pounding in his ears.

She'd given him a little friendly peck and he'd mauled her. She'd probably felt sorry for the poor guy who'd lost his wife, and then he'd thanked her by shoving his tongue down her throat.

She still hadn't said anything. He didn't blame her. How embarrassing. How fucking embarrassing.

He straightened. "It won't happen again."

"Yeah?" Her voice was rough.

"Yeah."

"What if I kiss you again?" she asked.

He clenched his teeth. God. "I'd rather you didn't."

She turned away and laughed. Not the happy kind. "Okay. Got it."

"I really am sorry."

"Got that too," she said.

A charged silence filled the car. He wanted to say something to heal the damage, but after a few long seconds, he opened the door and stepped out. "Thank you for the ride."

"No problem." She gripped the wheel with both hands.

"See you around," he said, shutting the door, berating himself for yet more inadequate words. He zipped his jacket up to his throat, realizing from his unsteady legs that he was still a little drunk, and didn't walk across the street until he was in the crosswalk with a green light.

He shook his head, disgusted with himself. Such a good citizen. The type to follow the rules, do what was right.

Screeching her wheels, April pulled an illegal U-turn from the curb and sped through the intersection. Fearless. Passionate. Alive.

He stood on the curb and watched her fade away into the night, telling himself it was for the best.

* * *

Work.

She was going to work.

Work, work, work.

On a Friday morning two weeks after whatever the hell had happened in her car that night with Zack, April picked up her morning's work from the printer and jogged out of the art room to catch the elevator.

Rita had been out for a few days. One of her children was really sick, and she'd had to stay home with her. April had been doing her best to manage without her, but the pressure was building. All of Rita's work had fallen into her lap, which was an effective distraction from unrequited lust, but exhausting.

The design assistants were crammed into the top floor near a row of women at sewing machines and men at cutting tables. It seemed like April spent an hour every day running back and forth between her second-floor cubicle and theirs on the fifth, but she wasn't going to complain. She didn't want to rock the work boat.

Unlike her years of temping assignments, designing graphics for exercise clothing was actually interesting. With her earphones on, engrossed in a project, she forgot to watch the clock and routinely forgot to take breaks. Twice that week already, she'd run out of Fite after the lunch hour, which made her late getting back to Oakland and baby Merry. Bev was nice about it—she still was on official leave, and didn't plan on going into Fite full-time yet anyway—but April felt terrible. She loved Merry, but work was rewarding in a way it had never been.

All those rewards, however, came with a price. As a temp, she'd felt invincible. Who cared if the cold automatons at the multinational investment company in Belmont hated her? She simply got another assignment.

Now she cared. She was vulnerable. When she designed a jagged stripe logo for a woman's running pant, she cared—actually cared—what happened to it. Would the design assistant pass it along to her boss? Would it make it into the line? Would an actual human being buy it in a store, wear it outside, and April might see her galloping down the sidewalk some day?

Caring was hard. It meant she hurried through the building to find the design assistant (who looked even younger than she did) with butterflies in her stomach, knowing the girl might curl her lip, tell her it sucked, and make her do it again—like she had yesterday.

But it was a real job, and she was going to make it work. Getting derailed with thoughts of clean-cut widowers with big sad eyes and hot lips was not an option.

She'd managed to bury the trauma of his rejection pretty well, although her pride stung, and she would never think about him the same way again.

He'd moved into the business offices on the ground floor, Virginia had told her, which she hoped would keep him busy and away from her indefinitely. Bev's grandfather, with the former CFO's help, had made a mess of the books before he died, and the company was still digging out of the hole. April didn't pay much attention to the business side of the family gossip, but she'd learned that much. He'd have plenty to do.

She hoped the books kept him warm at night; it certainly wasn't going to be April Johnson keeping him company. She'd heard the cliché *recoil in horror* before, but witnessing the dismay from a few inches away after sharing a kiss had stung. Her face burned just thinking of it.

She never should've kissed him. She had no idea why he responded the way he had, whether because of the generalized lust of a man in his prime, the reduction of inhibition from too much wine, or his physical attraction to her specifically. It didn't matter. When he realized what he was doing, he shoved her away with even greater enthusiasm than he'd pulled her close.

It was just the slap in the face she needed to focus on her job. Thank God she hadn't slept with him.

Yeah, right.

The elevator came, finally, and she got on. She looked over her design for a women's tank top and thought it was excellent. Stripy yet zigzagged. Great contrast between the electric blue and silver. When she reached the design assistants' floor—they were one down from the designers, who were at the top—she strode down the hallway, feeling confident and almost cheerful. Teegan would like it. It was just what she'd asked for, after rejecting the last three tries.

Teegan had her back to the entrance to her cube when April approached. Her hair hung down her back in a glossy brown curtain that came to a slight point at her spine, a shimmering arrow pointing at her skinny little butt. She wore Fite today, though it was all black synthetic stretch without any of the big color logos, just the tiny silver *F*.

Kind of boring, really. So many of the designers wore all black. It was depressing.

"Teegan?" April asked.

Teegan didn't move. April peeked around to see if she was on the phone, but no.

April took a step closer. "I've got that stripe design you wanted."

"Give me a minute," Teegan said, still not turning. Then she picked up a pen, made a note next to her desk, and turned. Hostility shot out of her eyeballs like automatic fire from a first-person shooter video game. "What?"

Now, in the old days, April would've had no problem with girls like Teegan. Teegan was younger, she was stressed out, she wasn't particularly bright—who cared what she thought?

But these days, girls like Teegan could do actual damage. April found her hand shaking slightly on the printout as she handed over the blue-and-silver stripe design. "I made the changes you requested."

Tilting her head, Teegan looked at the design without touching it. Then she tilted her head the other direction and wrinkled her nose. "No. Try again."

"Excuse me?"

"It's still not right. Try again."

April was finding it difficult to speak. Perhaps because her teeth were clamped together. "Did you have any specific suggestions?" She pitched her voice high to overcome the urge to snarl.

"You're the artist," Teegan said. Long pause. "Right?"

April's face burned. *Stay cool.* She rolled the printout between her fingers. "I'll see what I can do."

"And please be quick about it," Teegan said. "This is taking you way too long. It's just a little stripe. I was hoping you'd be able to do more for us."

The burning moved to April's neck. Her head was engulfed in shame flame. "Oh?" she managed to ask. "Like what?" Her voice was miraculously polite. And no flames shot out of her eyeballs. Another miracle.

"Well, for one, we needed an all-over floral for this T-shirt idea Jennifer has," Teegan said. Jennifer was her boss, the creative director for the Women's line. "But we'll find a real artist for that." Then she got up and walked out of the cubicle.

After thirty seconds or so, April realized she wasn't coming back. Teegan had just ended the conversation in as charming a style as she'd begun it.

April had to hold her hands against her sides to stop herself from tearing up the stripe and sprinkling it over the take-out salad open on the desk. When she had regained some of her composure, she marched down the hall to the stairwell, as mad at herself for having tears in her eyes as she was at Teegan for being a spiteful she-prick.

She let the door to the stairwell bang behind her. She jogged down the stairs, clutching the cold handrail for balance, squeezing her eyes shut to stop the tears. *Hold it together.* She'd lock herself in a stall in that bathroom on the first floor that nobody ever used until she was her tough, sassy self again.

It was stupid to get upset. Teegan wasn't the global authority on artistry. She didn't hold an official seal or have any real power —she was a little person in a little job in a little company in a huge universe. April was an artist and was immune to the slights dished out enthusiastically by unhappy, unfeeling women in low-paying creative fields.

Biting her lip, she stopped on the landing. She wasn't going to make it to the bathroom. The storm was coming, like it or not, and rain was gonna fall. Better just let it strike, clean up quickly, and carry on.

With a long exhale, she let herself cry. Not loudly, but deeply. She let the humiliation wash over her from top to bottom, up from her toes and down her cheeks.

It was good, just what she needed to continue. A little endorphin rush. A system reboot. And the dark stairwell was just fine. She didn't need to waste time huddled in a smelly bathroom —she'd be back at her desk in two minutes, good as new.

A low voice shocked her out of her sniffles. "April?"

Chapter 12

OF ALL THE people to find her crying on the job. Stretching her damp cheeks into a smile, April lifted her chin and looked down the stairs at her darling, overbearing brother. "Hey, Liam, what's up?"

"What's the matter?" He jogged up the stairs to reach her, brushing the blond hair off his forehead as he neared. He kept moving until he was on the same stair as she was, no doubt so he could scowl down his nose at her.

"Nothing." Wiping her face with the back of her hand, she continued down the stairs. "Relax, all right? I'm fine."

He caught her arm. "Are you *crying*?"

"Not anymore," she said. "Could you please let go? I've got work to do."

"You never cry." He loosened his grip but maneuvered around her to block her way down. "What happened?"

"Nothing," she said. "Seriously. I've got to go."

"Who were you just talking to?" He looked her up and down, saw the printout rolled up in her hand. "One of the designers?"

When he made a move to take the paper from her, she lifted the waistband of her Fite high-performance travel trousers and shoved it underneath. "None of your business."

He frowned at her crotch. "I can't believe you just did that."

A sharp edge of the paper was poking her in the inner thigh. She wiggled involuntarily to get more comfortable. "I'm surprising, aren't I? Now, let me go on my way. I'm sure you've got plenty of real work to do."

"You might as well tell me," he said. "I'll find out what happened on my own."

Her left thigh stung. The paper must've cut her skin when she shoved it under her pants. She put her hand in her pocket, caught the edge of the paper roll, and moved it sideways. "Nothing happened," she said.

"Then why were you crying? You never cry."

"Sure I do," she said. "I did just now. It was very refreshing. Now I'm done and I'm going back to my desk."

He grimaced, looking as if he, too, had a paper cut in a delicate area. "If somebody is going around making the support staff cry, I need to know. Bev made me promise. She has this thing about people crying in bathrooms."

"I wasn't in the bathroom, was I?"

"Just tell me, Ape."

"Nothing's going on."

His face hardened. "You may be my sister, but you're also one of my employees. If you want to continue in this rewarding occupation, I strongly suggest you answer my question."

Anger flowing into her, she wrenched her arm free. "If you want to fire me, go ahead. Until then, I'll be at my desk. Working. Until you fire me, which would be really stupid with Rita out."

Swear to God, the next time he threatens to fire me, I'm quitting. Steaming with anger, she ran down the stairs two at a time, dislodging the paper under her pants. It slid halfway down her left leg and jabbed her in the back of the knee.

She stopped and made sure Liam hadn't followed her before

kicking the paper out at her ankle and shoving it into her pocket. She would redo the design. She didn't know how, but she'd make several different stripes in different colorways and present Teegan with a blizzard of options before she went home this afternoon. No. This evening. She'd stay as long as it took.

* * *

Zack didn't notice Liam standing behind him in his cubicle in the finance department until he rapped the desk with his knuckles. Pulling out his earbuds, Zack spun his chair around and stood up. "Liam. I didn't realize you were there."

"Sorry to interrupt," Liam said. "Have a minute?"

Zack cast a longing glance at the spreadsheets on his desk. He'd immersed himself in a decade's worth of bookkeeping, unearthing all kinds of irregularities that Bev had already warned him he'd find, especially in the months between her grandfather's death and the start of her tenure. "Of course."

"When we hired you, you said you were a barometer for corporate culture. That you'd be able to tell us about the company from the bottom up in a way a team of auditors couldn't do."

Zack had an uneasy feeling about where this was headed. "Yes."

After looking behind him, Liam sat on the desk, leaned forward, and lowered his voice. "I need to find out who made April cry today."

"Excuse me?"

"She won't tell me. I need to know. It was one of the designers or their assistants."

The thought of April crying made Zack angry, but he was surprised to see her brother cared much about it. "What did they do?"

"I don't know," Liam said. "That's what I need you to find

out."

"How—but—how do you know—anything happened?"

"I found her crying in the stairwell," Liam said. "Look, you've got to understand. April's not like that. She's tough. She loves to make a scene, but not like that. Not crying."

"She wouldn't explain?"

Liam shook his head. "She won't. I need you to spend some time in the design cubes and let me know if there's anything Bev and I need to worry about. Corporate culture-wise."

Zack had hoped he was done working with the design team. They made him nervous. Backing away from Liam, he pointed at the array of spreadsheets arrayed on his desk in paper, and digitally on two monitors above them. "I was just making progress into the finances from last year Ed Roche was alive—"

"Ancient history," Liam said. "We need to make sure we've got a future. We lost two more assistants just last month. Our best patternmaker took early retirement. And Rita's going out on family leave, no idea when she'll be able to come back."

"I just heard about that," Zack said. "Sick kid?"

Liam nodded. "My sister would've been a great resource for keeping me and Bev aware of what's happening in the trenches, but she's acting as if I'm the police, sending her in to spy on the mob."

Zack sympathized with her. "I can give you general feedback, but I'm not going to ask about April in particular. It would be too obvious, given she's your sister."

Liam looked as if he was going to argue, then he nodded. "If there's a problem, you'll see it. She goes up there multiple times a day. Just make sure you've got a seat in the middle of all of them so you can see what's going on."

"What should I say? I've already talked to all of them. They thought they were done with me."

"Why say anything?" Liam asked. "You don't have to explain yourself to them. Just ask for an empty seat. With the way they drive people out the door, there should be plenty to choose from." He was already walking away.

Zack waited until Liam had been gone for a full five minutes before gripping his skull in both hands.

He'd have to see her again. Hiding out in the finance department had saved both of them from that awkward encounter for a little while, but the reprieve was never going to last forever.

One thing he was pretty sure of now: Liam didn't know. Doubtful he'd be asking Zack to help now if he knew about the drunken groping after the family dinner. The man went out of his way to protect his baby sister from design assistants. What would he do about the business consultant jumping her at the BART station?

Zack rubbed his face, stifling thoughts of doom. The benefits of getting between Liam and April were few. Whatever—or whoever—had upset her, she didn't want him to know about it, and she would be unhappy with him interfering. If it were important, she would've talked about it with her manager, or even Liam.

Or would she?

What if he could avoid the hassle of moving up to the design floor by just talking to her?

The more he thought about it, the more he liked the idea. They'd bump into each other around the building one of these days anyway. Now was as good a time as any. It would also give him the chance to apologize properly.

He tucked his spreadsheets into a drawer, shut down his computers, and went to look for her. Being a lecherous fool, he'd memorized her schedule and knew she often worked a full day on Fridays.

She wasn't at her desk, but she'd left a note in large, neat block letters handwritten over the discarded printout of a blue polka dot bike short: RAN OUT FOR COFFEE. BACK ASAP. APRIL.

He strode out the hallway to the lobby. Virginia, the geeky receptionist, had her head bowed over her phone as it beeped the tune of a familiar game, and didn't look up as he stepped outside.

Filmy mist shrouded the city, typical for early February. Not quite rain but enough to make him pause and zip up his jacket. With the weather, she probably hadn't walked too far. He was looking up and down the street, trying to decide which way to walk, when she appeared out of the fog with a cup of coffee in one hand and a white paper bag in the other.

Pulse accelerating, he strode in her direction, admiring today's outfit: hiking pants, floral poncho, ballet flats. Somehow, on her, it was sexy. She was small but rounded, most of it centered around her lower half. The hiking pants hugged every curve as she walked. By the time they were face-to-face, he'd forgotten why he'd come out to find her.

"Hi," she said, moving to walk past him.

"Wait." He held out a hand but didn't touch her. Had he ever seen her in the daylight before? Even under the clouds, the filtered sun lit up her brown hair, brought out strands of red and gold. Freckles dusted the bridge of her nose. Her eyes...

Her eyes seemed to say he was crazy. "What's the matter?" she asked.

"I need to talk to you. Got a minute?"

"Not really," she said. "Rita's out and I'm swamped."

"Please. We'll just walk around the block. It's good for us.

You'll be back at your desk in five minutes."

"No. Can't. I've got to finish this thing before the weekend." She started to move away.

"Your brother just came to talk to me about you," he said.

She stopped.

"Walk?" he asked.

She glanced at the sky, opened the paper bag. "Sounds like I'm going to need this ASAP." Out from the depths of white paper came a sugar-dusted, cinnamon-colored cookie as big as her face. After a huge bite, she turned an inquiring gaze on him.

"He's worried about you," Zack said, starting to walk. "Did something upset you today?"

"Jeez Louise." Crumbs flew out of her mouth. "He sent you to spy?"

"Afraid so."

"That overbearing turd. I love him, really I do, but he's got to let me handle this on my own."

"He's concerned about company morale."

"Just an excuse. He's forgotten I'm not eleven anymore."

"Was it Teegan?"

She took another bite. "I'm not squealing, copper."

"He told me to find an empty cubicle on the design floor and find out if there's anything wrong, corporate culture-wise."

"Of course there's something wrong. There's too much work and not enough time. Same as it is everywhere." She sipped her coffee and winced. "Ouch. Hot. I'm never good at waiting."

"Was somebody angry at you for being late with a project?"

"No, it was just"—she took another bite—"one of those things. I got a little stressed out. Liam found me and overreacted."

He knew that wasn't going to be enough of an explanation to save him from sitting in the design area. "If you tell me more about it, maybe I can get him off your back without sharing the whole story."

"It was nothing. *Nothing*. I'm not a child. I'm not *his* child."

"He's concerned about the high turnover. Assistants have quit. Freelancers don't like to come back."

"Well, I'd like to," she said. "I'm very happy. I'd like to stay at Fite for as long as they'll have me. Put that in your report. April Johnson is a happy camper. Like a girl scout on smack."

"This won't be on any report," he said. "Just a casual conversation."

"That goes to my brother the CEO and PITA." She lifted the coffee to her mouth. "April Johnson. Happy camper."

"Girl scout," he muttered.

She shoved the last, palm-sized piece of cookie into her mouth. "Exactly."

When they reached the corner, he stopped and looked back at the Fite building at the end of the street. "He said you never cry."

"I cry all the time," April said. "I'm crying right now."

He wished she would talk to her brother so he didn't have to interrupt his nice, logical financial analysis just when he was getting started. But Liam was right. He wasn't an auditor, he was a big-picture guy. He was supposed to unearth the subtle problems. "Funny, you don't look like you're crying," he said.

"On the inside," she said.

He scrubbed his face with both hands. He was going to the design floor. "Yeah. Me too."

Chapter 13

THAT EVENING AT five, April snatched the last of her designs off the printer in the hallway and ran up the stairs two at a time to the design floor.

Stripes, lightning bolts, polka dots, checks. Green, black, blue, silver, gray. The stack of designs in her hand was as thick as her wrist. She'd arranged them by shape and color so Teegan could flip through them without getting overwhelmed.

Her phone vibrated in her pocket just as she was opening the door at the top of the stairs.

It was a text from Bev. *Will you be back before 6?*

April swore. The journey home, though only fifteen miles, took over an hour via public transit.

Sorry! More like 6:30, she wrote. She'd promised to babysit Merry tonight so Bev could go out with Rose. Some wedding planning thing. The wedding was two months away, which seemed like a long time to April, but apparently was soon enough to make Rose panicked about the final preparations. Bev planned on taking her out for Thai and a movie, followed by gourmet ice cream on College Avenue—which sounded pretty good to April, too.

Bev had been working from home this week, eager to get back to Fite, but Merry wasn't making it easy. Liam was going to stay home for a few mornings next week so Bev could come in, but with Merry fussing about the bottle, it was hard for Mom to get away. Tonight was supposed to be a much-needed break for Bev as well as Rose.

April shoved her phone in her pocket, unable to wait for Bev's response. Teegan was expecting her, and stopping now would only make her later getting home.

Teegan was at her desk, thank God, eating another salad. A dinner salad, apparently. Teegan made a point of working longer hours than anyone else.

April took a second at the entrance to her cubicle to catch her breath. Then she said, "Hi. Here are a few more design options for you."

Mouth full of lettuce, Teegan eyed her without moving.

"For the running pant," April added.

"You did that already."

April placed the stack of printouts on her desk. "You asked for more options."

"What is that? That's like a whole ream of paper."

"I wanted to give you plenty of choices," April said.

Teegan frowned at the stack. "It would take me all night to go over all that."

"It's not as bad as it looks. It's arranged by design, with several colorways of each." April grabbed the stack and separated it out into categories. "Stripes are here, but I also tried out a few other —"

"You're obviously paid by the hour," Teegan said. She still wasn't moving away from her salad to take a closer look.

April's face heated. She tried to dredge up the calm of her last yoga class, where the instructor had encouraged them to embrace the opposite of whatever negative force was driving them down.

But the only thing she felt like embracing right now was a pair of pinking shears, with which she would cheerfully slice Teegan's glossy, glassy hair into ribbons.

"You said you wanted options," April said.

"Not that many. Besides, Jennifer decided to use the first one."

"The first—"

"From yesterday," Teegan said. "It sold well last year, so they're just going to run it in the new color. I don't suppose it's in that pile of yours? We need the Sunset Pink over River Rock."

April crossed her arms over her chest to restrain herself. An entire day's work, wasted. "You told me to come up with something new."

"That was before I saw what you could—and couldn't—do. We're using last year's design. We had a great freelancer last year."

The pinking shears weren't strong enough for what she wanted to do to Teegan now. Not pointy enough. She'd need some of the forearm-length stainless steel blades the cutters used on the production floor.

Teeth clenched, April scooped up the pile of designs Teegan had never looked at. "Last year's stripe?"

"The first one."

"Which colors?" April found a pen and flicked off the cap. She focused on the ballpoint, remembering a movie where the guy had killed somebody with a pen. Or was it a mechanical pencil? She scanned the desk for other writing options.

"Sunset Pink and River Rock," Teegan said, dripping with impatience.

April wrote it down in a shaky script. "I'll do it right now."

"Don't bother." Teegan closed the plastic lid of her salad. "Jennifer's gone for a week. Just make sure it's on my desk before next Friday."

Next Friday. Seven days. To print out the original design, which consisted of two parallel lines of identical width.

A masterpiece. Only a real artist could've made *that* sucker.

Paid by the hour, my big round ass. For once in her life, she *hadn't* been squeezing out the minutes for a few bucks—she'd actually cared.

What a mistake.

Clutching the stack of paper that represented hours of wasted life she'd never get back, April walked out of the cubicle without a word and down the stairs to her own floor, feeling disconnected and weightless, like a body floating in a swimming pool.

Her cellphone vibrated again. Now what? She dumped the stack into the recycling bin and glanced at the screen.

Never mind about babysitting, Bev said. *Liam's home early. Enjoy ur freedom!*

April stared at the phone. She was tired, but she'd been looking forward to a few hours with Merry. Even considering her niece's explosive digestion.

She packed up her things with a sigh. Maybe it was just as well. Aunt April was in an explosively shitty mood of her own. Better to keep all that bad energy away from an infant. Better to be alone.

She kicked the door as she walked past.

Being alone was overrated.

* * *

Zack had heard every word.

He'd done as Liam instructed and had moved himself that afternoon to the empty cubicle between the assistants for Women's and Men's. When April had come up and had her illuminating conversation with Teegan, he'd been on the other side of the flimsy wall, trying to concentrate on the data he was juggling into colorful graphs and failing.

He believed that the consulting work he did was good for everyone, especially the folks at the bottom of the corporate ladder. But right then he felt sleazy. He preferred to do his observing openly, obviously, not hidden like a weasel.

Not that furtive surveillance couldn't produce results. With him, Teegan had been agreeable and pleasant, even funny. In their short interview, she'd told him that her boss, Jennifer, wasn't always easy to work for, but that the designer was talented and creative, and Teegan was grateful to learn from her.

To his credit, he hadn't completely believed her. But he hadn't expected the enthusiasm for petty cruelty she'd just showed with April. Because he could hardly jump up and take April's side, he'd banged the phone handset into the receiver, typed as loudly as he could on his sleek laptop, and rustled papers—just to remind Teegan she wasn't alone. It had made no difference.

April departed, and mere seconds later, Teegan grabbed her jacket and bag and walked past him, chatting on her phone with a friend about which bar to meet at.

Zack gathered his things and walked to the elevator, caught up in his thoughts. He wouldn't tell Liam about the incident. If he did, April would hate his guts, and he wouldn't blame her. She wanted to handle this on her own, and he thought she should. Having her big brother come in and fix it personally wouldn't do April any favors in the long term. Teegan was probably testing her to see if she was going to appeal to her family, or if she was one of her own tribe. Needing to see if April could be trusted.

Besides, Zack had his own reputation to consider, and running to the boss about overheard conversations wouldn't help him any. Big-picture issues, yes. Individual incidents, no. It would ruin his rapport with the staff, at all levels, going forward.

He reached the lobby, wishing he felt more at peace with his decision.

Then he saw April walking toward him, and all possibility of peaceful thought went out the window.

"Hey," he said. His usual charming self.

Had her cheeks already been that bright shade of pink, or was it his doing? "Oh," she said. "Hi."

He didn't want her to think he'd been lying in wait for her, so he turned and opened the door to the street. "Have any plans for the weekend?"

"Definitely," she said, striding past him. The false spring of the month before had succumbed to a winter storm blasting the California coast from the northwest. Rain pelted both of them in the face as they headed out into the night.

Zack opened his umbrella and offered it to April, who had lifted her bag over her head as a makeshift shelter.

"Something fun, I hope," he said.

"What?"

"This weekend. Your plans. Fun." The sight of her lips glistening with rainwater had obliterated all the verbs from his mind.

Well, not all. *Lick*, *taste*, and *suck* remained.

He couldn't do this. He wouldn't be that guy. That creepy guy. He had to be professional. He slowed his pace so she would walk ahead, get away from him.

But April put the bag down at her side and looked up, letting the rain strike her in the face. After a few long seconds, she lowered her head and fell back to walk beside him. "I've just figured it out."

"Figured what out?"

"Everything. Life." She tilted her head back again and

grimaced—it might've started as a smile, but a large droplet smacked her in the eye.

He fought the impulse to move the umbrella over her. "This just happened?"

"Just now. Want to know what it is? The secret of happiness?"

He was worried she was going to be cold on the train ride home. Her wet hair formed ringlets around her face. "I'd love to know," he said.

"The trick," she said, "is not minding."

"Ah," he said.

"I mean that in the Zen way, not the masochistic sociopath way."

"Thanks for clarifying," he said. "Are you sure you don't want to borrow my umbrella? I only live a few blocks away."

"That's right. You do. The best commute I ever had was when I lived in Liam's condo and worked downtown."

He moved it over a few inches. At least her shoulder wouldn't get wet. "Here. Take it."

"I am one with the rain." She pushed it away. "I am the willow. I bend, I do not break."

"You can bend and stay dry at the same time."

"Nope," she said. "I'm tired of cowering. I'm going to walk with my head high, damn it."

He wanted to point out that holding the umbrella with the handle allowed placing one's head at any altitude one wished, but he understood she was making a philosophical point. "Heading home?" The BART station was two blocks ahead of them to the left. His condo was straight ahead. He should say goodbye.

"I had a really shitty day," she said. "But look at me—I'm totally fine." She held out her arms and embraced the sky.

"Want to go get a drink?"

Well, now he'd done it. It was probably a very bad idea, as bad as ideas come.

She looked at him and sighed. "I thought you'd never ask."

Chapter 14

FEELING RECKLESS, APRIL led him to her favorite bar south of Market Street, not too far from his condo. It was a yuppie bar, of course, couldn't be helped, but not too trendy, and they had excellent pita chips.

She would've preferred to relax with Virginia, who finally had forgiven her for almost getting her into trouble with Zack months earlier, but even a man who looked queasy after kissing her was better than going home to her mother on a Friday night, especially after a day like today.

"What would you like?" he asked, gesturing at the bar. It was blissfully free of any theme other than *drink*.

"Promise not to laugh?"

"I may do so eventually," he said, "but I'm usually pretty good at stopping myself."

She smiled. He really was kind of cute. "I'll have an appletini."

"Seriously?" he asked. She scowled and he held up his hands. "Just kidding. I'll get two."

Because the rain hadn't scared enough people away, she had to fight a damp, thirsty Friday-night crowd to find two empty chairs for them at a cramped table near the bathroom. Very romantic.

Which was perfect, of course. She didn't think she was going to jump him again—she'd never before wasted her time on a guy who wasn't interested—but it was good to avoid temptation when she was feeling so vulnerable.

She watched him through a gap in the crowd. He had a Clark Kent thing going on, no doubt about it—that dark hair, the glasses—she really, really liked the days he wore glasses—the square jaw, the sensual lips... Her belly tingled at the memory of his kiss.

She looked away, chewing a fingernail. Not that she was going to sleep with him, but did he have to swear so adamantly that he wouldn't touch her, either?

The trick is not minding, she told herself. When he arrived with two colorful martini glasses, she was able to greet him with a smile. They could be pals. Both outsiders, neither of them fashionistas, new to Fite, oddballs in life—they'd be pals.

She reached into her bag for cash to give him. "I thought you were kidding about getting one for yourself."

"What's that?" He frowned at the bill in her hand.

"I'm paying for my drink."

"My treat," he said.

She paused, but she'd never been one to turn down a free cocktail, so returned her cash to her wallet. "I'll get the next round." She sipped the enormous basin of sweet, alcoholic liquid in her hands, wishing she'd ordered an Irish coffee, because she'd started to shiver. Like so many of her good ideas, dancing in the rain hadn't withstood the test of time. And she'd always put on a show for an audience. If Zack hadn't been there, she probably would've run like hell for the train and been halfway home—and dry—by now.

And alone with Mom and her poop-eating dog.

Zack was looking around the joint with that studious, owlish expression of his. "Is this a gay bar?"

She laughed. "God, no. I've gone home with—" She stopped herself before she shared her fun-loving, sexually liberated past with him. "With... the knowledge that this is definitely *not* a gay bar. There are women here, see?"

"Mostly men, though. And lots of women like going to gay bars because they don't get hassled."

"You know this how?" she asked.

He ran his thumb along the rim of his glass. "My late wife. Meg. And her best friend. They used to go to a place in Brooklyn just for that reason."

"Are you *sure* it was for *that* reason?" she asked, then realized she'd just joked about his dead wife being a lesbian. "Oh my God, I'm sorry—"

His hand touched hers. "It's all right." He smiled. "It's much better to make jokes than tiptoe around like I'm going to burst into tears."

"Tasteless jokes."

"Even better." He moved his hand away from hers.

Well, one thing was working out—she wasn't cold anymore. In fact, she was feeling rather warm.

Awkwardness settled between them like a racist uncle at a wedding. They both shifted in their seats, their gazes darting around, settling on anyone but each other.

"So," she said, finally. "How was your day? Other than Liam moving you up into—"

Into the design assistant cube farm. How had she forgotten?

"It was fine," he said. "Other than that."

She'd just realized why he'd asked her out for a drink. "You heard me, didn't you? When I had my conversation with Teegan."

He lifted his glass for a long swallow. "I heard."

Her body tensed. "Well. I suppose I know what Liam will

want to talk about this weekend. He'll probably make a special visit tonight, with Merry in tow." She drained her martini and felt the booze tingle under her skin.

She'd have to convince Liam to do nothing. That would be a challenge. Her brother was a corporate workaholic with an Olympic medal—doing nothing was as foreign to him as wearing pink lace panties.

Well, she *assumed*. Months of living in his condo hadn't unearthed any secret kinks of her big brother's other than how he liked to alphabetize his bookshelf by title and got twitchy if she returned one to the wrong place on the shelf.

"I didn't tell Liam," Zack said.

"Monday, then."

"I won't tell him."

"Why the hell not?"

He put his drink down. "Do you want me to?"

"No."

"Why not?" he asked.

"Because it's none of his business."

"Well, technically, that's exactly what it is."

"I'll handle it myself. Teegan is just playing alpha to see if she can get away with it. She'll get bored eventually."

He nodded. "I agree."

"You do?"

"Don't feed the trolls," he said.

"Exactly!" She picked up their empty glasses. "Another round?"

"No... yes. Sure."

She stood up. "You're really not going to tell Liam about the pretty mean girl shitting on his baby sister?"

"If Jennifer, Teegan's boss, encourages her to treat all of the support staff, freelancers, and coworkers with petulant inconsideration, and she's not the only one who does, then I'll include that observation in my general report on the team, which I provide at the end of the month."

"And you'll leave me out of it?"

"I might change my mind if you keep asking." He pointed at the glasses in her hands. "How about a beer this time? I'm not colorful enough for the stuff you drink."

Another urge to kiss him struck her, but this time she had the willpower to hold herself back. She'd taken home enough men from this bar—too many hookups that went nowhere. "You got it," she said as a shiver racked her.

It was just her wet clothes. Nothing to do with the way she wanted to swim in his dark blue eyes.

She got two pints of lager and scanned the crowed for familiar faces. It had been over a year since she'd met the last guy from here she'd gone home with. Well, to Liam's home. And he'd interrupted them just when things were getting fun.

She sipped her beer as she walked back to the table, feeling older and wiser. She didn't miss dating. Her more tender parts missed the physical contact, the rush of pleasure, the naked embrace, but the rest of her was glad to be out of that game. None of the guys had ever been as great as she'd hoped. Not as funny, not as kind, not as smart. Although she'd had quite a few one-night stands, and relationships that lasted a week or so, she'd always hoped it would turn out to be forever. That the cute guy with the dimple in his cheek and the twinkle in his eye would be the one to understand her, to love her...

She was smarter now. Her last boyfriend had been such a loser, yet she'd hung on to him for months, squeezing him like a withered slice of lemon over iced tea, unable to give up on the hope there could be *more*. How couldn't there be? How could she be so wrong about people, about men, again and again? That guy at the bar wasn't a secret, misunderstood genius—he was just another self-absorbed dork with an obsidian earring and a Japanese tattoo.

She placed both pints on the table and flopped into her chair. Her underwear had crept up her ass, glued in place by the damp pants—the Fite hiking trousers she'd worn in an attempt to fit in and impress.

"You know what I need?" she said, toasting him with her beer before chugging the first quarter of it. "I need a makeover. I obviously don't have the knack for this corporate uniform thing."

"You?"

"Admit it." She poked him in the shoulder. He was wearing a blue button-down shirt again, this one with tiny white stripes. By newly formed habit, her fingers itched to measure the stripe width, get it into the computer. "You've noticed I'm not the most fashionable chick on the planet."

His mouth curved in a half smile. "I'm hardly one to judge. Luckily, that isn't part of my job description."

"But you know how to look serious. People take you seriously."

"I'm a guy. It's a sexist world."

She appreciated that he was aware of his male privilege, but she also knew he was trying to change the subject. "It's okay," she said. "I've gone to a lot of trouble to be unique. I like it. However... I'd like to be able to blend in when I feel like it, and I've got to admit I'm going to need help."

He looked at her, then down into his glass. "I like your clothes."

Fuzzy, happy feelings coated her like dandelion fluff on a

spring day. "You do?"

He nodded. "You make an impression."

"Not the right one, though, maybe, don't you think?" She moved her chair closer to be heard over the crowd. "It would be harder for assistants like Teegan to dismiss me if I had a different look."

"I don't know," he said.

"Don't worry about hurting my feelings." She took another drink. It was mostly true; she'd taken great pride in nonconformity. But it had always been a choice, not a default position, and she wanted to prove to herself she could adapt if it suited her. "You've got to admit that if I weren't wearing a funky outfit today, Teegan might not have been so quick to treat me like a disposable diaper."

"Speaking of which, how's your niece?"

"Don't change the subject," she said. "Well, will you help?"

"Change diapers?"

"Change me," she said. "I want some of that corporate style you've mastered to rub off on me."

"I'm sure they're laughing at my style—my total lack of it— more than they're laughing at yours."

"Nobody laughs at you," she said.

"Like I said, it has nothing to do with what I'm wearing."

"It does. Look at that shirt—all buttoned up. Literally."

Frowning, he plucked at it. "It's a shirt with buttons."

"Exactly."

"All this time, it was the source of my power," he said, shaking his head. "I never made the connection."

The second drink had clarified everything. She stood up so fast she bumped his arm and spilled his beer. "Let's go."

"Go?"

"Shopping," she said. "Union Square is only a few blocks away."

He licked the spilled beer off his knuckles. "Right now?"

The sight of his tongue momentarily derailed her. *Oh, yeah, right now, babe, let's* go.

She pulled out her phone. "It's not even seven yet. Macy's is open late tonight. Did you have something better to do?"

"You don't want me to come shopping with you, surely," he said.

"I surely do."

He laughed, and his whole face softened. "No. You need a woman. Or at least a guy with a clue." He put his hand on her arm and tried to pull her back down. "Finish your drink, and we'll both go home."

Her heart began to pound until she remembered he obviously didn't mean *together*. "I've already finished it."

"Why not ask your brother's fiancée, Rose?" he asked. "She looked like she'd be able to help you."

Jealousy nibbled at April's ego. "She's too busy right now getting ready for the wedding," she said. "Besides, she's not good at looking boring. She has no experience with it."

"Which is why you want me?" he asked, eyebrows raised.

"Exactly."

"Stop, you're embarrassing me."

"Come on. It's not too late, but it will be if we don't get going," she said.

"It's raining."

"I'm already wet, and you have an umbrella."

"I'll still get wet," he said.

She narrowed her eyes. "You owe me, remember? If you're really sorry about what happened two weeks ago, you'll prove it."

He drained his drink and stood up. "Union Square?"

"Yes! This will be so much fun." She patted him on the shoulder.

No, stop doing that. He felt way too good to keep doing that. Strong, broad, male. And whenever she touched him, something flickered in his eyes.

"So much fun," he said.

* * *

He blamed the appletini.

He sat on the couch outside the dressing room, trying to tune out the loud overhead TV broadcasting a feature about dieting cats.

It had come to this. He couldn't even sleep with her, and he'd let her drag him into a department store on a Friday night. His shoes were soggy. He needed a toilet.

And he was going to have to look at her body repeatedly and share his opinion.

Yes, he would say. *Perfect.*

He was in such trouble. He was swiftly careening into full-blown obsession. If only he'd devoted more time to dating this year, he wouldn't be as desperate. Every little tilt of her hips or smile on her lips made him want to push her against the wall.

"What do you think?"

She stood before him in an outfit a grandmother on a gambling bus to Reno might wear: a baggy floral blouse, a pink cardigan, and tan no-iron trousers.

"Great," he said. "We have a winner." He'd already decided he wasn't going to participate in any meaningful way.

Not the meaningful way he'd like. Wasn't that exactly why he was so unhappy?

"Seriously," she said. "I see women wearing this sort of thing to work all the time."

He bit his lip and nodded.

"It's hideous, of course, but isn't that the point?" she asked.

"Shall I meet you at the register?"

"You don't like it," she said.

"It's great."

She crossed her arms over her chest. "Fine. You pick something out then."

"I said—"

"I'm in the first room on the right." She spun on her heel. "The more you fight this, the longer it'll take."

He sank down onto the vinyl sofa and looked up at the TV. The fattest cat he'd ever seen was scowling at him through the screen.

He got up and strode out into the store to grab the first outfit he saw. She'd already shared her sizes with him, but he'd forgotten, so he had to eyeball it. He found a pair of dark khaki pants. And then a sky-blue, pinstripe button-down shirt. Exactly what he was wearing.

Grinning, he returned to the dressing room. "Here you go," he said, flinging them over the slatted door.

"Nice," she called out. "We'll be twins."

"I'm sharing my secrets, and this is how you reward me?"

He went back to his couch and the TV. They were still interviewing the family with the huge feline. Royal weddings got less coverage.

Then she came out of the dressing room with a gleaming smile on her face. "We've got a winner!"

She looked terrible. The shirt and pants fit her well, and she'd buttoned and tucked herself together neatly, but she looked *wrong*. Like every androgynous clone in corporate America.

Like him.

"Take it off," he said.

She crossed her arms over her chest. "Excuse me?"

He stood up and pointed at the interior of the store. "I'll find you something else."

"No need. This is perfect."

"It isn't."

"It is," she said, pivoting on her heel, showing him the buttoned welt pockets on her ass. "You picked out the perfect size, too. Thanks."

He strode over to her. "That's all wrong for Fite. It's too conservative. You're an artist, not an accountant."

She went inside the dressing room and banged the door in his face. "They don't want somebody who looks like an artist. They want somebody who looks like you."

"Just because some design assistant was yanking your chain doesn't mean it had anything to do with the crazy stuff you like to wear," he said.

She pulled the door open. She'd put her old clothes back on. "Crazy. There you go. Crazy isn't the look I'm going for anymore."

But he liked her look. Too much. "At least try on something a little more... I don't know... fashionable. More... I don't know, feminine. Like what the design assistants wear."

"I already know I can't wear that crap. The heels alone would kill me. I'd trip on the stairs. I wouldn't even be able to get out of the house." She slung the blue shirt and khaki pants over her arm and marched past him. "These are the perfect compromise. Comfortable, wash-and-wear, and they don't clash too bad with my combat boots."

"Not wearing the boots would be enough of a makeover. You don't have to—"

But she was already gone, disappearing past the racks and displays to find a register.

The TV was now broadcasting a commercial for chocolate-frosted-bagel breakfast cereal. No doubt that's what the cat had been eating.

He caught up to April at the opposite end of the store, where she was already handing over her credit card. Her hair had dried unevenly around her ears, sticking up at odd angles. Her lips were curled in a smile. He thought about kissing her.

Out on a Friday night with a woman he found irresistible, and here he was. Damp. Too sober. Frustrated. And she hadn't even taken his advice.

"Are you in line?" a woman asked behind him.

He jumped aside. "No. Just waiting for..." He trailed off, avoiding eye contact with the dark-haired woman, who held a red-and-black sliver of fabric that might have been underwear.

Why hadn't he brought *that* to April in the dressing room?

He rubbed his eyes. This had been a mistake. Just because he had iron self-control didn't mean he should torture himself.

April bounced over to him, hugging a shopping bag to her chest. "I got three of the shirts and two pair of the pants. I'll have to drive out to Concord this weekend to get a few more. Each store only has a couple per size, you know?"

"I'll walk you to BART," he said.

She bumped her shoulder against his as they headed for the elevator. "You aren't really mad, are you? Just because I didn't take your advice?"

"I'm not mad."

"Yeah?"

"The trick is not minding," he said.

Chapter 15

IT TOOK APRIL almost three weeks to admit her new clothes weren't doing the trick.

Teegan and the other Women's design assistants had become increasingly difficult to work with. They asked her to do things one day and then backtracked the next, never admitting they had said otherwise. April's hours sped by every morning in a haze of sketches and swatches and screen print designs, a parade of work that never ended, that she never completed.

One morning in late February, she hurried out with Virginia to the coffee truck in the alley for a quick caffeine fix.

"If these guys were really smart, they'd serve liquor," April muttered.

It was already eleven, she wouldn't be in the office the next day, and she had one hour to recolor six stripes, lay out a logo on a T-shirt, match a new palette into the computer, and... there was something else...

Right. Go to the bathroom. She'd had to pee for over an hour. At this rate she was going to get a bladder infection, no matter how much cranberry juice she chugged.

Always afraid of offending anyone, Virginia looked around and asked in a whisper, "What happened?"

"They don't like anything I do," April said.

Virginia scrunched up her face. "I know."

"You do?"

Virginia gave her a sympathetic nod. "I hear them bitching while they wait for the elevator in the lobby."

"About me?"

"Sorry," Virginia said.

April paid for a bottle of iced tea and an apple that would probably taste like Fite Performance Cotton, but she was desperate for nutrients that didn't come out of a bag. "The main problem is they make me redo everything, and then I get behind. It's really annoying."

"Any way you could pin them down better on what they want before you waste too much time?"

"I do. I ask millions of questions and make them write down what they want before I do anything. Then they see it, exactly what they asked for, and it's like *I'm* the crazy one."

"At least you get paid by the hour," Virginia said.

"But it's stupid. Inefficient."

Virginia paid for her hot chocolate and a granola bar. "Are you coming in tomorrow? We could splurge on dim sum."

"I wish, but I've got Merry all day." April took a bite of her apple, and it was worse than she'd feared, mealy and bruised. She frowned at it, tempted to ask for her money back but not wanting to add to the bad energy already spoiling her mood. "I have to watch her this afternoon, too. I'm going to get really behind."

Merry was five months old now, rolling around the house and getting into even more trouble. April loved being with her, and the proud parents had insisted on paying her nicely—but her babysitting hours, because of Bev's work schedule, were usually during business hours, and she kept running out of time.

With Rita still out—she'd filed for family leave, and nobody knew when she'd be back—the workload was snowballing. The design teams had permission to hire more freelancers, but none had appeared, and April was skeptical Jennifer or Darrin would bother. Easier to dump it in April's lap and complain.

"I'll have to come in early Monday morning," April said. She couldn't believe she'd reached the point in her life when she would regularly get up before five a.m., but what else could she do?

"I heard Rita's other kid is sick, too," Virginia said.

"She left me a message," April said. "Her older daughter had double pneumonia. She spent a night in the hospital. And her six-year-old has always had really bad asthma, and of course it flared up at the worst time."

They walked back through the back door, nodding at George, who scowled.

"Rita's a single mom," April continued. "I can't imagine how she's coping. Hopefully I can keep things from totally falling apart while she's away."

"You're just a freelancer," Virginia said. "Don't kill yourself trying to cover for her. They'll hire more people if you can't handle it."

But she wasn't just any freelancer—she was the family slacker, the baby. She *had* to handle it. She *would*.

When she went back to her desk, she saw the pile of clothes, boards, swatches, and paper. Her stomach twisted. Less than an hour now to get it done. And they'd hate it anyway.

She sat down and got to work. Whatever she didn't finish, she could get in between six and eight Monday morning.

The phone rang. Teegan's line.

On the third trill, April picked up the receiver and slowly put it against her temple, as if it were loaded. "Yes?"

It was a man's low, calming voice. "Just thought you might like to know they've all gone to LA for the rest of the week."

At first she thought it was God. Or an angel. "Zack?"

"In case they forgot to mention it to you," he said. "It was a spur-of-the-moment thing. They just left for the airport."

"Who?"

"The entire team."

"Teegan?"

"All of them. Men's and Women's. Designers and assistants. They decided to go shopping," he said.

"Just like that?"

"You're one to talk," he said. "Spontaneous shopping trips are your specialty."

"But..." She looked at the pile of work on her desk. "Do they want this shit or not?"

"Sorry. Not privy to their inner workings. So to speak. Just couldn't help watching them all run off with their suitcases."

"If they had suitcases, they must've known they were going at least last night," she said.

Zack was silent.

"Thanks for letting me know," she said. "I'll... talk to you later." She hung up.

Virginia appeared in the opening of her cubicle. In a daze, April looked up at her. "The entire design team just went to LA."

Virginia nodded. "I was coming to tell you. I saw them go a few minutes ago."

April got to her feet, gesturing at the mess of her desk. "Teegan said she wanted it by noon. Today." April picked up the top sheet, flung it back down.

"Who was it who just called you?"

April felt her face flushing. "The business consultant. He's using a cube in their department and overheard."

Virginia laughed. "Zack, you mean? 'Business consultant.' As if I don't know his name."

"Yeah, well, he thought I'd like to know."

"Nice of him," Virginia said.

April hadn't told anyone about the kiss. That way it was easier to pretend it hadn't happened. But now the memory washed over her, leaving her hot and achy. "He's just doing his job. He was hired to improve morale."

"Starting with yours."

April sat down. "Watch it."

"He likes you."

"Who doesn't?" April asked. "Other than the design team of Fite Fitness, that is."

"Do you like him?"

"This isn't sixth grade," April said.

Virginia nodded. "I'll bet you lunch something's going to happen between you two."

"Save your money. He never gets involved at work."

Virginia's brown eyes widened. "He told you that?"

Too late, April turned away and began rearranging the swatches of fabric and sketches on her desk. "I don't want to talk about it."

"He must be interested. He wouldn't call you like that otherwise."

"Trust me," April said, "he'd rather gnaw off a limb than touch me again."

Virginia whistled softly. "Again?"

"Nothing happened."

Virginia cocked an eyebrow.

"Over a month ago," April muttered. "So don't waste your

money. It's not going to happen."

"A hundred. I bet you a hundred it does."

"You're throwing your money away," April said.

"I doubt that. Deal?"

To get rid of her, April agreed, and Virginia finally returned to the front desk. April looked at all the work on her desk, finding it difficult to motivate herself to do any of it.

Her phone trilled again. Teegan's line. She picked up, her heart skipping. "Why do you keep using her phone?"

"She has you on speed dial," Zack said. "Big yellow sticker next to your name."

"Surprised it's not a bull's-eye," April said. She loved his voice, deep and rich.

"It is slightly round. Should I draw a black circle in the middle?"

April put her hand over her heart, felt its ridiculous dance under her palm. "What are you calling about this time? Not that I'm not thrilled to hear from you."

He paused. "I was headed your way at lunch. Thought I could offer you a ride."

"To Oakland?"

"I have a meeting with Bev at their house," he said.

"You could take BART."

"I'm continuing on to Bakersfield for a few days to see my parents. I actually rented the car just for that reason."

It was only Thursday. Interesting that he wasn't waiting until the weekend. "Is everything all right?"

"Why wouldn't it be?" he asked.

He obviously liked his privacy. She'd try to respect that, but it wasn't her strong suit. "When are you leaving?"

"Noon. Meet you in back. I'm parked in the alley." He clicked off.

She set down the receiver and stared at her screen, where the latest version of a polka dot Fite logo flickered in pink and blue spots.

He seemed rigid, but made his own rules. He was aloof but went out of his way for people.

For her.

She brushed her fingers against her lips, remembering.

The phone rang again, this time from Liam. "I just talked to Jennifer," he said. "She called from the cab. She said Teegan expected you to revise the sketch for the 534 hoodie before they left for the airport. She's asking me why you didn't get it done yet."

Teegan had specifically told her two hours ago that she would do all her own sketches. And having her boss call her brother... that was a new level of slime.

But April's thoughts had drifted to Zack, and latched on. *I hope his parents are okay.* Why hadn't he waited until the weekend?

She glanced at the clock. Not much time until she'd meet him. A different kind of stress pulled at her now.

She opened up the sketching program on her computer, made the revisions in three seconds, and put it on the network, all the while holding the phone at her ear.

"What should I tell her?" Liam asked.

"The sketch *is* done," April replied. "I just checked. Maybe Teegan was looking in the wrong network folder. She's not exactly a computer genius."

"Good to know," Liam said. "Thanks. Sorry to bother you."

Smiling, she hung up, pulled out her compact, and reapplied her lipstick, realizing that, indeed, her morale was *much* improved.

* * *

Zack tried to hand a few bucks to George at the back door for watching his car—parking spaces in San Francisco were as rare as affordable housing—but the old guy waved him away, wrinkling his nose.

"Save it for a haircut," George said. "You're a few weeks overdue."

Zack ran his hand through the waves flopping over his eyes. "More like a month. I haven't found a place I like to get it done."

"What's not to like?" George asked. "You got hair, they cut it off."

Zack didn't explain that the quarter-inch of white stubble at the base of George's skull didn't need as much skill as his own hair. In the wrong hands, his thick, cow-licked waves would look ridiculous, with tufts sticking out at odd angles unless he plastered it down with gelatinous goo that worked for only an hour or two.

His mother would tell him to get a haircut, too. His father would tell him his mother was right and then haul him to Quickie-Cut himself.

Maybe that's why he hadn't cut it yet. It would give him something to do with his parents while he was home, even if the results would lead him to wear a hat for the next month. His parents were even more introverted than he was, happiest when they were at work on their own solitary tasks. They were slow to talk, reluctant to pry, and always went to bed early. He spent most of his time at home reading on the couch.

He thanked George again and got into his rented Mazda, keeping one eye on the back door for April. His promise not to talk to her brother about the way Teegan was treating her was becoming increasingly difficult to keep. The drive over to Oakland would give him the chance to... he didn't know what. Suggest she ask for help. Now that he'd been in the design assistant area for almost two weeks, he was convinced that Teegan —and the other assistants—were trying to sabotage her in particular. While they weren't always nice with other support staff, they didn't laugh about them once they'd left the room.

He saw April pop out of the back door, scan the alley for him, and jog over, looking much happier than he'd expected. If Teegan had hoped for tears and a resignation letter, she'd failed. April was rosy-cheeked and smiling.

An increasingly familiar hunger struck him.

She climbed in and caressed the plastic dash. "Sweet wheels. Went all out, did you?" She put on her seat belt. "Let's bail this jail."

Her uniform was different today. She continued to wear the conservative trousers, but the poncho had returned. And pink safety pins pierced her ears like a punk rocker's.

"You look nice," he said, starting the car.

"Let's not kid ourselves."

"I'm not kidding."

She held up a hand and made a dismissive gesture. "Sorry. You look nice, too."

Luckily, his ego wasn't entangled with his appearance. Turning his attention to the narrow pavement, he snaked his way through the busy city streets to the Bay Bridge.

After ten minutes of silence, when they were careening away from the city on the bridge over white-tipped black water, she asked, "Are you sure everything's fine?"

"So far as I know."

"Have you visited them since you got here?" she asked.

"You're curious," he said.

"Sorry," she said. "It's just because it's a Thursday. Who goes to Bakersfield on a Thursday?"

"Oil tanker drivers?"

"Which describes you to a T," she said.

He smiled. "I'm just overdue for a visit, that's all."

"Nobody's birthday?"

Usually he avoided talking about his family, but at that moment, while the shadows of the top layer of the bridge flickered over the road, he heard the words pour out of him. "My parents never celebrate birthdays. They were raised in a religion that didn't believe in it."

He squeezed the steering wheel, waiting for the outrage that usually came when he told people that. Not celebrating birthdays got more of a reaction than finding out his first wife had died at twenty-six.

"Interesting," she said. "Were you raised in that religion too?"

Surprised by her mild tone, he relaxed slightly. "They left the church when I was a baby. But they never tried to be, you know, like other people." He cleared his throat. "They're very private people."

"Unlike me, obviously," she said, making a face. "Sorry. I thought you'd have to have a really good reason... or a bad one... to miss a workday."

"Well, since the design team would be in LA anyway, I figured it would be a good time to take off."

"I was such the last to know, wasn't I?"

"If I'd realized you didn't know earlier, I would've called," he said. "I heard Rita is out on family leave."

"Both her kids are sick."

"Bad luck."

"Yeah. Poor babies," April said. "I thought about getting some candy or toys for them, but I don't know what little kids like these days."

"I was talking about you," he said. "Does Liam have any plans for getting somebody in there to manage the department?"

"I was going to ask *you* that," she said. "But no, I don't think so. The assistants have to do more of their own work until she gets back."

"Or lay it on you."

"I'm not going to worry about that. It's much too nice out. I love spring, don't you?" When he didn't say anything, she added, "Thanks for calling to tell me they'd left, by the way. That was... nice."

He felt himself blush. For Christ's sake. "You're welcome."

The car became very small and quiet for a few minutes. Then April cleared her throat. "So, you're going to meet with Bev?"

"Yes."

"I think she's looking forward to getting back to work. She asked me to babysit Merry on Fridays from now on."

"All day?"

"For a little while. She's going to work one or two full days a week, with hours from home on the other days."

"That's a lot of babysitting for you, isn't it?" he asked.

"It's the deal we—" She fell silent.

"Deal?"

"Nothing. Forget it."

"I don't want to know, do I?" he asked.

"You really don't."

"Was this Liam's idea?"

"I forget whose idea it was. Mine, probably. I wanted to work in the art room at Fite, they needed help with Merry. It just made sense."

"It makes a lot of sense for them, I agree," he said.

"It makes sense for *me*. I wasn't going anywhere. If I took another temp job, I was going to jab my eyes out with some stranger's hole puncher."

"Sounds messy," he said.

She crossed her arms over her chest. "So, why are you going to the house?"

At that moment he was driving through the Oakland Maze, a region of tangled concrete spaghetti where the major freeways collided at the edge of the bay, and he couldn't respond for several minutes.

"It was on my way," he said finally. "And I won't be in the office tomorrow."

"What does Bev want to talk about?"

"You're full of questions," he said.

"And you're full of answers."

He smiled. The truth was, stopping by had been his idea. He was on his way to the Central Valley anyway, they hadn't met in person for a few weeks, he knew April was headed this way...

"Will you be scheming for a dinner invitation, too?" she asked.

He lifted his chin. It had occurred to him. Not that he'd admit it. "I've got a long drive ahead of me."

"Just as well," she said. "Mark won't be there until Sunday, when the whole family gets together. Maybe you can find a way to get Mom to invite you to that one," she said. "Casually mention you'll be driving past the house at around, say, four o'clock."

He got off the freeway and came to a stop at a red light. She was playing with him. She tried to be so tough, as if she couldn't get burned by this attraction between them—as if only he could.

It made him want to teach her a lesson.

Lifting the sunglasses above his eyes, he turned his head, met her gaze. "How about you?" he asked, pitching his voice lower.

"Will *you* be there on Sunday?"

Her tongue darted out and flicked across her lips. "I'm always there. I live there, remember?"

He dropped he glasses over his eyes and grinned as he drove around the corner. "Then maybe I'll see you there."

Chapter 16

HOW COULD I be so stupid? April asked herself. It was Sunday afternoon. She stood in the kitchen, staring out the window at the early evening fog shrouding San Francisco and the Golden Gate. *I practically invited him to dinner.*

"Did you baste the birdie?" Trixie called out from the living room, where she was playing the piano. Zack had called from the road from Bakersfield and expected to arrive any minute.

April poured herself a glass of iced tea. "Yes!" she called, taking a sip. The unfortunate fowl was already out of the oven and resting under foil. Stool was sprawled on the floor by the refrigerator, on his back with all three legs in the air. She squatted down and scratched his belly, smiling as he panted his appreciation.

Dogs were better than men in so many ways. Because of Zack, she'd changed her outfit six times, settling on an old sundress with combat boots (a classic combo). She'd painted her nails. She'd put on her favorite cobalt-blue eyeliner.

She'd cooked a chicken.

"I'm such a dork," she whispered to Stool. His adoring look said he didn't agree.

So much better than men.

Bev and Liam wouldn't be joining them because they'd taken

Merry up to Lake Tahoe to take pictures of her in the snow and pretend she would remember any of it. Mark and Rose, though, were already at the house, arguing about the honeymoon again while Trixie played Beethoven's "Wedding March" on repeat.

Why was she so nervous? They weren't going to have sex with each other—what did she care? Why bother? He was just passing through. He was nice, but he wasn't long-term material.

Or *she* wasn't.

The kitchen timer began beeping.

"He's here!" Trixie stood in the kitchen doorway. "You go answer the door, I'll take out the bird."

Wiping her hands on her hips, telling herself to calm down, April walked past her into the dining room. "Never mind the timer. It's already out." She strode to the front door and flung it open. "Welcome."

Zack stood there in dark jeans and a snug long-sleeved T-shirt. His cheeks were slightly sunburned. The hazy sunlight lit up his blue eyes. No glasses today—she wondered if he wore contacts. To stop herself from staring at his eyeballs, looking for lenses, she turned her gaze lower.

Oh, my.

She'd had no idea he had shoulders like that. Or muscles. Of course she figured he had *some* muscles—how else could he pick up his laptop?—but these were bigger than anyone would need to pick up a laptop. Or a desktop. Hell, a *desk*.

"Hi," he said. "I hope I'm not late."

Her throat tightened. Unrequited lust had never lasted this long before. It had been *weeks*. She should've been over it by now. Was there some kind of illegal additive in his shampoo?

"You're not late," she said. "Come on in."

A scream from the kitchen made them both turn in surprise.

Another scream.

"Mom?" April jogged away from him through the house to find her mother playing tug of war with Stool.

Oh, no. He had the chicken. Her perfectly browned, basted dinner was hanging out of his mouth.

She fell to her knees and joined her mother in a high-pitched, frantic struggle to free the slippery bird. Stool had already consumed half of it.

"I thought you only liked poop, you crazy dog," April gasped. The bones could choke him, especially since he was snapping and gulping it down like an alligator.

Her mother flung a dripping handful up into the sink. "I think he got a wing."

April wrested a drumstick away from him, but only the bone came away in her hand. She hooked her fingers through his collar and dragged him off to a corner.

What scraps remained of her gourmet meal were smeared across the tile floor.

"He's still breathing, so I guess he survived," April said, with mixed feelings. She took a moment to recover from the shock. "I can't believe he climbed up on the counter. I had it pushed up against the back wall."

Her mother sighed. "Just too tempting, I suppose."

Mark, Rose, and Zack crowded the doorway. "Anything we can do?" Rose asked.

"You two go back to your honeymoon planning," Trixie said. "April and Zack will go out and get us emergency takeout. That's okay with you, isn't it Zack? Just down to College for something. Whatever you like."

"He's been on the road all day," April said.

"I really don't mind," Zack said.

Trixie beamed. "Thank you so much. Maybe it'll be nice to get out and walk around? College has dozens of great restaurants. Order whatever looks good. We don't have any special dietary needs."

Zack looked at April. "We'll have to take my car. I'm parked behind you."

She released Stool, who promptly commenced mopping the floor with his elongated pink tongue, and walked to the sink to wash her hands.

She wondered if her mother had actually handed Stool the chicken or if she'd moved a chair over to the counter for him. She'd probably removed most of the bones first. Trixie Johnson wouldn't have fostered dozens of dogs over the years if she didn't love them so much.

"We'll be right back," April said to her, her voice firm.

Trixie flung a morsel of chicken in front of Stool's eager snout. "Take your time."

April grabbed her coat and walked with Zack out to the car. When he got behind the wheel, she put a hand over her eyes.

"I'm so sorry about this," she said. Her fingers still smelled like chicken.

"I really don't mind."

"Mark's favorite restaurant is Zachary's Pizza," she said. "Chicago-style."

"How about you?"

"His favorite is Zack's Special. You could joke and bond over the name. Then he'll be so grateful, he'll hire you to be his right-hand tech minion."

He backed out of the driveway. "I thought you said you were sorry. You're being kind of argumentative."

"God, you're right. I am sorry." She pointed. "Turn left here.

It's faster."

He signaled at the stop sign and headed down the hill. "I'm interested in working with lots of people. Your brother Mark is just one of them."

"Uh-huh."

"I'm a solo consultant. I have to network if I want to survive," he said.

"I completely understand," she said. "By the way, he really, really likes this pizza. I don't think you should let the opportunity to make him so happy pass you by."

He made a face and kept driving.

"How were Mom and Dad?" she asked.

"Great."

"That's good." She studied the shape of his skull. Some barber in Bakersfield had gone a little nuts with the razor. "I like your haircut."

"I doubt that."

"I do. It's the kind of—" She closed her mouth. It was the kind of style she liked to rub with her palms, soft and bristly, like a toothbrush. She shifted in her seat and slipped her hands under her thighs. "The kind of haircut that's very practical."

"Number four. My father suggested number one, which he feels is the better value, but I'd rather not have a haircut that requires sunscreen." He sighed. "Honestly, I still think I'm going to have to buy a hat."

She could hear the love in his voice. "I got a haircut with my mother recently as a bonding experience, too," she said. "It's only now starting to grow out."

"I like it."

"Well, I like yours, too," she said.

He glanced at her and she felt herself go all tingly again. *Oh, calm down.*

Shaking it off, she looked away and pointed at the road ahead. "Turn right on College. It's near the BART station."

"Will pizza be all right with your mother for the Sunday meal?"

"Please," she said. "She's lucky if we give her any."

"I really don't mind doing this, you know. It gives me something to do."

She'd better watch the complaints. She didn't want him to know her mother was trying to set them up. "Nice of you. Turn left up there. We might find parking under the tracks."

It took over ten minutes to find a parking space, and by the time they walked inside the packed restaurant, her stomach was growling. She inhaled the thick, savory aroma of tomatoes, garlic, and roasting cheese. "You're going to love this pizza," she said, maneuvering through the throng to the counter, where she ordered two stuffed specials and paid in cash, refusing to accept the bills Zack pulled from his wallet.

"Please," he said. "It'll make me feel better."

"Save it to buy yourself a hat."

He laughed. She grinned back at him before internally kicking herself and dragging him back out to the sidewalk.

"The deep dish takes longer to cook," she said. Only then did she realize she'd chosen takeout with a seventy-minute wait time. Now what were they going to do?

Her gaze fell upon the burrito place across the street. Five minutes, max, *that* would've been. Slap some beans and chicken inside a tortilla, sprinkle a little cheese, salsa, splurge on some guacamole, and off they'd go.

She never had been the type to plan things very well. "We should've called ahead. Now we're stuck here on the sidewalk."

"I wouldn't mind walking. I've been stuck in that car all day."

"I should've brought Stool. He's got a meal to work off," she said.

"Quite an impressive move for such an old dog. Getting up on the counter like that."

"I'll say."

"Your mom took it pretty well," he said. "My mother would've gone ballistic if my dog ate her dinner. She won't even let *me* in the kitchen when she's cooking."

"I was the chef tonight," she muttered.

"Oh." He laughed. "Sorry."

"Yeah."

"You should've let me buy the pizza. I distracted you when you came to the door."

He certainly had.

They walked past a bar and grill. Since it was early, and the place looked new, half of the seats at the bar were empty. She stopped and turned. "How about a drink?"

He paused for a split second. "Sure."

"We don't have to. I just thought it would be a convenient place to wait."

"It is." He opened the door for her, and within a few minutes, each of them had a beer in hand and a seat by the window with a view of trendy folk of Oakland and Berkeley walking past on the street.

He nodded at a dad pushing an orange-and-black stroller with enormous wheels. "Those things cost more than many cars do."

"Certainly more than mine," she said.

They drank in silence, staring out the window. After a few minutes, he asked, "Where does your dad live?"

She swallowed a mouthful of beer. "Oh. He's dead."

He closed his eyes. "That was stupid of me. I should've known better than to—"

"Don't worry about it. People ask me that all the time." She put her glass down. "It was a long time ago. I was still in junior high school."

He shook his head. "Professional consultants should be better at making polite conversation."

"It's really okay. Though... I admit, I'm surprised you didn't know. Given the BurnBar and everything." She grinned at him over the rim of her glass. "You must've done a quick Internet search on the family before you took the job, no?"

Her father had invented a popular energy bar decades ago, sold the overnight success to a huge corporation, and retired on the proceeds. Her mom lived off of the remainder, although April had no idea how much of the principal was left. Enough to eat, not enough to go to Tahiti every weekend. April used to worry about what would happen to her mom if the money ran out, since she herself wasn't much of a breadwinner, but then Mark had confessed to being a tech millionaire, and that put her mind at ease. Except for making her feel even worse about her own (lack of) accomplishments.

Zack rubbed his thumb along the water droplets clinging to the outside of his glass. "That's right. I did read something about that. I don't know how I forgot."

"It's all right. We weren't close." She took a deep swallow. Why had she said that? No need to admit her own dad hadn't had time for her.

"I used to say that about my own parents," he said. "But as I get older, I realize we're closer than a lot of other people. Just in a different way."

"Yeah, well, my father and I barely knew each other. He was on the road a lot with Liam swimming, or taking Mark to chess camp, trying to turn him into Bobby Fisher. I was just a little girl. I didn't have any talents and I wasn't even very pretty." She smiled to show she didn't care. Nope, didn't care.

He didn't smile back. "I find that hard to believe."

A pang of something both sweet and painful hit her in the chest. "Ask Liam." She was already at the bottom of her pint glass. "Or Mark. He's got lots of not-so-nice things to say about our father. It'll be the opening you need to chat him up at the wedding and sign him on as a client."

"Yes, because unearthing family trauma is always great networking."

She laughed, for real this time. "I'd hire you. It would show you've got a heart and a brain. That you're not just a bean counter spouting buzzwords."

"Hey. I need my buzzwords."

"Your rate on return for the process solutions in a disruptive ecosystem is..." She stumbled, unable to come up with more bullshit.

"Below expectations at this juncture. We need to diversify to achieve synergy," he finished.

She bumped her shoulder against his. "You're in the right field. It comes naturally to you."

"Years of practice, actually. I worked in a big firm for a few years after I got my MBA. It's taken years to weed out some of the language. I fall back into it like a drug habit sometimes."

"You have a drug habit?" She looked him over. "You don't even hold liquor very well. I can't imagine you on the hard stuff."

"I don't hold my liquor? Excuse me?"

Maybe it was the booze in her own veins, but she felt reckless.

"Every time you have something to drink, you end up doing something you regret." She held his gaze. "With me, at least."

He stared back at her for a few minutes. "You might be surprised about what I regret," he said in a low voice. He drained his glass and stood up. "Let's see if that pizza is ready."

She had trouble taking her next breath.

* * *

Zack waited until after dinner to chat with Mark about his new tech start-up. April—who had taken off her sweater and now was driving him insane with a view of shapely bare shoulders as she played fetch in the living room with her dog—had made him paranoid about looking too obvious about his networking. Even if he wasn't looking to snare Mark as a client, he was curious about the health website he'd founded, the apps he'd developed recently, how it was this quiet, geeky guy had a Midas touch Mark didn't even want or admire in himself.

They talked about the huge cultural rift between the East and West Coasts, even within high tech, and the early burnout of some of the brightest talent.

"I'm a geezer at thirty," Mark said, putting his feet on the coffee table.

Rose pinched his nose. "Thirty-one. And you are not."

"I am," Mark said. "I just want to be left alone. I'm like some grouchy old guy holed up in the basement, working on his model airplanes."

April threw a tennis ball into Mark's lap. "You've always been that way."

The old dog wandered over on his three legs and sat at Mark's feet, gazing up at him like a starving orphan.

"Are you sure you fed him, April?" Mark asked, placing the ball between Stool's two front paws. "He looks hungry. I know he tried to eat the chicken, but maybe that wasn't enough."

April snorted, walking over to her dog. "He didn't just try. He succeeded. And he had his full dinner, too. He's just a big faker." She bent over and scratched him behind the ears, cooing and kissing.

Zack watched her and forgot what he was talking about. Old age? Model airplanes?

How far gone was he if he was jealous of a dog?

"I'll get you another coffee, Zack," Trixie said.

He got to his feet. "Thank you, but no. I need to be going."

"How about a cookie before you go?" Trixie asked.

"Mom," April said. "He's had a long day. Let him escape."

"I'll pack them up for the drive over the bridge," Trixie said, walking to the kitchen.

"Watch out for that one," Mark muttered. "She adopts people. Doesn't care how old you are."

"She's wonderful," Rose said. "I'm only marrying you because of her, actually. You'd better be nice to her."

Mark's voice lowered. "You don't *always* like me to be nice."

When they started making out on the sofa, Zack was glad he'd already started walking to the door. April and Stool followed him.

"You don't have to wait for the cookies," April said. "They're only from Trader Joe's."

He put on his coat, zipped it up. He was having trouble leaving April's company. He wanted to kiss her. He wanted to pin her to the wall and slip the strap of her sundress off her shoulder, nibble his way down to her breasts. He wanted to hear her call his name, moan when he touched her, cry out when he made love to her. He wanted to feel her sweaty bare skin against his, lose himself in the taste and feel of her, wake up to her curled up against his side in the morning.

And then do it again.

He opened the door and stepped outside. When he got back to New York, he'd make a serious effort to find a woman without any contacts with his business life so that he could build a relationship that wouldn't sabotage his career. One that wouldn't make him feel like he was spiraling out of control. "I really have to go. Thank your mother for me, will you?"

She followed him out onto the porch—gently herding Europa and Luna, who were dancing around Zack's ankles, back into the house—and closed the door behind her. Her gaze pinned him in place. "What did you mean earlier?"

"About what?" he asked, but he knew. He knew.

"About what you regret."

Turning, he moved closer, his blood thickening. "And what I don't," he said.

Her tongue darted out, moistening her lips. "Ever tempted to not regret it again?"

Desire rushed through him. "Yes."

"Is that why you're here?" She was fiddling with a string at the neckline of her dress, tying and untying the bow.

He reached out and stilled her hands. The bones of her fingers were surprisingly delicate. Her pulse thrummed under the soft skin of her wrists.

Releasing her, he said, "Yes." His voice was low and quiet, barely audible.

"Or maybe it was to see my brother Mark again?"

He shook his head slowly, silently telling her *no* at the same time he said aloud, "I admit it. I couldn't resist the thought of seeing him again."

"I thought so. He's got a special charm all his own."

Their gazes were locked on one another. "That he does."

"Well, don't let me keep you. You must be dying to go to bed." Her fingers returned to playing with the bow at her throat. "You've had a long day."

He could only nod. What insane impulse had led him to this house? This wasn't a safe place for him to be, this charming old house with the dogs and the brothers and the warm-hearted mother...

And her.

"Good night," he said, finally tearing himself away.

He didn't take a steady breath until he was halfway to San Francisco, careening over the Bay Bridge, the cold, black water below as treacherous as his impulses.

Chapter 17

MARK AND ROSE'S wedding was the first Saturday in April, and although the morning was grim with a heavy fog that covered the West Coast from Eureka to San Diego, by early afternoon it was sunny, dry, and warm. Both the ceremony and reception would be held at the JSP Vineyard Inn, a winery up on a mountain ridge, where a sharp wind rustled the garlands of white roses and bouquets of blue and pink wildflowers strung between the seats and tables.

The ceremony was in thirty minutes, and Rose was still in her jeans. Nobody had been able to find her until April spotted her pretty blonde head near the Dumpster behind a storage building.

"I hope it's not too cold," Rose said, eyeing the hillside. Below them to the east was Silicon Valley and the south waters of the bay. To the west, where the wind came from, was the Pacific Ocean. And to the north, peeking out of tendrils of lingering morning fog, were the hills and skyscrapers of San Francisco.

"Even the garbage has an incredible view," April said. "You're going to have the most beautiful wedding anyone has ever seen. Which, by the way, is in less than a half an hour."

"But is it too cold?" Rose reached over and stroked April's bare arms under the sleeveless lavender gown she'd chosen at the last minute. As much as she liked black, April didn't want anyone to think she wasn't happy about this wedding. "Aren't you cold?"

"Not at all. It's sunny, and it's only going to get warmer," April told her.

"There's still time to move it inside. The great hall has a good view."

April put her arm around Rose and guided her to the inn, a squat, beamed building next to the winery itself. "Everything's fine. Go get your dress on before it's too late and you have to walk down the aisle in your jeggings."

Because Mark had more money than he knew what to do with, and an aversion to publicity and attention, he had reserved and paid for every room in the inn for their wedding guests, even though the entire guest list only filled it halfway, and many lived within an hour's drive. He'd also booked it for the entire week so out-of-towners could enjoy a mini-vacation on his dime. Many of the guests had arrived the day before and were already walking around the grounds, mingling and enjoying themselves.

"I think we should move it inside," Rose said. "Don't you think?"

"I think there's enough bubbly for you to start drinking it now," April said.

"I can't drink. I'd throw up."

"Get it over with now before you put on the dress," April said.

She shepherded Rose through a side door to a suite on the ground floor set up for the bride's attendants to get dolled up. Rose's best friend, Blair, sat on a chair letting—with some trepidation, judging by the tension in her jaw—a woman apply eyeliner to her lids with a long, sable brush.

April had already had hers done. She wasn't convinced the professional makeup and hairstyling for the bridesmaids was necessary, but she was twenty-seven and had been through the paces several times already. She knew it was insane to argue. What the bride wanted, the bride got—even if that was friends who looked like drag queens.

"Where's your mom?" April asked her.

"In my room with the dress." Rose pulled away and looked out the window. "Is that rain? Those clouds look like rain."

April squinted. Except for the fog over the city, the sky was as blue as a swimming pool from horizon to horizon. "What clouds?"

Rose walked over to Blair. "Don't you think we should move it inside? My mom told me it would be too cold up here in April. I promised her it would be perfect."

Blair, frozen with the makeup artist's mascara wand near her eyeball, said, "Will you please find your mother and get dressed? I really, really don't want to stand out there without you."

"Serves you right, after you eloped with my boyfriend," Rose said.

"Only because you dumped him first," Blair said. "He still mumbles your name in his sleep."

Rose stopped to stare at her old friend. "He does?"

Blair laughed. "You've really lost it, haven't you? I'm so sad John couldn't come. He would've loved to see you so nervous. April, can *you* get her to put on her dress?"

John, Bev's cousin, had dated Rose but was now with Blair—after more than a little drama. April was too polite to point out Rose had come out way ahead by ending up with Mark.

"I'm trying," April said. "She's ignoring me."

"I need to talk to Mark," Rose said. "He'll know if the weather will be okay. I bet he could write a program on his phone to forecast the odds of an adverse weather event. He's like that, you know? I need to talk to him. Not for me, for my mother. So she doesn't worry."

April slipped her arm through hers. "I just saw him. Come with me."

"But—" Blair moved to stand up. "It's bad luck for the bride and groom to see each other before the ceremony."

April shot her a quelling look over her shoulder and asked silently, *What room?*

Blair settled back into her seat. *Seven*, she mouthed back.

April led Rose out of the room and down the hall.

"You saw him down here?" Rose asked.

"Yeah, talking to Zack."

"Zack's cute," Rose said. "In case you hadn't noticed."

"Mm," April said.

"Definitely has a Clark Kent thing going on. Take it from me —nerdy guys have hidden depths," Rose said. She lowered her voice. "Definitely worth uncovering them."

Since the nerdy uncovered guy Rose was alluding to was her brother, April smiled tightly and walked faster. When they reached the door at the end of the hall, April rapped her knuckles against it as if the building were on fire. "Here we are."

Rose patted her hair. It was already braided in an elaborate updo. "He's in here? But—"

The door flew open. There stood a large, middle-aged blonde woman in a flowing dark pink dress—Rose's mother, Kim. She and April had met at the rehearsal dinner the night before.

"Rose! Where the hell have you been?" Two strong arms flung around the bride and hauled her inside.

"No, wait." Rose craned her neck around to look out into the hallway. "I need to talk to Mark. I think we need to move the wedding inside. It's cold, don't you think? Not now, but it might —"

The door slammed shut between them.

"See you soon!" April called out.

The door opened a crack. Kim peeked out. "Sorry. Thank you."

April grinned. "My pleasure. Good luck."

The door shut again. She heard the deadbolt engage, then the chain.

Letting out a relieved breath, April returned to the main dressing room, feeling silly as she wobbled along the hallway in the unfamiliar heels. She'd found a vintage dress in a dusty lilac silk with lace trim that seemed to look pretty good, but the delicate fabric clinging to her breasts and hips made her feel out of character, artificial, exposed.

Blair was already finished, and stood by the large rear window admiring the view. The two of them were the bride's only honor attendants, while the groom had Liam and Sylly Minguez, Mark's old friend and business partner.

Given the size of the facility and the unlimited budget, they could've had a dozen in the wedding party on each side and hundreds more on the guest list, but Mark was a reserved, introverted guy, and Rose had a small family.

April joined Blair at the window. "You look nice. I wouldn't let her put the false eyelashes on me."

Blair turned, smiling, and put a hand on her chest. "You look gorgeous. I wanted to tell you earlier. I've never seen you... you know..."

"In a dress?"

Blair laughed. "I know, right? I never wear dresses either. Look at me. I made her pick it out. Most bridesmaids would kill to be able to wear whatever they wanted, but I didn't want the responsibility. I took her to the store and made her pick it out."

April admired the elegant blue dress that flattered Blair's petite figure. "Whoever picked it out, it looks great. You look great."

"We *sort* of match," Blair said, moving her hip next to hers and comparing. "Shades of blue and purple. Right?"

"It's not a Broadway show. We don't have to match."

"That's what Rose said. But it's hard to break tradition, don't you think?" Blair asked.

"Not really," April said. "I usually have a harder time trying to follow it."

Just then Rose burst into the room finally wearing her wedding dress but holding the sling-back silver heels in her left hand. "Don't tell her I'm here!" She slammed the door behind her and ran past the table and chairs to the attached bedroom.

Kim flung open the door. "Where is she?"

April and Blair looked at each other. Then they both looked at Rose's mother and said in unison, "The bedroom."

"She's not herself," Blair said. "She needs her mother right now."

"Totally agree," April said.

Blair looked at her watch. "Oh my God. We were supposed to be out there five minutes ago."

"Doesn't matter," April said. "They'll wait."

"I hope I don't faint," Blair said.

"I hope you do. Spice it up a little bit."

"Thanks," Blair said, laughing.

"I never listen to the vows," April said. "I'm so busy looking at people in the audience, trying to figure out if they're happy these two people are getting hitched, how the bride is swaying from side to side because her feet hurt, how the best man is kind of green because he's hungover and worried about the ring in his pocket.

By the time the lucky couple is married and kissing, I've missed the important bits and I can't wait to get that glass of champagne."

Rose appeared in the doorway. Her mother held her shoulders with both hands.

"It's time," Kim said simply.

They all walked out of the building to the corner of the garden near a stone fountain where the wedding party had practiced the night before. The guests were already sitting in their chairs. Three men in tuxedos stood by the minister under an arch overflowing with tiny pink roses.

"Oh my fucking God," Rose whispered. "I'm getting married."

"Now *those* are vows," April said, waving at the crowd with her bouquet as she walked down the aisle into bright sunshine.

* * *

Struck between the eyes.

Arrow to the heart.

Smacked upside the head.

Zack sipped his third glass of champagne and watched April dance with the ugliest guy he'd ever seen. She didn't seem to notice how repulsive the stranger was, which annoyed him.

Over the deep end.

He tried to tell himself it was just the pretty dress, the pretty hair, the pretty setting. But his heart was beating too fast for *pretty*. Or even *gorgeous*. This was something else, something darker and faster and burning, smoking hot.

God, he wanted her. It was ridiculous how much he wanted her. They were so different, so incompatible. He knew that yet wanted her anyway. Oh, yeah. Perhaps it was *because* she was off limits—the sweetness of forbidden fruit, calling to him...

Mark's voice broke through his cloud of lust. "I told her I didn't want any dancing, but she just laughed at me."

Zack turned to him, belatedly offering his glass in a toast. This brilliant, reclusive man could be a priceless business contact. Zack had pushed his way into his family, crashed the happiest day of his life, and yet he'd almost forgotten to make the easiest of gestures —congratulating him on his marriage.

"You're a lucky man," Zack said.

"So true." Mark watched the two-dozen well-dressed bodies on the dance floor for a few moments. "I wonder when we can leave."

Zack's gaze had locked on April again. The dance was a recent pop hit, and she shimmied and bounced like a supermodel in a video.

No, much better.

He'd pictured her body more times than he'd admit even to himself, but his imagination had wildly underestimated the sultry curve of her hip, her calf muscles, her elbow, the hollow of her collarbone, the freckles on her left shoulder...

"Well, it was nice talking to you again," Mark said, starting to move away.

Zack came out of his daze. They'd talked at the house, but not to the point that he felt comfortable asking Mark about working together. When Zack gone home to visit his parents, his father had been impressed when he'd heard his son had met the founder of WellyNelly, one of his favorite websites. He'd encouraged Zack to pursue the connection, the first time his father had expressed an opinion about Zack's career.

"I wanted to tell you again how much I admire your work," Zack said. Oh, Christ. That was lame.

"Oh, right. Thanks." Mark glanced away.

"Not that I understand the tech. I mean, I try." Zack gulped his drink. He wouldn't have been so nervous if he hadn't just been obsessing about the man's sister for the past two hours. Weeks. Months. "It's the way you've created viable businesses from scratch, with your own idea and genius—"

Zack saw Mark flinch, and knew he'd made a mistake.

"You should talk to my friend Sylly," Mark said, taking a step away. "My best man. He's got the kind of genius you're talking about. I just write code."

"But you're the spark, the epicenter, the—"

"Excuse me. Rose wants me to dance. Better get it over with, can't escape her forever, wouldn't think of trying." He ducked his head and hurried away through the crowd. As Zack watch, he tapped Rose on the shoulder—she had been cheerfully dancing with Bev and the baby in a sling—and held out his arms for his new bride.

Damn it. I drove him away.

He'd come across as a shallow opportunist. More than he wanted Mark as a client, which would thrill his father, Zack wanted to learn from him. Mark seemed like a man who never settled for the conventional life inside the box. What was his secret?

Zack had gone solo and had a reputation among his consulting clients for clear thinking, fresh ideas, and plain speaking.

But he still felt like a cog in the machine. He thought it was financial insecurity, that when he had enough saved up, he would feel freer. But instead, as his personal wealth grew, his sense of entrapment tightened. He felt more bogged down than ever. And empty.

Missing something.

Someone.

April was dancing with that Sylly guy now, Mark's business

partner, another excellent contact.

Handsome bastard. Why was he touching her? Nineties pop was hardly a waltz, but he had one hand around her waist—over sheer fabric he could see through from twenty yards—and another woven through her fingers. He was smiling big, perfect white teeth at her.

Zack put his glass on a caterer's tray and considered his options.

For the first time, he realized work wasn't his only option. He didn't *have* to sacrifice everything for his career.

He had other options. He did.

His heart thudded in his chest as he smiled. Even after a couple of drinks, he didn't want to make a scene.

He'd wait. But not from over here—he'd have to get closer, then make his move as soon as the song was over.

Chapter 18

APRIL COULDN'T HELP peeking at Zack. He stood at the edge of the dance floor doing his all-important networking

He looked good in a tux. He'd told Rose, who'd told April, that he hoped she didn't mind him being a little overdressed, but he'd invested in it a couple of years ago and liked to use it whenever he could.

Of course he looked good. Everyone looked good in a tux, even women. They should all wear tuxedos, all day, every day. Like penguins. Look how happy they looked. And fancy. Happy and fancy.

April pushed Sylly's arm off her hip for the tenth time and gave him a mocking look. "I'm ticklish."

Sylly was also wearing a tuxedo, but she didn't care if he looked good in it. He was blocking her view of Zack.

Sylly grinned. "Really?"

"Does Mark know you're a horn dog?" she asked him.

Sylly pulled her closer. "Take a look." His gaze slipped over her shoulder.

She turned and saw Mark watching them with a scowl on his face. "Oh, that's ridiculous," she said. "You haven't even copped a feel yet."

Sylly brightened. "I'm allowed to cop feels?"

"Do you value your testicles?"

"Like the Visa ad," Sylly said, flinching. "Priceless."

April's smile fell when she realized she'd lost sight of Zack.

No doubt he was stalking Mark again. She never should've let him come. She should've warned everyone that Zack Fain was just an ambitious phony who had a tux because it made him look like a secret agent in glasses.

"That guy with you?" Sylly asked.

"No guy is with me."

Sylly's grin broadened. "I like the sound of that."

Although April had met Sylly a few times over the years, she'd never really talked to him. He was just the good-looking guy who'd taken the software and website Mark had developed as a teenager and turned it into a thriving business. Now he'd moved on to start up something new, also in software, but that was so typical around San Francisco, she hadn't bothered to find out what. Half of the baristas in the Bay Area had their own start-ups.

"You should talk to him," she told Sylly. The two businessmen could bond and leave her out of it.

"Not sure he feels like talking," Sylly said.

She turned her head and followed his gaze. Zack was standing two inches behind her, giving her a steady look that sent a shiver tingling down her back. He didn't say anything, just stared. After a moment, Sylly gave her a self-deprecating smile and released her.

For a moment Zack and April stared at each other, motionless under the thumping, frenzied beat of the hit pop song coming out of the speakers. Deep in his eyes she saw longing, frustration, determination. He frowned, searching her face, and all the smart-ass jokes and defensive moves she was so good at abandoned her. She felt her knees weaken.

But then he turned to Sylly and held out his hand. "Zachary

Fain. Sorry to butt in—but when Mark mentioned you were here —April, I hope you forgive me." He moved closer—not to April, but to Sylly. "You are Sylvester Minguez, aren't you?"

Sylly looked surprised but flattered. "I am." He held out a hand. "Zachary, you said?"

Without a glance at April, Zack pumped Sylly's hand in that boy's club way that had excluded women for centuries. "Fain. Zack Fain. I'm trying to remember where I last read about you— was it *Business Week*?"

Sylly smiled. "Could've been."

The two men launched into a discussion of other magazines and online business blogs that had featured Sylly or Mark over the past year. While they talked, the three of them were jostled closer to the head table, out of the way of the dancers. Feeling superfluous, April scanned the dance floor for another partner. The two she had were far too happy with each other.

"What you did with WellyNelly was miraculous," Zack said.

Mark had founded WellyNelly in his bedroom in high school when their father was dying of cancer. He'd wanted to make a forum for their mother to talk to other people dealing with serious illness—never expecting the financial success that followed.

Sylly put a hand on April's shoulder. "I owe everything to the groom. Mark was the miracle. I'm lucky to have met him." He slipped his hand to her other shoulder, drawing her closer. "And his family."

April wondered if she was imagining the way Zack's smile tightened. Was he clenching his teeth?

Was he *jealous*?

Instead of feeling gratified, she was annoyed. If Zack wanted her, why not do something about it? She'd given him plenty of chances—well, one was enough—and he'd blown it. Or not blown it. Not nearly enough blowing of the good variety.

She made eye contact with an imaginary friend across the room, waved, and stepped out of Sylly's grasp. "Excuse me, guys, will you?" She strode into the thickest clump of the crowd.

I hope they're very happy together.

Rose was standing with Bev near a table of people April vaguely remembered as Bev's relatives from southern California. Not her father—he was remarried, a busy Hollywood exec, and had sent his regrets—but Bev's mother, aunt, and sister were there, all looking fit and made up with ageless complexions and toned biceps. None looked at all like Bev. For one, they seldom smiled. Or ate. Their dinner plates were still heavy with food.

Before April could make a run for it, Bev latched on to her arm and dragged her closer. "Remember April, everyone? My sister-in-law?"

They eyed her with interest. Well, she got the impression it wasn't really *her*, but her hair, dress, and shoes. Staring at April's feet, Bev's mother said, "Those look comfortable."

April shifted her weight from one foot to another. Two-and-a-half inch heels shouldn't be comfortable for anyone, and certainly not for her. She never would've worn them if she didn't like Rose so much and wanted to look formal for her big day—yet still Bev's mother was talking about them like they were house slippers. Just because she didn't wear shoes that were slanted at a ninety-degree angle with toes as pointy as the Transamerica Building.

Rose still stood there, beautiful and glowing. Because she deserved a wedding without distant family members hating on each other, April smiled at Bev's mother and said, "Thank you." And then, because she really did like her new sister-in-law, she added, "Mark's looking for you, Rose."

"Oh, he is?" Rose put a hand on her chest—her ring flashed on a perfectly manicured finger with crimson nails, the same color as the roses in her bouquet—and smiled as she looked around for him.

April watched her admiringly. Rose really was gorgeous, a goddess in oils. April wondered how many drugs it would take to get her to pose nude for her. People who had never been art students might find it strange, but April had always wanted to draw Rose in the buff. Seeing her in a low-cut, well-tailored gown just reminded her of it. Nothing sexual—she'd been to college and knew from awkward trial and error that she only swung one way —but definitely sensual. Rose just had that magic that some women had.

"Maybe it's time to cut the cake," April said, hooking her arm in Rose's and drawing her away.

"Are there any alternatives to cake?" Bev's mother's voice piped out as they escaped. "I can't possibly eat so much sugar."

"Thanks," Rose whispered in her ear.

"Just don't throw the bouquet at me."

Rose's eyes twinkled. "I was the pitcher for my softball team in junior high."

"Please," April said. "Not tonight."

"It's not up to me. It's up to fate."

"Jesus."

"You never know," Rose said, pinching her cheek.

April withdrew her arm just as Mark collided with Rose in a full-body embrace.

"Where'd you go?" He smiled down at her, nose pressed against hers.

"I hope you're not going to be the clingy type," Rose said,

leaning back but smiling. Her cheeks blazed pink.

"Like plastic wrap, babe," Mark said.

April watched them, remembering a night years ago when she was sixteen and had just broken up with her boyfriend. Mark had been back from college for summer break, spending most of his days and nights alone in his room. When he'd found her crying, he'd fixed her a chocolate milkshake in the kitchen and told her she was lucky because she knew how to be with people. She may have broken up with this boy, but she'd already had more dates at sixteen than he'd ever had.

"Or ever will," he'd said sadly.

Now April felt her eyes burn. Look at him. So happy. She pushed Rose aside and bear-hugged Mark with everything she had.

"Gnuh," he said as his bones cracked.

April wiped her tears on the back of her hand and gave Rose a gentler embrace. "I'm so happy for you."

Rose drew back and looked at her with concern. "Are you all right?"

"I'm just so happy." Tears continued to flow down April's cheeks.

Mark handed her a paper cocktail napkin that smelled like cheese. "I know what you mean." He put an arm around Rose. "Somebody just told me we're supposed to be somewhere, but I can't remember why."

They excused themselves to find out while April got a grip. The music had turned slow and soft, romantic. Bev had escaped her family and was dancing with Liam, who gazed into her eyes like she was the center of his world—when he wasn't kissing Merry, in her carrier on his chest, on the top of her fuzzy little head.

Merry. *That*'s what she could do: she'd babysit. Adult life was aggravating, frustrating, and fraught with screwups, but she always knew what to do with a baby.

She glimpsed Zack and Sylly, still making entrepreneurial love to each other near the head table. Now they held drinks. Sylly was waving his hands as he talked. Zack nodded and laughed.

Get a room, she thought.

No. That's what *she* would do. She'd take Merry to the bedroom she had for the night and play peekaboo and eat through the minibar like a stoned caterpillar. The Hungry Hungry Bridesmaid.

But Liam and Bev wouldn't give her the baby.

"She's having such a great time," Bev said, laughing. "Look at her. I've never seen her so happy."

Liam nodded, stroking Merry's cheek. "She must love the noise. All the people."

April started to frown at the infant party girl but saw the wide-eyed contentment on her face and had to smile. "Watch out for her when she's older."

"Don't worry about that," Liam said, giving Merry a stern look. "I've already planted a cactus under her bedroom window. The giant kind, with five-inch needles."

April kissed the top of Merry's head, confident she'd have her dad wrapped around her finger for a long, long time, namely forever, and decided to go to her room and enjoy the minibar without a baby. She'd shared her love, given her congratulations, toasted her toast—she was done. She could be alone. Starting right now.

Her mother appeared out of nowhere and clasped her hand. "They're going to cut the cake," she said, dragging her through the crowd to the edible masterpiece—a tiered ivory cake sprinkled with violets—set up near the head table. "Oh, isn't this just wonderful," her mother said in her ear. She put both arms around April's shoulders and held her tight, as if she'd known the youngest child was a flight risk.

Ah, well, April was happy to see this part. Then she'd slip away.

The music stopped, everyone gathered around, and Mark and Rose did their thing with the knife and the feeding each other and the kissing and the laughing. Mark looked too happy to be self-conscious in front of the attentive throng. Even the photographer with the zoom lens didn't seem to faze him. Arm around Rose's waist, he smiled at nothing in particular and didn't seem to realize he had a glob of fondant on the tip of his nose, where Rose had put it.

Her mother let her go and rushed forward to hug them both. April stood alone in the crush, overwhelmed with emotion. She may have had more dates at sixteen than Mark would ever have in a lifetime, but she'd never had what Mark and Rose had now, or Bev and Liam—never even came close. She felt like an anthropologist in an exotic land, watching people talk with sounds her tongue couldn't make, eating the organs of animals she didn't recognize, dancing to music she could feel but not understand.

"They look happy," Zack said. He stood at her elbow, holding up two plates of cake. The rest of the crowd was moving to the tables.

"We're supposed to sit," she said.

He pushed a plate at her. "We can sit." He frowned, studying her face. "Are you all right?"

"Actually, I was going to go." She looked at the distant doorway at the other end of the hall.

"Why?"

When you had emotion that had nowhere to go and nothing to do, it tended to pour out of your eyeballs. Feeling the tears prick at her lids, April turned away and grabbed a drink off a tray. Not a new drink on a fresh tray—an abandoned one.

"Big day," she said with a shrug, not meeting his eyes. She rubbed her finger along the lipstick-smudged glass but couldn't bring herself to drink it.

He held out both plates. "Would you hold these? I'll get us coffee."

With a sigh, she put the glass back on the tray and took the cake. He gave her a sympathetic smile before moving away.

If she went to the room, she'd just end up watching TV and moping. Maybe it was better if she wasn't alone just yet.

"Champagne," she called after him.

He looked at her over his shoulder and his smile fell away. Maybe he was afraid she was going to kiss him again. Maybe she would.

"Please?" she asked.

He nodded and walked over to the bar.

She looked at the plates in her hands. Under the white chocolate fondant, the cake was dark chocolate sponge with layers of chocolate mousse. She inhaled a mouthful of cake off-gases, wishing he'd only handed her one plate—and a shovel—so she could start eating. She lifted one plate to her mouth and bit off a chunk of fondant and one of the candy flowers.

Oh, not candy: a real flower. Interesting. She swirled it around in her mouth, not sure what to do with it. Petals stuck to her tongue. She didn't want to eat it but didn't have a free hand to extract it. Bending over and spitting on the floor was probably against the Bridesmaid Rules.

Zack returned with two flutes filled to the top. "Let's sit over there." He nodded to an empty corner and walked ahead, his square shoulders flexing in the tux with the minor effort of carrying two glasses at chest height.

Her gaze dropped to his hips swaying under the tails of the tux jacket. Dangerous territory, hard to look away. She shifted up to the tips of his glasses poking behind his ears. Dark hair curled slightly at his nape, just over the white collar of his shirt.

Desire spread through her body like warm butter. Stifling another sigh, she lifted the plate and bit off another flower. At least she didn't feel like crying anymore.

He chose an empty table that had never been set for dinner, behind an easel displaying pictures of Mark and Rose as children. One sweet picture had a young Rose dressed as a penguin for Halloween. Another had Mark in front of a chess set. Painfully cute, both of them.

Zack put down the glasses, took the plates out of her hands, and pulled out a chair for her. She lifted the glass and gulped down half of it before her butt hit the seat. The flower petals got washed away in the deluge.

"Got forks?" she asked.

He took one out of his chest pocket, set it down next to her plate, and sat next to her.

The alcohol drifted through her body, lifting her spirits with thousands of sweet fermented bubbles. As she ate the cake, she chided herself for getting melancholy. It was probably just jealousy —of Mark and Rose, Liam and Bev—and that wasn't cool at all. Just because she'd been feeling a little lonely lately was no reason to withdraw and wallow in self-pity.

"The cake's good," Zack said.

She lifted her champagne and nodded. "No expense spared."

She tapped her glass against his and caught his gaze. "Thanks, by the way. I was starting to lose it."

"Weddings do that to people."

"Well, it's never happened to me before. I don't know what came over me," she said. "I hope you're having a nice time. How was it talking to Sylly? Snare him for your next gig?"

He looked down and pushed the cake around his plate. "We didn't get that far."

"He seemed to like you, though," she said.

"I wasn't bullshitting him, by the way. I did read about him somewhere."

"I believe you."

"I'm not sure he did," he said. "He wasn't in any hurry to set up a time to talk again."

"Maybe he's playing hard to get," she said.

His lips twitched. His blue eyes met hers. "Maybe."

Her pulse gave a kick and went off racing through her body. She tried to sip from her glass, but it was empty.

He pressed hers into her hand. "Have mine. I've had plenty to drink already." He reached up to his throat, loosened his tie. "Very generous at the bar. Stiff drinks. Unlimited champagne. My head is swimming."

She took his glass and lifted it to her lips. His spit had already mingled with hers once. What was the harm?

"I'm lonely," she blurted out.

His eyes widened. Then his dark brows met over the bridge of his glasses.

Oh, damn it. He thought she was going to assault him again. She went on quickly, "In the family, I mean. Now that both of my brothers are married, it won't be the same. Especially Mark. I was close to Mark."

"You can still be close."

"It's not the same. It won't be the same." She forced a bright smile. "But that's good for him. I'm so happy for him. He's been married to his computer for too long. He needs somebody who really loves him."

There. Good save. Now he'd think she was just sad because she wouldn't see Mark as much as she used to, not that she longed for hot sex with a meaningful, committed partner who understood and loved her at a profound level—a level her personal elevator had never reached. For all she knew, her building might have skipped that floor, like superstitious architects leaving out the thirteenth.

Looking over her shoulder, Zack put his hand over her wrist on the table. His touch sent shockwaves up her arm. "I think Mark and Rose might be leaving now," he said. "There's something going on by the door."

She was tempted to stay where she was, using sexual frustration to distract her from existential despair, but she didn't want to miss the goodbye. She stood up. "Let's go see."

She wiggled through the throng until she reached a giggling cluster of women gathered in a colorful ring in front of Rose, who had her back to all of them and was swinging her bouquet over her head.

Whack. Like a pie in a clown show, the bouquet smacked April right in the face. She didn't even have time to lift her hands.

She gasped, bending over in pain. Her left eyeball stung. Thank God she'd flinched in time. It wasn't just flowers in those things—the pretty blossoms were tied together with braided ribbons, wire, and tape, and it was as big as her head.

"Fuck," she whispered, picking it up.

Dozens of lenses from phones and cameras caught the

moment. She gazed out at them, blinked away the pain, and held up the bouquet like the Statue of Liberty brandishing her blazing torch. She'd light it on fire as soon as she found a match.

Zack was there, touching her arm. "Are you all right?"

Catching Rose's concerned look across the crowd of laughing faces, April glued a goofy smile on her face and waved the bouquet. The bride didn't need to worry about her new sister-in-law's skull fracture. "I'm fine," she said. "I've got a head like a rock."

The crowd surged forward to follow Rose and Mark to the car parked in the front driveway. April followed, rubbing her cheek, more distracted by the feel of Zack's fingers sliding down her bare arm than she was by the throbbing pain under her eyeball.

"We need to get you some ice," Zack said in her ear, his low voice sending tendrils of desire down her spine.

She let the crowd hurry ahead of her. Getting the best view wasn't as important as she thought it would be that morning when she painted abstract white roses all over their getaway car.

Zack slowed, too, and his fingers slid down her forearm and then over her wrist and knuckles to clasp her hand.

Her heart thudded in her chest. "Maybe I should lie down," she heard herself say.

Yeah. I need to lie down. Right now. Not alone, though.

"Are you staying here at the hotel?" he asked.

She nodded. Her head swam. "Are you?"

His thumb stroked hers. He didn't answer.

She turned and looked up at him. The world around them fell away, going dim and fuzzy and dark, leaving only Zachary Fain. She saw the stubble on his jaw, the crease between his eyebrows, the slight parting of his lips, and the darkening pupils of his eyes.

She didn't know if he wanted her, but if he didn't, he'd better make a run for it. "I'm room sixteen. Upstairs." She held his gaze.

His eyelids fell. She licked her lips and watched the tension flex in his jaw.

"Zack?" she asked.

He swallowed visibly. "Upstairs," he said.

"Yes."

His hand slid up her arm and over her shoulder to her cheek. Both of them were breathing heavily now.

"Sixteen?" he asked. His knee bumped hers, then his thigh. His face was inches away.

"That's what I sa—"

His mouth came down on hers. The kiss was deep and slow, unhurried, unbelievable. Her body responded like dry leaves blasted with a flamethrower after months of drought. If his other hand hadn't come up around her waist, pulling her firmly against his body and unbalancing her in the unfamiliar heels, she would've fallen over.

And then he lifted his head a few inches. "What luck," he said softly. "That's the same room I'll be in."

Chapter 19

HANDS SHAKING, ZACK moved away from her and scanned the reception hall.

She wasn't pushing him away. He was going to have her. Tonight. Right now. Desire burned through his veins.

Most of the guests had followed Mark and Rose out to the car, but some remained. If he stayed another minute, they were about to get quite a show. He'd never kissed a woman like that in his life. What was it about April that pushed him over the edge, over and beyond who he thought he was?

She was watching him with serious, vulnerable eyes—he didn't see any hint of the sarcastic, careful, tough girl in combat boots.

He didn't want to hurt her. She looked like a woman who could be hurt.

"April..."

She grabbed him by the lapels. "Don't you dare. Don't even think about it." She released him abruptly and turned on her heel, keeping her gaze locked on his as she walked away. "*Sixteen.*"

Heart pounding, he watched her disappear through the doorway.

Then he followed.

Ghosts tried to tag along: women in matching pink taffeta

from a different wedding years ago, his best friend still hungover from the bachelor party; his parents in their Sunday best; Meg. But he broke free of all of them, waking up from the bittersweet dream, seeing only the curve of April's neck under the flowers in her curly hair, the flow of her silk dress, the living, breathing movement of her body.

By the time she reached the curved redwood stairs that led up to the second floor, he was fully in the moment, an amnesiac who was grateful for what he had in the present.

She shot him a guarded smile over her shoulder. "Still with me?"

He stepped up directly behind her and brought up his hands to her waist, resting them on the flare of her sexy hips. Then he reached around to caress her stomach, leaning close to whisper in her ear, "I'm not going anywhere."

She pressed her round ass into his pelvis. "Good." Her voice wavered.

He was going to have her.

The sound of people returning to the hall to continue the party drove them up the stairs, hand in hand. He was in the lead now, his fingers entwined firmly in hers, pulling her along. When she tripped on the top stair, she kicked off her shoes without stopping, leaving them where they lay on the landing.

He paused, but she said, "Leave them," and rushed ahead.

He wasn't going to argue. They reached her door only a few seconds later, both breathing heavily, their hands roving close to one another in clumsy anticipation.

It seemed to take her an hour to find her key card— apparently wedged in her bra—and open the door, but then finally they were inside in the dim bedroom, quiet but for their labored breaths, and he had her in his arms.

Fears he hadn't admitted to himself vanished in the heat of her touch. When her tongue darted between his lips and danced across his teeth, he remembered what to do. When her breasts rubbed against his chest, his hands instinctively cupped them, when her fingers found the fly of his trousers...

He tore off the layers of his tuxedo, his shirt, his underwear, choosing to get himself naked first, which had always seemed more polite.

You're so silly, Meg had said once, laughing at him. *Flashers aren't polite.*

He waited for the surge of guilt to chill his body to uselessness.

Promise me you'll be happy, she'd said at the end.

I can't promise that. He wanted to. He wanted to give her anything. But he hadn't promised, hadn't been able to lie.

April was watching him, waiting. Eyes locked on his, she began to undress—not like a boy about to jump in a lake, as he had, but slowly, deliberately. Fingers trailed down her throat to unfasten the tiny button between her breasts. It was a pearl, and there seemed to be dozens more dotting the front hem of her dress, all the way down to her knees.

Tilting her head to one side, she pushed the delicate fabric off the opposite shoulder, exposing the thin, lacy strap of her bra. Then she slid her fingers across her collarbone, stroked her throat, and rubbed her lips until they were shiny with saliva.

Seeing the effect this had on him—his body, though rigid in parts, had not been paralyzed with guilt—she smiled around her fingers. "Get on the bed."

His pride woke with a start. If she thought he was going to roll onto his back like a service dog, she was going to be disappointed.

He moved closer to her, took the next button between his fingers, popped it open, and lowered his mouth to hers in a crushing kiss as he continued unbuttoning his way down until her dress fell away.

She melted against him, soft but enthusiastic. Her tongue tangled with his, her hands dug into his shoulders, her hips pressed closer. Finally the dress was off and the curvy body under his hands wore nothing but some flimsy fabric, which felt good, but wasn't her skin.

"Take this off," he said roughly.

She put a hand on his chest and pushed him away. "Get on the bed."

"You said that already."

"Yet here you are," she said, taking another step back.

He ran a hand through his hair, unable to look away from her nipples, tantalizingly erect under the thin fabric. He didn't want to argue with her. That would only delay things. Like his mouth tasting what he saw and what he was imagining and had been imagining for quite a while.

With a fierce look that told her he wasn't her slave, when of course he was, he turned and went to the bed. He tore off the duvet like a bullfighter with a red cape and lay himself down, face —and erection—up. Very up.

She followed him and stood at the foot. Tiny flowers still clung to her hair. Her eyes were huge, luminous, knowing. She was beautiful.

Under his ribs the lock snapped, the cell door opened, light poured in.

He reached for her.

Chapter 20

Looking down at Zack reclining on the white sheets, April wondered why she'd insisted on being on top. Maybe because this way she was able to get a really good look at him, naked in every way except for his glasses.

"You're still wearing your glasses," she said, lifting the hem of her slip over her thighs, not quite high enough to show him her panties.

His eyes followed her every move. "The better to see you with," he said in a low voice.

She shivered. He should've looked less intimidating, being butt naked, but he wasn't. Even with the glasses. He was just too beautiful.

She waited to catch her breath before lifting the slip the rest of the way and pulling it over her head. After flinging it onto a chair, she tried to regain her earlier confidence. The blazing look in his eyes made her falter, and it was hard to strike the seductive pose she'd intended without giggling.

He propped himself up on his elbows. "Come here."

She had to fight giggles again. And the urge to run. What was the matter with her? She'd done this a million times.

Well, not a *million*.

It's just he didn't look like himself sprawled out like that.

Looking at her like that. Wanting her like that.

She focused on his eyes behind the glasses and realized that his expression wasn't too different from his usual one. Had he wanted her all this time? She liked the idea of him lusting over her —secretly, just as she had for him.

Holding that delicious thought, she gave him her back as she unfastened the bra and shimmied out of it, throwing him sultry looks over her shoulder. His gaze made her hot. She stopped worrying and fell into the moves of the dance. Men loved this foreplay she did, but she loved it more. It transformed her from goofy chick to woman, delivered them both to a sensual, intimate sanctuary.

"April—please—"

She fingered the waistband of her panties, moving her touch around her hips, behind her back, rotating for a moment to show him the strain of the shell-pink lace. She didn't have much on top, but her ass, she'd been told, was miraculous.

Zack groaned from the bed. "Oh my God."

Down went the panties. She waited a moment, her back to him, then turned. Fighting down another wave of nerves, she got on the bed and crawled up his body on her hands and knees. His hardness brushed her nipples, her belly, and then, just slightly, between her legs. She held herself above him, not touching, and moved her face close enough to feel his breath. Then she shifted her weight to one hand and gently removed his glasses, setting them on the bedside table.

There. Now he *really* looked naked.

"April," he said roughly.

She rearranged her self above him. "Yes?"

He hooked a hand behind her neck and pulled her down to his mouth in a hard kiss that knocked the strength out of her arms. She fell on him, chest to chest, hearts beating against each other, lost in the onslaught of his tongue in her mouth. She felt his hands slide up her body and find her breasts, her nipples, then down and around to the swell of her ass. Caressing her, he slowed his kiss, gentle and light, and then he rolled her onto her back.

"April," he said, running one hand through her hair, kissing her forehead, her nose, her cheeks.

She couldn't think. It was moving so fast. Who was this guy? Where was this passion coming from? Why—

His tongue drove into her mouth. She spread her legs, suddenly urgent for him. "*Zack.*" Her voice sounded like a stranger's. "I want you."

His hand was there. *There*. She fell into a mindless pool. Who was this, what was this, why was this—

He raked his mouth across her cheek to her ear. "You're so beautiful," he said.

"So are you." She was dead serious, almost angry, but she felt him laugh against her throat.

"I want everything you have. All of it. Every piece of you." He stroked her skin from hip to shoulder, leaving a trail of fire wherever he touched. "Can I..."

She flung her head back on the bed, shaking with desire and need and fear, and forced her muscles to relax. "Do it," she whispered. She'd had sex, lots of it, she'd had quick times and fast times and hard times, but none of them felt like she'd been dipped in hot chocolate and set on fire and shot into space, none of them had been like this.

"Not yet." He stretched out along her, skin to skin, his long limbs pressing down on hers. His voice was husky. "I want to feel you." His feet stroked her calves, his knees caressed her inner thighs, and his belly, rough with hair, slid against hers until she cried out and begged him to just *do it*.

He paused, chest heaving. She watched him close his eyes. Then he was in motion, tearing open the condom, sliding his palms over her inner thighs, between her legs, exploring her with his fingers. Her thoughts splintered again, her awareness narrowed to the hot burning spiral in the center of her universe. And then his mouth found the pulse in her neck, and the slight pressure of his teeth ignited her like an explosive, his hands were in and out of her, everywhere. She let him take over, let herself sigh and moan and smile and gasp, let the pleasure rise up and arc higher until she was blinded, obliterated.

When he entered her with a well-timed thrust, she rose up to meet him, shocked to realize how much she wanted him, how much she didn't want it to ever end.

* * *

He slept the sleep of the erotically sated: joyful but turbulent. Wild dreams galloped through his mind, breasts and smiles and soft hands, the smell of sex, the taste of a woman's skin.

He dreamed of April's dark eyelashes, her pink nipples, how it had felt to be sunk deep within her. To want her and to have her, again and again.

But then she was gone, and Meg was there wearing nothing but his T-shirt and a pair of white cotton panties. He was stretched out on a leather couch at IKEA, trying to decide if they should buy it or wait for the wedding registry, when she climbed on top of him. Her lips found his.

"I love you," she whispered.

With a breathless jolt, he woke up. April's silky shoulder was under his mouth, her sweet perfume filling his nose.

Heart pounding, he flung out a hand to the nightstand, feeling for his glasses to read the green numbers on the clock radio.

1:34 a.m.

I should go.

He wiped the sweat off his brow, trying to clear his head. *Why?* a voice inside him said. *She's right there, soft and round and warm...*

He sat up, kicked his feet free of the sheets, watching April's form in the bed next to him, glowing from the faint bathroom light. Her eyes were closed, her breathing slow. Suddenly she sighed and reached out a hand, curving it around his upper thigh. His body sprang to life, wanting her again.

She could seduce him in her sleep.

He watched her, saw her flushed cheeks, her tousled hair, and felt cold at the thought of leaving her. But he shouldn't stay. The family would gather for breakfast in the morning, and not even he would have the self-control to disguise the erotic charge that was humming unhindered between them right now. He needed a little time to recover before he could attempt that.

He bent to kiss her shoulder, just a light touch, but when she rolled onto her back and the sheet slid away, exposing the swell of her breast, he couldn't stop himself from taking her nipple into his mouth and feeling it harden under his tongue.

Her eyes flickered open, her warm arms reaching around him, pulling him close, caressing the flexing muscles of his back. He moved up to her mouth, kissed her hard, slipped his hand over her hair to tilt her head, kiss her more deeply, disappear into the feel of her.

He noticed her hair was damp. He dropped kisses along her forehead, dipping his nose into the curls. "Did you take a shower?"

She nodded. "You were out to the world."

"I'm like that."

"You worked hard," she said.

"Didn't feel like work."

Her hands slipped down to his butt and squeezed. "Good."

He propped himself up on one elbow and brushed a curl away from her cheek, wondering how she did it, what it was about her. He stroked the peach fuzz at her temple with his knuckles, wishing they weren't in a hotel surrounded by her family, his clients, so many people.

The pain from his dream about Meg was fading to the shadows, but thoughts that he'd buried were now rushing to the surface. He remembered making love to her on a camping mattress of their first apartment, before they'd bought a real bed; the first time he'd proposed to her and she'd said no; the devastating moment the doctors told them the chemo would make her sterile.

April had no idea what baggage he was hauling around with him. He was too serious for her. The first time he'd seen her with her niece at her mother's house, he'd felt a bone-deep longing for her to have his children—*immediately*. It was nuts. She was young, fun-loving, lighthearted. She hadn't been shuttered up, half-alive for the past few years. *She* wasn't going to overreact to a single night together.

"I'm having a really nice time." She gave him an impish smile, tickling the hair on his chest. "How about you?"

He brought himself back to the moment. April's touch soothed, pleased, aroused him more than he would've thought possible. He wanted to close his eyes and drink in the sensation forever. "Very, very nice." He kissed her lightly on the lips. "But I think I should go, don't you?"

She leaned away from him on the pillow. "Why?"

"The morning would be awkward."

She dragged her fingernails across his nipple. "My mom would ask Mark to reserve the place for another night." She rolled her eyes. "For you and me."

"For—" He lost his breath. She was joking about getting married.

She kissed him. "Ha-ha. You don't think we could hide the afterglow?"

"Look at me. I'm radioactive." He sank against her, mouth taking hers, tongue teasing her lips apart. He had to be gone before morning, not necessarily right *now*. He found her earlobe and sucked it into his mouth.

She arched her back and spoke through a long, throaty sigh. "You want to have sex again?"

He circled his thumb over her nipple, felt it pucker. "Mm."

"Will you stay if we do?" she asked.

It took all his energy not to roll her onto her back and take her without another word, a sudden thrust, hard and demanding and unforgiving, just take what he wanted after months, years, of deprivation.

"Yes," he mumbled into her hair, forgetting everything, just wanting her.

She pulled him down to her mouth, and they kissed for a long, inspiring minute until she broke away and put her hand on his chest.

"No, you're right. You should go."

He ran a hand over his mouth and told his body to settle down. It wasn't listening. "What?"

"I wouldn't be able to keep my hands off of you." She slid a hand down his chest and grabbed him between the legs. "See?"

He clenched his teeth with a groan. "You'd do that... at

breakfast?"

"I might."

"You think that'll get me to leave?"

She released him and patted his shoulder. "Dismount, tiger. We'd better stop this now before we really get going."

"I could go afterward."

"No, you wouldn't," she said. "I can tell. One of has to show some restraint."

He couldn't bring himself to move. What if he never felt like this again?

"You can do it." She gave him a push, rolled out from under him. "Liam wouldn't understand. It'll be a lot better for you if he doesn't find out while you're still working at Fite."

She was right. But he still couldn't bring himself to climb out of the bed where he'd had her.

She pulled a sheet around herself, a vulnerable look coming into her eyes. "I was just trying to make it easier for you to go. Don't be angry."

He managed a smile, shook his head. "That's not the feeling." He was finally able to turn away and get to his feet. Finding his boxers on the floor, he pulled them on and hoped his body would get the message. Then he lingered for a moment, staring at nothing, fighting an anxious sensation that he'd gone too far and might not make it back.

April's quiet voice snapped him out of it. "Are you thinking about Meg?"

He turned and stared at her over his shoulder.

She put up a hand. "Sorry, it just came out. Forget it." She walked over to a table and poured a glass of water, shaking her head. "Sorry."

The sound of Meg's name on her lips, right after having sex, was strange, even painful, but it didn't stop him from wanting to get back into bed. He was even pretty sure he could do a better job than he had the first time.

"I'm thinking about you," he said. "About how you give the hottest striptease I've ever seen in my life."

She smiled around the glass. "Thanks. I've got to admit, I've had a lot of practice."

The way she said it made him wonder if she wanted him to ask how many times or say it didn't matter. "Professionally?"

She set the glass down with a thud. "No." Then she laughed. "Thanks."

"Thanks?"

She put a hand on her hip, smiling at him. "How many B cup strippers do *you* know?"

"Offhand?" He walked over to her. "I'd have to check my notebook." He poured himself a glass of water and drank it in one long, thirsty go.

He looked around the room. The rest of his clothes—including his tux, which he'd treated like a baby until last night—were in a pile near the TV.

Not last night. Still tonight.

He made himself get dressed. It wasn't nearly as much fun putting them back on as it had been ripping them off. He had to crawl around on the floor to find his socks and shoes before moving his unwilling legs to the door. She followed him, flushed and tousle-haired, wrapped in the sheet.

He stroked her cheek. "I'll call you."

"You don't have my number."

"Of course I do." He collected names, numbers, and email addresses like tickets. You never knew when you might want to talk to somebody. He even had Trixie's.

He opened the door, checking his pockets for his wallet and keys, and was surprised to find her at his elbow, smiling slyly up at him. "You were awesome, by the way."

She did something to him. He didn't know how or why, but she did.

"Thanks." He stole a kiss. "I aim to please."

As he nurtured the glow of their last words, hoping the hope of a man who'd seen heaven and wanted to die and see it again, he turned from the closing door and saw Liam Johnson standing two feet away, a baby in his arms, staring right at him.

And the hope died.

Chapter 21

ZACK LET THE door slam shut at his back, although he knew it was too late. Liam had seen—and heard—his sister in the doorway.

He felt his neck redden. Was his fly up? He couldn't look now, or he'd be asking for Liam to look, too.

Of all the bad luck. What could he say? Liam was standing there like a stern father in a '60s TV show. And it got worse: he was holding Merry, who wasn't at all merry, unless she screamed and arched her back when she was feeling good.

Which reminded him of April...

What timing. Shit. Was his fly really open? He had to look.

No. He had to keep his head up and hold Liam's laser-eyeball gaze. "Evening."

Liam adjusted Merry in his arms, teeth so tightly clenched his jaw muscles were rippling. There was a moment of silence as Merry inhaled, during which Zack realized just how loud she was screaming, but as soon as she'd refilled her lungs, she cranked it up again.

Maybe Liam was upset because of the baby's crying, not because of him sleeping with his sister.

Zack gestured to Merry. "Anything I can do?"

"Anything you can *do*?" Liam's voice was acid.

"Look," Zack began, but Merry drowned him out. What could he say, anyway? He lifted his hand and waved vaguely toward the stairs at the end of the hall. "I'm leaving now."

"You certainly are."

As the last thought of returning to April's room vanished, Zack nodded and walked away. He imagined that the baby's screams mirrored Liam's opinion of his romp with his sister. He sped up when he reached the stairs, and by the time he was on the ground floor, he was jogging. The remaining wedding guests had moved to the bar, and he heard laughing, shouting, happy voices. He could still hear Merry, too, or maybe that was the electronic pop playing over the speakers.

He almost got into the wrong car three times because every other car was a damn Prius—next time he'd borrow a different type of vehicle from the car share company—and finally he was driving down the narrow, twisting road along the ridge and down through the hills to return to San Francisco, the present and the past an uneasy stew in his mind.

He got a beer out of the fridge as soon as he got home. And then another one soon after. And another. When he was standing at his—Liam's—bedroom window and finishing off his third, he decided he needed to talk to April right away. It couldn't wait until the morning—she should know that her big angry brother had seen them together.

What should it matter, really? Zack was thirty-million years old, an old man who got older every day, apparently at twice the rate of normal men. And adorable, sweet, beautiful April wasn't half as young as she looked, the doll. He wondered if she had gone back to sleep.

She answered on the fifth ring. "Huh?"

"It's Zack."

"What time is it?" she asked.

"Look at the clock. You don't need glasses like I do. It's right there."

There was a pause. "Four oh six," she said. "Fuck."

"Can't. I'm too drunk to drive."

"Is this a new side of you I'm learning about?"

"I'm making up for lost time," he said.

She let out a long sigh. He heard a bed creak. "You know, I'd just fallen asleep."

"I know how you feel. I was asleep earlier. Once." He rested his head on the glass. It fogged up under his boozy breath. "Before you kicked me out."

"You said you wanted to go."

"You made me do it," he said.

"Sorry." She sounded like she was smiling.

"Yeah. Well. Liam saw me. Which is why I'm calling."

"Saw you when?" she asked.

"As I was leaving."

"Wait a minute—he saw you leaving my room?"

"Mm. He was standing in the hall."

"He doesn't necessarily know which room is mine," she said. "Maybe he assumed you slept with somebody else. There were lots of women at the wedding."

"Were there?"

"Didn't you notice?" she asked.

"I was only looking at you."

The phone went silent for a couple of long seconds. "That's nice."

"I want to see you again," he said.

"I'm sure you will."

"Liam will probably fire me on Monday. How about dinner

Monday night?"

"He can't fire you just because you fooled around with somebody at his brother's wedding," she said.

"He knew it was you, April. He didn't look happy."

She didn't speak for a moment. "Hm. He's going to be annoying."

"That's what I thought. He already annoyed me so much I ran down the hallway to get away from him being so annoying." He went to the kitchen and dropped the empty bottle into the bin with a crash. "He might annoy me all the way back to New York."

"I'll talk to him," she said.

He rubbed his eyes, trying to clear his head. He wished he knew if they were starting something serious. "How about an early dinner tomorrow night?" He didn't need to figure out their relationship. Baby steps. "Well, it's tomorrow already, so, what I mean is tonight."

"I don't know. Now you've got me worried about your job."

"I'll make pizza from scratch," he said. "It's really good, takes a lot of time, and it's really good."

"You said that twice."

"It deserves it," he said.

"All right. What time?"

"Really?"

She let out a breath. "How drunk are you? Will you forget this and I show up and there's no pizza?"

"Not that drunk. Come at six while I start the dough. We can talk while I work."

"You're always working," she said, and hung up.

* * *

April didn't wake up until noon, when the cleaners knocked on the door. She'd missed the checkout time and had to scramble into her jeans and a T-shirt, gather her stuff, and stumble out to her car without a shower or free breakfast.

Anxiety she hadn't felt the night before bloomed with a vengeance. He'd been drinking when he called her last night, probably trying to drown his fears that he'd ruined his career by sleeping with her.

When he sobered up, he'd probably regret going to bed with her. She could withstand a little horrified recoiling in a double-parked car after a quick kiss, but if he rejected her after last night, after all those kisses, the sweet words, the erotic abandon—

Something had shifted inside her. She'd finally shattered that control of his, but the breaking only made her want him more, or more of him. And it scared her. *He might annoy me all the way back to New York*, he'd said. She wasn't in control of him; she wasn't in control of herself. Just the type of situation she'd sworn to avoid.

She blasted the radio as she drove, her mood sinking and headache growing with each mile. On a whim, instead of taking the road down to the Peninsula and over the bridge to the East Bay, she turned west to drive down to the coast, desperate to get away from people who knew her, breathe in the cold salty air and empty her mind for a little while.

She didn't know how long she walked along the shore wrapped in the fleece blanket she kept in the car, but it wasn't long enough for her to figure out if she'd just had the happiest or saddest night of her life. She finally got in her car and drove home.

The first thing she did when she walked into the house was go into the kitchen for coffee and painkillers. There she found a note from her mom under a glass of homemade tomato juice:

Walking the dogs. Such a beautiful day.

She probably rushed home early that morning to be with the

dogs, since she hated leaving them alone. Had her mother guessed about her and Zack? Probably. The woman had magical powers.

April sipped the juice—spiked heavily with Tabasco sauce, the family remedy for hangovers—and gazed out the window at the rain. It was just a drizzle, gray and wimpy, the kind of precipitation that was too pitiful to do much good for water supply or agriculture but lingered for hours or days, making you depressed.

She didn't know if her mom thought it was a beautiful day because the rain was beautiful, or because it didn't rain yesterday and spoil the wedding. Knowing her mother, it was probably both. All glasses are more than half full at all times, even when they're empty.

April coughed down the last of the flaming tomato juice and was on her way upstairs to take a shower when Liam burst through the front door.

"I'd like to talk to you," he said.

There wasn't enough Tabasco sauce in the world to put her in the mood to talk to Liam right then. She continued on her way up the stairs. "My personal life is none of your business."

"Damn it." Liam strode over and stood on the bottom stair. "He works for us."

"For you. Not for me."

He made a rude noise. "You're family. And you work at Fite."

She reached the top stair. "I'm not going to talk about it."

"Couldn't you leave just *one guy* alone?"

She stopped and turned. "Excuse me?"

"It just would've been a lot easier if you hadn't seduced him."

"How do you know *I* seduced *him*?"

"Oh, come on," he said.

Anger washed over her. "Listen to yourself. What right do

you have to talk to me that way?"

He clamped his lips together and glared at her, but doubt had crept into his eyes.

She pointed at him. "You owe me an apology."

His gaze moved to the ceiling.

"You absolutely do," she continued, moving down the stairs to look him in the eye. "Let's hear it."

He held an incredulous expression for a long moment before ducking his head with a sigh. "All right. I apologize. But—"

"Apology accepted. Now I'm going to go take a shower." She turned, marched up the stairs to the bathroom, and slammed the door.

One guy. She couldn't leave just one guy alone.

She swatted the towels hanging from the old chrome hook behind the door, knocking them to the floor.

Had she been the one to start it? She remembered him being nice with those two plates of chocolate cake, and him suggesting she get some ice after the bouquet smacked her in the face, and then she was inviting him to her room for sex.

Damn it. Liam was right. It was her fault.

But he'd helped.

Her shower was so long, it drained the hot water heater. She walked naked to her room, the nakedness designed to repel Liam in case he was waiting for her outside the door. Nothing made him run away faster than her parading around in the buff. Such a prude.

But, happily for both of them, he wasn't there. She slammed her bedroom door, pulled on her baggiest sweatshirt and a clean pair of old, soft jeans, lay down on her childhood twin-size bed, and stared at her phone.

She knew Zack's number. Of course she did. And his email

and permanent address in New York. She skimmed personal information as effectively as an unelected government official.

She looked at his name on the screen. She hadn't snapped a photo of him yet to go with the number—

And she shouldn't, because it had gone far enough. She'd been lonely and vulnerable and he'd given her cake. Of course she'd slept with him. That didn't mean she had to do it again. It would be safer for both of them to just cool it.

Then again, why should she do what Liam wanted her to do?

Rebellious impulses inside her launched a civil war. Her mind swam with options, desires, obligations.

Oh, hell. She should at least talk to the guy. She tapped his name.

He picked up on the second ring. "Hello?"

The sound of his voice made her go soft all over. "Hi," she said, a little breathless.

"Are you calling to cancel?" he asked. "Because if you are, I can't talk right now."

She put her hand over her eyes, smiling. *You can do this.* "I just saw Liam. I don't think I should come over." No, that sounded wishy-washy. "Actually, I can't. I can't come over."

"You're a grown woman in the twenty-first century," he said. "Why would you let a male relative tell you what to do?"

Her heart flipped upside-down. He didn't regret it. He hadn't changed his mind. He was willing to risk the career that meant so much to him, for her. She wanted to race over, throw her arms around him, kiss him silly.

He wasn't playing fair.

"You can't mean that," she said. "What about your job?"

"The damage has been done."

She winced. *Damage.*

"In for a penny, in for a pound," he continued.

All of the implications of what they'd done crashed down on her. What if he really did lose his job because of her? He was leaving in a month or two—was it worth it? Hadn't she vowed to stop sleeping around?

"Here's the thing," she said. "I like you."

"April. You don't have to dump me to get out of eating a slice of pizza."

She sat up. "I'm not dumping. I'm explaining."

"It sounded like dumping. You'd started the I-like-you speech."

"Look, I'm tired. I didn't get much sleep last night."

"You don't need to say that. If you don't want to see me, just say so," he said.

"I *am* saying it! You... you..."

"We'll eat early. I've already started the pizza dough. Lunch is never serious," he said. "Come over anytime." And then he hung up.

She cried in frustration at her phone and threw it on the bed. The sound of four dogs clattering over hardwood floors reached her from downstairs. The rain was coming down harder now, which meant they were probably wet, muddy, and stinky—especially if Stool had indulged in his favorite treat.

With a smile, she got off her bed and finger-combed her wet hair.

Stool. The perfect solution. He'd be the perfect chaperone. He'd chew on furniture, steal the pizza, and make it impossible to get into bed.

She was halfway down the stairs before she turned around and put on her sexiest black bra and panties under her old clothes.

It didn't mean anything. Even normal people didn't wear

underwear with holes in it, just in case they were in a car accident and ended up at the hospital on a gurney with cute doctors looking at them.

It means nothing.

A little over an hour later, she pushed the buzzer to the condo in San Francisco, remembering fondly the year she'd had a key of her own. The view from the top floor of the modern high-rise near the Bay Bridge was even better than the one from her mom's house: twinkling city lights, the arc of the bridge over the ever-changing water, the hills of the East Bay.

Zack's voice crackled over the speaker. "April?"

She pressed the button. "I've brought company."

Silence. Then, "Great," and the door buzzed.

Stool pulled on his leash as if the finish line for the Iditarod were inside the elevator just ahead of them. She couldn't imagine what power he'd had when he was young and four-legged; she was having trouble staying on her feet. They scrambled into the elevator and looked at each other—Stool so excited, his tongue was hanging halfway to the floor, and April afraid she looked the same.

Zack was waiting for them upstairs in the hall outside the unit's door. When he saw Stool, his face lit up. "Tripod!"

"Please respect the name I've given him," she said.

He bent over and scratched Stool behind the ears. The dog's reaction was similar to hers the night before: lots of panting, closed eyes, generalized loss of muscle strength.

"I can't call him that," he said. "It seems disrespectful."

"Wait until he chows down on a big turd and then sticks his tongue in your mouth," she said. "You'll appreciate I've given you a harmless way to get even."

Stool jerked free and galloped into the condo. "Stool!" She

started to run after him, but Zack hooked an arm around her waist and pinned her into the corner.

"Thanks for coming," he said, breathing hard. He gazed deeply into her eyes but didn't make any move to kiss her.

Her heart thudded against her ribs. He felt strong and solid. And the sight of him in a baby-blue gingham apron and old khakis rolled up at the ankles—and those glasses, those damn glasses—was more exciting than the tux or the birthday suit.

He smelled good, too. Man and pizza. Her two biggest vices, all in one. God help her.

"I better get Stool," she said, breaking free and hurrying into the condo. "Before he destroys the furniture."

Zack closed the door and went into the kitchen. "There isn't much to destroy," he said. "What can I get you to drink?"

"Water. Nonalcoholic water."

"I'm not trying to get you drunk," he said. "I have juice, mineral water, milk…"

"Milk. I'll have a glass of milk." *That* would put her in a virginal mood. They called them milk*maids* for a reason, right? And milk made her think of babies, which, ironically, never made her think of sex. Although thinking of babies and milk did make her think of Bev's pale-gray expressed breast milk, which still made her a little queasy when she had to handle it. "Scratch that. Juice or mineral water. I don't care."

"I could mix them together."

"You're a problem solver," she said.

"That's why they pay me the big bucks."

"Do they? Are the bucks big?"

Something she couldn't read flickered across his face: a combination of a smile and a frown. "Sometimes."

"I hope you're not charging Bev and Liam too much," she

said. "They just got Fite out of the red. We weren't sure they were going to make it."

"I reduced my usual fee," he said.

"Really? I was just kidding. Why?"

He looked at his hands. "Why don't you look around? Make yourself comfortable. I have to stir the sauce."

Sensing a topic he didn't want to discuss, which made her suddenly eager to pursue it, she followed him into the kitchen. Liam used to cook for her when she lived in the condo. They'd talk about his unlikable girlfriends, her forgettable boyfriends, and then watch their favorite comedians on TV and laugh at the same jokes.

It wasn't the same since he'd married Bev. They didn't laugh like friends; they'd regressed to bickering siblings. She missed those days.

Zack went to the fridge and took out a carton of orange juice and a bottle of Calistoga. "Don't you want to look around?"

"Don't have to. I used to live here." She watched him pour the drinks. "I had a temp job not far from here, so I slept on Liam's couch."

"When was that?"

"Around when he met Bev." She took the glass he offered, brought it to her lips. "I had to move out when they... you know."

"Three's a crowd."

"Yeah."

"Is that when you moved back home?" he asked.

She sighed. "No, that was just a few months ago. Before that I was living with a guy who I don't want to talk about."

His gaze sharpened. "Boyfriend?"

"Unfortunately." She scowled into her glass. "Stool was his dog. He took off one night and left him behind. The landlord told me to get rid of him or move out, so I moved out. It's nearly impossible to find an apartment that takes pets, so I went home. My mom used to run a dog rescue, so that was an obvious move."

"He 'took off one night'? Did *you* know he was leaving?"

She glanced at him. "It wasn't anything serious. We'd only been together a few months."

He didn't say anything for a moment. "What an asshole."

"I know. His own dog." Zack looked shocked, so she added, "Yeah, yeah, and me too. I've already psychoanalyzed myself. My expectations were much too low."

"You could say that."

"Anyway, when I saw how much help Bev and Liam needed with Merry, I started babysitting and decided to stay longer than I'd planned."

"It's nice you're so flexible."

She snorted while she was drinking, inhaling orange juice into her sinuses. After she finished coughing, she said, "That's a polite way of saying I'm a total slacker."

"Slackers don't work two jobs," he said.

"Merry isn't a job."

"You undervalue yourself," he said.

He was probably just sweet-talking her to get her into bed, but it hit home. "You sound like my mother."

"She's right."

An awkward silence grew between them. Why were they talking about her? She hated talking about herself. "So, why were you willing to reduce your fee for Fite?"

He turned away and got busy stirring the sauce over the stove. "It was only a slight reduction. I knew it would be a tough sell, given the company's problems."

"That's not really what I mean. Why did you want to work at

fite at all?"

"A few reasons," he said.

"Such as…"

"My parents are here."

"Like, six hours away," she said.

"Closer than New York."

"Okay." She picked up a bell pepper and rubbed the smooth skin with her thumb. "Why else?"

"I wanted to expand the geographical reach of my client base," he said.

"You missed California," she said.

"Basically."

"Well, those are good reasons. I wonder what the real one is."

He lowered the heat, turned to her, and crossed his arms over his chest. A droplet of tomato sauce clung to his apron, mere centimeters from the bright white shirt underneath. "You'll mock me."

"Maybe. Will you tell me anyway?"

"I want to get into high tech," he said. "See where I'm going with this?"

"Like software and stuff?" she asked.

He nodded.

She stared at him. "You knew about Mark before. Before you even came out here." She put the glass down on the counter and took a step back. "He's your whole reason for coming to California at all."

"No." He followed her. "There were many reasons. He was just one of them."

"The wedding must've been quite a coup," she said.

"I told you I was interested in meeting him. I told you."

"You did." She ran a hand through her hair, nodding. "You

did. I thought it was more spur of the moment, though."

"I'm not usually very spontaneous. In case you hadn't noticed."

She didn't know what to say. He hadn't told her the whole story, but until last night, why would he have had any obligation to?

Even now, he didn't have to tell her anything. She was just the crazy little sister, the freelancer, the one-night stand.

So far.

While she chewed on her lip, she realized Stool was too quiet. Where was he? Silence was much worse than barking, whining, or crunching.

"Stool?" She strode out of the kitchen, casting her gaze over the tables and sofas for three-legged tornadoes. She paused at the bedroom door, hearing gulps and afraid to look inside. What could he be eating?

She peeked around the corner. "No!" She flung herself onto the bed, where Stool was ripping a tuxedo jacket into black ribbons. "Eating shit is better than this, you crazy dog!" She threw her body over the remaining fabric and caught his collar. Stool smiled at her with the lining of one sleeve dangling from his teeth.

"Well, that's one way to get you into bed," Zack said from the doorway. "Good dog."

Chapter 22

ZACK'S FEELINGS ABOUT seeing his best garment destroyed faded when he saw the agony on April's face. As she played tug-of-war with Stool, her face turned red, and tears flashed in her eyes.

"I'm so sorry," she said, yanking on a scrap black fabric. "So sorry, so sorry. My dog has an eating disorder. I'll pay you back. It's my fault."

"I'll be right back." He went to the kitchen and took a palmful of Italian sausage, already sautéed with fennel and ready to go on the pizza, out of the fridge. "Stool!" He added a whistle.

Immediately he heard the sound of three paws scrambling down the hallway, and then the dog was there, sliding around the corner of the cabinets, eyes wide, tongue flapping.

"Sit," Zack said. Stool sat. Zack gave him the sausage.

April came into the kitchen, holding the shredded remains of his suit in her arms. "You *fed* him?"

"Best way to get him out of my room." He took the suit from her—shoving aside the memory of the price tag that flashed in his brain, the special brush and storage bag he'd bought to care for it, the confidence he'd felt yesterday when he'd put it on, knowing she would see him in it—and gave her a smile. "It's okay. Accidents happen." He went to the bedroom, hung the ruined suit coat in the closet, and closed the door so Stool couldn't return for seconds.

When he returned to the kitchen and saw April standing by the front door wearing her coat and holding Stool by his leash, his breath caught.

She leaned over and stroked Stool's ears. "I don't want him to ruin anything else."

"Look around. What else could he ruin?" There was a cheap bistro table with two chairs, a used futon, and a cardboard shipping box he used as a coffee table. Liam had rented it to him unfurnished, and Zack hadn't seen a reason to make much effort.

She pointed at the floor. "That's wool carpeting," she said. "What if it reminds him of grass?"

"I'll wash it." He walked over to her and reached for the leash. He still couldn't take a proper breath. Her fingers felt cold and tense under his touch. "Please. Stay. I was just about to put the pizza in the oven. You can't leave now."

At their feet sat Stool, rock-still except for his quivering nose, his gaze locked on Zack's face.

"One sausage and he's yours for life," she said.

Zack tried to swallow his laugh, but she must've heard the strangled sound come out of his throat because she flushed pink and swatted him on the arm. "*I'm* not so easy," she said.

Finally giving in to temptation, he swept her up into his arms. "Not even pepperoni?"

Her body remained stiff, so he released her slowly, claimed the leash, and brought Stool with him into the kitchen. A hostage.

"You're courting disaster, letting him in there," April said.

"The worst has already happened."

He heard her groan. "Send me a bill for your suit. I'll pay you back."

"Right."

"I will!"

Hopeful she was getting comfortable, he dropped Stool's leash and washed his hands before putting the pizza together. He'd already rolled out the dough and baked it halfway. "I mean, I'm not sending you a bill." The sauce pooled in the center of the pie before he spread it around.

She reached past him and stole a sliced mushroom. "You should."

He slapped the pizza together and shoved it into the oven. "There. Not long now."

"My companion animal and I will wait in the other room." She'd retrieved Stool's leash and held him against her side. "I don't want him doing any more damage."

Zack watched her walk away, struck by how deprived he felt just from her move into another room.

This is dangerous.

He'd invited her over with one goal—a sober but enthusiastic replay of the night before—but hadn't thought ahead to the moment after that, when she got up and went home. Because as soon as she left, he'd have to get right to work getting her back again, sweet and wet and frisky again, such as tomorrow night and the night after, and possibly, it would certainly cross his mind, during lunch one day.

Leaning against the counter, he stared at his hands. What was he doing?

Last night, he'd offended the client he hoped would be his ticket to a new phase of his career, and he hadn't given it a second thought. He could've called or made an appointment for tomorrow, or looked for another client, like that friend of Mark's. But he hadn't bothered. Getting April to his condo had consumed him utterly.

That morning, he'd woken with a smile on his face, feeling like he could fly. But he wasn't flying, he was *falling*. He'd jumped out of an airplane without a parachute, and the hard earth was down there waiting for him.

He'd assumed he could be like other men, and have sex with a cute girl without overreacting. For God's sake, he was thirty-two, a widower, a successful businessman, not a seventh-grader who proposed to the first girl who'd agreed to go to the movies with him.

In a daze, he checked on the pizza. The heat from the oven blasted some sense into him.

It was his upbringing. What he felt when April walked ten feet away was good old-fashioned lust, same as it was for other men, but the firm morals drilled into him as a child couldn't let him admit it.

Sex and guilt were miserable companions. If anyone could help him separate the two, it was a woman like April.

He mixed up another nonalcoholic cocktail for her and plated the salads. After they ate, he'd get her back into bed. He'd just come out of a few long, lonely years, and didn't want to begin any more.

Proud of his pizzas—he liked to serve it on the pan, like at a restaurant—he carried it directly from the oven out into the living room.

It was empty.

At that moment, the earth rose up to meet him. He felt the blow deep in his guts. She'd left, she'd actually left, and she wasn't coming back.

He closed his eyes and let the hot pan burn through the dish towel and singe his fingers.

She didn't really want him, not enough. Last night had

changed his life, but for her it was just—

"Hey," she said. She came in from the balcony with Stool and a roll of newspaper. "I let him pee on your Sunday paper, is that all right? Don't worry—it was the *Chronicle*, not the *New York Times*." She laughed. "I didn't want to go all the way downstairs, especially since they don't allow dogs in most of the complex." She walked past him into the kitchen.

He heard a cabinet shut and the water come on. Heart pounding in his throat, he set the pizza down on the bistro table.

She returned, drying her hands, and stood beside him. "That does look good. You were—"

He drew her into his arms and kissed her. She hadn't left. He stroked her hair away from her cheek and kissed his way to her ear, dizzy with wanting her so much. "I thought you'd gone."

She tilted her head, offering her neck. "I..." She let out a little groan. "Thought about it."

"Bad idea." He ran a hand down her arm and entwined his fingers in hers, nuzzling her neck and breathing in the warm, delicate sweetness of her skin. "You're staying."

"No kidding."

"I'm going to make love to you." He was going to have her beneath him, push against her silky thighs, drive into her until she cried out, scratched at him and demanded more. "Right now."

Her body sagged against his. "I knew this was going to happen."

He lifted her sweatshirt and palmed her warm, smooth stomach. His fingers moved up to her bra, pulled down the lace, freeing the rounded flesh and finding the sensitive peak at its center. Enjoying her gasp, he said roughly, "I wish I had."

She lifted her hands to the back of his head and pulled him closer. Her tongue slipped into his mouth, sending bolts of desire shooting through him.

He wanted her. He didn't know what the future held and he didn't care. He clasped her hand and led her to his bedroom, where he locked the door, quite willing to let Stool enjoy the pizza on the table if it earned him a few minutes with this woman with big gray eyes and a laugh that shattered his icy heart.

As her hand slipped under the waistband of his pants, all he could think about was tasting and holding and taking her until he'd forgotten there was anyone else in the world but the two of them.

* * *

She liked the feel of him, hard and velvety-warm, and would've laughed at the stunned look on his face if she weren't so aroused herself.

"You like that?" she asked.

His eyes darkened, staring at her. "I like."

His husky voice knocked the smile off her face. Shivering a little, she stroked him, felt him get harder and bigger under her hand.

Clenching his jaw, he put his hand over hers, holding it still. "My turn." He pulled her hand out of his pants, clasped both wrists, and lifted them both over her head as he pressed her against the closed door. Heart thudding, she gazed up into his serious face and tried to breathe.

"Don't move," he said.

She didn't move.

A small smile curved in the corner of his mouth. "Good," he said, licking his lips. He took a step back and looked her up and down before shaking his head, taking the hem of her sweatshirt in his fists, and sweeping it up and over her head.

She started to lower her arms, but he seized her wrists again, pinning her against the door. "I just want to look at you." He raked his gaze downward. "Okay?"

She stretched up, hitching her hip to one side, and nodded.

He released her and stepped back. "You didn't really look like yourself last night. This is more like how I imagined it."

"How you imagined... what?"

"Undressing you." He reached for the waistband of her jeans, heat in his eyes. "You were wearing these jeans at dinner at your house that night."

"I was?"

He popped the button. His fingernail felt rough against her stomach. "When you kissed me."

"You kissed me back."

"Not as long as I would've liked," he said, unzipping the fly.

"I thought you didn't want me."

His palm stroked her belly, slid around her waist to her back, under her panties, over her bottom. The jeans gaped open and moved down her hips.

"I wanted you," he said roughly. Her jeans fell to the floor, and his gaze followed them down. "Jesus. You're so beautiful."

She felt heat rush into her veins, flaring wherever he looked—breasts, thighs, toes. Then he stepped forward and took her in his arms, his mouth slanting over hers, wet tongue sliding inside, making her so weak she had to cling to him.

The night before at the wedding, she hadn't had a chance to see him clearly. In their formal clothes, away from their normal lives, the lovemaking had felt like a fantasy. But this was real.

She put her hands on his chest and put a few inches between them to undo the buttons of his shirt. "Not so buttoned-up now, are you?" She licked the hollow of his throat.

"I'm not really that uptight." Breathing hard, he reached

around and unfastened her bra, then palmed her freed breasts. "I'm the rebel in the family, remember?"

As his thumbs raked across her nipples, she sucked in a breath. "Sure." Her fingers got back to work. Each unfastened button exposed another few inches of his chest. His hair was dark, the smell of him intoxicating. She took one nipple into her mouth and teased it, smiling as he groaned.

"I'm not," he said roughly. "It's just a facade."

"Mm." His hair tickled her nose. Wrapping her arms around him under the open shirt, she cuddled up against him, just enjoying for a moment how warm and safe it felt to be together, part of her afraid of how intense it had gotten so fast.

He ground his hips into her pelvis, reminding her they were just getting started, and she felt the heat fill her up again, felt her mouth go dry, every inch of her aware of every inch of him.

Their gazes locked. Talk stopped. He shrugged off his shirt and watched her with dark, serious eyes as she unbuttoned his pants and pushed them down over his hips. He was hard and ready, pushing at his boxers, and she swallowed over the dryness in her throat before hooking her fingers under the waistband and jerking them down.

She had to take a moment to drink in the sight of his erect maleness, the broad shoulders, the thick hair darkening his chest, his strong, muscled thighs. No more business casual. God. Her knees wavered.

He hooked an arm around her and pulled her to him, pressing open-mouthed kisses along her jaw. "Do you like it fast or slow?" His breath was warm and moist on her skin.

She couldn't breathe. "Fast," she whispered. "I like it really, really fast."

Before she knew what was happening, his hands were roughly

claiming her bottom, shoving her panties down her legs to the floor. Then he was driving her to the bed, tumbling her onto her back, climbing on top of her, kissing her mouth, her ears, her neck, her breasts, her belly, then pushing her thighs apart and burying his face deep inside her. His hair on the soft skin of her inner thighs was almost as delicious as his tongue everywhere else. She heard a scream, realizing with a gasp as she clutched the sheets that it was *her*, arched her back and, laughing, gave herself up to the pleasure, the gentleness and the roughness, the blinding delight.

And then he was inside her, thrusting hard, calling her name, and she was gasping his, digging her nails into his back, crazy with him, crazy for him, and they lost themselves in the frenzy and came together in a silent shout, and then collapsed: damp, entwined, spent.

Later, through a distant, sleepy fog, she felt his lips brush her temple, soft as a breath.

"April," he said.

Chapter 23

On Monday morning, April walked into the art room a minute after eight, sipping her coffee and thinking about how much she liked Zack's laugh. It came at you all at once, a tsunami of mirth, knocking you over with its sudden force. After the hot sex, he'd made a second pizza—on sliced sourdough bread this time, since the dough was long gone—and they sat in bed listening to her funniest stories about temping in San Francisco over the past five years. At one point he laughed so hard, he flipped off the edge of the mattress and landed on the floor, laughing harder when Stool lunged for his sausage.

It was impossible not to like a guy like that. She was almost ready to give up trying. Or pretending she was trying at all.

As she sat down in her seat, she saw the pile of work she'd left there the Thursday before, not recognizing any of it or what she was supposed to be doing and when. She could've blamed her poor memory on the wedding, but that wasn't it—she was preoccupied with skin, muscle, sexy blue eyes, laughter, and orgasms.

She'd done it again. She'd sacrificed her goals to get laid. She'd cashed out the kids' college fund and wasted it at Vegas. She'd fallen off the wagon, been kicked out of rehab, violated parole.

She sipped her coffee and turned on her computer, smiling.

Being bad always felt so good. The worst part about what she'd done was that she didn't regret what she'd done, not yet.

An evil voice in her head told her he only wanted sex, that he might look like a nice guy with depth, the kind of man she'd never been with before, but he was really the same: he was just lonely and wanted to get laid. She was fun and easy, a natural candidate, and soon it would be all over and she'd never see him again.

She told the voice to shut up. Even if it was true—and part of her was even more terrified to think it wasn't, that this was serious—the damage was done. They'd crossed the line. And would do it again soon.

Smiling, she ran a finger over her lips. They had plans scheduled for the following night—dinner and a movie, their first real date. They would've gone tonight, but she was babysitting Merry. She'd almost asked Bev if she could find somebody else to sit, but stopped herself because she didn't want Liam to find out.

She glanced at the clock on the computer, wondering if Zack was in the building.

No. He wasn't working today; he was preparing something for a previous client, the one he'd had before Fite. He'd told her he usually had two or three jobs going at once, the only way he could reliably make a living.

"Just like me," she'd said.

He'd pulled her close, spooning her. "Two peas in a pod."

It was hard thinking about that inevitable future, knowing how soon it was coming. His six months at Fite ended in May. Come June, he'd be starting another job at the other end of the country, over two thousand miles away, his home.

She'd always been reckless, but this was an entirely new level of peril for her. She really liked him. Respected him. She wanted to bring him little presents and see him smile, surprised, and then look at her with appreciation, admiration, desire...

Maybe six weeks was long enough to get him to change his mind about moving back to New York. She'd always worked fast —hell, for her, six weeks with one guy was like six years for somebody else. He could find another job out here. He was interested in high tech, wasn't he? Why look for software companies on the East Coast when Silicon Valley was right here?

Struggling to get her mind in the present, she launched the drawing program and scrolled through the files. Teegan expected a dozen sketches and a screen print design for the new baby line before a ten o'clock meeting. She had to hurry.

Before she knew what she was doing, she had her cell phone in her hand and was starting a text. She got as far as *hi xoxox wassup cutie* before she deleted the message, turned off the phone, stuck it into the bottom of her bag, pushed into the back of a drawer, and locked the cabinet shut.

The first step was admitting you had a problem. Zack was a problem. She had him. She'd had him more than once, actually.

Problem, problem, problem.

Then again, maybe the only problem was wanting him and not having him. Wanting him and having him was *no problemo.*

Shoving aside the memory of him giggling on the floor with pizza sauce on his chin, she worked on the sketches over the next hour. The tug of the phone in her drawer, her only link to him, was a constant, nagging pressure. If she were a smoker craving a cigarette, she'd have a chance to light up in the alley during break time. She'd stand around with other similarly afflicted coworkers, getting her fix, enjoying a little camaraderie.

She tried to imagine the reaction if she and Zack got their fix there, too.

This was insane. She needed somebody to knock some sense

into her. She picked up her desk phone receiver and called Virginia. "Power walk during lunch today?"

"What about the baby?"

"Not until two today. I thought we could walk to the Embarcadero and back."

"Why?" Virginia asked.

"What do you mean? It's good exercise."

"Did something happen at the wedding?"

April rubbed a plastic seam on the phone. "They got married. Is that what you mean?"

"You know it's not," Virginia said.

"Look, if you don't want to walk, just say so."

"It depends if you're going to tell me what happened," Virginia said.

April sighed. "We can stop by the ATM so I can give you your hundred bucks."

"I knew it." Virginia's voice was both eager and wistful.

The light on her phone started flashing. It was almost ten. She still had the baby T-shirt to do. "See you at noon." She hung up and switched over to phone mail.

Teegan had left a message, wanting to know when the polka dot running pant logo would be in the system for her to make colorways for the meeting.

April's stomach turned inside out. Logo? She swallowed and called Teegan back. "Which running pant logo are you talking about?" She heard the dread in her own voice.

Teegan paused for a full five seconds, long enough for the coffee in April's stomach to curdle. "What do you mean, *which* running pant logo? How many do you think there are?"

April knew that was a trick question. There were countless running pant logos, but Teegan was implying that the one *she* needed was obvious. Sadly, April didn't know what the fuck she was talking about. Had the memory been obliterated in the afterglow of her hedonistic weekend?

No time to figure it out now. April scrolled through the computer for all the recent work she'd done. "Do you have a file name?"

"You haven't done it?" Teegan asked flatly.

"No. But if you—"

The sound of the receiver hitting the cradle struck April's eardrum. She jumped back, not expecting such a violent end to their conversation. Teegan was bitchy and critical, but never overtly enraged.

Heart beating fast, April held the phone for a second before putting it down. Then she stared at it, waiting for it to ring. The meeting was in twenty minutes. There was time for her do it if it was important. She'd proven she could be fast.

When the phone didn't ring, April opened up the design she'd started for the baby tee—a chain of daisies, nothing fancy—and exported a copy into Teegan's folder, where she'd asked her to put it earlier.

The usual procedure was for her to email when she was finished, but the meeting was in ten minutes now, and she might not see it in time.

She rubbed the intensifying muscle spasm in her shoulder for a few seconds before dialing Teegan's number again. For good or ill, it went to voicemail. She left a message letting her know the daisies were done, and hung up.

Nobody called or emailed for the remainder of the morning. She sat at her desk, working through other projects, cleaning up old ones, checking Teegan's folder for any sign she opened it and made revisions, seeing no change.

At noon she packed up and walked to the lobby, eyes locked on the elevator for sign of Teegan or her team leaving for lunch.

Virginia handed over the headset to a woman from purchasing who covered reception during lunch, and followed her out onto the street.

"You look terrible," Virginia said, looking her up and down. "Did you sleep at all last night?"

"I couldn't." April looked up at the sky: no rain, no sun, just gray. The cold wind felt good on her face. "I was home, just couldn't fall asleep."

Virginia looked behind them at the Fite building entrance. "Nobody can hear us. Tell me everything."

"Everything?"

Virginia stuck her rubber band in her mouth while she pulled her hair into another ponytail. "Mm-hm."

"You were right. I couldn't resist him. Spent Saturday night with him and then went to his place yesterday. We're seeing each other again tomorrow night." April unbuttoned her jacket and sucked in fresh air. "God, what a shitty day."

"Yeah, your life sounds rough. Sex with a hot guy all day and night. Poor you."

April smiled weakly. "Teegan's gunning for me. I don't know what's going to happen."

"She scares me."

"I just don't understand why she hates me so much. I do good work for her. Great, actually. If she gets me fired, she won't have anyone." April was certain Teegan did want her fired, and would use today as evidence against her. "I just don't understand why."

"Kate Huck—she's a merchandising assistant in Women's—says Teegan wants Rita's job. It's her only shot at management."

"But Rita's coming back. She's just on family leave."

"Everyone expects Rita to get promoted," Virginia said. "Bev likes her. She's turned people she likes into vice presidents."

"That's crazy."

"I'm just telling you the rumor."

"Teegan can't even draw," April said. "Can she?"

"I don't know. Maybe she figures she'd hire freelancers to do what she couldn't."

"Leaving her to do what, text her friends and take selfies all day?"

"Hey," Virginia said. "Don't knock the life until you try it."

"I did try it," April said, snorting. "It loses its appeal after a few years."

Virginia turned the conversation back to Zack, wanting to know everything, and April shared as many details as she was comfortable sharing, which was not as many as usual. Something about Zack, knowing he wouldn't like to have his sexual prowess described on Mission Street, no matter how complimentary she was, kept her vague and euphemistic in her descriptions.

When they got to the hot dog stand at the Ferry Building, the only meal they could afford at the trendy spot, she turned toward the buildings at the base of Bay Bridge and wondered if Zack had anyone to talk to about her. If she was important enough for him to want to.

Six weeks. She didn't need to make big plans, or expect the sort of perfect ending her brothers had—she just needed to convince him to stick around a little while longer, maybe another six months.

Surely that wasn't too much to ask of the universe. Not a lifetime; just a small piece of one. Then he could escape to his high-powered life in New York, and she'd... get back to her own art at home, and save up the money from making polka dot screen prints for Teegan and other fashion minions to get her own place. Or not. But she didn't need to figure that out now.

While she ate her hot dog, she tried to think of charms, sexual and otherwise, that would make leaving her unthinkable come the first of June.

If only she could think of some she hadn't used already.

* * *

For the rest of the month of April, they enjoyed themselves.

Never at work—although April had tried to lure him into a closet on the second floor filled with fabric remnants one morning, which he escaped (barely) at the last minute—but their evenings and weekends were a pleasure-seeking, goofy wonderland.

May arrived, hot and dry, and they still hadn't talked about the future.

A few times April had woken up in the middle of the night in a panic, pinned under his sleeping arm, tempted to prod him awake to discuss the looming issue.

They talked about the native plants of California as the wildflowers in the hills faded under the dry heat of impending summer, and she set aside her pastel drawings of sky-blue, cup-shaped *nemophila* to paint the increasingly golden hills.

They talked about her wardrobe, which had reverted back to her original unmatched, punky goodness, and how terrible she looked in khakis and twin-sets.

"So awful I lose my hard-on to even think of you wearing those clothes again," he breathed into her ear one night as his hand played her like a virtuoso's.

She laughed, not offended in the least. For one, she was about to come, and two, it was obviously untrue. He was always ready for her. He was like her first boyfriend in high school, except with self-control. Amazing self-control.

They talked about that, too—how great they were in bed together. That meant a lot to both of them. April had been with a lot of partners, which she knew could make some guys feel like they were auditioning for the role of Best Ever against a vast, faceless pool of masculine talent. And he'd lost Meg, the woman he'd chosen as his lifetime partner but who had died so young, and he was still mourning.

Which was another thing they didn't talk about.

Maybe the perfection of their sex life was why they never talked about the future. Within seconds of experiencing the slightest uneasiness, they tore off each other's clothes and spent another heavenly hour or three in bed, and the issue, whatever it was, forever unstated, was dropped.

Although she only spent the night at his condo a few times, and never had him overnight at the house, her mother guessed what she was doing and with whom.

"I haven't seen you this happy since you were ten years old," her mother said one afternoon as they gave Zeus, the male Chihuahua mix, a suppository.

With her pinkie finger gently probing the little rectum, April bit back a laugh. "You pick this moment to tell me?"

"Careful." Her mother readjusted her hold on the dog's little body. "He's got a funny look on his face."

"I bet he does." April withdrew her finger. "There. I think it'll stay up there this time."

"Terrific," her mother said. "You have a magic touch."

April released Zeus onto the tile floor, where he danced around for a moment before scurrying out of the bathroom. "That's a gift I could do without." She snapped off the latex glove and went to the sink.

Her mother patted her on the arm. "And not only with animals, I think."

April groaned. Her mother was just the type to ask her if she had ever done something similar with… "I need to get going. Zack and I are going hiking today. Got to see if I can find my boots."

"I hope you know he's welcome here anytime," her mother said. "I wouldn't mind."

"Thanks. But…"

"You like your privacy."

"Yeah."

"I can wear earplugs," her mother said. "I wouldn't hear the all the sex noises even if I wanted to, which I don't." She held up her fingers in a Scout oath.

April put her hands over her ears. "I wish I were wearing them right now. Don't talk about listening to me have sex. Just. Don't."

"I swear, your generation sees and does all kinds of kinky things—which sounds like a value judgment, but it isn't, I just don't know what else to call some of the things I see on that computer—yet you're still too prudish to have a little conversation. Like fifteen-year-old boys."

April had heard this sort of comment before. "Less talk, more do," she said. "I'd better get going. Zack will be here any minute."

Her mother looked into the mirror over the sink, fluffing her short hair with her fingers. "I'm tempted to tell him myself that he's welcome to stay here overnight. All that driving back and forth across the Bay Bridge in the dark isn't easy on either one of you."

Not wanting to subject Zack to that, April found her boots and hurried outside with Stool and her backpack, meeting Zack in the street just as he was signaling to turn into the driveway.

"Why the big backpack?" he asked, jumping out to help get

Stool into the backseat of the ride-share Chevy Volt. "Will we be camping?" He gave her a wolfish grin. They were headed for one of Oakland's vast, wooded regional parks not far from the house.

She clipped Stool's leash to the seatbelt and settled her backpack next to him. She'd filled it with a few of her portfolios and sketchbooks and hadn't yet decided if she was going to show them to him. "Just a few things. Water, energy bars, you know."

Zack gave Stool a scratch behind the ears and her a long, lingering kiss before starting the car back up. "Cool."

It wasn't until fifteen minutes later when they were starting their hike from the trailhead's parking lot that she told him. "I brought some of my drawings, if you're interested. But they're kind of heavy. We should probably leave them in the car."

He reached into the backseat and lifted the backpack. "They're not heavy, they're your art." He kissed her on the nose. "No way I'm missing the show."

"We could do it when we get back from the hike."

"Nice try, but no." He wriggled his arms into the pack, loosening the straps to fit his broad shoulders, and then gave her a longer kiss against the side of the car. "You smell like heaven. How do you do it?"

"Must be my shampoo," she said, leaning into him. "I'm not wearing anything else."

His hand found her breast and stroked her over the thin cotton of her T-shirt. "I wish."

Eventually they broke apart and began their hike up a steep narrow trail into a cathedral of redwoods, and then up higher to a rocky, sunny ridge, where they collapsed onto fallen logs to catch their breath and have a drink.

"Let's take a look," he said, reaching past the water bottle in her pack to a charcoal-stained spiral notebook.

She shot out a hand to stop him. "Hold on, not that one." She pulled out a larger vellum pad. "This."

"Why'd you bring that one if you're not going to show me?"

"A mistake."

With a raised eyebrow, he accepted the vellum pad and opened it to see a series of pen-and-ink botanical studies—mostly California wildflowers. "You've showed me a few of these already."

"No, these are older ones."

Nodding, he looked at each page, offering his praise and asking a few questions about the plant names, until she turned her head to drink from her water bottle, at which time he lunged forward and pulled out the charcoal pad before she could stop him.

"No!" she cried, but it was too late. He was already staring at the page in his lap. The dry trail had coated his knees with caramel-colored dust, but his fingers were clean.

"Wow," he said.

She leaned back and gazed at the sky. The fog had burned off in the east but lingered like white smoke in the west. "I was afraid you might be offended."

"How could I be offended? You enlarged my penis to twice its actual size. You should write a note at the bottom warning people, like on a mirror."

"Warning what people? Your other girlfriends?"

"Exactly. I don't want them to get their hopes up."

She let out the breath she'd been holding. Not every man was happy to have his girlfriend draw nude pictures of him, certainly not without his consent. "I should've asked you if it was all right," she said. "Truth is, I couldn't help myself."

"I like the sound of that."

"Huge relief, let me tell you," she said.

"Seriously, why didn't you ask? Did you really think I'd mind?"

This was even more awkward. She glanced back at the sky. "Well, you see, I was relying on my imagination."

"Well, sure, since I think I'd remember if you'd ever whipped out your notebook when we were in bed together."

"Nooooooo," she said, drawing it out as long as she could to buy time. She twisted the cap on her water bottle. "Not my memory. My *imagination*."

He looked up at her, eyes wide. "You drew these before... *before*?"

"Mmm," she said.

His playful expression faded. He looked at the drawing, falling silent.

Big mistake. She'd made a big mistake. "I'm really sorry. I think I'm sort of confessing here so I can rid myself of the guilt I've been carrying around. I never thought we'd actually get together. I... took what I could get." Oh God, she was just making it worse. "Look, we can destroy them. I'll burn them all in one of the barbecue pits near the car." She reached forward to take the notebook back.

"Like hell you will," he said, springing to his feet with the drawing pad under one arm. Wiping the sweat off his upper lip, he squinted in the distance. "We can get back to the car faster if we take the other trail."

"You're so angry you want to go home," she said. "I understand." With a sigh, she lifted the backpack.

"I'm so angry I want to go to the craft store," he said. "And get this sucker framed ASAP."

"No, you're just humoring me. You're horrified and disgusted with me."

He pulled her against him, knocking the backpack to the ground, and spoke into her ear. "I want you more than I've ever wanted you. And that's saying something."

"But—"

"Do you have any idea how badly I wanted you all winter? No. You couldn't. I've *burned* for you, April. I've—I've abused myself, wanting you, you know what I'm saying?"

She grinned. "Really?"

"And to find out you thought I was, well, worth your talents… I can't tell you what it means to me."

"I've been using my talents on you for weeks," she said. "Hadn't you noticed?"

He glanced around them before moving his hand over her ribs, down her belly, and between her legs, where he lifted the hem of her lightweight running shorts and slipped his finger under the elastic of her panties. Trailing kisses down her neck, he nibbled the tender skin, sending sparks down to her toes.

She rotated in his arms and jumped him, arms slung around his neck, legs clamped around his hips, her mouth open on his.

He grabbed her bottom and kissed her deeply, the strokes of his tongue synchronized with the motion of his hands.

She broke the kiss and said, her voice ragged, "I'd do you right there if it weren't for the poison oak." Then she glanced over his shoulder and saw two women with a dog approaching on the trail, which made her think of Stool. Her eyes found him rooting around in the undergrowth a few yards away without a leash. Reluctantly, she unclamped her legs from Zack's hips.

He dropped his hands, letting her slide to the ground. His chest was heaving. "If only I'd rented a place on this side of the bay."

She gazed to the west, where San Francisco twinkled in the

distant sun. The two women, close enough now she could see the amusement on their faces, turned and disappeared down a different trail.

"It's only—" She cut herself off. *It's only for a few more weeks,* she was going to say. After that, then what? It wasn't as if he was moving into the other house next door. A short drive across the bay was nothing compared to a cross-country flight.

"An hour is an eternity," he said, kissing her loudly on the cheek. "Let's head back. I'll put a leash on the troublesome triped."

While he chased after Stool, April slung the backpack over her shoulders, watching his handsome backside scramble around the wilderness, fearing that she was the one who couldn't stay out of trouble.

Chapter 24

ON A THURSDAY morning in early May, Zack held his weekly status meeting with Liam. Bev usually joined them, either on the phone or in person, but at the moment was too busy with the creative directors in preparation for her return to full-time work to join them.

Zack sat in a chair across from Liam at a conference room table, his palms sweaty, fidgeting with his pen. Liam hadn't said a word about him and April. It had been weeks since Liam had seen him coming out of April's hotel room. Had the Olympian decided to stay out of it, or was he waiting for the right moment to strike? Outright hostility would be easier to take than this polite chill.

Zack had finished the bulk of the surveillance work. He wouldn't call it that out loud, of course, but others had pointed out his methods were similar to a secret agent's on a mission, quietly collecting data from the shadows, avoiding involvement, averting violent conflicts.

Now his work was mostly analysis and communication—the final report, which he could do from home on his laptop.

"Sylvester Minguez called me up the other day," Liam said. Their corporate baggage—their coffee, phones, laptops, bagels, and notepads—cluttered the table between them.

Sylly, the businessman behind Mark's success from the

wedding, owned a start-up in New Jersey, and had shown some interest in Zack's consulting talents.

Since Liam hadn't asked him a direct question, he just nodded. He didn't know if Liam had a problem with him landing new clients with his family's help. Not to mention landing a girlfriend with it.

"I told him you were easy to work with," Liam continued, "but that we hadn't received your final report or implemented your ideas, so we couldn't say yet how the whole thing was going to pan out."

"I understand," Zack said. "It's too soon. He should call the other names I gave him. Clients from a few years ago."

"I'm sure he will. Sounded like he would."

The rush of satisfaction Zack should've had was tempered by the new complexity of his personal life.

New Jersey. And Sylly had mentioned June 1 as a start date, less than three weeks away. The job was perfect—high-tech, just like he wanted—but there was so little time. A few weeks of sleeping together wasn't enough time to pressure April to commit to anything. She probably wanted to keep it light, exciting, fun. If he told her he was chucking his clients on the East Coast and staying in San Francisco to be with her, she'd think he was crazy. She might refuse to see him again.

How could he blame her? He *was* crazy. Love hit him all at once, like a meteor, a blizzard, a hurricane. Their relationship wasn't strong enough to survive a direct hit from that kind of storm.

"I should have my final report to you and Bev a week early," Zack told Liam. At least he could reassure him he had this assignment under control. "Since you didn't want me to audit the financial side, I had a lot of extra time."

"I noticed you spent a little time going over the books after all," Liam said.

"I had to have some idea of what the company was up against. The numbers were pretty bad two years ago. It helps explain the morale, some of the tension."

"The numbers still aren't as great as we'd like," Liam said.

"But you're out of danger."

"For now."

"When you read my report, you'll find a lot of ways you can keep the recovery on track," Zack said. "The Annabelle Tucker publicity is great, but it won't last forever."

"*She* won't last forever," Liam said. "Not as a pop star. She's going to Princeton in the fall, taking early retirement so she can become an oncologist, Bev said. We're looking at other celebrities, but unfortunately, Bev didn't babysit anyone else with the star power of Annabelle Tucker."

"You know brand identity and marketing isn't my specialty," Zack said. "My report focuses on the internals—the management structure, morale, work flow, compensation, retention, training, all the other human issues."

"Sounds good." Liam picked up his coffee and leaned back in his chair, signaling they were done for now.

Zack wanted to mention the trouble April continued to have with Teegan but knew it would only make the situation worse. He shut his notebook and slipped it into his pocket, holding on to the pen—the one from the gas station, the one that April had admired months ago—as a prop. He'd become quite attached to the little thing.

As he rose to leave, Liam suddenly said, "One last thing— what kind of relationship do you have with my sister?"

Zack dropped the pen. *Here we go.* Clearing his throat, he

leaned over to find his pen on the floor under the table. He bumped his head as he straightened, meeting Liam's bland gaze with stars in his eyes.

"I'm not sure," he answered finally.

Liam's expression didn't change. "But she knows you're leaving?"

As much as he'd love to discuss his love life with his client, Zack felt that the close family relationship made such a pleasurable chat impossible. "I can't discuss this," he said. "I'm sorry."

"Sylly said he'd want you right away," Liam said. "He wanted to know if you might be done early, like before Memorial Day."

"I'll be in San Francisco through May. I told him that."

"Still, that's only a few weeks away," Liam said.

"I'll have time to get your report done well before then, don't worry."

Standing up, Liam shut a four-inch binder with a loud *smack*. "It's not the report I'm worried about."

* * *

A week later, while he was getting ready for a date with April, Meg's older sister, Sarah, pinged him for a video chat. He'd had the laptop open after a meeting with an old client in Boston; she must've seen he was online.

He put down his tie—he'd just decided that was a stupid idea, anyway, since April was hardly the tie type—and turned on the camera.

Sarah looked a lot like Meg, although she had been almost ten years older: straight brown hair in a bob, brown cardigan, pearl stud earrings. Unlike Meg, she held a toddler on her lap. "Look, Max, it's Uncle Zack!"

"Hi, Max," Zack said, waving. Max, her youngest, had just

turned three.

"Max and I were wondering when you'll be coming home," Sarah said.

"Hummus!" Max shouted, pointing off camera.

"He misses me terribly, I see," Zack said.

Sarah let him down, and he disappeared. "He does, but we just got back from the store."

"Ah."

"You look nice," she said. "Going out?"

He froze. Sarah would know what a big deal it was, him going out with a woman. She'd been trying to set him up for over a year, aggressively, and he'd fought her off. "Uh…" He couldn't think of one of those escape statements that wasn't a lie but didn't tell the truth, either.

His laptop was much too high-res, because she saw right through him. A smile lit up her tired face. "Zack, are you going on a *date*?"

He rubbed the corner of the laptop screen, tempted to snap it shut. He wished he weren't such a terrible liar. "Yes."

"Really?"

"Did Max like his hummus?" he peered into the blurry suburban kitchen behind Sarah's head. Both she and her husband were lawyers, but they worked in local government, and their house was modest.

"What's her name?" Sarah asked.

"I don't want to talk about this," he said. "I'm sorry."

"Of course you don't, but you have to. Who else are you going to talk to about it?"

"I don't want to talk about *it* with anybody," he said. "And it's getting late, anyway. I should be going."

"You can't even tell me her name?" Sarah pouted. "It's not like

I know her, right?"

"You don't know her."

Sarah smiled. A bag of baby carrots in Max's little fist appeared on screen.

"Open, Mommy," Max said.

Never breaking eye contact with Zack, Sarah dug a hole in the plastic bag and returned it to the waiting chubby fingers. "Is this a first date, or have you known her a while?"

Zack glanced at the clock at the top of the screen. He only had a few minutes before he had to leave to get April's house by seven. "A little of both. Look, I'm sorry, but I don't have time to explain."

"Lucky you." But Sarah was still smiling. "I hope."

He felt his neck get hot and hoped she couldn't see it. "Thanks for calling," he said. "Is Max still there? Tell him bye for me."

"Tell me her name and I'll let you go," Sarah said.

"April." He intentionally left off the last name. He didn't think Sarah followed his clients that closely, but she was a lawyer and had an astonishing memory for detail.

Sarah put a hand on her chest. "April in April. How prophetic. Have a lovely time." Then she raised her voice. "Max! Come say bye-bye to Uncle Zack!"

A huge hand, pink and blurry, waved in front of the camera, and then they all said their goodbyes for a second and third time before Zack hung up.

His heart was beating too hard. It was like the night years ago when he'd told his parents he couldn't share their faith. He'd cut something, publicly, that he'd held to himself for too long. He wasn't the same person he'd been and he couldn't pretend that he was. But it was hard. He didn't want to hurt anyone. He wanted to be the man they wanted and needed, the one they'd loved.

Sarah had smiled, but the grief was there, looking over their shoulders, casting a shadow, reminding them of what could've been.

Poor Sarah. She'd loved Meg, her baby sister, so much. It killed him to remember the look on Sarah's face when he'd told her it was over, her baby sister was gone.

As much as he'd loved his wife, her family's grief had dwarfed his. He'd carried the guilt of that with him for years. There simply hadn't been any time to love her as much as she'd deserved.

Zack rubbed his face and stood up, wishing Sarah had chosen a different moment to call. Now he was stuck in the past again. April was the fun, buoyant type—she deserved a guy who was as happy and lively as she was.

Could you fake that?

He checked himself one last time in the mirror and ran out the door.

Chapter 25

"I CAN'T BELIEVE I never ate there before," April said as she and Zack left the little Nepalese restaurant in Berkeley. The evening breeze blowing along Solano Avenue was refreshing after the rich, stuffy air of the restaurant—and an hour and a half of stilted conversation. During that time, Zack had said two dozen words at most, and only when the situation demanded it.

She paused and watched him walk ahead a few paces. Still not a word out of him. Until now, she'd given him the benefit of the doubt, thinking he might've been tight-lipped inside the crowded restaurant because they'd sat wedged between two other couples. But it looked like the problem was with him.

"We have ten minutes to make it to the theater," he said, staring at his phone as he continued to walk away from her. "I hope that's enough time to find parking."

"Are you all right?" she called after him.

He looked up from his phone, saw she wasn't next to him, and spun around. "Excuse me?"

"Are you all right?"

"Sure. Of course." He gave her a tight smile. "Why wouldn't I be?"

"Maybe you'd like to skip the movie. It's okay with me if you do. I don't want to sit there feeling like you're suffering through it."

Or my company, she added silently to herself.

"I don't understand. Don't *you* want to see it?"

Apparently, he didn't feel like being honest with her. She'd never been much of a therapist, drawing people out of themselves.

Yes, it was definitely better to call it a night. She was afraid she might pick a fight just to break apart that fortress of silence of his, and that wasn't part of her Six Week Charm Offensive at all, now faltering in week four. "Actually, no. I think I'd like to go home," she said. "Maybe we could get together later this week."

"What do you mean, maybe?"

"I mean if you're up for it."

He frowned. "What's your problem?"

From the spark in his eyes, the first she'd seen all night, she realized he was hungering for an argument. Her ex-boyfriend had been like that most of the time, letting off steam by debating every little thing with her, no matter how trivial, and it had been fun for a while—ragingly great makeup sex—but exhausting and destructive. She wasn't going to have that kind of relationship again. Not with Zack.

She looked up the street to where he'd parked his shared car, a yellow Mini this time, as bright as a buttercup. "Do you think you could drive me home?"

He stared at her. "Are you serious?"

"Yes." She smiled politely, but inside her chest was tight. Was it her table manners? The way she'd chatted with an old friend who'd happened to be seated near them?

Was he initiating his departure sequence?

When he didn't move, she pivoted and started walking down the street, away from the car. "Never mind, I'll catch a bus." She chided herself inwardly for lacking patience with him, but she couldn't bear to look at his unexpressive face another second. She waved at him over her shoulder, forcing a smile to show there were no hard feelings.

He didn't move at first. Then he jogged after her. "April, hold it."

She kept walking. "It's no big deal," she said. "It's been a long day. Maybe we could have lunch tomorrow."

He took her arm. "I'll drive you home." He sounded tired.

Maybe that's all it was—a lack of sleep. He'd mentioned he'd been up late the night before and then was up early for a phone meeting with a client. He'd been having a lot of those, planning his business for the rest of the year. He didn't hide the fact that they were all in the northeast, a fact that was causing her recurrent stomach cramps.

She slowed and looked at him.

"It's the least I can do," he said. "Come on."

She stopped. It would take her forever to catch a bus and then transfer to another one that went up into the hills. And she didn't want him to think she was angry at him and then start looking forward to babes in New York who weren't so touchy. "All right. Thank you."

They walked wordlessly to the car. She got in, biting her lip to stop herself from asking him questions about what was on his mind. If she was quiet and gave him a chance to talk, he'd open up on his own. Now that he knew it was important to her, he'd come up with some cursory explanation of whatever it was—trouble with a client, a failed investment, intestinal parasite, whatever—and she'd nod sympathetically. They'd part on friendly terms, she'd suggest lunch again tomorrow, and then instead of eating, they'd end up in bed at his place.

But he drove through the Berkeley city streets to Oakland and then up into the hills without a word.

She tried to remember if the dinner date had been her idea, if she'd pressured him into it. He was usually the one to initiate getting together—not because she was shy, God knew, but because he was so wonderfully eager. Maybe he was uncomfortable with her taking any initiative in the relationship. He did have an old-fashioned streak as wide as a ten-lane California freeway.

Well, if that was it, he'd have to get over it.

When he pulled into her driveway, she was thoroughly annoyed with herself for letting the date go on as long as it had. What the hell had happened to her pride? She was cowering in the passenger seat like a freshman cheerleader with the captain of the football team. If she sucked up any more, she'd swallow her lips.

To hell with it. If he wanted to talk, he'd talk. If he wanted to be with her, he'd find a way. She liked him, that hadn't changed. She couldn't control whatever strange brew of emotion and biochemicals was bubbling inside him.

She opened the door and put a foot out on the driveway. "Thank you for dinner and the ride."

He cleared his throat. "You're welcome."

She climbed out and slammed the door, turning her attention to the house with a sigh. Lights spilled out of the windows on the ground floor, warm and glowing, and her mother's piano music faintly peppered the evening quiet. She'd snuck into the house after curfew many times when she was a teenager, never appreciating what she was running away from.

Older and wiser, older and wiser.

Next door, Liam and Bev's house was also bright and stirring with life. Just the day before, Merry had eaten her first slice of watermelon—rind and all. The mess in her diaper a few hours later had been spectacular.

"Are you all right?" Zack asked.

She'd just been standing there like a zombie. He probably thought she wanted something from him. A good-night kiss would've been nice, but she'd gotten the message. "I'm great." She waved, headed for path through the lavender. "Have a nice night."

She heard the beep of his car alarm setting and his footsteps following. "I'll see you to the door," he said.

"Gentlemanly of you," she muttered.

"Better late than never."

She glanced at him as she pulled open the screen door. His eyes were fixed on hers, sad but intent.

"Is there—are you feeling—" She clamped her mouth shut. No. She wouldn't pry. She would learn self-restraint if it killed her. The door swung open and she turned to him with a polite smile. "There. I'm in," she said. "Thanks again."

"How about dinner tomorrow?"

She studied his face, not understanding him at all. "Okay," she said finally.

"My place?"

They couldn't keep on having sex instead of talking. "Mine," she said.

He nodded and then kissed her quickly before ushering her into the house and walking away.

* * *

April was so unbalanced by the bad date with Zack, she lingered in the kitchen with a cup of herbal tea, waiting for her mother to come by on her way to bed and keep her company for a few minutes.

Stool sprawled on his side at her feet, as motionless as roadkill. She sipped her chamomile tea, a small smile lifting the corner of her mouth, remembering the day she'd adopted him. He had unfortunate gustatory preferences, but he was worth it. She reached down and scratched his warm belly.

Her mother appeared in the kitchen doorway. "Back so soon?"

April met her gaze and nodded.

"Trouble?"

She nodded.

"Let me get my own cup. Just a minute." Her mother put a kettle on the stove—she didn't believe in microwaving much of anything—and went through the cupboards, getting her cup, her tea, a saucer. Finally, the water boiled, she poured, and she sat across from April at the old table, an expectant look on her face.

"Did you know his wife died of cancer?" April said without preamble. "She was younger than I am now."

"I thought there might be something like that."

April set down her cup, surprised. "You did?"

Her mother nodded. "I thought so in January, when he came for the picnic."

"I can't believe it," April said. "How do you see those things? You can't find your car in the parking lot at Target, but you know a complete stranger is nursing a tragedy in his past."

"People are a lot more interesting than cars. I pay better attention."

April sipped her tea and considered upgrading to vodka. "Well, you were right. He's kind of screwed up."

"Aren't we all?"

"He still loves her," April said. "I can feel it."

"Love isn't a pie," her mother said.

"Love isn't—what?"

"Always plenty to go around." Her mother put her hand over

hers. Her fingernails were trimmed short and unpolished. "But maybe you're right." Her gaze drifted to the floor, where Stool was running jerkily in his sleep. Did he have four legs in his dreams?

"Right about what?" April asked.

Her mother gave her a pat, her smile falling. "About Zack." Her voice sounded tired.

April pulled her hand away. "In what way?"

"He's not right for you. Or, what I mean is, you're not right for him."

April couldn't speak for a moment. "Why do you say that?"

"Oh, don't look like that, honey," her mother said. "I just mean... he's not the kind to play the field. He plays for keeps. He's the serious type."

April managed to say, "And I'm not, right? I'm not serious?"

Her mother batted big sympathetic eyes at her. "You're wonderful, but you're not serious the way Zack is serious. He's more than halfway in love with you, anyone can see that. An all-or-nothing kind of man. I just don't think you're ready for that kind of commitment. You're a free spirit."

"Here I thought you were trying to set us up," April said.

"Maybe I was. Before I'd met him, before I'd realized how deep his feelings run. I think it's been good for him to have a little fun, but I'm worried he's going to get hurt."

Her mother was worried about *him* getting hurt. "I'm capable of love, you know." She sounded ridiculous. If her mother didn't believe that, who would?

"This is a time for you to focus on yourself as a person. You've started a new career, which is wonderful, but you're still living at home."

April's face heated. "I thought you didn't mind—you'd even like having me around—" She heard the strain in her voice.

"But you'd love to have your own place. You're more than ready for it."

Standing, April walked to the sink and poured out the rest of her grassy beverage. "You're right. I'll get my own place as soon as I can find one."

"I've blown it, haven't I?" Trixie came over and caught her hand again between both of hers. "I love you just the way you are. I love having you around as long as you want to stay. You're my baby. I love you."

"I'm not—" April's voice cracked. She could hardly say *I'm not a baby* and then start crying. Smiling tightly, she kissed her mother on the cheek and drew back, nodding. She had to change the subject or she was going to lose it. "I'm having trouble at work with some of the design assistants. Since Rita's been out on leave, they've ramped up the hate. It's kind of wearing on me."

"Not you. You're invincible."

"You'd think so, but it turns out I have a few weak spots," April said.

"And you don't want to talk to Liam and Bev about it," her mother said.

"I need to handle this on my own."

"And Zack?"

"He'd like to help, but I don't want him interfering either."

"It's complicated now," her mother said. "No wonder you're upset."

"Yeah."

"Well, the night is young. You have time to get a really good night's sleep before tackling all of this tomorrow. It always seems worse at night. Go to bed, take some melatonin, and borrow my lavender eye pillow if you'd like, and I'm sure you'll wake up fresh and ready in the morning."

April nodded, realizing her mother's company wasn't what she'd needed tonight after all. A few shots and grunge music blasting in her ears would've been a lot more therapeutic.

After a hug and another few soothing words that didn't, her mother said good night and left her alone in the kitchen.

So. She finally got involved with a genuinely nice guy, and her own mother didn't think she was good enough for him.

Chapter 26

THE NEXT MORNING, April arrived at work to find Rita standing near the color printer.

"You're back!" April cried, beaming at her.

Rita picked up a stack of printouts and smiled back. "I decided to come in at the last minute."

"Your kids are better?"

"Back in school, trying to get caught up," Rita said. She made a face. "Them and me both."

April strode to her desk and put down her bag. "It's great to see you. I'm so glad they're okay. That must've been horrible for you."

Rita hovered in the opening of her cubicle, saying nothing. April assumed she was lost in her own thoughts, reading through the printouts, but then she realized her boss wanted to talk.

April didn't like the awkward look on her face. She stood up taller. "What is it?"

Rita looked behind her, chewing her lip. "We need to talk."

April's mind flew back over the most recent drama with her biggest fan upstairs. "Is this about Teegan?"

"The situation has escalated to such a point... I'm not sure what I can do. If the design team really doesn't want to work with you, I'm not in a position to override them. I haven't been here, you know?"

Romantic drama and fitful alcohol-dazed sleep had already worn her down. She rubbed her eyes, trying to think clearly. "I'm not sure what to say. I did the best I could."

"I'm sure you did," Rita said. "It's not fair to judge you based on a few complaints after you'd been left here on your own after only a couple months, but that's all I have to go on. I've been gone. I don't really know what's been happening."

April hadn't even taken off her jacket yet. She looked at her bag, slumping sideways on the desk next to a pile of T-shirts and sketches. "Are you going to fire me?"

Rita didn't meet her eyes. "Well, you're a freelancer, so, technically, you're not actually an employee that would be fired."

Since she'd been kidding, shock temporarily pushed the air out of April's lungs. "Not technically."

"I'd like to set up a meeting with your brother, but he's not in the office today."

 April nodded dully.

"I'll see if I can set something up first thing tomorrow," Rita said. "It might have to wait until Monday, if he's not back."

April glanced at the red blinking light on her phone, the pile of unfinished designs. "I should get to work. Teegan's not the only one waiting for me."

"Yes, I know," Rita said, sounding pained.

April picked up a swatch of elastic orange fabric and began yanking it between her fingers, taking out her anger on it. "You got other complaints?"

"People didn't seem to believe I was on an official leave of absence," Rita said. "I had too much phone mail to listen to all of it, and the email covers four pages, but I got the idea. I was going to work from home the rest of the week, catching up, but after I started going through it, I realized I had to come in and deal in person."

Partially recovered from her shock, April sat up straight. "It can't be *that* bad."

"April, I'm really sorry, but I'm not on very strong footing myself right now. I've been gone for over two months. That's a really long time. I'm lucky they didn't replace me."

"They couldn't, could they? Legally?"

Rita lowered her voice. "My kids have been back in school for a while. I... needed more time to be with them. I wasn't ready to come back. Bev and Liam were very understanding."

April let that sink in. "They *should* be understanding. Sounds like you needed to recover." She could relate.

"Thanks." Rita smiled faintly. "But they should've hired somebody to cover for me. It wasn't fair to dump it all on you."

"I was doing fine," April said. "Really. I do good work. I know this sounds catty, but Teegan seemed to have it in for me. Seriously."

Rita looked doubtful. "We'll try to clear the air in the morning. Just do your best until then."

As inadequate as you assume that'll be, April thought.

Coffee. She'd need coffee before she could face the rest of this day. She dug into her wallet for a few bills. The truck in the alley would have to be good enough. There wasn't time to walk to her favorite café.

But just then a young woman with long brown hair appeared behind her with a men's bright-red track jacket and a presentation board as big as she was. April had never seen her before.

"We need this by ten," the woman said.

April smiled tightly. She'd never thought her own manners were exemplary, but working at Fite had changed her mind.

"Good morning. I'm April Johnson. You are..."

"Darrin sent me. You know him, right?"

"He's the creative director for the Men's department," April said. "And who are you?"

"We'll start working on it right away, Hayley," Rita said.

The petite brunette rolled her eyes at April and walked away.

"What is the matter with people around here? No time for a simple introduction?" April stood up. "Seriously. What is it about this place?"

Rita held out the board and jacket. "You'll want to do this first. Darrin could be an ally for you against Jennifer and Teegan, if it comes to that."

April took it from her and set it up on her desk with shaking hands. She didn't have the temperament to roll over and take the abuse this job seemed to require, she just didn't have it. Surely Rita could see the steam coming out of her ears. Her face had to be as red as the men's jacket in her hands.

"No problem," she said in a flat voice, opening the program on her computer.

April *knew* she was good. For months she'd done amazing work with few resources and no support. And they were going to shit-can her.

She could've thrown the Men's presentation board on the floor and danced the Macarena all over it. But she didn't care enough about Teegan or Fite to fly off the handle and make things worse for herself.

So she worked. She quickly completed the variegated stripe pattern Darrin so desperately needed, designing several color options and printing them out—possibly before the charming Hayley had even made it back to her desk.

Then she worked steadily through the rest of the pile, a

paragon of talent and efficiency.

Rita left their office around ten to "put out fires" upstairs—April bit back a joke about always having been a pyromaniac—and didn't return before noon, when April needed to leave so she could get home to Merry. Her plan was to take Merry to the tot park and get inspired by the toddlers staggering around the sandbox. Merry loved to watch the babies who'd mastered the walking thing, and April was eager to soak up the happy baby energy and some spring sun. She was going to count her blessings and put Teegan and Rita out of her mind until she could defend herself in the morning.

Unfortunately, when she got home an hour later, and then walked next door to pick up her niece, Bev met her at the door. Her eyes were fretful, her lips pinched with worry.

April stiffened. "What happened?"

"Oh, April, this is the worst timing."

April's gaze finally found Merry bouncing happily inside her plastic entertainment center. She looked fine, eight months old but as big as a toddler, but that didn't mean anything with Merry. She cried when she was healthy. "Is it another ear infection?" Merry had already had two in her short life, one in each ear.

Bev caught her arm and led her inside. "Come in. We have to talk."

Jesus. What now? April closed her eyes for a second before joining Bev on the sofa. She put her hands on her knees and waited for it to hit.

"We've found a permanent nanny," Bev said in a rush, her blue eyes huge and melting. "I'm so sorry. I was going to wait a little longer before we even started looking for a long-term, full-time person, but Alicia just moved up here from Orange County and called me up out of the blue. She was the nanny for one of my best friends in high school. I mean, not my friend, my friend's baby. She's six now. The baby, I mean—which means she's not a baby anymore, of course—"

"You found a nanny," April said.

Bev took a deep breath, let it out. "Forgive me for babbling. Yes. We think so. I wanted you to know as soon as possible."

Finding a loose thread on her jacket, April followed it to the seam and snapped it off. She should touch that up with a needle later to stop it from completely unraveling. "Her name's Alicia?"

"Yes, she's originally from Venezuela. She's in her early fifties, used to own a bakery, and has three grown children of her own. She showed me pictures."

"How long have you been interviewing?" April asked.

"No, we weren't. That's why I feel so bad. It all happened so fast. We never would've started this process without telling you first. You've been a fantastic help, but you never signed on to be full-time or permanent and we wouldn't expect you to." Bev gave her a weak smile. "Liam is teasing me that I only want to hire her because she's a professionally trained pastry chef."

"It's okay. You told me from the beginning you were going to get a full-time person."

"Yes, but not today!"

April swallowed. "Today?"

"Well, she's going to come by every day for a little while so they can get used to each other." Bev put a hand on her arm. "We'll always be grateful to you. Anytime you want to be with Merry, just say so. We'll tell your mom the same thing. Liam thinks she might be upset."

"Why?"

"Because of you," Bev said. "He thinks your mom secretly wanted you to be our full-time nanny, keep it all in the family."

April smiled. "Yeah, Mom likes having me around, but I don't think she'd be angry or anything."

"Well, I didn't think so, but you know how your brother is."

"Yeah, I know how he is," April said, imagining their impending meeting with Rita. Now that she wasn't needed as a babysitter, he wouldn't be under any pressure to put up with her at Fite. "When is the nanny coming today?"

Bev ran a hand through her dark hair. "In an hour."

Chest constricting, April stood up. "Okay." She forced a smile. "We'll go to the park another time, then." Careful not to glance at Merry, whose chubby cheeks would make her lose it for sure, April made for the door.

"I hope you will," Bev said.

April turned. "Of course I will."

"Whenever you have time. I mean that. We've told Alicia that the family will come first."

April managed another smile as she stepped out into the midday sun.

In a daze, she walked over to her mother's house. She picked up the forgotten morning newspaper, flicking off a snail as big as a plum, and went inside.

She didn't want to talk to her mother. She didn't want to talk to anyone. She herded all four dogs into the living room, gathering their leashes for a walk, grateful none of them could talk.

She didn't even want to talk to Zack. Although they'd done a great job of avoiding tough conversations so far, they couldn't keep it up forever.

Chapter 27

As soon as he got home from work, Zack dropped his backpack next to his cardboard coffee table and threw himself onto the couch.

Every hour he felt worse about the way he'd shut down at the restaurant last night. He'd been aware of it at the time—he'd seen himself eat and drink without making eye contact, smiling, or chatting, but he'd been powerless to overcome the old, familiar ice that had crystallized around him, turning him into an untouchable statue. It wasn't that he was thinking concrete thoughts about Meg, remembering her face or conversations with her. It was the grief, just the heavy, drowning essence of it, that had dogged him since his conversation with Sarah.

He pulled his shirttails out of his pants and stared at the sky out the window. A smudge of grime on the glass distracted him. He got up and tried to rub it off with his thumb, but it was on the wrong side. He turned away in frustration and stalked into the kitchen to make coffee. He didn't really want any but needed something to do with his hands.

Time to get his head screwed on straight. If he could figure out how.

He poured some coffee beans into the grinder and flipped the switch. The harsh, high-pitched whine pierced the air, sharpening his thoughts.

Some things, perhaps, he couldn't do by himself. Since Sarah was the one to trigger this problem, maybe she could be the one to bail him out. He used the landline to call her at home.

She was immediately alarmed. "What's wrong?"

"Nothing," Zack said quickly. "I just—nothing. Is this a bad time?"

"Hold on, let me tell Robert to watch Max. This sounds serious."

"It's not—" But Sarah was already yelling at her husband to come and get Max, turn on a video, she'd be a while. Then he heard a door slam and Sarah's breathing as she returned to the phone.

"There. All set. Go ahead."

Zack deeply regretted his impulse to call. "It's really nothing, Sarah. I had a few extra minutes and thought I'd check in. I had to cut you off the other night."

"Because of your date."

The phone fell silent. "Yes," he said finally.

"I look forward to meeting April."

Zack closed his eyes. She was so eager for him to find someone else. She had been for a long time.

He poured hot water into his coffee press, "Sarah..."

"I shouldn't pressure you." She sounded amused. "It's just so hard not to. You're so obviously embarrassed about it."

"I'm sorry." His voice was rough.

"Oh, don't be."

"You were all so good to me," he said. "Look, whatever happens, I want you to know how much I appreciated it."

She paused. "You sound like you're about to jump off a bridge. What's going on?"

"Nothing." Everything. "I was just thinking about you. All of you."

"Wow, this thing is serious," she said.

"Thing?"

"With April."

He held the press down over his coffee, counting the seconds. "It was on my mind before I moved out here. How much I appreciate all of you."

"Appreciate. There's that word again. Appreciate for what?"

He took a breath. "You know. Taking me into the family."

Her voice became impatient. "Of course we took you into the family."

"You didn't have to. You barely knew me. Hell, Meg barely knew me."

"Don't say that. You know time doesn't work that way, not when you're living at the hospital. My God, you were always there. Every morning, every evening. How could we *not* love you?"

He was grateful, he was, but in his tired moments, he admitted to himself it could be a burden. "It's been four years, Sarah. I haven't done anything since then to merit the kind of loyalty your family has shown me. Your dad still refers clients to me. Just last week your mom sent me an email saying she missed me, that I'd been in San Francisco too long. And you... you want me to get married again."

"Everyone has to grieve in their own way." Her voice fell. "You're a piece of Meg. We want you to be happy, like we'd want her to be happy. And we don't want to let go."

"I know." He pinched the bridge of his nose. "I know. But..."

"But what?"

Zack had to say it. If not now, he never would. "It's a bit much. It has always seemed a little like"—he swallowed over his hesitation—"maybe you were overcompensating."

"What? I have no idea what you mean."

"I loved her. No matter what I tell you now, I don't want you to think I blame her, or that I resent her for anything, because I don't. I wouldn't give up a moment that we had together."

"Of course you loved her," she said. "But what—"

"She was about to break up with me before she got the diagnosis, wasn't she?" he asked.

She paused. "No."

"It's all right," he said. "I meant what I said. I understand."

"She was having doubts about getting married so soon, that's all. Engaged after only two months."

"But we weren't engaged," he said. "She turned me down."

"You were living together when she got sick."

"Yes, but she didn't want to get married," he said.

"But I remember her telling us, me and Mom, right before you moved in together. It was Mother's Day, and we were having brunch at this cute place with mimosas that would knock your socks off at eleven in the morning. She said you'd bought her a ring but you were going to live together for a year before telling anyone else about it."

"She was lying," he said, the anger in his voice for himself, not poor Meg. "She wouldn't commit."

"What?"

"She was worried about what your mother would think about moving in together so soon." He poured his coffee into the sink and dumped the grounds into the bin. "She confessed a few days later, when we were buying a shower curtain at Target. We got in a huge fight. She wanted me to play along with her whole family thinking we were getting married, even if she hadn't made up her mind yet."

Sarah was silent for a long moment. "She always did care too much what other people thought of her," she said softly. "Especially Mom."

"If I hadn't loved her so much, I would've ended it right then."

A long silence grew. She let out a sigh. "I'm so sorry. She did love you. I'm sure she did."

They'd rushed the wedding so they'd be full partners when she began treatment, so she'd have more to live for. The pressure to tie the knot "while they still could" had been overwhelming. Not just from him, but from her whole family.

"I think maybe you're not so sure," he said. "And neither are your parents. I just want you to know it's OK. I'm OK."

"Oh, Zack." It sounded as if she were crying.

"I think I'd better hang up before I say something else. Give my love to Max."

"No, wait—"

"Love you too. All of you." He pressed the button and set the phone on the counter. His shoulders felt lighter, as if strings pulled him to the ceiling.

He'd done it. He'd finally said it out loud. The sympathy for the poor sap who'd loved a little too quickly, too deeply, had finally come to an end. It had nagged at him for years. Now Sarah knew that he knew, and she could tell the rest of the family. They could all, finally, stop trying to make it up to him.

He could move on.

He picked up the phone and called April.

* * *

April was at the dog park with Stool and her mom's three Chihuahuas when Zack called. She was still reeling from their bad date the night before, the threat of losing her Fite job, and the nearing end of her routine days with Merry.

"Look, I'm sorry," she told him, "but I'm not up for anything tonight. It's been a long day." She kept a suspicious eye fixed on Stool, who sniffed the bark chips for feces like a teenager looking for stray Cheetos under the couch cushions.

"Anything serious?"

"No, just work," she said.

"Just work?" he asked in mock horror. "Since when is work 'just'?"

She smiled, not that he could see it. "My point."

A long pause stretched between them. Then he said, "I'm trying to think of how I can redeem myself for last night."

"It's not necessary." She readjusted the phone at her ear, wary but enjoying the sound of his voice.

"It is to me," he said.

"Just answer me this," she began, "is it anything to do with me?"

"No," he said quickly, emphatically. "Nothing to do with you."

Nothing to do with me. He hadn't mentioned having any other relationships since his marriage. Could *she* be his first?

April twisted a strand of hair between her fingers. Did she want to be? "Is something wrong at work?"

"No, that's going fine."

"What, then?"

"I'm not sure you'd like to hear this."

She had to ask. Her mouth was dry. "Were you thinking about Meg?" It hurt to talk about it, but it would hurt more not to.

He didn't answer right away. "Her sister called me last night, right before I came over. I started thinking about the old days, when Meg was in the hospital, and it kind of put me in a mood."

Closing her eyes for a moment, she let out a deep breath. "I wish you'd told me."

"I'm sorry."

"I went through cancer with my dad. If you ever want to talk, I can take it."

"Thanks." He cleared his throat. "Really, it means a lot, that you understand."

Except she knew she didn't really understand. She'd never lost a partner, a husband, the love of her—

"I'd better go," she said. "Stool is watching a Great Dane take a dump and I don't like the way he's licking his chops."

He laughed. "Have you eaten? I'll come by and cook something for you. You won't have to go anywhere."

"You don't have to do that. It's late, you must be tired…"

"Please," he said. "I've been beating myself up all day for ruining our date last night. I need you to put me out of my misery."

"Watching Stool has kind of ruined my appetite."

"Avert your eyes and think of chicken curry."

She coughed. "Not working. The Great Dane has diarrhea."

He groaned and laughed along with her. "Pasta with grilled vegetables, then. Nothing brown. And I'll leave whenever you say the word."

She pulled out the wad of plastic bags in her pocket, ready to intercept Stool's meal, but the Great Dane's owner was already there with a long-handled plastic scoop. Thank God.

"Okay," she said. "But not for the night. I need to sleep." She could've used her mom down the hall as an excuse, but they both knew Trixie Johnson was an earthy, sex-positive, and grandmother-oriented woman.

"Deal," he said.

And so he drove over to make her dinner. As soon as he

stepped foot in the house, her mother announced she was out to the movies, grabbed her jacket, and was gone. And two hours later, April watched Zack's long, deft fingers dry the last dish. She loved the look of his dark hair against his fair skin, the strong bones of his wrists, the flex of his forearm muscles. He had a deliberate grace to his movements, in the kitchen and in the bedroom. Never hurried—well, never in a bad way. Confident but careful.

Through a vulnerable haze of longing, she watched him pour her a second glass of chardonnay. The grilled vegetables had been good, especially with the Spanish cheeses he'd brought over from a gourmet shop in San Francisco. His skills were apparently limitless.

"I like a man who cooks for me," she said, too tired to edit what she said. "It's very sexy."

It was just after nine, and the city lights of the Bay Area outside the window below them flickered in the night.

He hooked an arm around her waist and brushed his lips along her cheek. "You're beautiful, you know that?"

She closed her eyes and felt his breath on her temple. "Thanks." She tilted her head, hoping he'd kiss her neck. "So are you."

He smiled against her skin and did as she hoped, kissing his way across her jaw to the thrumming pulse under her ear. "I hope tonight made up for last night."

"You don't have to be perfect, you know."

He tensed a little before putting his other arm around her. "I like to try anyway." He found her mouth and teased her lips with his tongue, and the playfulness turned demanding. Deepening the kiss, he pressed her against the counter, wedging his body between her legs.

Her exhaustion melted away. Clasping the back of his head, she sucked his tongue into her mouth and hooked her legs around his hips. With a groan, he lifted her higher, clearing the counter with an urgent sweep of his hand.

This was good. This was easy. She knew how to do this.

Then why was her heart beating so fast? If he weren't holding her up to the counter, she would've fainted to the floor.

She cared. She cared in that deep, sticky, helpless way.

Oh, God.

She held him and closed her eyes and waited for the panic to subside. At that same moment, however, he lifted her T-shirt and began kissing the swell of her breast above her bra, and she opened her eyes and saw her five-year-old self's white handprint on red burlap hung on the wall behind him, right next to the framed photograph of Liam and Mark dressed as bottles of ketchup and mustard for Halloween.

"Not here," April said, catching his face between her hands.

He looked up at her. "I don't want to drive all the way back to San Francisco again."

"My room," she said.

"Are you sure?"

Was that why she was so nervous? Because she'd known she was going to invite him to stay? This was her home, home of the real April. Nobody had ever shared her bed here before. She nodded.

"Thank God." Licking his lips, he glanced down at her chest before helping her off the counter. "I don't know what it is you do to me, but it's a lot. More than a lot. It's unbelievable."

"Believe it, baby." She smirked, trying to lighten the mood, but her knees wobbled as her feet hit the floor.

His dark eyes caught hers as he ran a hand up her cheek and

clasped her face. "I'm serious, April. You have no idea what you're doing to me. I've been obsessed with you ever since..." He stared for a long moment before turning abruptly, clasping her arm to draw her out of the kitchen. "Upstairs?"

She held back. "Ever since what?"

He looked at her out of the corner of his eye. "Ever since I met you."

Her heart skipped a beat, tripping over itself as it broke into a run.

"You almost called security," she said.

"Even then I knew you were dangerous." He caught her hand.

She led him up to her room with its pink-and-black decorating scheme from her high school years, wishing she'd done a little revamping when she'd moved back in last November. Her easel was balanced on top of an antique steamer trunk near the window, a box of pastels overturned beneath it, and an uneven stack of sketches spilled out of a plastic basket.

She also hadn't put away her laundry that morning; it was clean and folded, but piled at the foot of the bed. She jogged ahead and moved it aside, then picked up the old romance paperback from her pillow, plucking out the lime-green panties she'd been using as a bookmark before she shoved it onto an overflowing shelf near her suitcase. She hadn't put that away in the closet, thinking it was a good reminder that she was only passing through.

The bed was small, but at least the sheets were clean. She felt an odd twinge of discomfort. Nerves again. The real April was on full display.

Zack came close and stood behind her. He slid his hands up her arms and played with her hair, stroked her neck, moved back down her body. While he kissed her throat, he moved his hand under her shirt to pull down the cup of her bra. Teasing her nipple between his fingers, he lifted her shirt over her head and pulled her hard against him, his hips grinding into her bottom.

Her body didn't respond with its usual charge, as if some of the wires weren't connected properly. She looked out the window at Liam and Bev's house and found her thoughts drifting to Merry's new nanny, Bev's return to Fite full-time, her own failures.

"Are you all right?" Softening his touch, he moved around until they were face-to-face. He kissed her lightly on the lips, smiling. "April?"

Her mom was worried about him getting hurt. That was cute.

"You're leaving soon," she said.

His smile fell. He kept his hands on her shoulders, but moved back a few inches. "Yes," he said.

Her heart pounded in her ears. "Any chance you'll stick around?"

Chapter 28

APRIL'S STOMACH TIED itself in knots as she waited for him to reply.

Finally he said, "I've signed a contract. With that friend of Mark's." His thumb drew a circle in the hollow of her collarbone. "It's a software start-up in New Jersey."

"Yes," she said. "I know."

"This doesn't have to be the end," he said, "just because I'm leaving."

She squirmed out of his arms and went over to the window. He'd repeated it twice now; he was really going.

"April?"

"What did you have in mind?" she asked. "For this not ending?" She tried to keep her voice calm.

"Will you turn around and look at me? I feel like you're angry."

Was she? She stared down at Bev's new minivan in the driveway next door. She'd been angry at Bev for hiring a nanny so suddenly without consulting her about the choice. She was just the flaky aunt, but she and Merry had a special bond. Bev and Liam should've introduced her to the woman and asked her what she thought before plowing ahead with the deal, just as a courtesy.

But angry at Zack? What had he ever done that she could be

angry with? He'd supported her at work, helped her with her family, pleasured her in bed—and the entire time he'd been clear about his ambitions to grow his business back in New York, where he lived, and where he had always stated would return before the first week in June.

He'd done nothing wrong except be wonderful and temporary. Temporarily wonderful. Wonderfully temporary.

She turned. She'd had a lot of arguments with guys over the years where her temper fueled her jets, told her what to say, but that was no help now. The secret deep inside her chest was too small and new to blaze forward with demands, ideas, exclamations.

She didn't want him to go. Desperately. What could she say?

Crossing her arms to cover herself, she licked her dry lips. "If you don't want to end it, what did you have in mind?"

He paused. "Come with me." Eyes blazing, he strode over to her. "There are dozens and dozens of garment companies that need graphic designers. You've got a portfolio now. You can charge a higher hourly wage—you're not charging nearly enough, by the way—and work more hours."

Her mind went numb. Following him to New York had never occurred to her, not even once.

Well, she'd never claimed to be the genius in the family.

"New York would be great for you," he continued. "You'd love it. The more I think about it, the better it sounds. Not for me—and it would be, I'm not denying that—but for you. The opportunities are unmatched anywhere in the country or even the world."

"Hold it." Chest squeezing, she walked away from him to retrieve her shirt from the floor, where it had fallen next to the hamper filled with her sketches. She saw the top page, a drawing of a lemon tree in black cross-hatching, and remembered the afternoon the summer before when she'd drawn it. Had it only been a year ago she'd been alone, ignorant of Zack's existence, happily immune?

Her mom didn't think she was the long-term type, and maybe she hadn't been. Until now. Zack had changed everything. She'd tasted something and now she wanted more—but not at any price. She wasn't going to give up the best part of her life—her mom, her brothers, her new sisters-in-law, and, of course, Merry— for a career. Not his and not hers.

He hadn't even considered staying. He talked about his contract with a client he'd never met as a holy unbreakable bond.

She'd been so stupid.

She pulled the shirt over her head and turned to face him. "I'm not going to leave my family."

"It wouldn't be forever. Have you ever lived away from home? It might be good for you."

Her shoulders stiffened. "Oh, would it?"

"I'm speaking from experience. Putting a little distance between you and your parents—or parent and brothers—can really help you find yourself."

"Except it isn't me I'd be finding, is it?" She heard the rising edginess in her own voice. Maybe she was going to fly off the handle after all. "I'd be giving up everything that's really important to me so that you can get that juicy tech contract you've always wanted."

"I live in New York. My job here was only six months long, and part-time at that. You always knew that."

"I live in Oakland," she said. "I don't care about your job. I do care about my family. You always knew that."

They stared at each other. Her bedroom felt small,

suffocating. The lamp on the desk sent his face into shadows that made him look unfamiliar—a sinister, unlovable relation of the nice guy she'd fallen in love with.

Love. Maybe it was all an illusion. Just a trick of the light.

He crossed his arms over his chest. "So," he said, and nothing else.

She was hurt and afraid, and neither feeling was tolerable. "I can't believe you assumed I'd give up everything and follow you to New York."

"I can't believe you won't even—" He moved to the door. "Never mind. It was just an idea. I figured you're probably done with Fite soon, and the baby has a full-time nanny, so it seemed perfectly logical to suggest other career options to you."

She filled in his sentence for him. *He can't believe you thought he might put yourself ahead of his career.*

"I don't believe in putting a job ahead of the important things in life," she said.

"And your life is more important than mine?"

"It's not less important," she said.

"It wasn't just the—but I understand. I get the message." He strode to the door, rubbing his mouth with his hand. "You don't want to come. No big deal. We never made each other any promises, did we?"

Without another word, he was gone.

She stood near the bed and stared at the empty spot where she'd last seen his back, not believing he'd walked away in the middle of their conversation.

I understand. No big deal. No promises.

That was *it*? She wasn't going to move to New York, so he was going to bail like a drunken sea captain in a hurricane?

Just like that?

She ran to the bedroom doorway and heard his footsteps on the stairs and then the slam of the front door. Moving over to the window, she shoved the curtains aside just in time to see him climb into his ride-share Mini and back out of the driveway.

She turned away from the window, her breath tight in her chest.

No big deal.

She kicked the hamper over. Sketches poured out like gold doubloons out of a pirate's treasure chest.

They'd finally had a real conversation, acknowledged the elephant in the room, and he'd picked up his toys and gone home at the first sign of trouble.

She kicked the hamper again before sitting on the bed.

He'd left her.

Easily.

* * *

She didn't know how long she cried, but it was too long. When the need for a tissue was too great to put it off another sniffle, she climbed to her feet and staggered to the bathroom.

In the mirror over the sink, she saw her face, splotchy and tear-streaked, and was disgusted with herself. She ran cold water into the basin and submerged her face. The sobbing stopped—impossible if you couldn't inhale for another go—and she willed herself to calm down. The cold water helped. Eventually, she lifted her head and dried her face on an old bath towel she'd had since she was a kid. Ladybugs with lasers—it was some gender-bending attempt by the towel manufacturer in a more daring decade, and she'd adored it.

Standing in the bathroom with her damp T-shirt sticking to her chest, she held out the towel to study it, seeing the edges of the primary design, only about five inches square, and the drop of the repeating pattern across the terry cloth.

Cute ladybugs, but she could do better. She never got to draw, really draw, at Fite. The existing fashion lines were too conservative and adult—stripes and dots, abstract shapes in block colors. Imagine what she could've done with Fite Baby, if they'd begun development on that while she was there.

Not that they'd make towels. Who made stuff like that, anyway? She pulled the frayed label up to read some words that ended with *NY, NY.*

Figures. She flung the towel over the shower curtain bar and marched out of the bathroom. She wasn't going to follow a guy she'd been dating for just over a month to the other side of the country. She'd end up living with him. It was no use lying to herself, that's what always happened, that's what she would do. Then she'd immediately be at a disadvantage. His life wouldn't have to change. His toothbrush wouldn't even have to move.

Then, when there were troubles, and there would be, she'd be homeless again, except this time in New York on the other side of the country, where she had no friends or family. They might not even allow dogs in his building, and she wasn't giving up Stool for some emotionally constipated widower who couldn't even say goodbye when he walked out on a date—or a relationship— certainly not when the only fallback plan she had was for a career, which she'd never cared that much about anyway.

And New Yorkers would make fun of her clothes.

She went downstairs to make herself a drink before her mom came home. Funny she wasn't there already. The movie had to be long over by now, and she didn't like to drive at night so usually came straight home.

She picked up her phone from her purse on the way to the kitchen and saw a message from Liam.

It was voicemail, not text.

"Sorry to bother you," he said, "but I thought you'd like to know Mom is in the hospital."

Chapter 29

Within thirty minutes, April stood with Liam in the emergency room of the same big city hospital where they'd both been born. Their mother had been wheeled away before April got there.

"I didn't know people got appendicitis when they were older," April said, pulling at the fringe on her poncho. "A friend of mine had it when we were in high school. They said most people get it when they're young." She tried not to worry—it was a routine procedure, caught early—but the thought of her mother on a gurney made her want to yell at somebody.

"Not everyone," Liam said.

"Why didn't she call me? I can't believe she just checked herself in and left you a message."

"And she left me the voice mail at the office," he said. "If I didn't call in to check them every night before bed, I wouldn't have heard it until I got in to work tomorrow morning."

April shook her head. They were already prepping her for surgery. "She should've called me. Crazy woman."

"Sounds like she'll be able to go home the day after tomorrow. Maybe another day to recover, given her age."

"She's barely sixty, not ninety."

"Still," Liam said, "there are more risks."

When they found out which waiting room they should go to, they headed out of the chaotic, crowded emergency room to the elevator.

"I can't believe it happened so quickly," April said, hitting the button. "She was fine, totally fine, just a few hours ago. She was going to the movies."

"She said it had been bothering her for a few days. She did make it to the movies, though. Even bought popcorn." He smiled. "Which she made me promise to get out of her car and bring home to Bev so it didn't go to waste."

They found the waiting room, more cloth and padding on the chairs than in the emergency room, and sat down together near a potted palm.

April took out her phone. It was just past eleven. No messages. Her mother had driven herself to the hospital so as not to spoil her daughter's date. April didn't know if she should admire her or see her as a cautionary tale of excessive maternal, or grand-maternal, instinct.

She put her phone away and looked at her hands. "She didn't call me because Zack was at the house."

"Figures." He crossed one ankle over his knee, sighing. "Having Merry hasn't slowed her down. If anything, it's made her greedy."

"It's not that kind of relationship. Me and Zack."

"Of course not," he said. "When has reality ever mattered with her?"

"Why do you say that?"

"You know what I mean. A first date is just a baby shower waiting to happen. All it needs is cake and presents."

"No," she said, "I mean about me and Zack. Why 'of course not'?"

He gave her a serious look. "Am I wrong?"

"I just wondered why *you* thought that."

"Forget I said anything," he said.

She put her elbows on her knees, propped her chin on her hands. "No, you were right. We broke up."

"Sorry," he said, and fell silent.

"Really?"

"Oh, no. Don't ask me that. Please."

"But you weren't angry about us being together," she went on.

"It's none of my business."

"You used to make my love life your business," she said, realizing she sounded hurt.

"That's because you were living in my condo and your business contaminated my personal bedding."

She waited a long moment before asking, "Did you like him?"

He groaned, threw his head back. "We're not talking about this."

"We are, actually."

"Not here," he said. "Not now."

The waiting room was empty except for a man on the other side of the room with his head propped against the wall, half-asleep. The administration desk behind the window to his left was empty.

Suddenly exhausted, she slumped against Liam and rested her head on his shoulder. "He's moving to New York."

"That's where he lives." His words were hard, but his tone had softened.

That only weakened the control she'd been holding over her tears. Everything had gone to hell. With a deep breath, she squeezed her eyes shut and counted her blessings. Her brothers were pretty cool, even Liam. They'd married great women. Her niece was brilliant and feisty. Her mother was in the hospital with a mild ailment, hardly anything to fall apart about.

Her eyes burned anyway.

How could he end it so easily? Just walk away without a glance over his shoulder?

She wasn't good with abandonment. Her father, even before he'd died, had never made any time for her. Was that it—she kept chasing guys who were like her father? Was it as simple as that?

How pathetic. She refused to be so predictable. "Would you beat him up if I asked you to?" she asked.

"After he turns in his report," he said, "it would be my pleasure."

Her smile stretched across the rough fabric of his jacket. "Really?"

He paused. "I would've fired him already if Bev hadn't stopped me," he mumbled.

"Fired him? Why? Not because of me?"

"Of course because of you. I hired him to dig into Fite, not my baby sister."

"You can't fire somebody because of that," she said.

"Sure you can. He's a consultant, not an employee."

"But you have a contract," she said.

"I would've found a way."

She was still smiling. "Thanks." She lifted her head and looked up at him. "I'm glad you didn't, but it's nice you wanted to."

"I wish you weren't so..." He trailed off.

"Slutty?"

"I did not say that."

"You didn't want to make me cry," she said.

He laughed, putting an arm around her shoulders. "Optimistic. You think there's more there than there is. Some of these guys you've dated… they're not good enough for you, April. Not half as good as they should be."

She enjoyed the compliment but didn't think that had been the problem with Zack. He was brilliant, hard-working, loyal, considerate. If anything, she'd aimed too high. Until he'd walked out on her tonight, she would've said he was more than she deserved.

That was a disgusting thought. She should be grateful he left. She couldn't imagine spending the rest of her life with somebody who had that power over her.

Grateful, grateful, grateful.

"What did he do?" Liam asked.

Memories of their times in bed together flooded her mind. She pulled away. "What do you mean?"

"If I'm going to beat a guy up, I'd like to know why."

"Never mind about that."

He let out a frustrated breath. "Great. I have to keep working with this guy. Now I don't know what to think."

"He has to go back to New York for his next job, that's all." She made her voice light. "I wanted him to stay."

Liam didn't speak for a moment. "Did you ask him to?"

She pulled away. "I did, actually."

"Son of a bitch," he said.

"I know, right?"

Liam smacked his fist into his palm. "He's going down."

"Tempting, but I wouldn't want you to get hurt."

Liam sat up taller. "Please."

"You're not getting any younger." She was joking around to cheer herself up, but now she was thinking about her mother and where they were, the operation underway, and she deflated into her chair. "Seriously. This is between me and Zack. Except there isn't anything between us anymore."

Liam picked up an ancient *Sunset* magazine and flipped through the pages. Soft-focus photos of ideal West Coast homes and gardens danced before their eyes. "I can't believe it," he said.

She looked at the slipcovered sofa and colorful throw blankets displayed on the glossy pages. "I know. As if a real person's house could look like that."

He slapped the magazine shut. "Not this. You."

"What?"

"I can't believe you're giving up. April Johnson, the girl who went on strike in seventh grade. The woman who ended up in custody for hours because she wouldn't walk through the scanner at the airport." He studied her. "You must really care about this guy."

"If I cared, wouldn't I fight for him?"

"Maybe you only fight over things you don't care about," he said. "That way it doesn't matter if you lose."

April cursed under her breath. "Hit me while I'm down, why don't you?"

"It only hurts because I'm right."

"Wait until tomorrow, when Rita and Teegan and Jennifer convince you to fire me," she said. "Maybe then you'll feel guilty."

"I'm not going to fire you," he said.

It should've come as a relief, but she felt nothing. "With the rest of my life in the shits, I'm not sure I care that much about my job right now."

"Well, that's good, because I can't promise Rita will keep you on." He ran his hand through his blond hair. "I'm leaving the decision completely up to her. I can't possibly be objective, especially now."

"Why not now?"

He put an arm around her shoulders, bumping the side of his head against hers. "Because all I want to do right now is make you happy, Ape." He twirled a strand of her hair. "I love you, you know."

Although she did know, hearing it was damn nice.

* * *

Zack stared at his hands. They held a pen. The cheap pen from the gas station. The love pen, he used to call it—not entirely as a joke.

He was at home, only one night after their fatal last date, outlining a few ideas for his next job in his notebook and thinking of the way she used to tease him for carrying one all the time. Once they'd been watching TV at his place and he'd pulled it out —ideas strike at any time—and she'd confiscated it and drawn a picture of a dead man holding a daisy with a thought bubble rising above his head: *If only I'd spent more time at the office.*

He'd torn out the page and kept it in his wallet. He saw it every morning when he bought his coffee. On his way to work.

Everything reminded him of April. He couldn't get away from her.

Except he could get away from her, because she would never consider following him. She found the idea unthinkable, outrageous, insane. Whatever they'd had, however profound it had felt to him, wasn't enough to merit a plane trip across the country. He was loving too much, too soon, all over again.

He dropped his pen on the cardboard coffee table. If only they'd had more time. They'd only been coworkers until a month ago. Chucking her life to be with him on the other side of the country after five weeks of sleeping together would be idiotic. Of course she wouldn't do it.

Imagine how she'd feel about *marrying* him.

He tore his hand through his hair. He thought he'd been so

careful not to scare her away. He'd held back telling her how he needed her, how much he cared, how much he wanted.

And blown it anyway.

To take his mind off his misery, he did what he always did: turned his obsessive attention to his work. The next job at the tech start-up in New Jersey was only weeks away, and he'd have to start researching the new company immediately. He never walked into a new place without having a clue about what was wrong with it, where they might need him, why they'd *really* hired him.

Sylvester Minguez had given him the address, a few names, the website and press releases, but that wasn't nearly enough. Sixty-three employees, most hired within the past year as the economy picked up and another tech bubble began to swell from the panting breath of positive-thinking capitalists.

He'd have to fly back. He couldn't do this from the wrong coast. There were three guys putting up most of the money. He'd sit down with them face-to-face somewhere, buy them food and drink, hear the pitch that had gotten them to pony up the cash. Zack wasn't a tech guy, and he wouldn't know if their product was flawed at an engineering level—but he knew people and process, and he'd find a way to improve whatever they were doing, give them a chance to survive.

It was just the kind of project he'd dreamed about for years, a chance to get into the new economy. No more garment companies or gum-ball machine manufacturers. High tech. The future.

He booked the first flight to New York for the next morning and then took out a fresh notebook to begin brainstorming ideas about questions to ask the venture capitalist guys.

His mind blanked.

He got up and made a fresh coffee, returned to his notebook.

Still nothing.

He'd spent the day finishing up most of his report for Fite, so it wasn't that job that was interfering with his concentration.

He put the pen against his lips and saw April's face.

His stomach twisted. If he hadn't invited her to New York, but instead casually mentioned how he planned on returning to San Francisco before the end of the year for his next assignment and wondered if she'd be interested in continuing what they'd started, then maybe he wouldn't have found out how little she cared about him. He'd be sitting here now in blissful ignorance.

He shoved the pen into a box of other pens and selected a different one. He had to stop thinking about her or he'd never get anything done.

That was the moment Sarah decided to call. As the phone rang, he looked at her photo on its screen, determined not to answer. But before he knew it, he'd hit the button and was saying, "Hey."

Sarah let out a breath. "I didn't think you'd pick up."

"I almost didn't." But he figured he couldn't feel any worse.

"I've been thinking about you all day," she said. "I couldn't sleep last night. We have to clear this up. I was afraid you'd avoid me for months because you were afraid of talking to me."

"OK. Shoot." The image of a handgun appeared in his thoughts.

"Is something wrong? You sound terrible."

"Didn't sleep well either last night," he said. On impulse, he added, "April and I..." He stopped, not sure how to describe what had happened. "I'm flying to New York tomorrow."

She let out a long breath. "You broke up?"

He put down the pen he was still holding. "I think so. Yes."

"I'm sorry."

"Really?" he asked.

Neither spoke for a moment. Then Sarah said, "I thought I was angry at you last night," she began, "but I've given it a lot of thought. I'm not angry."

"You were angry?"

"I was disappointed you thought it would change anything. Like you were freeing us from some unpleasant obligation."

His mood lifted a millimeter from the bottom of the pit. He hadn't really wanted to lose them. Sarah was like the sister he'd never had. He couldn't think of anything to say.

"You don't have to get rid of us when you find somebody else to love. We can share."

"I thought you should know that I knew the truth."

Sarah made a frustrated noise in the back of her throat. "The truth is she loved you. Maybe you've convinced yourself she didn't because you have to live without her, I don't know. Maybe you wouldn't have gotten married as soon as you did, but you loved her, and she did love you, and I'm just so glad she knew"—her voice faltered, and she paused a moment before she went on —"she knew love like that before she... died."

Neither one of them could speak for a long moment. Pressure building behind his eyes, Zack finally said, "Thank you."

"You're welcome."

He let out a long breath. "Well. It doesn't matter now."

"Of course it does."

"Not anymore," he said.

"Because you've broken up with her?"

He put his hand over his eyes. It killed him to hear her say it. "Yeah."

"I'm sorry it didn't work out with April." Her tone softened. "But it will someday with somebody, and every one of us who loved Meg will love who you love, and you sure as hell better invite us to the wedding."

"There isn't going to be—"

"Someday. Somebody," she said. "We'll be there. Understand?"

What did it matter what he said? It wasn't going to happen. There hadn't been time.

"I understand," he said.

Chapter 30

THE NEXT MORNING, April called in sick at work—Rita had already heard from Liam that their mother was in the hospital, and didn't hold it against her—and returned to the hospital with a bag of quinoa pomegranate scones from her mom's favorite bakery. She'd stayed late the night before, waiting to see the surgery had gone well before she went home to doze fitfully for a few hours.

Her mother was asleep when she arrived, in spite of the nurses chatting at the foot of her bed, her roommate's TV the other side of the curtain, and the bright sun coming in the windows.

April stood at the foot of the hospital bed with its industrial steel bars and buttons and twisted the hem of her poncho into a knot. The sight of her mom lying there with tubes coming out of her, looking two decades older than she had last week, made her stomach hurt.

Maybe she needed an appendectomy herself.

At that moment, her mother opened her eyes. Her tired face lit up with a smile. "Honey. How long have you been standing there?"

"Just got here." She walked over and hugged her over the steel bars and the plastic tubes. Then she lifted the pastry bag up to eye level. "Hippie scones."

Her mother's smile widened but her eyes darted to the door. "I'm not sure I'm allowed. They're very strict, you know."

"Oh, come on."

"They're good even when they're stale. Leave them. I'll eat them when I can." Her mother reached out to a bouquet of lilies on the nightstand. "Are these from you, too?"

"Nope. Probably Mark." April found the card. "Yep. Mark and Rose, wishing you a speedy recovery."

Her mother's mouth dropped open. "But they just got back from their honeymoon."

"That was weeks ago."

"You shouldn't have bothered them."

"You had surgery," April said.

"Just a little tummy ache."

"They had to remove an organ."

"Not like I ever used it."

April grinned. She didn't seem sick at all. "When do you get to go home?"

"Soon. They seem to think I'm old. It might take a little longer."

April leaned over and inhaled the sweet smell of the lilies. Not her favorite scent, but her mother loved them. "They don't know you the way we do."

"Thank you for staying with me so late last night. I'm glad you finally convinced Liam to go home, though," her mother said. "Silly boy. He's got enough to worry about. What about the baby?"

"They put her up for adoption," April said.

"Don't tease."

"Nobody wanted her, though. Too high-maintenance. People like girls to be quiet."

"Not everyone." Then her mother lowered her voice. "Although I think my doctor could learn how to whisper. You'd think she was auditioning for Broadway."

"She seems to have fixed you up pretty good," April said.

"I'm fine. I took a promenade with the nurse all the way down to the elevator." An impish smile curved her lips. "A very nice-looking man from Kansas City."

"Get his number?" April asked.

Her mother frowned. "Are you having a rough patch with Zack?"

"I didn't mean for me. You said he was cute, so I thought *you* were interested." Her mother had had many men interested in her over the years, but she'd never reciprocated.

"He's too young for me," her mother said seriously. "So you are having a rough patch?"

"Nope."

"Oh. That's good."

April couldn't help herself. "What do you mean? You said I should dump him to save his tender feelings."

Her mother put a hand over her mouth, dragging the IV tubes over her chest as her arm moved. "Did I say that?"

"And no, we're not having a rough patch," April continued, "we're having a death spiral off a cliff."

Her mother didn't say anything, but her eyes were sad.

April suddenly regretted saying anything. It wasn't the time to rant on her shoulder. "It's okay." She forced a smile. "Maybe I'll run into that nurse of yours. Sounds like he's on the night shift. That's good for romance, am I right?"

"He's not as handsome as Zack," her mother said. "What happened?"

April stroked the hair off of her mother's forehead. "I'll spare you the gory details. As soon as you bail yourself out of this joint, we're going back to the salon. These layers need some work."

"You hated the cut you got last time."

"But I got to have it with you."

Her mother cupped her cheek. "What happened, honey?"

"He's moving back to New York."

"And?" her mother asked.

"And? What do you mean? He's leaving, end of story."

Her mother's face fell. Sinking back against her flat pillow, she turned her gaze to the ceiling. "I don't believe it."

April felt a stab of annoyance. Wasn't this what her mother wanted? "At least this way I can't hurt him, right? That should be some consolation to you."

Her mother's gaze drilled into her. "Are you sure? He's really leaving?"

Nodding, April twirled one of the lilies in the vase. "These are beautiful. I wonder where Mark ordered them. Of course, it was probably Rose. She has style, that girl. Can't believe she married Mark, of all people."

Her mother clasped her arm. "I only said what I said to get you thinking. Knock some sense into you. You've always lived in the present, which is so wonderful about you, but sometimes you're so happy floating down the river in your raft, you don't see the waterfall. Until it's too late. You know?"

"Raft?"

Her mother put her hand on her throat. "I'm so thirsty. There should be a cup of water over there somewhere."

April found it and helped her take a sip. "You were playing me?"

"I was afraid he wouldn't know how much you cared about him. You've got such a way of hiding your feelings. Your father was the same way."

"Dad?" That had to be a joke. "I'm nothing like him."

Her mother gave her a small smile. "You're more like him than either of your brothers. All that passion, the temper." She squeezed April's arm. "So much love, but it's hidden under all the other drama."

"I asked him to stay. He left anyway."

"That's it? You asked him to stay and he ran out of the room screaming? Nothing else was said?"

April almost smiled in spite of herself. "There was something in there about me moving to New York with him."

"But he didn't want you to?"

"No! How could I do that? Leave you and Mark and Liam and Merry?" April asked. "It was *his* idea, of course. I thought it was a cop-out."

Something amused twinkled in her mother's tired eyes. "I see."

"What do you think you see?"

"Listen, sweetheart, I'm really tired. I think I'd like to sleep a little more." Her mother handed her the empty cup. "Before you go home, do you think you could pick me up a pair of earplugs and an eye mask? If I don't get a few hours of decent sleep, I'll never recover. Could you do that?"

"Sure," April said, suspicious. Her mother had another crazy idea in her head, one that seemed to make her happy, even if she was wrong and there was nothing to be happy about.

But April could hardly keep squabbling with her when she was laid out in a hospital bed. "I'll run to the store right now. If you think of anything else you want, send me a text." She made sure her mother's phone was in reach, next to the water.

"That's my girl," her mother said, closing her eyes.

* * *

With their mother in the hospital and a cluster of already scheduled design meetings, Liam rescheduled the meeting with Rita for the following Friday, more than a week away. Yet another confirmation of April's low status; they couldn't even make time out of their busy schedules to get rid of her.

Pending her status, Rita had suggested she take time off and not even come into the office until the meeting. "It'll give everyone a chance to cool down," she'd said.

"Or light the candles for my going away party," April had replied.

Rita hadn't laughed. "I'm going to give you plenty of time to give your side of the story. You want to prepare a few notes for the meeting. Show everyone you take it seriously."

April had hung up, wondering what she'd ever done to suggest she didn't take her job at Fite seriously. She'd once worked an entire week in an insurance company wearing mismatched plastic flip-flops while she played games on her phone eight hours a day —*that* was not taking a job seriously. But Fite? She'd actually printed out samples of the work she'd done there for her portfolio. She'd sketched out draft concepts while she was home, off the clock—when nobody had asked her to. She'd indulged in that holy American value of *showing initiative*. Fat lot of good it did her.

But Fite was just a job, like any other job. Just work. She had years of practice shoving career issues out of her mind. She'd find another way to pay the bills.

Brushing Zack out of her mind, however, wasn't so easy. She kept imagining him falling off the bed, laughing; the way he'd call her at Fite to warn her Teegan was on the way downstairs; the intensity in his eyes when he listened, really listened to her talk;

the sensual curve of his lips before he kissed her. Without Fite or babysitting, she was stuck at home, wandering around the empty house in a daze, with only Stool and three worried Chihuahuas for company, unable to stop the thoughts about what might've been.

They would've been happy together. If he'd given them time, given her a chance.

If he'd loved her.

Enough. She decided to take over Liam's old room. The dude was married and owned his own whole damn house next door, so why would he care? Mom was tied down to a hospital bed with IV shackles, so she couldn't stop her from shoving Liam's furniture into Mark's old bedroom—seriously, their mother was managing a museum—and moving her easel and art supplies into it. By the time she returned from the hospital, which could be as early the next morning, the studio would be set up. Mom would probably be too weak from the surgery to put up much of a fight.

April had never pretended to be a selfless martyr. If the world didn't like it, the world could get the hell out of her way.

Out of consideration for her mother, however, she also cleaned the bathroom and fixed the leak in the kitchen sink. And took the dogs in for their flea and tick meds, and paid the cable bill.

When her work was done, she and the four dogs relaxed on the floor of her new studio eating microwaved chicken nuggets in the fading light of the setting sun. Nicely diffused light, she noted —it would be perfect for painting. When she lost the job at Fite, she'd have plenty of time to paint.

She peeled the greasy breading off a nugget and fed the chicken to Stool. She didn't like the idea of getting fired. She'd tried to convince herself she didn't care, but she did.

She cared, and more every second.

Zack was gone, or soon gone, and she'd need to find a way to recover from the hole in her chest. Her new studio was nice, but it wasn't hers. It would help her develop the freelance business she'd begun to imagine, but she'd still be living with her mother. And being kicked out of Fite now would be like starting a career with a black mark on her record when she deserved fifteen gold stars, happy faces, and a glittered *Way To Go!* sticker.

No. She couldn't let Teegan win her campaign of evil.

If there was going to be a Trial of April, she'd have to prepare, like Rita said. And boy, was she going to *prepare.*

What was that line about bringing a gun to a knife fight?

She was going to bring a freaking *nuke.*

* * *

"Zack?" the man asked.

Zack looked up from the grape he'd speared in his salad. He and the three venture capitalists sat outside at a bistro table wedged off a side street in midtown Manhattan. "Yes, Tom?"

The tall, balding guy next to him raised an eyebrow. "I'm Tom. That's Tim."

Zack should've been mortified. He never got names wrong. But if two men named Tim and Tom are going to go into business together, they should use their last names. "Sorry." He shoved his fork into his mouth. To him, the grape might as well have been a cow's eyeball. He rolled it around in his mouth and swallowed it without chewing.

"Are you all right?" the third man asked. His name, no kidding, was Tony. That second syllable made all the difference, and Zack hadn't forgotten it once.

Although he did think the guy was a jerk, the kind to keep tugging up his shirt sleeves so his Rolex was on constant display.

"I'm fine," Zack said. If he hadn't forgotten his notebook at his hotel—his apartment was sublet to a visiting professor for another two weeks—he would've had a question to fall back on when his mind wandered. At the moment, it had wandered to Antarctica and was shivering with the penguins. Ten minutes earlier, it had been flying past Jupiter.

Better than California.

"Sylly's already hired you?" Tom—no, Tim—asked.

Zack speared another eyeball. He'd called Liam. April hadn't been fired yet, but only because Trixie's emergency appendectomy had postponed the meeting. The day after tomorrow, she'd be finished. Zack's report wouldn't save her—too little, too late.

"Fly in late last night?" Tim—no, Tom—asked.

Zack looked up. He liked Tim. Tim was in his late thirties with black curly hair and a nose that leaned about fifteen degrees to the left, like a dented sundial. "No, I've been here since last Friday." It was almost a week later. He'd walked out on April and flown to New York and there was no chance on God's green earth she would ever move here to be with him. He'd had another undeserved shot at happiness and blown it.

The second grape caught in his throat. He inhaled sharply, feeling his air supply cut off, wondering if three men who had devoted their fragile, brief mortal lives to acquiring wealth would know the Heimlich maneuver.

He wasn't sure he cared whether they had.

As he clutched his throat, stars flashing before his eyes, he silently cursed the staff in the kitchen who couldn't be bothered to slice a grape in half. He was going to die without ever seeing April again because of a lazy sous chef. She'd assume he'd died happy, fraternizing with his beloved capitalists on the streets of New York City, never suspecting he loved her and had just decided she should know it, even if she laughed in his face again. Which she almost certainly would.

But the grape dislodged itself, and he covered his mouth with a napkin and waited for his pulse to return to a steady pace.

"You all right?" Tim asked.

Zack nodded, wiping away a tear. "Choking."

"I'll say," Tony said.

Zack put his napkin down. He didn't like Tony and didn't expect the man would become more lovable with repeated exposure. Did a guy like that have a woman who loved him? He didn't wear a ring, just the status-telegraphing timepiece. Zack couldn't imagine Tony giggling in bed with a cute, funny girl he adored, who adored him. He couldn't imagine Tony having the kind of genuine friendship and happiness he had with April.

Had had.

Zack signaled for the waiter, giving Tom and Tim an apologetic shrug. "It's good we had this meeting," he said, pulling a few bills from his wallet. "I realize now this isn't going to be a good fit. I think I should go. Not waste any more of your time."

Tony rolled his eyes but Tom and Tim argued politely for a minute before wishing him well and shaking hands goodbye.

Within two minutes, he was around the corner, breaking into a run.

Chapter 31

At 8:46 a.m. the following Friday morning, April walked into the conference room off the lobby with her laptop, a portfolio case, and a swarm of butterflies in her stomach. She'd slept four hours out of the eight she'd been in bed the night before and had bags under her eyes so large they wouldn't fit under an airplane seat. The chill in the room made her shiver. She found the thermostat and cranked it up ten degrees. She wanted her audience to be comfortable. Cold women were unhappy women. Liam wouldn't care—he was the one who set the temperature in the building, which was why it was arctic—but Rita, her primary audience, would.

After checking her makeup—with a spike of rebelliousness she hoped she wouldn't regret, she'd gone ahead and worn her usual cobalt-blue eyeliner—she set up her laptop and connected it to the projector. She'd prepared a professional, unemotional slideshow to make her case.

Jennifer was going to have a very bad day.

"I'm not sure you should be smiling like that," Virginia said, walking into the room. She held out two cardboard containers, each holding four steaming coffees. Behind her, grouchy George from the back door carried a pastry box.

"You guys can't come in here," April said, glancing at the clock on the wall. 8:55. "There's a meeting in a few minutes."

George dumped the pastry box on the table. "Cool your spurs. We're not staying."

Virginia set the coffees next to the box. "We wanted to help."

"Those are for me?" April asked, unbalanced by the gesture.

"For Christ's sake, don't start blubbering," George said. "It'll melt that paint you slather all over your pretty face."

"Aw, George." April had to chase him halfway out the door to give him a hug. "I owe you one."

"Empty words," he said, swatting her away.

When he was gone, Virginia said, "No matter what happens, let's catch a movie tonight. Would you like that?"

"Deal. It can even be a comic book movie," April said. Virginia had stopped wearing her cartoon T-shirts to work, but her apartment was still decorated like a nine-year-old boy's bedroom, with superheroes and video game posters all over the walls. "You've been incredibly nice. Even if you did take my hundred bucks."

"Text me when you're free," Virginia said. "Now kick some ass."

Just then Liam appeared in the doorway, Bev at his side. Virginia bolted past them through the door without another word.

"Thanks," April called after her as she offered Liam and Bev the coffee and pastries. "I didn't know if you two would be here."

"I can't believe it's come to this," Bev said. "I don't approve."

Liam gave her a loving smile. "Softie."

"No, it's good," April said. "This crap's been building for months. It's great to finally get it out in the open."

"I wish you'd told me about what was going on," Bev said.

"That's what they wanted me to do, go crying to you. Then

they'd never take me seriously," April said. "No, I had to deal with this on my own."

Bev sat down, shaking her head. "There's no such thing as being on your own."

"You ordered the donuts, didn't you?" Liam asked Bev, looking at the pastry boxes with amused disgust.

"I would have, but Virginia and George already had it covered," Bev replied.

April looked up from the projector, worried she was losing control of the situation. Bev and Liam looked too cheerful, too relaxed. "I hope you two aren't here to put your thumbs on the scale. I've got this."

"We don't expect any freelancer," Bev said, "no matter whose sister she is, to deal with the most impossibly difficult—"

Just then Teegan entered the room, Jennifer right behind her.

"Situations," Bev finished, clearing her throat. She clasped her hands together on the table and gave both women a tight-lipped smile. "Good morning."

Teegan glanced at Jennifer before mumbling, "Hi" and averting her eyes.

Jennifer flashed a cold smile of her own before sitting in the corner near the door and pulling out her phone, as if she wasn't really a part of the meeting. Teegan seemed to look for a chair similarly remote but had to settle for one at the table. She shot April smug, malevolent glances, stroking the tablet in her lap as if it were a Persian cat.

"I hope I'm not late," Rita said, bursting into the room. She paused when she saw Bev and then helped herself to coffee and a bear claw before she sat down. "I had to do a rush job for Men's that couldn't wait."

At that moment, the creative director for that department,

Darrin, entered with his phone at his ear. His new assistant, the charming Hayley, trailed behind him holding a liter-sized bottle of Diet Coke.

Everyone was there. The party could begin. Bending over her laptop, April adjusted the window for the presentation, trying to keep her hands busy as she got a grip. Her nerves were sending up last-ditch alarms in desperation: *wah wah wah, SOS, abandon ship.* Even if Bev, Liam, and Rita believed what she was about to tell them, they might forgive Jennifer's bitchy shenanigans because of her design talents and her seniority, asking April: what did she expect from a fashion designer, hugs and cookies?

No, she could expect that from Bev, the former preschool teacher. *She* was the nice one—so nice she'd probably forgive Jennifer and Teegan for conspiring against her for months. And if Bev was forgiving, Rita would fall into line. April would have to suck it up. She'd have her job, but so would Teegan and Jennifer, and nothing would change.

"I've prepared a presentation," April said, checking the whiteboard behind her for the projected title page of her slideshow.

Nothing would change...

She picked up the whiteboard eraser and wiped off an imaginary streak of marker. The projector lit up her arm with the Fite logo.

How could nothing change when she herself had changed so much?

Zack had asked her to come with him. It hadn't been halfhearted—he'd really wanted her to. His eyes had lit up like a patrol car chasing a Ferrari going ninety-five in a school zone.

He'd wanted her to come with him. What had she said? Something about *never.*

She turned back to the group of big fish in the little pond of San Francisco fashion, and wondered why she'd ever let them get to her. All those years she'd put half her heart into her job and all of it into having a good time, she'd been right: making money didn't matter.

He'd wanted her to join him in New York.

Finally, she understood what he'd done. Impulsively, emotionally, irrationally—he'd asked her to run away with him. Yes, he was already living there and would enjoy many conveniences she would lack—but he'd done it. He'd offered his heart. She realized now it hadn't been planned, it hadn't been in his notebook or his calendar. He'd broken all of his typically anal-retentive safeguards in asking her.

And she'd thrown it back in his face.

She frowned at the screen of her computer, vaguely aware of all the eyes watching her, her heart beating with renewed excitement.

Holy shit. She was going to move to New York.

If it wasn't too late.

Chapter 32

ZACK WAVED HIS thanks to Virginia, who had seemed surprisingly happy to see him, and opened the conference room door.

Eight heads swiveled his way: Rita, Teegan, Jennifer, Darrin, Hayley, Liam, Bev... and April.

She stood at the head of the table, her back to him, wearing a turquoise sweater over a slinky black skirt with an asymmetrical hem that brushed her combat boots. She turned her head and looked at him.

His heart seized up for a moment. And because his throat had gone dry, he could only nod at the group, holding up his little notebook as if he were the court stenographer, before silently finding a seat at the end of the table.

Liam caught his eye, sending a tight-lipped warning look that Zack interpreted to mean *not a word*.

"Uh..." April said, staring at Zack.

The room fell silent.

"You have a presentation?" Bev asked.

"Yes. Thank you," April said. She jerked her attention back to her computer. "I do. This presentation has a few interesting data points all of you should be interested in, whether it's me or another artist you'll be working with."

Not wanting to distract her again, Zack turned his gaze to the whiteboard on the wall, where the projector was aiming the show. If his memory was right, the words FITE ART were flickering in the same color palette she'd come to find in this same conference room months ago, when she'd tripped over his feet. He remembered her bright blue jeans, the attraction he'd felt from the beginning, not admitting to himself then that he'd always been a love-at-first-sight kind of guy and had already had his second sighting.

He'd been lost from the beginning.

As the slideshow began to play, he gripped his notebook in his lap, wishing he hadn't been a few minutes late. He'd had two informers about the meeting: Virginia had sent him an email the night before, apologizing for bothering him but suggesting he might maybe want to know about April fighting for her reputation. And Liam had sent a text an hour ago, telling him to drag his ass over if he hadn't already skipped town.

He didn't know if April was going to forgive him for walking out without a word, but he was going to do his best to help her defend herself at Fite. In his briefcase were a dozen copies of the section of his report addressing the design division, with particular detail about Jennifer, Teegan, and the Women's team. Nothing most people with eyes couldn't see for themselves, but it was good to have an outsider put it down in black-and-white.

Ten seconds into the presentation, however, he realized April wasn't going to need his help. A colorful bar graph illuminated the wall—one that immediately showed how difficult she'd had it the past few months.

"Here's a chart showing the trends in art room work requests over the past year," April said, "to freelancers such as myself."

"But you've only been here since November," Teegan said.

"Which is why I pulled the data for longer. So you can

compare. Get a frame of reference." April's sharp gaze flickered over to Zack, who couldn't help but smile at her. He liked graphs. This one showed a spike in project requests of 126 percent in November... and 557 percent in the month Rita had gone on leave. It was like a pastel Mount Everest.

"That can't be right." Liam stood up and walked over to the whiteboard. He tapped the projected graph. "Spring is big, but it isn't that big. And why does it keep going? It should go down after we moved on to the summer deliveries."

April reached under the table and lifted up a stack of papers tall as it was wide. "Here are the hard copies of the project requests," she said, dumping it on the table with a thud, "if you want to check my numbers."

Zack bit back a grin and saw that Bev, sipping her coffee, was doing the same.

"Leave them with Rita," Liam said. "If anyone wants to see for themselves, they can."

The silence in the room seemed louder than it had a minute earlier. Everyone, even Jennifer and Teegan, were frozen in place, staring at the stack of paper.

"If you sit down," April said, "I'll show you the next slide. It gets even more interesting."

Liam raised an eyebrow at Zack and reclaimed his seat. Zack drank in the sight of April at the top of her game, fighting for herself. It was killing him to keep a straight face.

"Here are the work requests broken up by department," April continued.

There, in living color, a picture told a thousand words: the Women's department had sent the art room 764 work and revision requests from March through the day last week when Rita had told her to stay home. That averaged out to—Zack factored in five workdays per week over three months—over a dozen requests a day. All of the other departments—combined—had, on average, only three requests per day.

Most damning, in the most recent week, when April had been kept out of the office, Jennifer hadn't asked for a single sketch, screen print, stripe, polka dot all-over T-shirt, or logo. Not one. And in the months prior to April's starting at Fite the previous November, the work requests from the Women's team were a low, steady line, about four per day.

Darrin actually laughed out loud, smacking the table with both hands, the impact sounding like gunshot. "Jennifer, what have you been smoking?"

"Shut up," Jennifer said. She'd put away her phone and sat up as if she were strapped into an electric chair. "It only looks like a lot. I'm sure she recorded every little thing she did. Walking up the stairs to talk to the design team, saving a file to the correct folder, answering her phone. I wouldn't be surprised if she filled out a form to go to the bathroom."

April patted the stack of work requests. "No, they're all actual projects. Take a look for yourself."

Without a glance at anyone else in the room, even Bev, Jennifer fixed her gaze on Liam. "I'm sure she tried as well as she could, but I heard she never got it right the first time. Never. She must've counted each revision as an entirely new project. I heard that just a few weeks ago she insisted on a special form just to print out a single page."

"Who did you hear this from?" April asked.

Jennifer looked annoyed to be interrupted. "Who?"

"Yes. If you remember," April said.

"It was Teegan. Obviously. My assistant."

"Associate," Teegan said. "I got promoted Monday."

Jennifer's eyes rolled skyward.

"Is this about that time you asked for the printout for an abstract all-over triangle design for a tank bra from a few years ago," April began, her cheeks flushed in an adorable way that made Zack's chest ache with longing, "but you couldn't remember the name of it, or the line or the season—or the actual year, it turned out—so you ended up describing it to me from memory and I had to completely redesign it?"

Teegan didn't reply.

"Teegan?" Bev asked, her tone sweet as always.

"Yes," Teegan said. "We needed it right away, but she couldn't get it to us until the late afternoon. We missed the FedEx delivery."

Jennifer shot to her feet. "That's what I'm talking about. Rita would've known what we needed without wasting an entire day's work."

"Sounds like you don't know yourself what you needed," Liam said, making Zack want to cheer.

"Rita would've had it for us in three minutes. And the company would've saved a thousand bucks, or whatever it costs to have your—April here," Jennifer said.

"I'm not sure I would've known what you were talking about, actually," Rita said.

Jennifer's tone turned warm, best-friends-forever. "You would've. You totally would've. You're amazing."

"But Rita was on family leave," Bev said.

"I know, and it was such a tragedy." Jennifer reached out and squeezed Rita's arm.

"Not at all." Rita leaned back in her chair, but her arm was still captured in Jennifer's grasp. "Both of my children are back in school now."

"I mean it was a tragedy you were out so long," Jennifer said.

Rita freed her arm, her fair cheeks flushing a splotchy pink. "Actually, I chose to extend my leave so I could spend some healthy time with them. I'm a single mom, so there's never enough time, and when my youngest got better—" She cut herself off and looked at Bev, then Liam. "Anyway, thanks for letting me do that."

"You were on *vacation*?" Jennifer asked. "How long have your kids been back in school?"

Rita's face was still flushed. "No, I was—"

"You don't have to explain," Bev said. "I'm sure Jennifer wouldn't want to discuss *her* personal matters in the middle of a design meeting." She gave Jennifer a smile that wasn't as beaming as her usual expression. Zack detected lightly veiled disgust.

"But we were totally screwed without her." Jennifer flung out her arm, jabbing a finger at the graph on the wall. "Look how much it cost the company to rely on somebody who didn't know what she was doing! I'm sure there isn't a page in this presentation that talks about *that* little problem."

With a toss of her gorgeous, sexy, wonderful head, April clicked to the next slide. "Although I disagree with the claim that I'm unqualified, I did think it was good to show how much all that busywork cost the company. I've made a few charts with the monthly invoices and total workload for all freelancers—again, broken up by division."

The first chart showed the Women's team was responsible for over ninety-six percent of April's billed hours. The second showed that she was paid a third less, and considering most of her days were part-time, she did twice as much as the average freelancers who had worked the year before her.

April shook her head sadly. "I had no idea I wasn't charging enough by the hour. I'll remedy that in my next job." She lifted her head and held Zack's gaze. "Wherever it is."

<h1 style="text-align:center">Chapter 33</h1>

ZACK'S HEART JUMPED into his throat. *Wherever it is?*

"San Francisco just can't compete with New York," April said. "In terms of opportunities."

Liam looked at Zack for a moment, then back to April. "Sometimes you just have to go for it." His tone was bland.

"That's what I was thinking," April said.

Zack dug his fingernails into his leather notebook, aware his own face had turned hot. He had to grit his teeth to stop himself from shouting out.

She'd changed her mind about following him to New York. Even though he'd left her without a word, even though she'd have to give up her family and friends, everything she'd known.

"You'd certainly do well there," Zack said, his heart pounding in his ears. "But I'd miss working with you."

"Your job at Fite is almost over anyway," she said.

"That's true," he said, not caring that the rest of the room hung on their every word, heads swiveling back and forth like a crowd at Wimbledon. "In fact, I've just signed on with a new client in San Francisco. I start next week."

Her voice rose. "San Francisco?"

Nodding, he put his notebook on the table and reached for one of the cinnamon buns jutting out of a cardboard box, hoping nobody noticed how his hand shook. He wanted to grab her instead and run out of the room, but she needed to bring her meeting to a triumphant conclusion first.

Pointing the bun at her, he said, "Sorry to interrupt. Please continue."

She stared blankly. The sound of Jennifer's annoyance—sighs, snorts, seat-shifting—filled the room.

"I'd love to see the rest of the slideshow," Rita said.

April didn't break eye contact with Zack. "I could email it to you, Rita."

Bev reached over the table and tapped a button on the laptop. "As long as we're all here..."

Lost in April's eyes, Zack smiled, happiness flooding him. He wouldn't mind having Bev as a sister-in-law. She was nice. Not as nice as April, who had mastered a totally different, superior-in-every-way kind of nice, but just fine.

He was getting ahead of himself. Just because April was willing to move to New York didn't mean she wanted to spend the rest of her life with him, bear his children, sign a marriage certificate. She was a free spirit. She might want to keep him as her personal sex slave, and only that until she grew tired of him.

No, she loved him. He felt it.

Liam's low voice broke into his thoughts. "Tell us about this chart, April."

Finally, she turned away from Zack. "Oh, this one shows the percentage of designs requested of the art room that actually make it into production and into stores."

"You're kidding me," Liam said, leaning back in his chair, eyes scanning the room.

None of the departments had very high production rates— the highest was for Men's, at 56 percent—but Women's was staggeringly low.

"Eight percent?" Bev asked. "In other words, ninety-two percent of what the art room is doing for the Women's team doesn't go anywhere?"

Jennifer's voice rose. "That's garment. That's how it always is. Everywhere."

"Actually," Zack said, "the data here shows quite the opposite. Look at last year. Much better, by at least half. Or the Men's division—"

"Men's is always like that," Jennifer said. "Black, charcoal gray, a few stripes, a pop color that's on trend, the end. Darrin could run the same line year after year and nobody would notice."

Clearly enjoying the show, Darrin popped a blueberry scone into his mouth. "I wish. I tried that once, but Liam caught on." He smiled at Liam. "Smart man."

"Suck-up," Liam muttered.

"It wasn't too bad before I went out on leave," Rita said, "but it did seem to me, Jennifer, that you were giving April an especially hard time."

"Why are you singling me out?" Jennifer demanded. "It's Teegan's name on most of those project requests. Not mine. I never worked directly with her."

Until now, Teegan had sat with her mouth shut and her eyes wide. "But you *told* me to give her a hard time—"

"It has been impossible to get decent design assistants in this company," Jennifer said. "We're too small, too pathetic, and we don't pay nearly enough."

"Can't afford to if we spend all our money on work that goes into the recycling bin," Liam said.

Teegan was visibly close to bursting, her mouth opening and closing like a broken garage door. "I—I—I was only doing what she told me." Her wild gaze scanned the crowd, settling, to his surprise, on Zack. "*You* know. *You* were there. You heard what she was like."

"I never heard her talk about the art room," Zack said with regret. "She always met with you in her office." And in spite of his repeated requests, Jennifer had always closed the door.

The overhead fluorescent lighting lit up the tears pooling in Teegan's eyes. "I can't believe this." Her voice cracked.

"I think maybe we should take a little break," Bev said, squeezing Teegan's arm. "How about we go for a walk around the block and you tell me whatever you want to tell me. I'll listen."

Jennifer stood up. "God help us, the preschool teacher is on the case. Is that what it takes to get ahead around here now? A few tears?" She backed up to the door, eyes scanning the group for an ally, finding none. "Maybe I should cry, too."

"Go ahead," April said.

"I hate this place," Jennifer said. "I can't wait to leave."

"Turns out we have that in common," April said. "We can't wait for you to leave, either."

Jennifer shot her one last hateful glance before striding out of the room. Nobody called out or chased after her.

Teegan closed the cover on her tablet and hugged it to her chest. "Am I—are you going to fire me?"

"Let's go on that walk," Bev said, gesturing to the door. Teegan nodded, and they went out together.

Liam stood up and said to Darrin, who was eating a croissant, "How about you get back to work. This isn't Starbucks."

Looking pleased as shit, the Men's designer stood up. "Ah, Jennifer. She's been stewing for a while," he said, licking his fingers. "Talks all the time about how she hates the direction the company's taken, the bigger sizes, the mainstream silhouettes. She misses Ellen and the old ways. She's been interviewing for months but thought she might take down your baby sister on the way out as a little bonus. She hates your whole family."

Offering April a friendly shrug, he left the room with his assistant carrying his coffee in his wake.

And then only Liam, Rita, April, and Zack remained.

Glancing first at Liam, Rita told April, "In case it isn't obvious, I'd be happy to keep you on. If you're willing. And if you stay in town. Although your brother might want to hire you as a business consultant instead. You seem to have a knack for numbers."

Liam eyed Zack. "You didn't help her with any of that?"

April punched him in the shoulder. "Of course he didn't. Give me a break! How can you *never* take me seriously?"

"Years of practice," Liam said.

"I did better on my SATs than you did, you booger," April said.

"Then why can't you use grown-up words?" Liam asked.

"What's the fun in that?" April asked.

Zack stood up, ready to start shouting. He'd waited long enough. "April," he said, his voice low. "Care for a walk?"

"Big morning for walks, isn't it?" Rita said, grinning as she walked to the door.

Liam followed Rita. "Time to get back to work. Mail me the files for that presentation, will you, Ape?"

Zack didn't wait until they were gone to capture April's hand and bring it to his lips.

"April?" Liam asked.

Her skin smelled like dry-erase markers and sweet jasmine. Zack dropped kisses along the knuckles.

Liam cleared his throat.

"Get lost, Liam," Zack said, looking up into April's eyes.

* * *

Zack's kisses sent shivers up her arm, down her spine, and into her heart, where they collected in a pool of bubbling, overflowing warmth.

The click of the door as Liam left signaled they were finally alone.

"I'm sorry I left," he said.

"I'm sorry I didn't follow," she replied.

He put his arms around her. "I love you."

Tilting her hand to cup his face, she felt the roughness of his whiskers, the heat of his cheek. "I love you, too."

It should've been hard to say, but it was the easiest thing in the world.

His eyes closed. He looked as if she'd slapped him. "Thank God."

"The job in New York didn't work out?"

"Not without you," he said, pulling her into his arms.

"What did you tell them?" He felt so good it was hard to listen to what he was saying. "Are you in trouble?"

"Big trouble. I was hoping you'd visit me in prison."

She stretched up against him, fingers tunneling through his hair, and kissed the hollow of his throat. "I totally would."

"That's nice," he said with a sigh, stroking her bottom. "My life would revolve around our conjugal visits."

"How is that different from right now?"

"So true." He tilted her chin back and kissed her.

Crazed with longing and relief, she pushed him against the wall to kiss him back. Covered with a metal grid for hanging presentation boards and clothing designs, it rattled at the impact.

"Would your brother and sister-in-law mind if we had a

conjugal visit right here?" he asked, flipping her around so he was the one pinning her against the grid, caressing her breast over her sweater, sending tendrils of desire to her core.

"Virginia will scare anyone away."

After a hard, probing kiss, he lifted his head and said breathlessly, "I was just kidding. My place?"

"I want to hear more about how you couldn't live without me."

"I couldn't live without you," he said, licking her earlobe.

"It took me a few days to figure it out, but I finally did." God, he knew just how to touch her. She arched her head back. "We can move to New York. I mean, I can. You already live there."

"Not anymore. I'm here now."

"What about your career?" she asked.

"What about it?"

"Will you resent me if you crash and burn and lose everything as your years of work go down the drain?"

He lifted his head. "You know something I don't?"

"It's tough out here. You might not be able to do as well here as you did back east."

Smiling, he kissed her forehead. "I'm willing to take that chance. How about you? Can you give up the opportunities in New York? You were right. You'd make more money, have more clients."

"Give up leaving Merry and my mom and my brothers and California weather, and everything I know and love except for you?"

He stroked her lower lip. "Yeah."

"I can give it up." She wiggled against him. "For you."

They kissed for another long, dizzy minute until April started unbuttoning his shirt, having convinced herself that Virginia would protect them from interruptions. Brushing her lips across the hair below his collarbone, she inhaled the scent of him, swimming in the flood of her own emotions: gratitude, anticipation, relief, love.

"Oh, hello there!" Her mother's voice was like the lifeguard's whistle, commanding everyone get out of the pool. "Merry and I thought we'd come and offer our support. Are we too late?"

Reluctantly, April peered around Zack. "Yes." But Trixie had Merry with her—who, with a green cap and a one-piece red getup, looked like a strawberry with feet.

Heart squeezing at the thought of leaving her niece just as she was about to crawl, walk, talk, and get even more interesting, April looked up at Zack. "Are you sure you want to live in California? You won't regret it?"

"I'm sure." He kissed her forehead. "I never meant to stay away forever."

"What about your wife's family? You were close to them. They'll miss you."

Her mother cleared her throat. "Are you sure you want to argue with him, sweetheart?"

"I'll visit them," Zack said, catching her by the waist and turning to face the newcomers. "Morning, Mrs. Johnson. Merry Johnson."

Her mother grinned. "Call me Mom."

Oh, lord, April thought.

"April did a great job this morning," Zack said. "You would've been proud."

April felt her face get hot.

"I was already proud," Trixie said.

God, now I'm going to cry.

Moving between them, her mother handed Merry over to

April, then let out her breath and shook her arms. "She's going to be a bruiser like her father. Soon I won't be able to pick her up at all."

In spite of her strawberry outfit, Merry smelled like bananas. "You're still recovering from surgery, you crazy lady," April said, kissing Merry's petal-soft cheek. "What are you doing here? And where's the new nanny?"

"Merry and I wanted to make sure you two got things figured out," her mother said. She rubbed her hands together, reached for Merry again. "Looks like you did, so we'll be going now. See you at the house soon, am I right, Zack?"

April gave Merry one last kiss, pushed her into her mother's arms, and ushered the pair around the table to the doorway. "Not that soon."

"Remember, I can sleep through anything," her mother said.

Biting her lip, April waved at Merry—and her mother—before shutting the door between them.

Zack caught her from behind and pulled her body against his. While his hands explored her breasts, he nibbled on her neck, licking and kissing.

There was a tap on the door. "April?" Virginia's voice.

April covered Zack's mouth to stop its sucking action so she could answer semi-coherently. "Yes?"

"We can skip the movie tonight," Virginia said.

"Oh! Right!" April gasped as Zack slid a hand under her underwear and squeezed her butt cheek. "Thanks!"

"You're welcome," Zack whispered in her ear.

"How about next week?" Virginia asked.

"Great! Wonderful!" April said.

"I know, aren't I?" Zack replied, moving his hand around to the front.

April swallowed a squeal. "I'll text you!"

Sounding like she was laughing, Virginia said, "OK. Talk to you later."

After a moment, April said to Zack, "I think if we want any privacy, we should probably get out of here."

Zack held her chin between his thumb and forefinger, kissed her on the lips, and smiled the kind of smile that made her wobbly in all the right places. "We can go wherever you want," he said.

"Anywhere?"

He nodded.

"I just want to be together." She stretched up against him.

"Then we're both very lucky," he said, stroking her back. "Because that's exactly where I want to be."

Epilogue

ALTHOUGH THEY'D INITIALLY decided not even to discuss marriage until they'd been living together for fully one year—a pact that Zack's mother would've found unthinkable, had she known of it—it turned out that they lasted only four and a half months before the topic reared its veiled-and-tuxedoed head.

"Maybe we could get married on a boat," Zack said one evening as he watched TV. They had rented a two-bedroom apartment in Oakland halfway between April's mother's house and the BART station. She could visit family and get to work without too much hassle, and her part-time freelance income as a textile designer at Fite and at two new companies more than covered half the rent. She knew he had the bucks to cover a nicer place all by himself, but she made him squirrel that away for their distant future. She needed to feel that this first home was just as much hers as his.

Perhaps it was a little more hers than his, actually. She'd taken over the second bedroom—with north-facing light—and converted it to an art studio. Stool loved the little patch of land they had off the back porch, chasing bumblebees he never caught around the lavender and agapanthus and howling every time a siren wailed in the distance, which in the city was fairly often.

Tonight she was lying on the couch next to Zack, her legs over his lap, taking photographs of the ceiling with her phone. She'd decided that ceilings were very poorly represented in the arts. Theirs was particularly interesting, with an antique bronze chandelier retrofitted with LED bulbs, coved corners near the bay windows, and crown moulding from a more glamorous age.

When she heard his indirect marriage proposal, she turned her head to see what he was watching on the TV that had inspired it.

She sat up in a hurry. "You've got to be kidding me. *Moby Dick*?"

"I've always loved the ocean," he said. "And I love you, so it makes sense to put them together."

"You're watching a black-and-white movie about an obsessive crazy guy killing a whale, and suddenly you're thinking long-term?"

He grinned at her.

She whacked him in the shoulder. "How do you think this makes me feel?"

"Wanted?"

She tried to look serious. Failed. "Oh, totally," she said, laughter bubbling out of her. She'd thought he'd propose in a predictably conventional way, such as on one knee at a fancy restaurant or during a walk across the Golden Gate Bridge.

This was so much better. A lifetime of dick jokes was worth much, much more than any meal at a fancy restaurant.

"*Moby Dick* puts you in the mood for love, this is what I'm learning," she said.

"My mother always swoons whenever Gregory Peck comes on the screen."

"Oh, oh, oh," she said, clutching her stomach. She was laughing hard now. "You've brought your mother into it, too."

He crossed his arms over his chest, sinking lower into the couch. "Fine. We won't get married on a boat."

"We won't?"

Shaking his head, he pointed the remote at the TV and raised the volume. The mid-century orchestra blared into the room.

Not that she'd ever doubted him—not since she'd turned and seen him in the conference room at Fite and decided he was hers forever—but hearing him plan their commitment ceremony put a smile on her face.

"I love boats," she said, climbing into his lap and kissing his neck. She took another picture of the ceiling, getting some of his freshly buzzed scalp into the shot. The weekend before, they had visited his parents in Bakersfield; while he and his dad went to the barber, April bonded with his mother. Any cultural, religious, or style chasms between them were soon bridged by their mutual love of Zack, dogs, and living in the lovely state of California. April, it turned out, had been the answer to a prayer, even with her liberal politics, colorful language, and combat boots: she'd gotten Zack to move back home.

Zack wrapped his arms around April while Captain Ahab bellowed his frustration at the whale, the sea, the universe.

"I love you," he said. He didn't turn his head away from the TV, but his eyes were closed, and she felt the pulse at his throat accelerate under her lips.

"I love you, too." She tried to imagine wearing a wedding dress like Rose's elegant gown and failed. She tried to imagine being a whirlwind mother like Bev with her own multimillion-dollar business and couldn't picture that either. She knew she would spend the rest of her life with Zack, but she didn't know what it was going to look like. She'd travel her own path, find her own way, dance to her own tune.

Who said settling down was boring?
Not the way she was going to do it.
"I think a boat would be great," she said.

Author Note

Thank you for reading!

Would you like to get an email when my next book is released or on sale? Sign up at www.gretchengalway.com.

And if you enjoyed this book, please consider leaving a review online. It's ridiculously helpful!

Finally, I really love to hear from readers. You can find me here:

www.facebook.com/AuthorGretchenGalway

www.twitter.com/GretchenGalway

www.GretchenGalway.com

Happy reading!

Gretchen

About the Author

GRETCHEN GALWAY is a *USA Today* bestselling author who writes romantic comedies because love is too painful to survive without laughing. Raised in the American Midwest, she now lives in California with her husband and two kids.

To get an email alert about sales and new releases, please sign up at www.gretchengalway.com.